THE BALLAD OF DARCY & RUSSELL

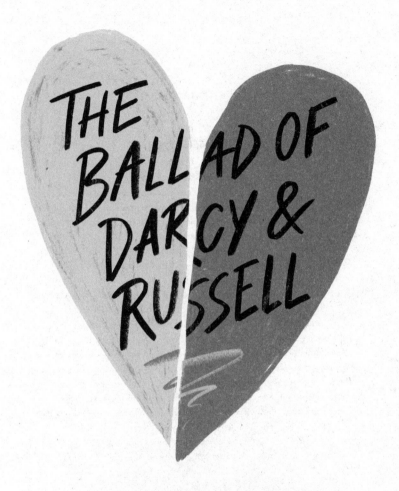

THE BALLAD OF DARCY & RUSSELL

MORGAN MATSON

SIMON & SCHUSTER BFYR

NEW YORK LONDON TORONTO SYDNEY NEW DELHI

SIMON & SCHUSTER BFYR

An imprint of Simon & Schuster Children's Publishing Division
1230 Avenue of the Americas, New York, New York 10020

SIMON & SCHUSTER BOOKS FOR YOUNG READERS
and related marks are trademarks of Simon & Schuster, LLC.
Simon & Schuster: Celebrating 100 Years of Publishing in 2024
For information about special discounts for bulk purchases, please contact
Simon & Schuster Special Sales at 1-866-506-1949 or business@simonandschuster.com.
The Simon & Schuster Speakers Bureau can bring authors to your live event.
For more information or to book an event, contact the Simon & Schuster Speakers
Bureau at 1-866-248-3049 or visit our website at www.simonspeakers.com.
Interior design by Hilary Zarycky
The text for this book was set in Adobe Caslon Pro.
Manufactured in the United States of America
First Edition
2 4 6 8 10 9 7 5 3 1
CIP data for this book is available from the Library of Congress.
ISBN 9781481499019
ISBN 9781481499033 (ebook)

To Adele Griffin
for friendship
and Wednesdays
and cake

ballad

noun

a song or poem that tells a story
a slow song about love

One night is not so long. In the scheme of things, it's just a blip.
But it's long enough. Long enough to fall in love. Long enough to
fall out of it. Long enough for your life to change forever.
—J. C. Richards, *Theseus's Sailboat*

A love song ain't nothing but a lie.
—Wylie Sanders

I
Because the Night

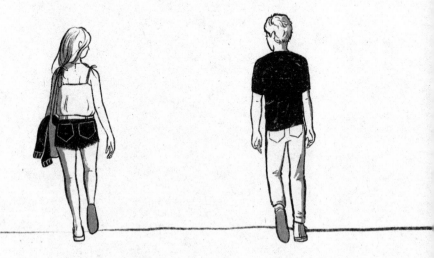

I stood at the foot of the stairs with my duffel bag, trying to remember if I'd forgotten anything. I was tempted to unzip the bag and start going through everything one more time, despite the fact I'd spent the whole morning channeling my nervous energy into making sure I'd packed properly.

"Got it all?" my dad asked. He was sitting at the kitchen table, frowning at the New York Times crossword.

"If I don't, I won't remember until I'm halfway there," I said, dropping my duffel at my feet. I stepped around the dog's food and water bowls as I crossed to the fridge, pushing the cards and photos out of the way so I could open the door. It was still early, but I'd woken up with a start hours before my alarm, with everything that was going to happen today scrolling in a loop in my brain. "That's the way this works."

"How are you feeling?" He turned to face me fully, setting the crossword down. I wasn't sure if it was because he was actually concerned or if he needed a break from trying to figure out five across.

"Nervous," I admitted. But it would have been weird if I wasn't, right? I'd never done anything like this before. "But excited, too."

"Well, have fun," my dad said. He gave me a smile that crinkled the corners of his eyes. "Be safe. Please come back in one piece."

"I'll do my best." I glanced outside, at the bright sun and the wind blowing the trees around. "It's nice out, but if you're going to the park, you should probably bring Zyrtec."

He grinned at me. "Duly noted."

I leaned over him to look at the crossword. "Fun fact—did you know that a person who creates crosswords is called a cruciverbalist?"

"I did not," my dad said as he picked it up again. "But I would appreciate any help you can offer on nineteen down."

I gave him a quick hug, then headed across the kitchen and picked up my duffel bag. "If I give you the answers, you're never going to learn."

My dad groaned. "This is revenge for me telling you that whenever you had a math question, isn't it?"

I laughed. "I'll call when I get there."

"Drive safe!" my dad called, already focused back on the crossword, muttering curses at David Kwong under his breath.

I stood there for just a second and looked at it—the quiet kitchen, my dad just where he was supposed to be, the clock ticking on the wall. I took in the scene—the one I knew I'd be missing all too soon—and let out a breath.

Then I picked up my duffel and headed out the door.

CHAPTER 1

Sunday
4:30 P.M.

Sitting alone on the floor of the bus station, I finally admitted to myself that the music festival might have been a mistake.

I was not normally a music festival–going person. I'd been to concerts at home in LA, of course—the Hollywood Bowl with my dad, the Greek Theatre or the Troubadour with my friends—but never a proper music festival, the kind that involved staying overnight. The kind that seemed to promise an *experience* like I'd seen in pictures on my Instagram and in cautionary-tale documentaries.

But when, six days ago, I'd gotten an out-of-the-blue call from Romy Andreoni—who I hadn't talked to since graduation two months earlier and, truthfully, not a whole lot before that—asking me if I wanted to go to Silverspun this weekend with her, I hadn't hesitated before saying yes. The Silverspun Music Festival—*the Coachella of Nevada!*—was located three hours north of Vegas, which meant it was not really near much else. That had seemed like a big part of its appeal then—that it was a real escape, and nobody else would be there other than the people who'd made a pilgrimage for the music. But now that I was stranded in the middle of nowhere, it was starting to seem like a bug, not a feature.

When I'd agreed to go to the festival, I could immediately see it playing out in my mind like a movie, the way I was sure everything would unfold. It would be an amazing adventure, all sun-dappled light and zippy montages, Romy and I running around and having fun and getting to listen to some of the best bands ever under endless western skies. And since I was going out of my comfort zone and taking a risk, like a heroine in a movie, I was sure I'd be rewarded with a great time, because that's how things worked.

Which was all seeming more than a little ridiculous, given what had happened.

I'd been an hour into the ride south on the post-festival LA-bound bus—alone, since Romy had ditched me practically the moment the festival had started—when I'd realized I was no longer in possession of the pouch that contained both my phone charger and the bulk of my cash. I didn't have any other form of money—I'd followed the advice of a website called Silverspun Secrets and had left my debit card and emergency credit card at home. But as I gripped my canvas bag and stared out the window, heart racing, I'd told myself it was okay—I still had enough cash in my pocket to get my car out of the garage at Union Station, and surely *someone* over the course of this seven-hour bus ride would lend me their charger. And if they didn't, it would be all right, because I'd be home soon enough.

And that was when the bus had shuddered and slowed, smoke pouring from the engine, which did not seem to be a good sign.

The driver had taken the next exit, for Jesse, Nevada, and we'd crawled to the station, the engine making unhappy sounds the whole way. We had all disembarked and headed inside, milling around until the driver came back and told us to get our bags off the bus, because things weren't getting fixed anytime soon. He told us that anyone wanting to get to LA tonight would have to first get themselves to Vegas, where another bus would be waiting. We were currently two hours north of Vegas—or an hour south of Ely. We could also get a bus in Ely, but it wasn't leaving until midnight. If we didn't take either of those options, we could wait here until seven a.m., when the replacement bus would arrive.

I had pulled up my ridesharing apps—despite the fact that the last time I'd checked my battery, it had been in the single digits—to see what my options were. And I quickly saw I didn't have any. The cost of a two-hour ride to Vegas was so eye-popping I couldn't consider it. Even getting to Ely was way out of my price range. My apps were linked to my debit card, and I didn't have enough on there to pay for it.

All around me, people who looked older—like in their twenties and thirties—had pulled out their phones. I watched them all booking cars and going outside to wait—everyone seemed to know someone, and nobody else appeared to be alone. For just a moment, I thought about asking one of them if I could get a ride—but would that actually be more dangerous than just staying put? And what if I didn't have enough money to cover my part of the trip—what then?

So I'd just grabbed my stuff—tent, duffel, canvas bag—and staked out a spot on the far side of the bus station, under a decorative mirror. It was becoming clear that I didn't have another choice—I had to stay here overnight. There were a handful of people still in the bus station who also seemed to be settling in—an older guy stretching out on a bench, a couple, a guy who looked around my age—which meant at least I wouldn't be alone here.

Trying to stop my thoughts from spinning, I did the math. The new bus would be here by seven, which meant I could be back in LA by noon—and my dad wouldn't have to know about any of this. When the bus had first broken down, I'd called him, even though my battery was already in the red. But none of the calls had ended up going through—he was spending the weekend fishing with my uncle Drew at his cabin in Shaver Lake, which had famously spotty reception. Finally, giving up, I'd just texted him that there was a slight bus issue but nothing to worry about. As I sent it off, I said a silent thanks that my dad wouldn't be back until Monday afternoon. I knew without question that he would *not* have been okay with me sleeping overnight—alone—on the floor of a bus station in Nevada, using my duffel as a pillow. But it seemed like that was exactly what was going to happen. There were no other options that I could see.

A slight wrinkle was the fact I was scheduled to fly out on the red-eye to New York Monday night—but considering it was Sunday afternoon, I wasn't in danger of missing it. And even though I had no real desire to get on the plane and start college in a godforsaken place called Connecticut, I also knew that I had to, and I didn't want to miss the flight my dad had paid for. I would just sleep here tonight, take the bus in the morning, and be home by Monday afternoon in plenty of time.

It was all going to be okay.

And if it wasn't going to be okay, it would at least be *fine*.

But even as I was trying to convince myself of this, it was like I could practically see my two best friends standing in front of me, looking at me with mirror-image skeptical expressions. Kaitlyn and Deirdre Meredith—aka Katy and Didi, aka KatyDid—had been my best friends ever since they'd arrived in my small Los Angeles town fresh from Colorado, like avenging angels come to rescue me from the horrors of seventh grade. They were Black identical twins, with upturned noses, dark eyes, long curly hair, and finely honed bullshit detectors.

Darcy. I told you so, I could hear the Didi in my head saying. Her tone was trying to conceal her joy at getting to use her favorite phrase, but not quite succeeding.

We did *warn you,* Katy chimed in. *What did you expect from Romy Andreoni?*

It's because she decided *it would be okay,* Didi said, her voice knowing.

Didi and Katy always seemed to see this as a giant flaw, but I just liked to stick to my decisions once I'd made them. Why would you want to walk around always second-guessing yourself? Sometimes, things actually *were* as clear as black and white. But my friends were always pointing out when I was doing it—sometimes in song. "And Darcy decides not to change her mind," Katy was fond of singing, to the tune of "Anna Begins" by the band that was her mom's favorite.

And it wasn't like I *never* rethought anything—I'd fully changed my tune about kombucha, something I frequently pointed out to them. But for the most part, I'd found that my first instincts and impressions were the right ones. Doubting that was where you got into trouble.

Darcy just thought she was going to be in a movie, Didi said, her tone pitying. *Like she always does.*

Well, she kind of is! The Katy in my head chimed in. *But it's seeming kind of more like a horror movie than anything else. Maybe she should have specified the genre.*

As I looked around, I realized she was right—I was in a deserted location, with a dying phone, stranded. Didi and Katy and I had started a movie club together, meeting every Friday night—it was called, creatively, Friday Night Movie Club. And since Didi always wanted horror, I had more than enough examples of situations just like this to compare it to.

But I immediately pushed this thought away and, trying to distract myself, I looked around. For the first time since I got there, I really took it in, the place that was going to be my home for the next fifteen hours. The bus station had clearly been the train station at some point in Jesse's history. There was a large sign taking up most of one wall—NEVADA NORTHERN PASSENGER TRAIN BULLETIN was printed across the top, with columns for Ely, Cobre, and McGill, and spaces for train times underneath that.

The former train station—now bus station—was a big, open space with high ceilings and tile floors, a wooden chandelier hanging over the center of the room. There were wooden benches and a line of wooden cubbies along the back wall, which once upon a time must have been for pay phones—with none still in there. TELEPHONES, the sign above the cubbies lied.

The ticket windows were all dark, with blinds pulled down in front of them. There were two bathrooms in opposite corners, with the gender signs represented by a cowboy with gigantic pants and a cowgirl with a lasso. There was a water fountain and, tucked in the back next to the empty pay-phone cubbies, a vending machine with a flickering fluorescent light. I sighed as I looked at it, with the knowledge that this was where my dinner—and probably my breakfast, too—would be coming from.

I pulled out my phone again to see the time, and then a second later, wished I hadn't. There was a wall clock, after all. My heart clenched as I looked at the battery icon—I was now down to just 2 percent.

Keeping my phone charged had been a nightmare the entire festival. There weren't enough charging stations, and the lines to get to them were epic. And the reception and Wi-Fi had been so spotty that they seemed to immediately drain any charge you did manage to get.

I looked at the angry red of my battery icon, feeling like it was judging me. In my regular life—when I wasn't in bus stations or music festivals in Nevada—my phone was *always* charged. It was one of the things I was forever bugging Katy about, since her phone was constantly dying, usually at the worst moment possible. "Two percent is for milk," I'd always tell her. "Not phones!"

Now that I was in this state, I was haunted by every time I'd used my phone casually, just because I was bored. The time I'd managed to get some service and had idly scrolled DitesMoi for some celebrity gossip (Scarlett Johansson had brunch; Wylie Sanders of the Nighthawks was locked in a courtroom battle with his much-younger wife, fighting over both their Telluride estate and custody of their three-year-old twins; there were rumors Zendaya was having relationship drama; pictures of Amy Curry's lavish Kentucky wedding). When on the bus, I'd reread two chapters of *Theseus's Sailboat* in my ebook app. It was my all-time favorite novel, and even though I had a hardcover *and* paperback copy at home, I kept a digital copy in my library so I could always have it with me.

But in retrospect, the biggest phone mistake was recording the Nighthawks set for my dad. I should have just recorded "Darcy," the song he'd named me after, and left it at that. Ever since college, he'd been a huge fan of the band—"the American U2," according to several rock journalists, even though my dad preferred to think of U2 as "the Irish Nighthawks." But he hadn't seen them live in years, not since the lead singer and front man, Wylie Sanders, had set up his

Vegas residency at the Wynn. When I'd suggested a few years ago that we could get tickets for my dad's birthday, he shook his head. "The Nighthawks belong in an arena. Not in a casino next to a mall in the middle of the desert." Then he'd smiled at me and bopped me on the head with his crossword (*New York Times*, Wednesday, half-done, pen). "But you're sweet to think of it, kid. Let's go when they're back at the Bowl, okay?"

So even though I knew I was flirting with disaster, battery-wise, I'd pressed record for the whole hourlong set, holding my phone above my head as I danced and sang along to the words I'd known my whole life, some of the very first songs I'd ever learned. And while I was glad to have the recording for him, I was paying for it now.

Okay, then, said Didi in my head. *So what's the plan, Milligan?*

I dropped my phone back in my bag and took a breath. I knew what I had to do, but that didn't make doing it any easier. I had to ask one of the people here if I could use their charger.

I looked around at the four people that were left, weighing my options. There was the middle-aged guy sleeping on one of the benches, an angry-looking red sunburn across his mostly bald head. There was the couple with headphones on sitting under the big clock on the wall, watching a shared tablet. And there was the guy across from me, the one who looked around my age.

Figuring he was probably the best candidate, I leaned forward to look a little closer. This guy was leaning back against the wall underneath the closed ticket counter, his face obscured. He was sitting cross-legged, bent over a thick book. Every now and then he would absently run a hand through his hair as he read. The very fact he had a book with him was like spotting a mirage in the desert. This guy had brought a book—a hardcover, no less—to a music festival?

I agree! the Katy in my head said approvingly. *Go ask the guy with the book. He's a snack.*

Don't say snack, my inner Didi said, rolling her eyes at her sister. *Just because* you *don't think so.*

I'm not disagreeing with your assessment, just your word choice.

I pushed myself up to standing, wondering how I was still having to hear their bickering when they weren't even here, and caught my reflection in the mirrored sign behind me.

WELCOME TO JESSE, NEVADA! WHEN YOU'RE HERE—YOU'RE HOME.

The lettering on the mirror was done in white and gold paint, peeling off in patches. The font was what I could only describe as *old-timey Western,* but I knew my dad, who ran his own advertising firm, Milligan Concepts, would have known the name of the font straight off.

This sign, combined with the chandelier and the sheer size of this building, evoked a kind of faded grandeur. It seemed to say that maybe at one point Jesse, Nevada, had been a real destination, a prosperous town, one that needed a train station this big to handle all the comings and goings. But it didn't feel that way now, from the little I'd seen of it as we'd limped into town, engine smoking. And the chandelier and the mirror's fancy script seemed to sit uneasily next to the vending machine with its fluorescent, flickering light. Like IKEA furniture in a Victorian mansion.

I stared at my refection in the mirror for a moment, just taking stock of myself—Darcy Milligan, eighteen years and three months old. I'd gotten some sun, despite the fact I thought I'd been really careful with sunblock. But I could see my cheeks were faintly pink (honestly the last thing I needed, since I was a champion blusher), and I had a new scattering of freckles across my nose and cheeks.

I had dirty-blond hair that was wavy—not curly, not straight, just sitting somewhere in that nebulous, often-frizzy middle. I had dark brown eyes—my dad's eyes—which were probably the thing about me most people commented on, since they were such a contrast with my hair and coloring.

And even though I wanted to look like my dad, scouring pictures to try to prove the resemblance, the fact was there in the mirror. It was in my strong nose, my thick eyebrows, my deep-set eyes. I was the spitting image of my mother, Gillian—I never called her *Mom*. Which seemed patently unfair, that she should be so present on my face when she hadn't bothered to stick around anywhere else.

But the last thing I wanted to do right now was think about Gillian. I gave myself a final look, brushing some dirt off my cheek and reasoning that I could have looked a lot worse, considering that I'd been sleeping in a tent for the last two nights. I smoothed out my shirt, even though I knew the wrinkles were beyond help at this point. I was wearing a variation on what I'd worn the whole festival—jean shorts and a tank top. This one was white and flowy, with an embroidered top. I had my dad's vintage Nighthawks sweatshirt in my bag for when it got cold—which I'd thought would be for the ride home, but would apparently be for sleeping overnight in a bus station. It was from when my dad was in college, and when he'd given it to me for Christmas when I was in eighth grade, it immediately became my prized possession.

I turned away from the mirror, confident that I looked like a not-dangerous, fairly normal—*Ha!* Katy and Didi said in unison—eighteen-year-old. I didn't look like someone who was about to abscond with a charger and disappear into the night, never to be seen again. Out of habit, I glanced for a second at my duffel bag and at the tent I'd borrowed from Katy and Didi—MEREDITH was printed on it in huge Sharpie'd letters—but then figured it would be fine.

I started to walk over to the guy with the book—when I realized he was no longer sitting there. Regrouping, I changed direction and headed over to the couple. I played with the pair of bracelets on my wrist as I walked. Everyone had gotten them upon arrival at the festival—mine indicated I was there on a three-day ticket, and that I was under twenty-one and not allowed in any of the beer tents, despite the fact that Romy had tried her level best to get inside all of them.

I stood in front of the couple, who were focused on their tablet. I cleared my throat, but neither of them looked at me, and I silently cursed their headphones for a moment before taking a step closer and nudging the girl's sneaker with my Birkenstocked foot.

She glanced at me, then tapped the guy next to her. They both pulled off their headphones and looked up at me questioningly. It seemed like they were in their twenties, probably. She was wearing a Charlotte Sands T-shirt, and he was in Bad Bunny merch.

"Hi," I said, giving them a small wave. "Sorry to interrupt."

"It's okay," the girl said easily, even as I saw the guy cast a longing look back at the tablet. "Kind of a crazy situation, right? Like, how can they not get a bus fixed faster?"

"Right? I know!" My words spilled out in a rush, and I realized it was a relief to acknowledge the weirdness we were all collectively experiencing. "I don't get it."

"You going to be all right here?" she glanced over to where I'd left my stuff. "Are you alone?"

"I'm okay," I said quickly. "I was just . . . wondering if either of you had a phone charger I could use? Just for a little bit! I, um, lost mine."

"Sure." She whacked the guy on the arm. He sighed, put down the tablet, and started to rummage in his backpack. I could see, frozen on the screen, that they had been watching *Scott Pilgrim vs. the World*, which I knew well from the Edgar Wright run Katy had gone on in movie club sophomore year. It was frozen on the party scene, when Scott first sees Ramona across the room and immediately falls in love—one of my favorite moments.

"Here you go." He held out a cord to me, and I eagerly grabbed it—only to realize a second later that it wouldn't work.

"Oh." I turned it over in my hands, as though I could somehow will the plug to change shape. "You don't have an iPhone charger?"

They shook their heads in unison. "Android," the girl said.

"Right," I said, handing it back. "Well . . . thanks anyway."

"If you need to call anyone, though," the girl said, her brows knitting in concern, "you can use mine. Just ask, okay?"

"I think that he had an iPhone," the guy said. He pointed to where the boy with the book had been. He shrugged. "I'm sure he'll be back."

I nodded, and gave them a small smile before I turned to walk back to my stuff. What if I really couldn't charge my phone? What then?

I was almost back to my corner when I felt a tap on my shoulder.

"I heard you were looking for me," a voice said.

I turned around—the guy with the book was standing in front of me. I could see him clearly now.

And my heart, for the first time ever, skipped an actual beat.

CHAPTER 2

Sunday

4:45 P.M.

I've always believed in love at first sight.

It was my favorite beat of any romantic movie—the crowds parting, the couple seeing each other, both people falling at the same time. That undeniable, ineffable spark, the feeling of knowing someone you just met. A look of shared destiny, of sudden understanding.

Whenever it was my turn to pick for movie club, I always went for romances. I didn't care if they were tragic and doomed, or earnest and sappy, or dramas, or comedies. As long as there was love in it—love that was never in doubt—I was in. Katy and Didi complained about this, since Didi always chose horror and Katy liked action and animated films—but I endured their haunted dolls and rat chefs and Tom Cruise endlessly running. When it was my choice, I wanted longing glances and dancing and banter and kissing in the rain. I wanted autumnal walks through Central Park, and racing through the airport, and shattering realizations in Paris. But mostly, I wanted that first moment.

And though I would have never shared this with Didi or Katy, I had always held tight to the feeling that someday it would happen for me, too. One day, I'd see someone and just *know*. Everything would be clear and simple.

I went to every middle-school dance hopeful for my own crowds-parting moment. (According to Didi, both *Romeo + Juliet* and *West Side Story* had a lot to answer for when it came to this particular idea. Which made sense, since they were from the same IP.) I'd come home from all these dances disappointed but still believing that at some point—at the *right* point—it would happen for me. It had to, right? That's what all the stories had told me.

And I kept on believing this despite the fact it had never come close to happening for myself. There was Brent Perkins, my first kiss at the slightly embarrassing age of fifteen. And then I'd dated Alex Petrosyan, my chem lab partner, for a month last fall before we both realized that we were better as friends. ("There was just no . . . chemistry," I explained to Katy and Didi, who groaned and yelled at me about puns.) There had been guys I'd kissed in the dark of backyard parties, slightly buzzed on warm beer, and guys I'd crushed on from afar, waiting for the moment in which they would finally notice me (a moment which, sadly, never seemed to arrive).

And while I'd had fun with guys, I had never slept with anyone, and I was more than fine with that. I wanted what I'd been promised—the fairy tale. Running to meet your true love across windswept moors. Eyes locking across a crowded room (or high school gym, or resort in the Catskills, or illegal underground dance club).

I wanted weak knees. I wanted the feeling of being swept off my feet. I wanted to know, from the first moment, that it was love. Meant to be.

I wanted that one perfect night.

And so I'd decided years ago that I would just hold out for that—knowing that at some point, it was bound to show up.

All of which to say, the first time I really saw this guy, and my heart temporarily forgot how to work, it seemed like the moment I'd been waiting for my whole life had—when I'd least expected it—shown up at last.

I was annoyed at myself that it had taken me so by surprise—how had I not been on guard for this possibility? But then a second later, I realized that this was *exactly* how it was supposed to work.

The guy standing in front of me was seriously cute. He was maybe an inch or two taller than my 5'7", and wiry. He had curly brown hair, sharply parted and pushed back, like he was a forties movie star, or Tom Holland. He had light blue-green eyes and cheekbones that honestly should have been illegal. He was wearing white Chucks, jeans, and a black T-shirt that fitted him perfectly. His ears stuck out the tiniest bit, which I was actually grateful for, since they were keeping him from being too intimidatingly perfect. He was smiling politely at me—he clearly had no idea that my stomach had started doing somersaults.

Pull yourself together, Milligan! my inner Didi yelled.

"Right," I said, trying to gather my wits and focus. "Sorry. What?" I cringed. *That* was what I was leading with? My moment of destiny arrived, and that was the best I could do?!

"Uh." The guy, looking politely confused, pointed at the couple with their tablet. "They said you were looking for me?"

I nodded as I tried to get it together and act like a reasonable human being.

But why start now? the Didi in my head chimed in unhelpfully.

"Yes." I knew my face was probably the color of a strawberry, but I also knew there wasn't anything I could do about it. "They mentioned that you have an iPhone?"

He shot a wary look at the couple, like he was suddenly worried they had been casing his belongings. "I . . . do."

"I just needed to borrow a charger," I explained. "I asked them, but they're androids."

His eyes widened in comedic horror. "They *are?*"

I laughed. "Android people."

"That's the most dangerous type of android," he said knowledgeably. "I've seen the movies. When robots can walk among us undetected, that's when we're in big trouble."

"But if they're undetected, how will we ever spot them? They could be here right now and we'd never know."

He looked at me for a moment, his eyes widening. "Well, I didn't really need to sleep tonight anyway. No big deal."

I laughed. "But um—*do* you have a charger that I could borrow? Just for a little bit. My phone's about to die." I pulled it out of my pocket just in time to see the little white dash-circle light up once before the screen went black—the iPhone death rattle. "And . . . it's dead."

The guy's smile dropped quickly, like he understood the gravity of my situation. "Oh man. I'm really sorry—I don't have a charger."

"Ah." I wasn't sure how this guy had gotten through three days at a festival without one, but he was probably wondering the same thing about me. Maybe he'd also attended with a flaky gym-class acquaintance who'd made off with his stuff. "I guess you lost yours too, huh?"

"I had been borrowing someone else's. And I just thought I could charge on the bus."

"Wait, is the bus still here?"

He shook his head. "They towed it."

"Oh."

He pulled out his own phone and looked down at it. "But mine's nearly dead too. So we're about to be in the same boat."

"It's not a good boat. I'd prefer not to be in this boat."

"There have been worse boats, though. Like the *Titanic*."

"The one in *Life of Pi*."

"I'm unfamiliar with that boat."

"There was a tiger in it."

"That *is* a bad boat."

I laughed again. It felt like something was bubbling up inside my chest, making me feel buoyant, like my feet could start to leave the ground and I might not even notice. I didn't even really care that I was down one person who might have a charger. "What do you think?" I nodded toward the sleeping man sprawled on the bench. "Should we ask him?"

"You mean . . . wake the stranger up and ask for a favor?"

"Uh . . . kind of?"

The guy took a tiny step toward me, causing my heart to start pounding triple-time. Not in a bad way—in an excited way. It suddenly seemed to me that there should be another option for adrenaline besides fight or flight. A more positive one, for good exciting things. Like *dance party*. Fight or flight or dance party.

"I just don't know if he's going to be in a good mood if we wake him up. He has a *sunburn* on his *head*."

I burst out laughing, then clapped my hand over my mouth. The guy was smiling—and it was a great smile, too, taking over his whole face and revealing perfectly straight, impossibly white teeth. "And how did that even happen? Like, if you don't have hair, how do you not at least have a hat?"

"These are all questions I'm sure he's asking himself right now."

"I mean, they were selling them all over the festival. He could have picked one up for the reasonable price of thirty bucks." I waited for him to chime in about how expensive everything at Silverspun had been—I had a rant about how a twenty-dollar burrito was contrary to the very spirit of what a burrito was supposed to *be* all ready to go—but he just nodded.

"Right, totally." He took a step closer to the guy. "I think what we need to do first is a recon mission."

"See what we're dealing with."

"Exactly. We should assess the situation."

I thrilled at the *we*. "I'm Darcy, by the way. Darcy Milligan."

He startled a little at that. *"Darcy?"*

"Yeah. Like the song." He just stared at me, his expression blank. "The Nighthawks song?" I was aware not everyone my age knew the band, but they *had* been the closing act of the festival.

He nodded, like he was trying to call the song to mind. "I think I've heard it."

"It's total dad music," I said with a laugh. "But—my dad was the one who named me, so . . ." I looked at him, expectant, and after a second he seemed to realize he was supposed to say something.

"Sorry! Right. I'm Russell."

"Russell," I echoed, tasting the name in my mouth. It was a great name. It somehow evoked autumn and guitar solos and road trips under wide-open skies. And best of all, I'd never met another one before, which meant he was minting this name in real time. My first Russell.

"Russell. Henrion," he added after a moment. He pronounced it with a slight accent—*En-ri-on*.

"Is that French?"

"Do you speak it?" He then said something in French, very quickly, and I nearly fainted. Katy, who had what could only be described as a shrine to Timothée Chalamet in her room, would have burst into flames on the spot. A *cute guy* was speaking *French* to me. It was almost too much to take. I cursed the fact that I'd taken Spanish and—for reasons passing understanding—Latin, all throughout school. What good were they to me now?

"Oh, um, no. I mean, *non*."

He smiled. "My mom's French. I wasn't going to be able to get away with not speaking it."

"Well—nice to meet you, Russell."

"*Et vous aussi.* That is—you too. Darcy." He held eye contact with me for a moment, and suddenly I wished that we were in a more formal environment, so that we could have shaken hands without it being weird. I wished we were in a Jane Austen ballroom, about to do the . . . pavane, or whatever. I had a feeling that if we touched, there would be an actual spark.

His mouth curled up in a smile on one side—god, I couldn't stop staring at his mouth—and as we kept looking at each other, I let myself wonder if maybe he was feeling the same thing I was. Maybe all he wanted was to reach out and touch my hand as well. Maybe the world had spun the first time he'd seen me, too.

Was it possible?

"Right." He tore his eyes away from mine and cleared his throat. "So. Our recon mission. I say we do a lap, see what we can see."

"Look out for any evidence of an iPhone."

"And if that fails, we can try to make noise or something so that he wakes up, and then we take advantage of the moment to ask him about chargers."

"Solid plan."

"Why, thank you."

He grinned at me and we crept toward the sleeping man. I saw the girl look up from her tablet and give me a small, understanding smile as I passed her.

We approached the sunburned guy, who was sleeping on his side. His head was even worse up close—a dark, mottled red, with patches that were already peeling. Russell looked at me and mouthed *Yikes* and I had to press my lips together tightly to prevent myself from laughing.

The guy's possessions were tucked under the bench he was sleeping on—a tent bag like I had and a large hiking-style backpack. Unfortunately, the backpack was zipped up tightly, and I wasn't about to go rifling through a stranger's possessions. It was one thing to assess the situation; it was quite another to cross that line. I met Russell's eye and shook my head, and I could see that he'd come to the same conclusion. Just as I'd started to take a step away, though, the guy let out a giant, rumbling snore. He rolled over on his back, and his arm flung over the side of the bench, his hand grazing the floor. His hand that had a phone in it.

An Android phone.

I pointed at it, and Russell nodded. We walked back to the other end of the bus station, near my stuff, out of earshot of the sleeping, sunburned, snoring, non–Apple user. Russell shook his head. "That's a bummer. What's with all the Androids in this bus station?"

"Thanks for trying to help, though."

"It might have been purely selfish. My phone's about to die too."

I nodded. Silence fell, and I realized I didn't know what happened now. My stomach plunged at the thought that this might be over. Were we going to go back to our separate corners now, after the banter and the French and the sparks? Was this just . . . done? It couldn't be, right? Not if this was what I was hoping it was.

"Okay," Russell said. "So I saw a few places in town as we were driving in. Not a ton, but it might be worth trying. Maybe we'll find someone who has a charger they can lend us, or a place we can buy one."

Relief flooded through me, like a cool drink on a hot day. This wasn't over. It was—possibly—just beginning.

"What do you think, Darcy? Want to explore?"

I nodded. In that moment, what I *really* wanted was a time-out so I somehow could have pulled Didi and Katy into a huddle and told them everything that had happened and was currently, right now, still happening. How did all the love-at-first-sight people in movies and books do it? How did they not have to grab their friends to fill them in? I wanted a pause in the adventure just to acknowledge that an adventure was happening.

Because something *was* happening. I could feel it in my bones. It felt like the curtain had just risen on a play I'd been waiting my whole life to perform, lines memorized and blocking down pat.

So even though I couldn't talk to Didi and Katy about this, I'd just have to save everything up to tell them all about it later. Suddenly, the stories from this weekend would not be about how Romy had screwed me—they would be about Russell. Romy's role in this whole thing had diminished—just like that, she'd gone from villain to footnote.

"I do," I said, then felt myself blush. "I mean, yeah. Exploring. Let's go for it." I slung my canvas bag over my shoulder, then picked up my duffel and the tent bag. Once I was carrying all of it, I could feel just how weighed down I was. "Oof."

"Maybe—" Russell started to reach for my tent bag, then paused and drew his hand back. "May I?" I nodded, and he took the tent bag from me. "'Meredith,'" he read.

"I borrowed it from my best friends. It's their parents' tent."

"Your best friends are siblings?"

I nodded. Occasionally, people had commented on this over the years. *Was it strange/Was I closer to one of them than the other/Did I ever feel left out?* And I never knew how to explain that it had always just worked, from the very first seventh-grade lunch period. And knowing Didi and Katy as I now did, I could see how it worked for them, too. That they were so close that someone who was only friends with one of them would have fractured them in some fundamental way. "They're twins. Identical."

"That must be fun."

"It really is." He gave me a smile and I drew in a breath, like I was preparing for all the questions I wanted to ask him. Because I wanted to know it all. Where he was from, and what his middle name was, and what his go-to pizza topping was, and what he'd wanted to be when he was five, and what he wanted to be now. I wanted to know everything. I got a sudden flash of a huge undiscovered country in the distance, just waiting to be explored, beckoning me.

Russell lifted the tent bag and crossed to the first bench, then slid it underneath. "What do you think? Feel safe enough?"

I nodded, and pushed my duffel underneath as well. After all, there were only three people here, and I couldn't imagine any of them stealing my stuff. And even if they did—they had no place to *go* with it. That was what had landed us all here in the first place. I slung my canvas bag over my shoulder—practically empty except for my Nighthawks sweatshirt, my sunglasses, half a granola bar, and my tiny toiletry bag.

"Do you want to put your stuff here too?" I asked. I looked around, but the only thing where he'd been sitting was a small black backpack

"I'm okay," Russell said as he crossed over to it and slung it on his back. As he did, his black T-shirt rose up a little, giving me a flash of his stomach, making my mouth go suddenly dry.

"That's really all you have?" I was trying to make the backpack make sense. I'd packed as lightly as I could—despite Romy bugging me about what I was packing in the run-up to the festival, texting me constantly about what I was bringing—but I still hadn't been able to do anything smaller than my duffel bag.

"Yeah. I . . . um . . ." He dropped his eyes to the tile floor and took a breath. "I had a fight with the guy I came to Silverspun with. I didn't want to head back with him, so I just took my bag and got on the bus."

"I had a similar thing! Romy, the girl I was at the festival with, headed off to Palm Springs with some people she'd met to 'keep the party going.'" Russell made a face at that, which reflected pretty much the way I'd felt when I heard Romy say it, and I laughed. It was kind of crazy that we had both washed up here in similar circumstances. It felt like it was more than a coincidence. Was it a sign?

It's totally a sign! Katy enthused.

A sign of what? Didi asked skeptically. *Maybe Sunburn Head was also ditched by his friends. Want to go hang out with* him?

Ignore her, Katy said. *It means something. It totally does.*

"Sorry about your friend."

Russell took a breath, like he was going to say something, but then let it out and just smiled at me. "It's okay," he said, his eyes finding mine and holding them. "In fact, right now I'm kind of grateful to him."

Heat crept into my cheeks, but I made myself keep looking right at him. "Me too," I said, then realized that didn't make any sense. "I mean, I'm grateful to my person. At the festival . . . who left . . ." My voice trailed off. "Anyway. Ready to go?"

He nodded and crossed to the door of the bus station and held it open for me. "After you."

I tried not to swoon at that—Didi was always talking about how straight girls were far too impressed by things that should just be baseline manners—but I also couldn't help noticing how nice his arms were, his biceps and forearms and large hands holding the door open. I glanced back for just a second at the bus station—my stuff stashed under the bench, the bald guy still snoring, the couple and their movie. The girl gave me a look that clearly said *Go for it!* and I smiled at her.

I tried to freeze the moment for just a second, pause it for posterity. Because I was pretty sure this was when everything started happening. This was Jesse and Céline getting off the train together, Tony and Maria ducking under the bleachers, Jack and Rose taking a turn around the deck. The moment that everything started to change.

I took a breath. And then I stepped forward, out of the bus station, into the Nevada afternoon—ready for our story to begin.

CHAPTER 3

Sunday
5:05 P.M.

I t was still warm outside, but not too hot. It *was* August in Nevada, but we were north enough that we weren't getting true desert heat—it had been warm during the days at the festival, but it had gotten really cold at night. The second the sun had gone down, the temperature had dropped, so much so that I'd been grateful for Romy's insulated sleeping bags and ended up sleeping in a long-sleeved T-shirt both nights.

"Well," Russell said, turning in a circle. "Huh."

I followed suit, looking around. I could see now—in a way I hadn't been able to tell from the highway—that Jesse must be in some kind of basin or valley. Because we were surrounded on three sides by mountains. They were dotted with green trees—and just looking at them, you could imagine, not too long from now, when they would be white-capped and covered with snow. We'd been able to see some mountains in the distance at the festival—but it was nothing like this.

But despite how gorgeous the scenery was, this didn't translate to the area outside the bus station. We were at the end of a paved road—I could see the highway just over some fencing, cars zipping by on it. The station had a parking lot with a few scraggly trees planted in the medians between the rows of painted lines. Across from us was a Mobil, and I was momentarily hopeful that we might be able to find a charger there before I realized that there were weeds growing around the pumps, and that the little mini-mart was boarded up. This clearly hadn't been a functioning gas station in a while.

"What do you think?"

I looked and saw that Russell had walked over to a brown sign that read VISIT JESSE, NEVADA! And then in smaller letters under it, PROSPECTING MUSEUM! HISTORIC DOWNTOWN!

"I think whoever made this sign really likes their exclamation points."

"I think more signs should do it. Get you really excited about merging ahead! Or exiting right!"

I laughed. The sign pointed to the left, down a paved, dusty road that ran between the bus station and the gas station, away from the highway. "Let's check it out. I can't say I've ever been to a prospecting museum before."

"It'll be a first for me, too."

We started walking down the road together. There was a sidewalk near the bus station, but it ended when we passed it, and then it was just the road with its yellow line, faded in places. There was nobody else out that I could see, and after having spent the last three days surrounded by more people than I'd ever seen in my life, it was giving me a bit of whiplash.

I glanced over at Russell. There was so much I suddenly wanted to say—so much I wanted to ask—that I wasn't sure where to start. He looked back at me, one eyebrow quirking up, and I wondered if he'd just had the same thought. "So."

"So," he echoed, smiling at me.

I cast around for what to say next. I wanted to just get to the point where we'd gotten all of the small talk out of the way, and we'd talk about . . .

I realized, startled, that I actually didn't know how this worked. In all my movies, you never actually heard the getting-to-know-you conversations. They were usually covered in a montage, with some pop song playing over it, and by the end of the montage, everyone was firmly in love.

We were kicking up dust with every step, and I looked down at Russell's white Chucks. "I'm worried about your sneakers."

"My *sneakers*?"

"I mean, aren't they going to get dirty?" They were gleaming white at the moment, including the laces. How had he managed to keep them so clean during the festival? It felt like everything I owned was covered in a fine layer of dust.

"I don't mind. I'll get to take home a souvenir of historic Jesse, Nevada."

"Still." I shook my head. "Maybe it wasn't the day to wear Converse."

Russell looked over at me with a grin. "Fun fact! Okay, so—"

"Wait—did you just say *fun fact*?"

He blushed, which I was actually kind of glad to see. It meant that I wasn't the only one getting embarrassed and turning red around here. And somehow, it made him seem more approachable— not just a guy with perfect teeth and shoes who had everything together. Someone who'd just said *fun fact* and whose ears were currently bright red.

"Um. Maybe? Never mind."

"No, it's good. It's cute." A second later, I wondered if I should have said that. It was like I'd just said the quiet part out loud, admitted why we were both out here wandering around together on the pretense of trying to find a charger. Or at least that was why *I* was out wandering around with him. But I was hoping that he liked me, too. He did, right? Otherwise, why all the eye contact and door holding?

And more than that—it was just a *vibe* I was getting. A sense from him that he was as aware as I was about the space between us, and when it widened or narrowed. How I was suddenly so much more tuned in to my hands and how near they were to his and how I could have reached out to him without even extending my arm all the way. I didn't think my stomach would be regularly swooping and dipping—as though I were on a roller coaster only I could see—if he wasn't feeling some of this too.

He shook his head. "My friends are always making fun of me for them."

I couldn't quite suppress a giggle. "For your *fun facts*?"

"Yes! Just like that. That's just what they do. In fact, Tall Ben—"

"Sorry, *Tall* Ben? That seems to imply the existence of Short Ben. Or at least Medium Ben."

Russell laughed, then took a breath, like this was going to be a story. "Okay, so there are two Bens. We've all been friends since fifth grade. And when we were younger, Tall Ben was really tall."

"I mean, I should hope so. Otherwise it's false advertising."

"Well, keep that in mind. It becomes relevant later. So there we were. Russell and the Bens—"

"*Excellent* band name—"

"But then in eighth grade, Regular Ben started to grow really tall. And now he's the tallest of all of us. He's like six inches taller than Tall Ben. But at that point, you can't just go around changing people's names. Tall Ben was just Tall Ben."

"So what happened?"

"Well, we decided to look at it like Starbucks. Where tall is actually the shorter drink."

"Or you could call the other one Benti."

Russell burst out laughing, like I'd surprised him. "Oh man," he said, shaking his head, still smiling as he slung his bag around and unzipped it, took out his phone, and unlocked the screen. "That's great. I'll have to tell them—"

"Your phone is still charged?" I asked, surprised.

He looked at it and shook his head, then dropped it back into his bag. "Just died."

"Sorry about that."

"You should be. The pun was so good it made me use the last of the battery in an attempt to share it."

"Well, I'm glad you liked it. Just like the Bens and your facts, my best friends always complain whenever I pun too much."

"These are the twins?"

"Yeah, Katy and Didi. Because . . ." I hesitated.

"What?"

"Well—I kind of make a lot of them," I confessed as I played with my Silverspun bracelets, hoping this wasn't a deal-breaker. "Didi is always saying how a pun is a joke nobody enjoys. Katy kind of gives me a little grimace whenever I make one, like she's acknowl- edging something happened, but nothing good. And my ex, Alex, said every time I made one, I was somehow causing him to get *less* funny." Russell laughed. "But I can't help it! It's how I was raised."

"How you were *raised*?"

"Well, my dad's in advertising. So it was just the coin of the realm in our house. Puns, wordplay . . . you need to be good at them to come up with taglines and product names, so it just became second nature. It wasn't until much later that I realized most people not only don't find them funny, but actively dislike them."

"Fools. Ingrates."

I grinned. "Thank you." The fear I'd had—that we wouldn't have something to talk about—was gone. Why had I been worried? This was fun. It was *easy*, like I'd always known it would be when it was right. We walked a few steps in comfortable silence before I realized something and turned to him. "Wait, what was the fun fact?"

"It's really okay."

"No, I want to know! You can't just dangle a fun fact and then not deliver on it. Fact, please."

"See, now there's been all this buildup. It can't possibly deliver."

"Um, I think I'll be the judge of that."

He looked at me with a half smile, and I smiled back, just reveling in how . . . right this felt? Like we were throwing a ball back and forth without having to talk about what sport we wanted to play or what the rules were. Just like we both automatically knew. "It's that Chuck Taylor was an actual person. Converse were essentially invented by him. He was a shoe salesman and part-time basketball player."

"Whoa." I thought about my own Chucks—cute, but with practically no support, and not a shoe I ever would have exercised in. "People used to play *basketball* in those?"

"Converse used to be the official shoe of the NBA! They were huge in the sixties and seventies. In fact, they were basketball shoes before they were . . . I don't know . . ."

"Walk-around shoes?"

"Exactly."

I slowed, then stopped as I looked around. "I think this might be it."

"I think you're right."

We were at the beginning of a street, what another brown sign—the same style as the one near the bus station—proclaimed as HISTORIC DOWNTOWN JESSE! EST. 1865. On either side, there were low one- and two-story buildings lining the street. They were made of dark red bricks or wood, and seeing this long street—with the mountains rising up behind them—made me feel like I was suddenly living inside one of the many, many Westerns my dad had made me watch over the years.

We started walking down the street—and I could see that most of the buildings had the raised or curved sections above them that screamed *stereotypical Western town*, like we'd just wandered onto a movie set. But it didn't look like any of the buildings were general stores or saloons any longer. Some were boarded up, but most seemed to have current businesses in them—A Touch of Class beauty salon, Jesse Chamber of Commerce, This & That Resale Emporium. But exactly none of these currently looked open. We passed the Prospecting Museum, which was next to the Stagecoach Souvenir Store—both closed. I realized it was getting later on a Sunday, and it maybe didn't seem like Jesse was the most happening town to begin with, but still.

We were walking down the center of the street—while there were a few cars parked in front of meters, there was nobody driving, so it felt like this was safe. I found I couldn't shake the feeling that we'd wandered back into another time. The iconography of all the buildings and the mountains rising up all around us were familiar in a way I hadn't been expecting. It could have come straight out of *Unforgiven*—except with lines on either side of the road for cars to park, and fire hydrants, and no Clint Eastwood looking for revenge.

"So when they said *historic*," Russell said, "it seems they meant it."

I felt a thrill, deep in my bones, that he'd been thinking just the same thing I had. "I mean, it was right there on the sign. We should have believed them." I looked around, struck by the quietness of the street. "It's weird to see it like this, right?"

"What do you mean?"

"Just—these buildings are probably the original ones! From, like, a hundred years ago, right? In the middle of whatever boom created this town?"

"Gold?" Russell asked, then frowned. "Wait—was gold just California?"

"I . . . don't remember. My fourth-grade teacher would *not* be happy."

"Did you do the Gold Rush in fourth grade? I'm pretty sure that's when we did the Spanish Missions."

"We did that in sixth. I remember it well, because I did a whole presentation in the style of a heist movie, and I called it *Missions: Impossible*." Russell laughed, throwing his head back, and I smiled, feeling something warm spread through my chest. "My sixth-grade teacher was *not* a fan. She called my dad and everything."

"That sounds amazing. I want to see it."

"I threw it out. Like, so long ago."

"Well, that's just wrong. It should have been preserved for pun posterity. Did you use the Lalo Schifrin music?"

"Uh—maybe? Is that who did the theme song?" Russell nodded. "Then yes. That's very impressive."

"What is?"

"That you know the guy who did the music."

"I heard a *lot* about him growing up, believe me. It was . . ." He stopped, and pointed to the side of the street. There was a storefront—dark, of course, advertising something called Silver State Adventures. From the illustrated sign, it looked like it booked mine tours and trips to a nearby hot spring. "So it must be silver, right?"

"This is the problem with having a dead phone. I can't Wikipedia Jesse, Nevada." I took a step closer to the store and looked in the window. "But it seems like this town must have popped up in a silver boom? They're advertising mine tours of *something*, after all."

"And I don't think there were gold mines, were there? Wasn't it just . . . people finding gold in creeks? What's it called—panning?"

We stared at each other, our shared lack of California mineral knowledge becoming clear to both of us. "But . . . the term *gold mine* has to come from somewhere, right?" I asked.

"You make an excellent point."

"And Nevada had to be the Silver State for a reason, right? And that's why California is the Golden State?"

"I thought—I thought we were the Golden State because of . . . like, sunshine?" He stared at me, his eyes wide. "Have I gotten this wrong my whole life? I feel like I need to rethink everything." I laughed at that, and Russell smiled, like he was joining in.

We kept walking down the quiet street, and I tried to imagine what it would have been like 150 years ago, before the (closed) vape store existed, when things would have been at their peak. I tried to picture a town so bustling it couldn't even have imagined an afternoon this deserted. "It's funny."

"What is?"

"Just being here. It's . . . like a place out of time, you know?" I was finding my thoughts even as I was speaking them. "I'm just thinking about all the people who would have come here. The ones who showed up from other places, ready to begin again . . . find a fortune and start over. Become someone else, someone nobody back home could recognize."

Russell nodded slowly as he looked around—it seemed like he was turning my words over in his head, which I liked. Like he wasn't just jumping in because it was his turn to talk.

"But that being said, I don't think we're going to find an iPhone charger here."

"I don't think we're going to find a *telegraph* charger here." I laughed at that, and Russell grinned at me. "Ready for another fun fact?"

"*Am* I!" I said, making my voice comically enthused. The second after I said it, I worried that Russell wouldn't get that I was kidding, like my ex, Alex, never seemed to. But he just smiled wider.

"It's not exactly related to telegraphs—but it's in the wheelhouse of old-fashioned phones."

"I'll allow it."

"So in the 1940s, people used to call the phone the Ameche."

"The *Ameche*?"

"Yeah. The actor Don Ameche had played Alexander Graham Bell in a biopic, and so it became what people said instead of *phone*."

"So what you're saying is that we're looking for an Ameche charger?"

He looked over at me, a smile forming on his face. "Exactly."

"That *is* a fun fact. How does one even come to be in possession of a fact like that?"

"There was this musical about ten years ago—*The Game of Telephone*. Do you know it?"

"No. But that's not saying all that much. I only know, like, three." I meant this as a kind-of joke, but Russell had gone stockstill, his face grave.

"Seriously?"

"Um. Yes? I saw *Hamilton* at the Pantages. And I'm pretty sure *The Music Man*, too . . ." Russell was still looking shocked by this, so I tried to think of any I'd seen put on at school. "Um . . . the one with the cats?"

"That's *Cats*. And that should *not* be one of your examples. How is this possible?"

"We weren't big on musicals in my family, I guess. Do Disney movies count?"

Russell shook his head. "No."

"Oh. Um—sorry. I didn't realize this was such an issue."

"It's not—I apologize. I know I can get a little . . . It's what I want to do. Musicals. To write them, I mean."

"Oh!" His reaction was making more sense now. "That's so cool. Like Lin-Manuel Miranda?" I was pulling out literally the only musical composer I knew, but hoping it would still get me some credit.

"Yes! Him, Sondheim, Jeanine Tesori, Pasek and Paul, Michael R. Jackson, the Lopezes . . . it's my favorite art form."

"That's really great." I took a breath to ask him if he'd be studying it in college—but then a second later, stopped myself. Because I suddenly realized I didn't know if he was starting school this year, like me.

I'd assumed he was around my age—but there was a possibility he was already in college. Or not in college at all. Or, more distressing, that he was a really mature-looking high school sophomore. I was all at once aware of the knowledge gulf between us, one that hadn't seemed to have been there with the fun facts and the puns. I didn't even know where he was *from*.

But *was* it such a big deal? In so many of these stories, it didn't seem super important. What mattered was how you *felt*. After all, Maria and Tony didn't know anything about each other before they were declaring their love and inadvertently starting a gang war. "*West Side Story!*" I burst out triumphantly. Russell raised an eyebrow. "Sorry. I just thought of another musical I know."

"That did kind of come out of nowhere."

"I think it came out of *somewhere*."

He just looked at me for a second, and then his face broke open in a smile as he got the joke. "I can't even believe you just said that." His eyes were on mine, and his face was full of wonder. "Who *are* you?"

"Darcy," I said, my voice coming out a bit strangled. "Like the song." My thoughts were spinning in every direction, and if I'd been in a musical myself, I had a feeling this would have been the moment I would have burst into song.

Calm down. And maybe get some basic facts about this dude, Didi advised, her tone dry.

Unnecessary, Katy insisted, sounding swoony.

We walked in silence for a few paces, and I tried to think about the best way to do this. I was realizing that most of the time when I'd met someone, there had been context. I was usually meeting someone through school, or through a friend—and either way, I had something of a backstory sketched in. I'd almost never just encountered someone out in the world like this, not tethered to anything. The two of us could have been anyone, from anywhere. And while I liked that idea in theory, it also meant I wasn't armed with baseline facts. But I wasn't sure how to go about getting them. I didn't think I could just demand *How old are you and where do you go to school?* without building up to it a little.

After a moment of silent deliberation, I finally asked, "Are you—studying musicals in school?"

Russell looked down at the ground for a moment. I was about to ask the question again—maybe he hadn't heard me, or was still reeling from my lack of composer knowledge—but then he turned to me and took a breath. "I am. I got into the musical theater BFA program at University of Michigan. I start next week."

"Oh, that's awesome." I was secretly relieved that he was clearly around my age, and couldn't help thinking that it was just one more sign that this was meant to be happening. Out of only five people at the bus station, two of us were the same age *and* had this kind of connection? It meant something.

It means teenagers are more broke than adults, Didi said skeptically.

Ignore her, Katy said with a sigh. *It totally means something.*

"What about you? Are you going to college?"

My stomach sank, the way it always did when I thought about what would be happening in about a day and a half. "Yeah. I'm going to Stanwich College." I tried to sound like a normal incoming freshman would, excited about going to school—like Russell had just sounded. I tried not to think about what it would actually mean when I showed up there, or about the note on the brochure that had been sent to me. I pushed all that away and took a breath to begin my explanation, which always seemed to be necessary, since most people on the West Coast hadn't heard of a tiny liberal-arts college in a nothingburger state. *It's in Connecticut. About an hour outside New York City. Yes, it* will *be a big change in weather.*

"In Connecticut, right?"

"Yeah—you've heard of it?"

"My—Montana, a friend of mine, knew someone who went there. She talked about it a lot."

I nodded, trying to pretend like I hadn't even noticed that *my.* I just silently hoped that he was talking about his ex and not a current girlfriend. Because otherwise, would he be out here with me right now? Would my heart be pounding this way if he wasn't feeling something too? I decided this Montana *had* to be his ex. It didn't make any sense otherwise.

"That's a long way from home," Russell said, then frowned. "Wait—where is home? I assumed LA, because of the bus, but . . ."

"LA," I confirmed, a little bit shocked that we'd gotten this far without establishing this. But I also kind of *liked* it. It was like, for once, I wasn't being defined by who I was or where I went to school or the people we had in common. Like I could just *be.* "We're in Raven Rock. Me and my dad." Russell didn't say anything, which wasn't that shocking. A lot of people hadn't heard of our town, a tiny, peaceful pocket in the northeast corner of the city. One main street, farmers market every Friday, and more frozen-yogurt shops than made any rational sense. "It's about as far east as you can be in LA without crossing into Pasadena. College of the West is there. Basically," I said with a laugh, falling back on the analogy I'd heard my dad use more than once, "picture Brentwood. Then take away all the assholes, drop down a few tax brackets, and that's Raven Rock."

Russell looked down and frowned and I wondered if he'd just noticed how dusty his Chucks had become. "I think I've been there," he said, sounding distracted. "There's that hot dog place, right?"

"Walt's?"

"I think so? With the pinball machines?"

"Yes! That's the one."

"It was so good."

"It really is . . . wait, where are *you* from?" Was there a chance that he lived in Glendale or Highland Park, just a few towns over from me? It didn't seem possible. I felt like I would have heard tell of him—this cute, smart, pun-appreciating guy—if he'd been anywhere near my orbit. Russell stopped, stared down at the state of his shoes, and sighed. "I did try and tell you."

"You did." He looked up at me and shrugged. "Ah well. There's something kind of creepy about too-perfect sneakers anyway, don't you think? Like you can tell they've just been boxed away and never worn." He frowned, like he was trying to call something to mind. "Sorry, you asked me something?"

"Where you're from."

"We live in Ojai," he said, naming a town two hours' drive outside LA. "Me and my mom and dad."

"Ojai there," I responded immediately, which was the joke I made basically when anyone said the name of that town. "Sorry. I bet you're sick of hearing that."

"You get used to it. It's practically the town motto."

"I can't believe you live there." I'd only been once, two years ago, when my dad and I went there to attend his friend Dave's second wedding. But it had immediately seemed magical—the rolling green hills; the tiny, perfect downtown; the outdoor bookshop; the people riding around on beach cruisers. All at once, I could picture Russell there—biking through downtown, the breeze ruffling his curls.

And the fact that he lived in Ojai meant we definitely didn't know any of the same people. A second later, I realized how much I liked this. I didn't want to play *who do you know*. I didn't want to find out that Russell knew Katy's former soccer teammate or Didi's ex-girlfriend's sister. We were in a historic downtown in the middle of Nevada, late in the afternoon on a Sunday, with the most beautiful mountains I'd ever seen surrounding us. There was nobody else around, and in the light that was just starting to fade, it seemed like maybe we were the only two people on Earth and that all of this had been conjured just for us.

"So have you always been in Ojai?" He looked over at me and I shrugged. "It just seems like a long drive for hot dogs."

"I mean, they were *really* good hot dogs."

"This is true."

"We're in LA occasionally—I think my mom had read about Walt's somewhere and wanted to make a pilgrimage. But yeah, it's just the three of us in the same house I grew up in." He laughed. "Pretty boring, huh?"

I shook my head. I could see it—Russell riding his bike up to a cute cozy cottage, a perfect small-town life. "Your parents are still married?" I wasn't quite able to keep a note of something—envy? longing?—out of my voice when I asked this.

"Yes," he said, then hesitated. "I mean . . . kind of? They're still together, but they weren't ever technically married."

"Oh," I said, not sure what to say to this. Russell looked over at me and laughed, then started walking again. I fell into step with him, our feet falling at the same time, like it was the easiest thing in the world.

"They *thought* they were. They were on this boat, and got married by who they thought was the captain, but then later they found out it was just a random waiter who didn't have the authority to marry anyone."

"I've always thought it's so weird that sea captains have the authority to marry people."

"You've *always* thought that?"

I laughed but kept going. "Yes! Like, why is it this one job in transportation that gives you this power? Why not train conductors? Or bus drivers?"

"I have never thought about it. Unlike you, who has *always* thought about it."

"I stand by what I said!"

"I guess . . ." Russell tilted his chin up, looking at the sky, like he was thinking. "Maybe it's because sea voyages used to be really long? And it's not like on trains, where you'd be stopping in places where there would be ministers or rabbis or judges or whatever. So it was more necessary."

"But these random ship people couldn't wait until they got back on dry land? They had to be married in the middle of the ocean?"

"I don't know. I mean, if you met someone on a ship—and you fell in love—maybe you wouldn't want to wait. Maybe you'd want your life with that person to start right away." He turned to me and something about his expression made my heart stutter again.

"I can see that."

"That's what my parents thought, at any rate." I took a breath, to ask more about his parents, what they did, when he turned to me. "What about you? You live with your parents?"

"My dad," I said with a smile. "It's just the two of us."

Russell's expression suddenly became more careful. "Is—is your mom . . . ?"

"They're divorced." I could see that he was waiting for more of an explanation, which I was used to by now. When a mom was the primary care parent after a divorce, nobody thinks anything of it. But when you tell them you're being raised by your dad, everyone feels entitled to answers, some *reason* this is all happening.

I thought about going into all of it—but what was the point? It wasn't even like it was a good story.

My parents met when they were both in college—she wanted to be an actress, he wanted to be a writer. They got married in a courthouse ceremony so Gillian could get on my dad's insurance— he'd gotten a job at an advertising firm, something to pay the bills while he wrote his novel and she auditioned. They were planning on having a proper ceremony at some point in the future, but that never happened, because a year later, I came along.

The fact that my parents had me when they were twenty-four meant my dad was a *lot* younger than most of my friends' parents. Didi and Katy thought it was weird I helped my dad's best friend organize his fortieth birthday party. "Our parents were older than forty when we were *born*," Katy had pointed out.

My dad always said this was part of the problem—that they had been too young to become parents. But whatever the reason, when I was two, Gillian left, going off to pursue an acting career. Since things hadn't been working for her in LA, she wanted to be free to try her luck in New York, then London. And then five years after she left, she married a British guy. She ended up having three kids with Anthony—pronounced the British way, *Ant-ony*, like the *h* was just there for decoration. I saw her intermittently throughout the years, but not often. And people would sometimes make sad faces when they heard I didn't have a mother, but I'd really never minded it. I barely ever thought about her, and we didn't keep any pictures of her around. The wedding pictures and early photo albums had, since I could remember, always been boxed away in the attic. The only picture of Gillian I had was in a shoebox under my bed, and I didn't feel the need to look at it much. You can't miss what you've never had, after all. I'd also never had a dog, or a motorcycle, but nobody seemed to get all upset about that.

The last time I'd spent more than an hour or two with Gillian was when I was seven, and she was performing in the Oregon Shakespeare Festival. Since then, the times I'd seen her could be measured on one hand, and never very long, the two of us making stilted conversation at slightly too-nice restaurants. She sent me Christmas and birthday presents that I always opened last, alone in my room—knowing that they would be just a little bit wrong. And even when she moved back from London last year, it wasn't like I wanted or expected anything to change. If it had been up to me, I would have been happy never seeing her again.

But then, this year, it had become very clear that it wasn't up to me at all.

I looked over at Russell, lit by the fading Nevada sunlight, and I realized the last thing I wanted to do was bring Gillian into this.

She didn't belong here, and a bare-bones CliffsNotes version was all she warranted. "She moved to London and got remarried. They have three kids."

"Oh!" He smiled at me. "You have half-siblings?"

"Uh—yeah. I guess." I'd only met Gillian and Anthony's kids once, at a very awkward dinner a few years ago. Their oldest daughter, Freya, sometimes tried to message me on Instagram, but I hadn't ever accepted her requests. It wasn't like we were going to become some happy blended family, so there wasn't any point. "I don't really know them," I said now, shrugging one shoulder like it was *just no big deal*. "They mostly grew up in London."

"Heck of a commute."

"Exactly." I looked over at him and smiled. "What about you? Do you have any brothers or sisters?"

"I'm the only kid my parents had. Which was really nice, in a way. It was just the three of us, so I didn't have to compete with anyone for attention."

"Yes! Like with me and my dad—we became a little unit." He gave me a nod of recognition that I thrilled to see. "It did always seem fun to have a big family, though. My friend Maud has three sisters, and her house is always busy and crowded and loud . . . but in a good way?" I shook my head. "I guess we'll never know."

We walked in silence for a few steps, and I could see the end of this street ahead of us. I wasn't sure what would happen when we reached it, and slowed down a little, even though we weren't walking that fast to begin with. "Is everyone telling you to prepare for the change in weather?" Russell frowned and squinted up at the sky, and I shook my head. "Sorry—not this weather. I mean, because you're going to Michigan. Ever since I told people I'm going to

Connecticut, all they're doing is telling me I'm not going to be able to handle East Coast winters."

"I know! And it's not like we don't have weather here. It does get cold in California occasionally. We'll be fine."

"Well—*I'll* probably be fine. Michigan seems like a whole other level of cold."

He laughed. "I think I can handle it. I've spent a bunch of time in Colorado, and it can't be that much worse, right?"

"So in addition to fighting off frostbite, you're going to be writing musicals? At Michigan?"

Russell nodded, his whole face lighting up. "Yeah. They actually have one of the best programs in the country. The top ones are USC, Tisch at NYU, Temple University, and Michigan. You have to compose an original musical to get in, and . . ." He stopped and turned to me, his brows drawing together. "Wait, why were we talking about musicals?"

". . . because you're studying them?"

"No, before," he said, the furrow between his eyes deepening. "I brought it up for some reason, and then discovered you'd seen zero musicals—"

"Three," I countered. "At least. Probably more. Um . . ." I tried to think back. I secretly liked that there was enough of our conversation to sort through—tangents and information and puns about his friends' names—that the answer wasn't immediately apparent.

"Sorry. I know this is annoying."

"No, I'm used to it. My dad is always doing this—he says that his train of thought jumps the tracks, never to be seen again. We spend a lot of time tracing it back, especially when he's working on a campaign." I stopped walking and concentrated, trying to find our way back. "Was it about that guy—the one who played Alexander Graham Bell?"

"Ameche!" Russell's expression cleared, like the sun breaking through the clouds. "Yes! That's it. Darcy, you're a genius. I brought up musicals because I was talking about *The Game of Telephone*. That's a musical," he added helpfully.

"Thanks for that."

"Anyway, it was all about how the telephone came to be invented, and Don Ameche basically functioned as the narrator."

"Huh." I was trying to be polite, in case this was Russell's favorite musical, but I was having trouble imagining something I'd want to see less.

"It only ran for a few performances in the West End, but I always had a soft spot for it. And, clearly, the Ameche fact stuck with me."

"So you're all about the facts, huh?"

He nodded. "And like your dad with puns, my dad is to blame for it. He's obsessed with *Jeopardy!*. He never misses an episode. When he's on the road—"

"Wait, what does your dad do?"

"Oh—he's a structural engineer."

"Got it."

"Building bridges, mostly. So he travels a lot. And when he's on the road he always makes sure to have *Jeopardy!* recorded. He's obsessed. He was even on it once—" Russell stopped talking quickly and looked away.

"He was? That's so cool! Did he win?"

"Yeah. But it's not that impressive."

"I think it is. I haven't seen it that much, but it always seems really hard to me."

"I promise it's not a big deal. The other people he was up against were kind of terrible at it. And he gave all the money to charity anyway."

"*Wow*. That's so nice of him." The picture of Russell and his family that was taking shape in my head—the cozy cottage, the happy family unit—suddenly added another dimension. Now I also knew they were super generous, too.

I mean, maybe. Maybe he only won, like, a hundred dollars, Didi pointed out.

We had reached the end of the street—a lone stop sign and a discarded Snickers wrapper. "I think our Ameches are out of luck."

"I think you're right."

I twisted my hands together. I wasn't sure what happened now. I didn't care that my phone wasn't going to get charged—I just didn't want this to be over.

"Wait." Russell turned his head, his eyebrows drawing together. He smiled at me. "Do you smell that?"

I turned where he had been looking and breathed in—the faint smell of meat cooking. "What are . . . tacos?"

He grinned at me. "Exactly."

CHAPTER 4

Sunday
5:45 P.M.

We tracked the taco smell down two blocks over from the historic downtown. And as we rounded the corner, we were back in the twenty-first century. On the other side of some bushes was a strip mall. Dollar General, Payday Loan & Check Cashing, a discount tobacco shop, a nail salon. And like the stores we'd seen on the main street, they were also all closed.

But that didn't really matter because there, in the parking lot, was a woman behind a folding table, making tacos. There was a grill with meat cooking on it, and the most amazing aroma wafting toward us. My stomach rumbled as I breathed it in, which made sense, since the last time I'd eaten had been at eleven a.m.—a fifteen-dollar pizza slice and seven-dollar can of soda.

There were a surprising number of cars in a parking lot where no stores were open, but a second later, I understood why. We weren't the only ones who thought tacos would be a great idea—there was a line of people waiting that had to be ten deep. I could see some people eating right there, sitting in their cars or on the little raised concrete barriers in front of parking spots.

"What do you think?" Russell asked.

"I think yes please," I said, and he laughed. We could have

walked around to the street entrance to the strip mall, but we both headed toward the scrubby knee-high bushes, cutting through to the parking lot.

He stepped through them first, then turned back and extended his hand to me.

My pulse started to pick up, and I took a deep breath, trying to steady myself. And then I reached out and took Russell's hand.

As soon as our palms touched and his fingers closed around mine, I felt a jolt run through me—like it went from my fingertips directly into my chest. And I flashed back to the bus station, when I'd somehow known that it would be like this if we touched. That it would be electric.

Russell's hand was big, almost enveloping mine—and I was so distracted by the fact that we were touching, that his hand was on my hand, that I wasn't paying any attention to what my feet were doing. I tripped over a rock and stumbled forward—but then Russell's arm was suddenly around my back, catching me.

"You okay?"

I looked up at him and nodded. My heart was thumping wildly in my chest, in full-on dance party mode—because flight was certainly the last thing on my mind. His arm was all the way around my waist and I was pulled in close to him, closer than I had yet been.

I could see now that there were little flecks of gold in the blue-green of his eyes. There were faint freckles scattered on his cheeks, an unplotted constellation. I wanted to trace it with my eyelashes. I wanted to run my fingers over it until I had it memorized.

As he'd wrapped his arm around my waist, my tank top must have gotten pushed up, because I could feel that part of his hand was touching the bare skin on my back, making it feel like it was on fire.

His other hand was still holding on to mine, and I could feel the blood pulsing in my fingertips—I was pretty sure I could feel his, too. I wasn't sure how any of this had happened, but I didn't want it to ever stop.

Russell was looking down at me, and I could see he was breathing a little harder now. I was too, like it was taking more of an effort just to be this close to him. And for a second, I thought about stretching up on my toes so that our faces would be level. I was so close to kissing him—only a few inches, a breath, and a bit of courage away. I could practically hear the orchestra starting to swell, the music kicking in . . .

Yes! Katy swooned. *Kiss him kiss him!*

No. Darcy. *Stop behaving like a damsel in distress,* Didi admonished.

Shh! Katy said. *Go for it, Darcy.*

But then Russell blinked and looked away from me, breaking this moment. He released his arm and I stepped down onto the asphalt of the parking lot. He held my hand a second longer, then let it go. "You okay?"

"Uh-huh." I tucked my hands into the back pockets of my jean shorts. Normally, I would have been blushing up a storm. But I somehow didn't feel embarrassed—just disappointed that his hand wasn't holding mine anymore, that his fingers weren't brushing against my bare skin. . . . I tried to compose myself. "Sorry about that. And thank you."

"Sure," he said. "My pleasure." We were still standing maybe a step closer than we needed to—it was a large parking lot, after all—and his eyes lingered on mine for a moment, then dropped down to my mouth before he looked away.

I felt a swelling in my chest and smiled—clearly, we were on the same page with the whole wanting-to-kiss-each-other thing. I had to fight down a wave of incredulous, happy laughter. How had this happened? How had the worst situation I'd ever been in turned around so decisively into one of the best? "Okay," I said, really needing to focus now. "So. Tacos."

We headed across the parking lot together, now definitely walking a little closer than we had been before, like we'd somehow crossed a threshold. Like I was pretty sure that wouldn't be the last time we touched. That there was more coming at some point.

When? Katy demanded.

We got in line, and the sheer number of people, combined with the truly heavenly smell, was convincing me that this was the right thing to do—and *so* much better than anything we could have gotten from a vending machine.

There was a chalkboard easel with a menu written on it. And as I scanned it, I crashed back down to earth. I had been so focused on the tacos—and then on Russell, his hands and eyes and heartbeat—that I'd forgotten about things like commerce.

The woman behind the table was selling tacos, burritos, muletas, tamales, and quesadillas. All of them were much cheaper than anything at the festival had been. But none of them were *free*, which meant I needed to do some math. I silently cursed Romy as I pulled my remaining cash out of my shorts pocket.

"What looks good?" Russell said, squinting at the sign. "I'm suddenly starving."

"Me too. I'm just . . . okay. So I have thirty-two dollars."

"I think that's enough."

"No—it's just—Romy, the girl I went to Silverspun with—"

"The one keeping the party going in Palm Springs?"

"The very same. She took my cash when we split up, in addition to my charger. I still have to pay to get my car out of the lot at Union Station, so I just need to do some math. . . ." It was eight dollars every twenty-four hours you had your car there. So I would need twenty-four for my car. "Okay, I think I have eight left," I said, tucking the rest of my cash in my pocket. "Should we split something?"

"I have some money. Why don't you let me get this? It's my treat."

"I can't let you do that."

"You're not *letting* me. I'm offering. What if the bus takes forever to get fixed and you need more to get your car out?"

This possibility hadn't occurred to me, and the thought of it made my stomach drop. "Only if you promise to let me Venmo you. You know, once I get my Ameche charged."

"It's really okay. I have . . ." He spun his backpack around and rifled through it. "Twenty bucks! More than enough for a taco feast."

"Well—thank you. That's really nice of you."

"I can't believe your friend took your money."

"Well—*friend* might be too strong a word. More like gym-class acquaintance."

Russell's eyebrows flew up. "You went to a music festival with a gym-class acquaintance?"

"Well, when you put it like that . . ." He laughed. "On some level, I knew it was a mistake. Didi and Katy certainly told me that enough. We had PE together, but it wasn't like we ever hung out just the two of us. I must have been really far down the list of people she was asking to go."

"So . . . why did you say yes?"

Seriously, Didi grumbled.

"I think I just . . . wanted this." I gestured around us.

"Tacos in a parking lot?"

"I mean, not no," I said, and Russell laughed. "I think . . . I just wanted an adventure. A little bit of the West to take with me. Especially because I'm leaving. Music and flower crowns and big horizons . . ." I glanced over at him and smiled. "But really, the main draw was the Nighthawks. When I saw they were closing out the festival, I was in."

Russell nodded and took a step forward even though the line hadn't moved much. "Did you guys get along okay?"

"Friday night was good." I flashed back to how the fairgrounds had looked after we'd first set up the Merediths' tent, everything still new and well-maintained, the crackle of excitement in the air. We'd dashed back and forth between all the stages, plotting out who we wanted to see. "But then she found some people to party with on Saturday, and I didn't see her again until I was taking down the tent and she grabbed her stuff."

"And some of your stuff, too, it sounds like."

"Yeah. But I really think it was an accident. We were just dividing everything up and she took my pouch by mistake."

"That's really frustrating."

"It's okay, actually." I looked over at Russell and gave him a smile. "And if she hadn't, I might not be here now. So I'm kind of finding it hard to be upset about it."

Russell looked down at the ground with a smile, the tips of his ears turning red.

We stood there for a moment in comfortable silence, the sound of conversation around us and meat sizzling on the grill. I looked back and saw that since we'd gotten there, three people had stepped into line behind us. I tipped my head toward them. "Looks like we came here at the right time."

"Have we somehow discovered a hidden Jesse gem?"

"Seems like it. Unless the line is because this is actually a secret speakeasy and we need to know the password."

"I'm sure someone would tell us. We look like we're down for a good time."

I nodded toward a white van, parked crookedly in its space. "The entrance is through that van. They've built an underground club. *Literally*."

"You know, I've actually been to one."

"A van club?"

"I mean, I *wish*. I meant I've been to a speakeasy. In Paris—Candelaria. It just looks like this little taqueria, but through the back there's a bar."

"Wow." I nodded, trying to pretend like this was just normal for me. Like my friends were also always talking about their time in *Paris* going to *bars*. "It's cool that they let you in."

He laughed. "I wasn't worried about that. I was with my . . . my cousins."

"Oh."

"They're twins," he explained. "And very cool. Astrid and Artie. They're the best." He smiled, like he was calling them to mind. "Have you been?"

"To Paris?" I shook my head, suddenly feeling out of my depth. But then a second later, I remembered Russell had said his mother was French. This suddenly didn't feel quite so intimidating—maybe he'd been there visiting relatives. "*Non.* Not yet, I mean. Hopefully someday."

"I just thought . . . because your mom." I looked at him sharply. "Because she was in London—I thought maybe when you would visit her, you guys went over there."

"No," I said, keeping my voice light, ready to move far away from this subject. "I've only been out of the country a few times. Mexico, Prince Edward Island—"

"Where's that?"

"Canada," I said, trying not to sound as scandalized as I felt. "It's where all the L. M. Montgomery books are set." Russell just looked at me, his expression blank. "See, this is how I can tell you don't have sisters. She wrote *Anne of Green Gables*, the Emily books . . ."

"Oh, right! Got it."

"And then we went to Panama a few years ago."

"Panama?"

We moved forward a step in line. The line really wasn't moving very fast, but I found I didn't particularly mind. "Yeah, my dad got their tourism account and was trying to help them rebrand. The official slogan before had just been 'Panama!' with an exclamation point. He was trying to come up with something a little more specific."

"That's so cool he's in advertising."

"It's fun to be around. Like when I was younger, I'd hang out at the offices a lot. I'd just be trying to write a book report on *Wonder*, and I'd hear adults going into full-blown meltdowns about what cereal mascots would and wouldn't say. And when he was working at home, during the pandemic, he'd let me pitch on taglines or concepts."

"That's awesome."

"It really was."

Russell looked at me, his head tilted slightly to one side. "But . . . ?"

I was a little taken aback by the fact that it seemed like Russell was able to read me so easily already—but then a second later, I realized this was a good thing. This was how these nights went, right? You got to know the other person fast. How else were you supposed to be in love by sunrise? "But," I continued, giving him a smile, "it's just . . . not what he set out to do. He wanted to be a novelist. There was this whole sci-fi story he was working on, back when I was in elementary school . . ."

"Did he ever try to get it published?"

"I'm not sure. I just know one day he was working on this book, and talking about it at the dinner table, and then it was like none of that had happened. I think maybe it just got to be too hard? Raising me, doing his job, and writing a book . . ." I wasn't about to tell Russell this, but it was ultimately one more thing that Gillian had taken away.

"Well . . . maybe he'll be able to now? Now that you'll be off to college?"

I nodded, even though I doubted it. Because I could practically see what the house would look like when I was gone—my dad sitting alone at the kitchen table. Me in Connecticut, him in Raven Rock, both of us unhappy.

"Next!" the woman called, and we all took a step forward.

Now that I was a little closer, I could see that by the table, there was a cooler filled with ice, with waters and cans of soda sticking out, and I edged up a step, trying to see more clearly. "You think she has Sidral Mundet?"

"What's that?"

"*What's that?*"

"Is it a kind of taco?"

"It's a drink," I practically sputtered. "A delicious Mexican apple soda that's basically pure sugar. Do they not have taco trucks in Ojai?"

"Of course we do."

"*Good* ones?"

"Really good."

"I don't know about that. If they don't have Sidral Mundet, I'm not sure I trust them."

"My favorite one makes their own tortillas *and* they have horchata on tap."

"Oh. Well—that actually does sound delicious."

"It's amazing."

"Still. I bet mine is better. Leo's, on Raven Rock Boulevard, across from the little Target. I can show you."

Russell smiled wide at me, like he could somehow see the same thing I could—this night, this feeling, just continuing, pulling us forward through time and space until there we were, the two of us holding hands outside my favorite taco spot. "Sounds like a plan. And I'll ask for an apple soda."

"Sidral Mundet."

"That's the one."

"Next!" the woman called, and I realized that four of the people in front of us had been in a group—which meant there was only one person ahead of us, a man who stepped forward to order. The back of his T-shirt read *The Nevada Independent*.

I breathed in the scene for a moment, trying to etch it into my mind. How many nights had I stood like this, waiting in line for dinner in parking lots and sidewalks? Knowing I was only moments away from a paper bag with foil-wrapped tacos or a burrito or a quesadilla sandwiched between two paper plates, red and green salsas on top along with the little plastic bag with lemon slices and radishes.

"Oh *no*," I groaned, as a terrible realization hit me all at once.

"What? You okay?"

"Decidedly not. I just realized this is the last authentic taco I'll have until Christmas, probably." I let out a breath. "Is it possible to be nostalgic for something when you haven't technically left it behind?"

"I'm sure there's a word for it. Probably a really long German one."

"I can look it up." I reached for my phone and then immediately realized this was futile. "No, I can't."

"Can you get some more tacos before you go? When do you leave for Connecticut?"

"Tomorrow."

"*Tomorrow?*"

"Yeah, I'm taking the red-eye to New York, and then the train to Connecticut. My dad and I have a whole plan. We're going out to dinner first—he's calling it the Last Supper. And then on the way to the airport, we're going to In-N-Out to pick up shakes for the drive, since I'm going to be without it for the longest time in my whole life."

Russell shook his head and folded his arms—god, they were nice arms, bare except for his watch. It was an actual watch, not an Apple Watch. A worn leather band, a white face with gold numbers and hands. "I didn't even think about the fact you're not going to be able to get In-N-Out for months. That's rough."

"But you won't have it either—I assume there's none in Michigan."

"Jeez, that's right. I guess I've been in denial."

"But at least there's good stuff in Ann Arbor. My friend Jack went there last year. He was always talking about that one deli . . ."

"Zingerman's?"

"Yes! He brought us back black-and-white cookies once; they were awesome."

"But maybe you'll have something like that—I'm sure they have something really delicious in Connecticut. Maybe they'll have amazing tacos there, who knows."

"They have *nothing* good in Connecticut. It's barely a state. Nobody even has a concept of it."

"That's not true. I'm sure there's *something*."

"Like?"

"Like . . . Yale? Hedge funds?"

"I appreciate the effort, but Connecticut is basically the beige of America."

"So . . . um, why are you going there? It doesn't sound like you're that excited about it."

"I'm not." I said this shortly, then immediately regretted it. I shook my head, trying to think of how I wanted to put this. "Sorry. I just—got a really good financial-aid package. One that was pretty hard to turn down. But it wasn't my first choice." I figured that Russell didn't need to know how exactly I'd gotten my free ride, or that it had been pretty much my *only* choice.

He nodded, looking right at me—like he was letting me know that if I wanted to tell him about it, he'd be listening. I considered this for a second, but then pushed it away. Tomorrow, and everything that came after it, had no place here, tonight, with Russell.

"Next!" the woman called as she handed the man in front of us a brown paper bag and a dripping can of soda, and I realized with alarm that I hadn't even made my decision yet.

"What did you want, Darcy?" Russell asked, and I couldn't help but notice how much I liked the way he said my name.

"I'll get a carne asada taco and a cheese quesadilla." I took a breath to order, just as Russell stepped forward and ordered for me in perfect Spanish. I just stared at him as he ordered for himself—a chicken burrito and an al pastor taco—then took a step back to stand with me while we waited.

"Sorry," he said, looking abashed. "I probably shouldn't have done that. I just wanted to impress you."

I felt a happy little flutter in my chest. "Well—it's working." I gave him a smile and tried to focus, even though it felt like it was getting harder by the moment. "I thought you spoke French."

"My mom's a translator. You had to pick up multiple languages in my house if you wanted to eat."

"That's so cool! How many languages does she speak?"

Russell frowned, his head tilted slightly to the side, like he was counting in his head. And with every second that passed, I got more impressed. I could just see them—Russell and his dad and mom, all sitting around their cozy kitchen table, multiple languages flying rapid-fire as they talked and laughed together.

"Five," Russell finally said. "French, English, Spanish, Portuguese, and Italian. But she's currently trying to pick up Korean, so let's say five and a half."

"So does she translate books?"

"Now she does. When she started, it was more in hospitality. That's where she met my dad, actually. He was in France and ended up hiring her to be his translator because he kept accidentally insulting people."

"So that's the opposite of building bridges."

"Exactly."

"More like tearing down bridges. And you can't have that."

"Okay, fun fact—"

"Oh yay!" I clapped my hands together, and Russell laughed. "Another one!"

"I can't tell if you're being sarcastic."

"I swear I'm not. I wouldn't do that to you. I'm no Tall Ben." I paused—something had just occurred to me. "You guys never went with Big Ben instead?"

"Okay, where were you back in fifth grade?" He swung his backpack down to his feet and started to unzip it. "I'll text him—"

"Dead phone."

"Right. It's hard to remember."

"The fact? Sorry I keep interrupting you."

"Oh—well, it's about French. Did you know it's one of the most precise languages? The vocabulary is a lot more limited than English. So a lot of contracts and treaties are written in French, because you can really drill down on the language and specificity."

"That is a fun fact. A fun French fact, even."

"Okay, *now* you're being sarcastic."

"Maybe just a little."

We stood there in silence for a moment, just the sound of the meat cooking, the faint hum of one of the cars idling in the parking lot, and two women sitting on one of the raised concrete parking blocks, eating their tamales and talking, with occasional bursts of laughter.

A gust of warm air—a desert wind—swept across the parking lot, blowing my hair across my face. I was pretty sure I had a hair tie somewhere in the depths of my canvas bag, but I didn't want to go looking for it right this minute, so I just tucked my hair behind my ears. "There's a line I love. It's about the moment you understand someone's humor without having to ask. How it's the turning point in any relationship—when you've found *the skeleton key to the soul*."

"What?" Russell asked, staring at me.

"It's from *Theseus's Sailboat*," I explained, knowing this would be necessary, since most people had never heard of this book. It had come out ten years ago, it wasn't a bestseller, and there had never been a movie or anything. I'd found it at the Raven Rock Library two years ago when I was looking through the New and Noteworthy section (it must have been mis-shelved; it was neither of those things). Looking back on it, I had no idea what about it had grabbed me—the cover? The title? The fact that my dad was waiting for me and I had to hurry? I could no longer remember, but I'd checked it out—and then I'd devoured it.

It all took place over one night on a small island off the coast of Maine. A twentysomething guy, Will, gets locked out of his hotel room—with a cat—and ends up spending the night walking around the island and talking with Emma, a marine biologist waiting up to see the first whales in a generation return to the harbor at dawn. In between the story of Will and Emma falling in love over the course of the night, there are cutaways to the summer camp on the other side of the island—this was admittedly my least-favorite part of the book. Well, that and the two chapters in the middle that were from the cat's point of view.

And even though I'd tried to get my friends to read it—even gifting copies to Didi and Katy for Christmas last year—neither of them had gotten into it. "It sounds like *Before Sunrise*," Didi had said dismissively.

"It's not like *Before Sunrise*," I'd protested, even though it was, a little. "It's Maine, not Vienna. And there's a camp! And a cat!"

"Pass," Didi had said, and no amount of arguing could get her to even give it a shot. But I kept at it, because I wanted her to experience just how wonderful it was. In my mind, it was the perfect book. The first time I'd read it, I'd immediately wanted to crawl inside the world that it portrayed. And that feeling had never gone away, despite two years and countless re-reads.

Russell was still staring at me, and I realized I probably hadn't been at all clear. "Sorry, it's a novel," I explained as he knelt down by the backpack at his feet and started digging through it. "It's actually my favorite novel. It's—"

He stood up, and I saw he was holding something in his hand—a battered hardcover copy of *Theseus's Sailboat*.

"Oh my god. What?" I took his copy from him, just staring at it. It was a different edition from mine—his cover showed a couple looking out at the water, a cat winding around their feet, a whale breaching in the background. This was the book, I realized, he was reading when I'd first seen him across the bus station.

"How is it your favorite book?" he asked. "It's *my* favorite book, and nobody's ever heard of it."

"I know! It's a tragedy! I keep trying to get my friends to read it, and nobody ever will."

"I did get Tall Ben to start it, at least. He couldn't get through the camp stuff."

"Yeah, that part can be rough. But if you just make it through—"

"I know! He's missing out."

We just looked at each other for a moment. What was this? How was this *happening*? Even in all my daydreams about what it would be like when I fell for someone, I hadn't allowed myself to imagine something this wonderful. Someone this cute, this easy to talk to, who just *got* me—and loved the same book I did. It was like opening up the most beautifully wrapped present under the tree and finding a kitten inside. A level of wonderful I hadn't even known to ask for.

"This is . . . crazy," Russell said. He took a tiny step toward me.

I looked up at him, my pulse galloping, his favorite book in my arms and my eyes locked on his. I took a step toward him. Everything in me was screaming for me to kiss him, or at least take his hand again, and—

"Ready!" the woman behind the table yelled. We both turned to her as she set a big paper bag with our order on the table. "Drinks?"

She didn't have Sidral Mundet, so I got a Sprite and Russell got a pineapple Jarritos. He handed over his twenty to pay, and as she counted out his change I noticed a little cardboard box on the table—selling candy for the Jesse High Teacher Supply Fund. There were bags of Skittles and Hershey bars, but then also less familiar candy—Big Cherry and Abba-Zaba.

"Want anything?" Russell asked. He picked up the Abba-Zaba and turned it over in his hands. "Oh man, I haven't had one of these in years."

"I'm not sure I ever have," I said as the woman set Russell's change down on the table. He bought the Abba-Zaba, too, and dropped the rest of the change in her tip jar. I started to walk away, figuring we'd be sitting on the parking blocks to eat like those women, when something occurred to me. I turned back and nodded at the candy box. "This high school," I said. "Where is it?"

CHAPTER 5

Sunday
6:30 P.M.

This was an excellent idea," Russell said as he looked over at me from where we were sitting across from each other, sprawled in the very center of the football field. It hadn't been very far to Jesse High—just a few blocks over from the parking lot. I'd thought that maybe we could eat on the benches by the front entrance—but then I'd seen the goalposts and had had a better idea.

The football field was AstroTurf, with the white lines of the gridiron spray-painted on. It wasn't a stadium or anything, just the field and some bleachers set up on either side. And right now, we had it all to ourselves.

"Why, thank you," I said. "I'm glad it's not *offensive*." Russell groaned, but in a way that seemed appreciative. I set the bag down between us and opened it up, unpacking our dinner and spreading out our football field picnic.

There were lights at all four corners of the field, turned off at the moment. It wasn't dark out yet, but the sun was thinking about setting. The moon was already rising, and a neon sign I could see beyond the football field was just beginning to glow. So even though the light was fading, I could still see everything I needed to—our tacos, the scoreboard, Russell's face.

"What do you think happened there?" I asked, nodding toward the scoreboard. It was an older kind, nonelectronic. Right now the score was Home: 69 and Visitor: 0.

Russell looked at it and then laughed. "I think some kids were having fun."

A second later, I got it and felt myself blush. "Oh, right. Anyway. Thanks again for dinner. I will pay you back."

"There's really no need. I was happy to do it."

"You're missing an opportunity here. You could really *hike up* the prices."

"You're unstoppable."

"I'm done now. I promise."

"Not on my account. I'm impressed. You must have loved the chapter with all the rejected names for the bakery."

"Yes!" I unwrapped the foil around my taco. "That's one of my favorite sections." We'd done this on the whole walk over to the high school—talked about *Theseus's Sailboat*, our favorite chapters, our favorite lines, our theories about the characters. Just finding anyone else who loved this pretty obscure book and getting to talk to them about it would have been miracle enough. But here, in the middle of nowhere, for this boy to pull it from his bag like a magic trick?

It *meant* something. It had to.

I breathed in the taco aroma for just a moment before taking a bite. "Okay," I said around a mouthful of carne asada. "That's good."

"As good as Leo's?"

"Not quite. But what is?"

"So," Russell started, then he bit into his own taco, and his eyes widened. "Uh-huh. Okay. Yep."

"Good, right?"

"Excellent. I hadn't realized how hungry I was."

I nodded and took another bite. It was better than anything I'd had at the festival, both food-wise and experience-wise—no waiting with crowds of people for overpriced, mediocre food that I was going to eat alone. "Okay," I said as I took a paper napkin from the bag, glad Russell had thought to grab a handful. "Explain to me your camp theory. You think the kids don't exist?"

"They *exist*. They're just in a different timeline than the rest of the story. It's Will, when he was a kid. He's the camper everyone calls Billy, the last summer that the whales were there."

"I don't know . . ."

"Think about it. It's too random otherwise, right? And this way, the whole thing comes full circle." Russell stopped to take a breath and shook his head. "I just can't believe I have someone to talk about this with."

"I know! Even if some of your theories are unsound."

"Unsound?"

I laughed as I lifted the top paper plate from my quesadilla, broke off one of the triangles, and offered it to him. "Want some?"

"You sure?"

"Of course."

"Thank you." He took the quesadilla triangle from me, our hands brushing again, sending another thrill all the way through me. "So where do you fall with the whole Ship of Theseus thing?"

Theseus's Sailboat was a reference to the thought puzzle of the Ship of Theseus—which I hadn't ever heard of before I read the book (and I had a theory that the book would have done better if it had a different title). The puzzle describes a ship that's been rebuilt over the years, plank by plank, until none of the first ship remains. And the question was if that ship could still be considered the Ship of Theseus even though none of the original components were there.

"You mean do I think it's still the same ship? Even though every part of it has changed?" Russell nodded. I'd never had to think about it before—but then again, I'd never had anyone to talk about my favorite book with before. "I think so," I said slowly. "I mean, the essence still remains, right? It's more than the sum of its parts."

"I think so too. It's just like us, actually—"

"Wait." I held up my hands. "I think I sense a fun fact coming. A football field fun fact!"

"Darcy."

"Friday Night Facts! Sunday Night Factball? I'm done now."

"Are you?"

"Probably not. But I do want to know the fact."

"Well—it was just that we're like the ship too. Our whole systems change over every seven years. So you're physically not the same person you were when you were a kid. But you're still you, right?"

I nodded, turning this over in my mind.

"It's actually why—" He stopped short and shook his head. "Sorry, that was about to be an un-fun fact."

"Well, now I have to hear it."

"You sure?"

"Positive."

"So." Russell cleared his throat. "It's, um, where the phrase *the seven-year itch* comes from. Because back in the day, when you had scabies—"

"Scabies?" I paused, a bite of quesadilla halfway to my mouth.

"Yeah, they're um, skin mites? And before people had antibiotics, they would have them for seven years."

I looked down at my quesadilla—I no longer had much of an appetite. I put it back on the plate and pushed it a little ways away from me.

"See? I told you it was un-fun. Not romantic at all." As soon as he said this, his eyes widened, like he'd just realized what he'd done.

I smiled down at the AstroTurf. Now that he'd said it out loud, it was just confirmation that we were on the same page—that maybe he liked me as much as I liked him.

You don't actually know him, the Didi in my head piped up.

She's getting to know him, Katy admonished her. *Leave Darce alone.*

A breeze blew across the football field, not as warm as the one in the parking lot had been. It was definitely starting to get colder, and I reached for my canvas bag. I dug out my Nighthawks sweatshirt and pulled it on.

"Oh," Russell said as he looked at my sweatshirt, eyebrows raised.

I looked down at it and laughed. I was used to it now, the image of Wylie Sanders, leather jacket open over his bare chest, staring soulfully at the camera. I would sometimes get double-takes when I wore it out and about, but I didn't care. It almost became like a shibboleth—people I didn't even know would nod at me, and random strangers would smile and give me a thumbs-up. Like a secret code among Nighthawks fans. "I know. It was my dad's. It's a lot, but fun, right?"

"I guess you're a big fan?" Russell was still blinking at Wylie staring out at him.

"I mean, my dad is."

"He *did* name you after one of their songs."

"This is the truth. I suppose a casual fan wouldn't have done that."

"So you're a fan too?"

I picked up my quesadilla again, thinking about it as I took a bite. The Nighthawks had always just been the soundtrack in our home. I would know the second I stepped into the house or got into the car what kind of mood my dad was in based on which song was playing.

He played me other stuff besides the Nighthawks, of course— we always had music on, our system connected so that you could go from room to room and not lose a note. But the Nighthawks were his favorite, the thing he always came back to the most, his touchstone.

"I don't know," I said slowly, realizing I'd never had to put this into words before. "They were basically the sound of my whole childhood. Like I knew the songs before I remembered ever learning them. They were just part of me—the way you don't remember learning your name."

"He played you Nighthawks songs when you were a kid?" I nodded, and Russell frowned. "Even 'South of the Border'?"

I laughed, impressed that he could pull that one out, when it seemed like he hadn't even been familiar with "Darcy." "That's a deep cut."

"I just can't imagine playing it for a little kid. I don't think I even heard it until I was thirteen or something."

"My dad didn't believe in the concept of kid music. He played me everything, so I learned these songs while having no idea what they were about. I sang 'Ecstasy Nights' for a first-grade talent show."

Russell stared at me, taco forgotten, a smile tugging at the corner of his mouth. "You did *not*."

"My dad got called into a meeting with my teacher about it. But I think secretly he was proud." Russell laughed. "But . . . I actually don't know if I would have liked them if I'd just heard them on my own, you know? Like, the Nighthawks *are* my dad. Do I love them because of the music? Or because I love my dad, and *he* loves them?" I shook my head and ran my hand over the fake grass. "I'll never know, I guess."

"I can see that."

"Did you see their set?" I flashed back to it—the way that when Wylie Sanders had run out onstage, everything that had gone wrong with Romy and the festival had melted away. I'd heard the first notes of "Saturday Night Falls" and been transported.

"Just the beginning."

"Oh man, you missed out. It was *so* great. He's so fantastic, and to just be there with all those other people . . . and he played 'Darcy,' which he usually doesn't do in concert anymore, and there was a moment in 'Fair Weather' where he held the mic out to the crowd, and we all sang the chorus, and . . ." I shook my head, the words spilling out fast. "And I know this isn't an original thought at all. But at one point I looked around, at this moment we were all experiencing, this magic that was happening for just the people right then. And you could listen to a recording of it, but the experience was only if you were there. The one we were all sharing." I stopped and took a breath, knowing that I wasn't even getting close to capturing how it had felt.

Russell smiled at me in the slowly falling darkness. "That sounds—really amazing. It's too bad your dad couldn't see it."

"Oh, I recorded the whole thing for him. Which is basically why my phone is dead."

"He'll appreciate it when you get home, though."

"I hope so. He's practically Wylie's biggest fan." I paused, considering. "Of the music, at any rate."

"What do you mean?"

"You know."

Russell just shook his head. But even if he wasn't a huge fan, he *had* to know about Wylie Sanders's personal life. It was just . . . out there, in the supermarket aisle on the cover of *People*, fodder for late-night hosts' jokes, memes on social media.

"Just . . . how it's kind of a train wreck. He's been married a million times, he has all these kids with different women, and his last wife was basically a teenager, right? And he and Candace Young are always in court. . . ." This was the most prominent of his breakups, mostly because it involved a movie star, someone as famous as him. They'd never gotten married, but had a son and, judging by the articles in *Us Weekly*, hadn't stopped fighting since. This was the only one of Wylie's kids who was in the press—the rest were pretty much out of public view, unless one of them behaved badly on social media. I seemed to remember a few years ago, his daughter—was it Dakota?—had been photographed skinny-dipping off a yacht. A yacht she'd borrowed without permission.

Russell shrugged. "I don't really know."

"Really? There was just a thing in DitesMoi. He and his child bride fighting over custody of their twins . . ." I reached for my bag to show him on my phone.

"Dead Ameche," Russell reminded me.

"Right. That *is* hard to remember."

"You like DitesMoi?" There wasn't judgment in Russell's tone, exactly—more like surprise.

"I mean, it's not like I read it a lot. Just for entertainment, you know?"

Russell nodded, his head bent as he stuffed his trash in the paper bag. I was about to ask him if he ever read it—when I looked up and caught my breath. And what was happening in front of me drove away all thoughts of Instagram gossip sites. There was a glorious sunset streaked across the horizon—apparently, while we'd been eating tacos, we'd missed the sky turning into a Van Gogh painting, purple and pink and orange mixing together across the huge canvas of the desert sky. The mountains were silhouetted and huge, and the whole thing was just breathtaking.

Needing to get a better view, I lay back, tipping my chin up, trying to take it all in. More than anything, I wanted to freeze this moment. So that when I needed to, I could call it back—the Technicolor sunset, the AstroTurf under my bare legs, the faint breeze blowing, Russell's profile as he finished his Jarritos. The feeling of pieces snapping, at long last, into place.

Russell set his empty bottle down, then he lay back too and looked up. "Wow."

"I know. I don't think I've ever seen one like this."

We just lay there next to each other for a moment, looking up, the silence easy and comfortable between us. I turned my head to look at him—he was so close to me. I could have reached out and touched him without even having to extend my arm all the way.

"Have you ever seen the Sistine Chapel?" Russell asked.

"The—what? In Italy?"

"Yeah."

"Not in person. I've seen pictures, though."

"Well—when you go and see it, there are all these signs everywhere saying you're not allowed to lie down. Like in every different language, and with pictures and everything."

"Okay."

"So I was there with my family, we were all together, seeing it as a group with a guide. And after they'd told us all about it, the rest of my family started to leave. And I saw my moment."

"You lay down?"

"I had to do it! I wanted to see it from that perspective—like Michelangelo would have."

"And?"

"It was incredible. Truly. It's almost too much to take in. Overwhelming, but in a good way."

"Did you get in trouble?"

"Oh yeah," he said immediately, and I laughed. "I only had a few moments before the guards were running toward me yelling in Italian and our guide was admonishing me." He turned back to look at the sky, folding his arms behind his head. "But I hadn't seen anything else that felt like that—until now."

I looked back at the sky. "I know. It's so beautiful."

"Yeah," Russell said. But I turned and saw that he was no longer looking up at the sky—he was looking at me.

My breath caught in my throat. I felt like we were on the border of an undiscovered country. At a threshold we'd been moving toward since the moment we first spoke. And it was scary and exciting—but right. Like every step had been in the right direction—and led us here.

I smiled at Russell, even though my heart was beating so wildly I was pretty sure he could probably hear it.

He looked at me for a moment longer, his eyes searching mine. Then he rolled over so that he was on his side, leaning on his elbow. He reached out and touched my face gently with the back of his hand, tracing the curve of my cheek and making me shiver. "Darcy," he said. A second later, he shook his head. "I honestly can't believe that's your name."

"What about it?"

"It's . . ." He hesitated. "Nothing. It suits you. You'll be what I think of when I hear the name from now on."

"And you're the first Russell I've met. I've never known another one."

"Most people say the kid from *Up*."

"That kid was awesome! Great Russell representation. You should be proud." He gave a half laugh, and then we lapsed back into silence again, but it wasn't simply comfortable now—it was charged, with everything we were on the verge of. I was all too aware that it would take just a single step for us to cross over. Like a line of dominos a breath away from tipping over and causing a cascade.

I summoned my courage and did what I'd been wanting to do since I first saw him bent over our favorite book at the bus station— I stretched my hand up and ran my fingers through his hair, tangling them in his curls.

Russell caught my hand in his, threading his fingers through mine, and even though his hand was a lot bigger, I couldn't help but notice how nicely our hands fit together, how good my hand felt in his.

He played with my Silverspun bracelets, and then kissed the back of my hand. When he did this, I felt a thrill that extended through me all the way to my toes. Then Russell turned my hand over and traced the inside of my palm with his index finger, slow spirals and lazy figure eights, making my breath come more shallowly. It was all amazing, just like I'd known it would be. We hadn't even kissed yet, and it felt like I was on the verge of exploding.

He ran two fingers around my palm in a slow circle, then bent his head, kissed my palm, and traced his mouth down my hand to the inside of my wrist.

I had never thought much about this particular part of my hand before. When Katy got a tattoo there on her eighteenth birthday, she cried through the whole thing, and afterward the tattoo artist told her she'd picked a particularly tricky spot for a first tattoo—the inside of your wrist is all nerve endings.

I understood that now. With Russell's lips, feathery and soft, tracing the inside of my wrist, suddenly I was feeling everything a lot more than usual, like every nerve in my body was suddenly awake. He kissed the inside of my wrist, and I gasped when I felt his tongue on my skin, his teeth scraping lightly over it.

He raised his head up and kissed my palm again, and then the back of my hand, like we had all the time in the world—and like he knew just what he was doing.

He traced his hand down my cheek again, and looked at me like he was drinking me in. "Hi."

"Hi," I said, slightly breathless, feeling very certain I was not going to be able to wait more than a few more seconds before kissing him. It was actually not going to be physically possible.

We hovered there for just a moment, in the space between, the anticipation building and stretching out—and then he tilted his head down, we both closed our eyes, and Russell kissed me.

I stretched up to kiss him back, our lips lightly brushing at first—but then it was like we both took a breath at the same time and started kissing for real.

And he was really good—and we were good *together*, finding a rhythm right away, our lips and breath fitting together as easily as our hands had.

Russell lifted my hand—he hadn't stopped holding it this whole time—and placed it above me in the grass, then traced his fingertips down my arm, all while continuing to kiss me. Which was good, because I didn't want him to stop. We were kissing in waves, almost—first fast and breathless, then slowing down, taking our time, exploring. But then he'd give a shuddering breath or lightly bite the inside of my bottom lip, and that would be all I'd need to start kissing him quickly again. My arms were around him, my hands running through his hair, trying to pull him even closer to me.

Russell broke away and kissed my neck. He started in the hollow of my collarbone, the little indentation there, then traveled slowly upward, finally stopping just under my chin, where I could feel my pulse thundering wildly. He rolled over a little closer to me, one of his legs tangling in between mine, and we were kissing again, faster now, like even that brief break had been more than either of us could handle.

I don't know how much time passed. I was just living in the moment—the AstroTurf tickling my bare legs and our lips and our breath and his heartbeat and our fingers twining together and Russell rolling me on top of him so I could look down, seeing him below me in the growing darkness, tracing his freckles with my lips the way I'd wanted to when I first saw them. It was like nothing existed except his lips and my lips and my hands tangling in his hair—when Russell pulled away.

"Sorry."

"About what?" I asked, pushing myself up to sit up with arms that felt wobbly. I knew, without a doubt, that if I tried to stand right now, I'd go crashing to the ground. I blinked, trying to focus. I felt flushed and kiss-drunk, like everything else had gone fuzzy around the edges.

He tugged at the hem of my sweatshirt, rubbing the fabric between his fingers. "I was just wondering if maybe we could do something about this?"

"Um," I said, looking down at my sweatshirt.

"Like turn it around or something?" He gestured to Wylie Sanders's circa 2002 pout. "It's just . . . kind of distracting? And," he said as he leaned closer to me, tucking my hair behind my ear and then untucking it so he could play with it, turning it between his fingers, "I really, really don't want to be distracted right now."

I laughed as I looked down at my sweatshirt. From his perspective, I could understand why it really might have been a little off-putting to see a shirtless, pouting rock star in this particular moment. "I could definitely turn it around. Or . . . I could take it off." I didn't let myself look away from him as I said it.

"That sounds really good," he said, smiling at me, and even in the darkness, which was falling fast, I could see his cheeks had gone pink. He reached over, cupped my head in his hands, and kissed me again—was that ever not going to feel miraculous?

He slipped his hands under my sweatshirt and started pulling it up, sliding up my rib cage. I raised my arms and he pulled it over my head. He didn't just toss it aside, though—he shook it out and then folded it neatly, setting it near my bag on the grass, like he somehow knew, without me having to tell him, that it was important to me.

"There," he said, turning to me with a smile. "Much better."

I laughed and leaned over to kiss him, running my hands down his arms, bare except for his watch. "We don't want you to be distracted."

"That's the last thing we want," he said between kisses. He was sitting up now too, and pulled me into his lap, so that my legs were around either side of him and I was sitting just a little taller than him, looking down.

I kissed his cheek, his temple—he closed his eyes when I did that and kind of sighed—his neck, his lips again—but then I drew back.

"You okay?"

"Yeah," I said, even as I untangled myself from him and looked around. "Do you think that the bathrooms here would be unlocked?" All at once, I was cursing myself for not going into the cowgirl bathroom back at the bus station. Why hadn't I anticipated that it might be the last one I was going to see for a while? I was suddenly regretting my Sprite.

He laughed, and I could see relief in his eyes—that I wasn't pushing him away, that this was literally just nature calling. "That's a very good question. And now that you mention it, one that I could also use the answer to."

He pushed himself up to standing and squinted over at the area behind the home bleachers, where there was what looked like a locked concession counter, and on either side of it, the bathrooms. "I'm going to go check." He bent down to kiss me once, quickly, before starting to jog over to them. "Be right back!"

I lay back against the grass. Like Russell had felt, lying on a floor in Rome and looking up at a painting on the ceiling, I felt overwhelmed—but in a good way—by everything that had just happened. While we'd been kissing, the sunset had almost totally faded out, and the first stars were starting to appear. I looked around the football field—the goalposts, the scoreboard. It didn't seem possible that these things were the same, but absolutely everything else had changed.

"All right," Russell said as he jogged back onto the field, and I sat up. "So, good news and bad news."

"Bad news first?"

He smiled. "Okay. So these bathrooms are locked. But! I walked to the top of the bleachers, and I think I saw somewhere we can go."

"Oh yeah?"

He nodded, and I pushed myself up to standing—and sure enough, my legs felt wobbly. Russell reached out his hand to steady me, and I gave it a squeeze. "In that case, lead on."

CHAPTER 6

Sunday

7:45 P.M.

I t turned out that the Silver Standard Hotel was only a ten-minute walk from the high school. Russell had seen the sign from the top of the bleachers, and we found the hotel with only a couple of wrong turns.

It was a three-story, smallish building done in a faux Old West style. There was a front entrance with a circular driveway and a parking lot around the back. The name of the hotel was spelled out under a neon ten-gallon hat that needed some repair—the brim of the hat seemed to have trouble staying on. FREE HBO! was painted on a sign that hung from the hat, and something about the font—and the fact that they were advertising this at all—made me think it was a few decades old. The VACANCY in the sign was illuminated, the NO dark—presumably, everyone who had been staying here for the festival had headed home as soon as it was over.

"Okay," Russell said to me as we stood just off to the side of the entrance. "So I'm betting the bathroom is past Reception—there has to be one somewhere in the lobby. I'd just go in, walk fast but not run—just like you have somewhere to be. They're not going to stop you."

"Are you sure?" I asked as I peered through the sliding glass doors, trying to get a look at the reception desk but just seeing a potted plant blocking my view. I looked down at my tank top and jean shorts, my Silverspun bracelets. Was I immediately going to be pegged as an interloper?

"Do you want me to go in first? I could scout it out, give you the lay of the land."

"Really?"

"Sure," he said with a smile as he squeezed my hand and leaned down to kiss me. Then he took his phone out of his bag and held it to his ear as he headed inside. "Uh-huh," I heard him say to nobody as he walked through the automatic glass doors. "Right. Interesting."

I took a step away from the door, still feeling Russell's kiss on my lips, and leaned back against the brick of the building, taking a moment to try to process everything. How was this happening?!

Oh my god! Katy shrieked.

Calm down, Didi muttered.

No. Shan't. OH MY GOD!!

It is *exciting,* Didi acknowledged. *I just don't want Darcy to lose sight of reality. She's not in one of her movies.*

Maybe she is, Katy swooned. *Lose sight of reality, Darce. Lose it entirely. Who needs reality? How often does something like this occur?*

What's going to happen tomorrow? Didi asked, startling me.

Which really *shouldn't* have been so startling, since this whole conversation was taking place inside my head. But I hadn't even allowed myself to think past one moment at a time, taking things as they came.

And I realized a second later that I didn't *want* to. This whole night felt like a miracle—it was turning me into the heroine of a cinematic love story all my own. Worrying about the future, by contrast, felt like the antithesis of sweeping romance. And a sweeping romance was what I had, for the first time ever, found myself in.

Darcy's deciding things again, Didi said with a sigh.

But she's right for once, Katy protested. *She shouldn't worry about tomorrow. Maybe there won't even be a tomorrow. There could be an apocalypse! There could be the Rapture! This could be the last night on Earth, and I think Darcy would really regret it if she didn't spend it kissing a cute guy.*

"Okay." Russell had returned, and as soon as I saw him, I smiled—automatically, like a reflex. He smiled back at me—maybe he'd just experienced the same thing. "So there was no problem at all. I just walked straight past the desk, and then the bathrooms are off to the left, down a little hallway."

"Awesome. I'll be right back."

I pulled out my (dead) phone and stepped through the doors into the lobby. A second later, though, I wondered if it would look suspicious for Russell and I to have done this back-to-back. One teenager walking through a lobby having a one-sided conversation was one thing. But two? In quick succession? I decided maybe I shouldn't risk it.

I dropped my phone in my canvas bag, but that half second of not looking where I was going must have been enough, because when I looked up again, I saw that there was a large dog barreling toward me, towing a small child who did not look like they were at all capable of handling this dog. The dog probably weighed more than the kid did. I tried to step out of the way, but the dog—it looked like some kind of Lab, but with a more squashed face—lunged toward me, jumping up, tongue flopping out of its mouth and tail wagging fast, whapping the kid every time.

"Down," I said, taking another step to the side and trying to give the dog a pat on the head. "Good dog. Nice buddy." We'd never had a dog. I'd begged for one every year until I realized sometime around fifth grade that we weren't ever getting one and stopped asking.

"Did you fill out the pet waiver?" I looked over and realized that the woman behind the desk was talking to me. She looked like she was in her forties, with red hair that appeared dyed, cut into a blunt bob. This hairstyle—and her expression—contrasted mightily with the cowboy hat that was perched jauntily atop her head.

There was a guy on the phone next to her and I saw he was also wearing one, so clearly this was part of the uniform at the Silver Standard hotel, not just a fashion choice.

"Oh," I said, taking another step away from the kid and his happy, drooling dog. "No. I'm not . . . with them."

"Brinkley!" I heard a voice call from across the lobby, and a harried-looking mom came running up. I didn't know if she was talking to the kid or the dog; both seemed possible. I used this commotion to edge past them, but I could feel eyes on me, and as I glanced back before taking the hallway to the left that Russell had told me about, I saw that the red-haired lady behind the desk was watching me, her eyes narrowed. I looked away quickly, and kept my head down as I pushed open the door to the bathroom.

When I was done washing my hands, I dug my tiny toiletry bag out of my canvas tote, beyond glad that it had come with me and hadn't ended up in my duffel. There wasn't a ton in there—a foldable hairbrush, mints, a lipstick, lip gloss. Also an emergency tampon, Advil, and liner, because I'd learned the hard way what happened when I didn't have those things on me at all times.

I quickly brushed the tangles out of my hair, popped in a mint, and then contemplated the lipstick before choosing the gloss and applying it quickly. After all—I was going to be kissing someone imminently, so lipstick probably wouldn't be the best idea. Just the thought of that was enough to give me that bubbling, fluttering feeling again, and when I met my eyes in the mirror, I could see just how different I looked. This was not the same reflection I'd caught in the WELCOME TO JESSE bus station mirror. My cheeks were flushed (no surprise there) but my eyes were practically sparkling. I looked about a thousand times happier—like I had a secret to tell.

Because things were *happening*. It felt like my whole life, I'd been listening to songs and watching movies and reading stories about things happening to other people, and now, finally, things were happening to *me*. This was my *Theseus's Sailboat*. My *Before Sunrise*. My one perfect night.

Go have fun, Katy practically yelled. *Why not?*

Why not? was the thought rattling around in my brain as I pulled out another paper towel, wiped away the droplets on the sink, and balled it up to throw it away.

Which was when I noticed, lying on top of the tissues and paper towels and chewed-up gum—a plastic key card. *Silver Standard Hotel* was written in fancy script along the top, and along the bottom—*Keep Exploring*.

I picked it up out of the trash, wiping it quickly on my jean shorts before pocketing it. This was the kind of souvenir I wanted of this night—especially since neither Russell or I could take any pictures. I'd want something to remember it, something to prove that I was here, that this had happened. Something I could pull out with a flourish when I told the story to Didi and Katy over FaceTime.

This, along with the persistent drumbeat of *why not*, was echoing in my head as I pushed my way out the door and crossed through the lobby—but I went in the opposite direction this time, not wanting to draw any more attention from the front-desk woman. I figured that there would be a side entrance somewhere. I picked a hallway at random and walked down it, trying not to look suspicious, focusing on the horseshoe pattern on the slightly worn carpet.

I saw the door at the end of the hallway and pushed out—I was now around back, near the parking lot. I figured I'd just walk to the front of the hotel—but then I turned my head and saw it.

And right then, it seemed like it was the thing that absolutely needed to happen now. And given what I'd just taken from the bathroom, it seemed like it absolutely could.

"Why not," I murmured, making a decision as I hitched my bag over my shoulder and started walking fast, hurrying around to the front of the hotel.

Russell was leaning back against the front entrance, one leg bent, and he smiled and straightened up when he saw me. "Hey. I thought you'd come out the, you know, door. You all set?"

"Uh-huh," I said, then looked back to where I'd just come from. "But I actually had an idea."

It turned out it really wasn't at all hard to break into the pool of the Silver Standard Hotel. It was located in the fenced-off area I'd noticed when I'd gone out the side door. There was a hot tub, and plastic loungers all around the concrete deck. The pool itself was medium-size, with underwater lights that cast a cool blue glow over everything.

"So I think this is a great idea," Russell said when I'd led him around the side of the hotel and presented the pool proudly. "There's just one problem." He'd pointed to the locked gate that required a key card to get in.

"Ah," I said. I took the key card out of my back pocket and held it up. "Problem solved." Russell just looked at me, eyes wide, like I'd pulled off a magic trick, and I laughed. "I found it in the bathroom. I figured someone must have checked out and tossed it. But maybe it'll still work?" I waved the key card at the sensor, and after a pause, the green light flickered on, and I pushed the pool gate open and we walked through.

We stood there for just a moment in the silence of the pool deck. There was one lone inflatable bobbing in the shallow end—a round red-and-orange float, with handles on the side. I looked at the lights changing as the water in the pool moved, and at the sky above us, huge and dotted with stars.

"It's nice that there's nobody here," Russell said.

I nodded and looked around—and then saw the sign near the door that led back into the hotel. NO LIFEGUARD ON DUTY. SWIM AT YOUR OWN RISK. POOL HOURS 7:30 A.M.–7:30 P.M. POOL FOR HOTEL GUESTS ONLY. TRESPASSERS WILL BE PROSECUTED. "I think technically it's closed."

"And we're not hotel guests. We're breaking all kinds of rules."

I smiled at that as I set my bag down and kicked my Birks off, leaving them under one of the loungers, then dipped a foot in the pool to check the temperature.

"How is it?"

"Nice," I said, pulling my foot back out. It was a good temperature—maybe a little colder than I would have picked, but in my opinion, that was way better than it being too hot.

Russell sat on one of the loungers and untied his shoelaces, taking off his shoes and socks. He pushed up his jeans and walked over to the deep end. He sat by the edge of the pool and put his legs in the water. I walked over to sit next to him, glad that I was wearing shorts and didn't have to worry about my jeans getting wet. Russell leaned back on his hands, then looked over and smiled at me. "Well—today is really not going how I was expecting it to."

I laughed. "Me neither." I leaned over to look at his watch, and seeing what I wanted, he lifted it up to show me. But even so, I took the opportunity to hold his wrist in mine, turning it so that I could see the watch face, but really so that I could just hold on to his hand, running my fingers lightly over his arm, but then I had to stop. You can only pretend to need to see someone's watch for so long, after all.

But as though Russell also felt it really had been too long since we'd touched each other, he brushed a lock of hair away from my forehead, tucked it behind my ear, and traced his fingers lightly down my neck. "Are you tired?"

I shook my head—I had never felt less tired in my life. "You know, if things hadn't gone wrong, our bus would be closing in on California."

"You mean we would have been on a *bus* this whole time?" Russell shook his head. "I have to say, I prefer this."

"Same."

Russell circled his feet in the water, brushing against my ankle for just a second. But that moment—his bare skin against mine—was enough to transport me back to the football field. I was about to touch his foot back, when something suddenly occurred to me, and I sat up straighter.

"Wait," I said, shaking my head. "Do you have to let your mom know?"

Russell just blinked at me, a dull flush starting to creep up his neck. "Um. I wasn't . . . um . . ."

"Oh—no," I said, shaking my head quickly. "I just meant, did you have to tell her that you're not going to be on the bus?" Russell was still frowning, and I suddenly wondered if I'd overstepped. "Sorry—it's not my business."

"No, it's fine. I . . . was supposed to stay overnight with the friend I went to Silverspun with, that's all. So she's not expecting me to be home tonight."

"The friend you had a fight with?"

Russell nodded and let out a short breath, eyes fixed on the water. "Yeah."

"Was it Tall Ben?" I asked, mostly just to break the tension. "Or Actually Tall Ben?"

It worked, because Russell laughed. "No. Nary a Ben attended Silverspun with me."

"How do you get to Ojai from Union Station?" I asked, realizing that for me, that was the end of the line, but Russell would still have a lot of travel to get home again. I would have thought there would be a way to get there without going through LA, but apparently not. "Do you take a train?"

"You can take a train. Or get a bus. . . . What about your dad?"

"What about him?"

"Is he going to be expecting you in LA tonight?"

I shook my head. "Thankfully, no. He's with my uncle at his lake house. He's not back until tomorrow afternoon. Hopefully I'll be home by then, and he won't have to know about this. He really wouldn't be happy about it." A second later, I realized what I'd just said and how this might have sounded to Russell. "I didn't mean you," I said quickly. Though if I was being honest, my dad probably wouldn't have been *super thrilled* about me being at a hotel with someone I'd met in a bus station. "I just meant he wouldn't be happy about the whole stranded-in-Nevada-with-no-phone thing."

"See, my mom *would* probably be happy about it. She has all these stories about backpacking through Europe with no phones or internet. She believes that we've all gotten too soft and isolated. And that the only way we can actually connect with people, and be our true selves, is when we step away from our devices." Russell said this with a kind of weariness, like he'd heard it a lot. He shrugged. "She always says that I need more grit."

"Well, she is French," I pointed out, and he laughed.

"Mais bien sûr," he said, so easily, his accent *so* good. It was honestly almost too much to take.

Please keep it together, Didi sighed.

Make him speak more French! Katy swooned.

"It is funny, though," Russell said after a moment of comfortable silence, our feet circling each other, coming into each other's orbits but not quite touching. "About how the smallest things can make the biggest difference and we don't even know it at the time?"

"What do you mean? Like the butterfly effect?"

"Kind of. I guess it's like—what if we'd just picked another bus to get on? We'd almost be home now, and we'd have no idea that there was this whole other thing that could have happened. Or what if our bus had worked instead? We wouldn't be here now. I wouldn't . . . know you. And that feels impossible." He turned to face me, more fully, his eyes searching mine. "Doesn't it?"

I made myself keep looking back at him and nodded. It *did* feel impossible—that there was any other way this day could have gone. "I guess you just never know, except in retrospect." I pulled my legs out of the pool, let the water drip off them for just a moment, then pulled them up in front of me. "Like, if I'd known what the result would be, I wouldn't have gotten barbecue the night before my history midterm."

"Oh no—what happened?"

It was only a second later that I realized I probably shouldn't have brought up a food-poisoning story in front of someone who I really wanted to kiss me again. It was probably the same way Russell had felt when he realized he'd started to tell his un-fun fact about scabies. "Well—let's just say nothing good. I was *really* sick, but I insisted on going in to take my test. It was, like, half our grade. I should have just waited, but I'd been studying before the evil brisket had come into my life, so I thought I'd do okay."

"And?"

"And I did not."

Russell laughed, but not in a mean way. "I'm really sorry."

"Yeah." I was about to leave it at that. But then I realized I could tell him the truth—even the stuff I normally kept hidden from other people. I felt in my bones that I could trust him—and more than that, I wanted him to see me, flaws and all, just like he was letting me see him. "It's actually—" I started, then took a breath. "I've never actually told this to anyone else. But that one test—it really brought down my GPA. And . . . I don't know if that was why, but I didn't get into as many schools as I was hoping. Just two." Even just saying it, I felt the shame flare somewhere in my chest, remembering the cascade of rejection emails while all my friends seemed to be swimming in acceptances.

"What was the other school?"

"Ithaca College. It's in upstate New York. And neither of them was my first choice, by any stretch. I wasn't even going to apply to Stanwich, but—" I stopped before I said something I didn't want to go into. I didn't want to explain why I was getting a nearly free ride, or the price I would have to pay for it. I hugged my knees, remembering a second too late that they were still wet. "Anyway. My dad said the choice was mine—but it's like it wasn't even a choice, you know? Because Ithaca would have just meant a ton of loans, and Stanwich was basically free. And it wasn't like I even really wanted to go to Ithaca in the first place, so . . ."

"I know what you mean. It—the same thing kind of happened to me."

"It did? But I thought—that you wanted to go to Michigan. To be the next . . . Evan Hansen."

"Evan Hansen is the character in the musical, not the composer. Nice reference, though."

"It's really all I have. I'm out now."

Russell's smile faded, little by little, and he took a breath. "I got rejected from USC's musical theater program. And from Temple's. And from Tisch. The musical I submitted as my sample—it just wasn't ready. And my dad told me that. And of course I should have listened to him—he would know, after all. And while Michigan is great, I just . . ." He shook his head. "It didn't turn out the way I was hoping."

I nodded as I looked at him, feeling somehow lighter, knowing we had this in common too. "I know how you feel. It's why I'm not looking forward to tomorrow."

"All because of some brisket."

"Right? Like if I'd ordered a burger or something, I might have ended up going to a totally different college. So you're right. You never know those little choices that are actually going to make the biggest difference."

"Wouldn't it be great if you could? If, like, you could get an alert on your phone—'Turn left ahead.' 'Don't eat that brisket.' 'Go talk to the cute girl in the bus station.'"

I smiled. "Oh yeah?"

"Yeah," he said simply. "As soon as I saw you, I was only pretending to read. I was just staring at the same page."

"It's a good thing you'd read the book before."

Russell smiled but didn't look away from me. "When that guy told me you were looking for me, it felt like the moment I'd been waiting for." He moved a touch closer to me and hooked his ankle around mine, entwining our feet. "It was like something out of a story."

I blinked at him, surprised but thrilled that he thought this too. "Like *Theseus's Sailboat*."

"Yes! Is that stupid?"

"No, I thought the same thing. It's like that, but . . . better. Because it's actually real. And . . . this can happen." I reached out for his hand on the concrete, getting a little zingy jolt the second I touched his skin.

I knew that when people had been together for a while, this wasn't a big deal at all. I'd seen the way that Didi would take the hand of whatever girl she was dating. I understood that eventually, things just became familiar and easier. But right now, in the newness of whatever this was, it felt like there were sparks and electricity every time I got close to him.

Russell picked up my hand and kissed it, looking at me over our entwined fingers. "Hi."

The lights around and inside the pool suddenly snapped off all at once, like they'd been on a timer. Now the only light was coming from the floodlights in the parking lot, the faint neon glow of the cowboy hat, and the occasional lighted window in the rooms above us.

I reached my other hand out and touched his face, cupping his cheek. He leaned his head into my hand, giving me the weight of it for just a moment. I traced my fingers over the planes of his face, like I was trying to memorize it. I ran my thumb over his lips and he kissed it. It was all more than I could take, and I leaned in and kissed him.

And it was as if we'd both been waiting for the same moment, the same downbeat of the music, because we were kissing like we'd never stopped. It was just like the football field again, but more comfortable now—this was just what we did. Less finding our rhythm, more settling back into it.

His arms were around me, and he was running his fingers under the hem of my tank top, touching my bare skin, making me shiver and gasp against his mouth as his hands spanned my waist and his thumbs traced circles on my stomach.

But after a while—I had no idea how much time had passed—I became aware that as nice as this was, sitting on a concrete pool deck was really not the most comfortable thing, even if you're really enjoying all the other aspects of the experience.

And Russell must have been feeling the same way, because when we took a break to catch our breath, he stood up, leaving wet footprints on the concrete. He pulled me to my feet, and then into his arms, pressing me close. We just stood there for a moment and I wrapped my arms around his waist, still a little amazed that I got to do this. "Maybe," he said, "we should . . ." Then he looked around and frowned.

I laughed at his expression, and Russell laughed too, the sound shattering the stillness of the night. A light flicked on in a room two floors above us. I looked up at it, worried for a second, but then dismissed it. Probably someone just wanted to read or something; it had nothing to do with us.

"Well," I said, gesturing to what was in front of us. "We could always . . . go swimming?"

He leaned back a little bit, like he wanted to see me better, and smiled. "We *could* do that." He slipped a hand up under my tank top again, letting his hand rest there, just above my hip bone. "I don't have a bathing suit, though."

"Me neither," I said, trying to ignore that the skin under his hand suddenly felt like it was on fire, and it was currently all I could think about. "I actually thought about packing one, but . . ." I took a big breath. How was it *me* who was proposing this? But all at once, it just seemed like the only thing to do. "I guess we don't really . . . need them?"

Russell leaned down and kissed me gently. "You make an excellent point." He pulled his hand away from my hip and touched the hem of my tank top carefully, like it was a precious garment, and not something I'd gotten on clearance at J.Crew Factory. "May I?"

I nodded, my heart beating a million miles an hour. Russell slowly, inch by inch, lifted up my tank top until he pulled it over my head, and the cool Nevada night air was hitting my bare skin and my dark red bralette.

"Oh," he breathed as he looked at me. He touched the strap carefully, like maybe it was made of glass and might shatter. "Red?"

I nodded. "Red."

"But . . . you were wearing white. Wouldn't it have shown through?"

I couldn't help but smile at his expression of utter bafflement. "Well, here's a fun fact for *you*. When you wear red under white, it doesn't show through. Something about the way it absorbs light and blends with your skin rather than reflecting it. I don't know exactly how." I paused for a second. "I guess I really didn't have enough facts in there, huh? But it always works."

"I'll say," Russell said, still gazing at me.

I laughed and touched the hem of his black T-shirt. "May I?"

He nodded, and I held his eyes as I started lifting up his shirt. He bent his knees slightly so that I could get it over his head.

"Um," I said, swallowing hard as I took him in, bathed in the moonlight and the blue lights of the hotel pool. Russell was thin but muscular, with well-defined stomach muscles and *really* nice arms. I wondered if he played any sports—it certainly looked like it. I regretted that I hadn't asked him back when he was clothed. "Well." I tried to get my thoughts in any kind of order, but at the moment, that seemed like an ask of monumental proportions. "I mean," I said, gesturing to him. "This is just unfair."

He looked at me, shaking his head. "Imagine how I feel." I realized I was still holding his shirt, and handed it to him. He handed me mine, and we both started laughing—with giddy delight at the whole absurdity of the situation. He put his shirt back on the lounger near his shoes, and I did the same with my tank top. I reached for the button on my jean shorts, trying to tell myself that this was no big deal. After all, I was pretty sure my underwear covered more than a lot of my bathing suits did. If we'd brought bathing suits with us, this whole thing would have been no big deal. But we didn't have bathing suits—and the fact that I was about to be in just my underwear in front of a boy I really liked made the whole thing seem really intimate.

I knew I was wearing the same kind of underwear as always—lacy stretchy thongs that I bought in packs of three. I was very glad I'd randomly picked the black pair from my duffel, and that it wasn't one of the ones with sprouting elastic and a stretched-out band. When I'd gotten dressed in the tent that morning, I had just been grabbing whatever pair was nearest, not thinking in the least that someone else would be seeing it before the day was over.

Offering up a brief thank-you to faulty buses and people who chose to use Android phones, I undid my jean shorts and stepped out of them, dropping them on the lounger with my tank top.

Then I turned and ran for the pool, jumping into the deep end with a splash.

The water was cool, and heavily chlorinated, and felt great. I stayed under for just a moment before pushing off the bottom and surfacing.

I smoothed my hair down—it looked like maybe another light in the hotel was now on, and I turned to Russell to mention it, but then I saw him and promptly forgot all about it.

He was walking into the pool from the shallow end, wearing navy boxer-briefs that showed long legs and even more stomach muscles, including those ones that looked like lines on either side of his torso. . . .

I ducked under the water for another moment, feeling like I needed to cool myself down. He dove off the last step into the pool and then surfaced a moment later, pushing his hair back. He swam over to me, grinning. "It feels great."

I smiled back. "I know." He dove down again, and when he surfaced he was swimming on his back.

"When I was little . . . ," he said, pushing himself through the water toward the end of the pool. I started doing sidestroke, keeping pace with him. "We spent all our time in my dad's pool. Like, you'd wake up in the morning and put on your bathing suit and not take it off until night, you know?"

"Yeah," I said, stopping to tread water. "What do you mean, your dad's pool?"

"Oh." Russell shook his head. "Sorry—that's what we call it since my mom never goes swimming."

"It's nice you have a pool at your house. My friends and I do the same thing at the Raven Rock pool—go early in the morning, don't leave until night. Stake your claim." I swam over to the shallower end until I could touch the bottom, then walked to the float. I ducked underneath it, surfaced through the hole in the center, and pushed off the pebbled concrete floor and swam back over toward Russell.

He smiled as he nodded down at the float. "Nice."

"I figured it was here—might as well get some use out of it."

"We used to play this pool game we'd invented, Brontosaurus. It involved a series of floats, and had all these crazy rules, and just got more complicated every year."

"What does a dinosaur have to do with swimming?"

He laughed. "Nothing. My older—Connor, my cousin, named it back when he was obsessed with *Jurassic Park*, and it stuck." Russell swam closer to me, and I could see there were water droplets on his forehead. His eyelashes, which were long and dark, had turned into damp triangles, and there was water beading on his neck, on his nice shoulders . . .

"So how do you play?"

"Play what?"

"Brontosaurus! I mean, we *are* in a pool."

He smiled, reached out and brushed some water droplets off my cheek. "That's really nice. But we need four people. And a ball. And ideally, a diving board."

"Can we do a modified version? I . . ."

"What?"

"Nothing." I dipped my head under the water for a second, smoothing my hair down. "Just weird déjà vu. I feel like I've heard about that game before? But that's not possible."

"So about that—fun fact—"

"We're getting an *aquatic* fun fact? An AquaFact! A fact that's anything but dry." Russell smiled patiently, like he'd already learned to wait this out. "I'm done now."

"I highly doubt that. Please interrupt me if you think of any more."

"I absolutely will. Wait! A fact that will hold water. Okay, *now* I'm done."

"It was just about déjà vu. There's an explanation for why we feel it. It's not that we're remembering something from the past, or getting a sense of the future. When you have it, what's happening is that your brain is coding a new memory as an old one, that's all. Like something being put into the wrong folder. Nothing mystical."

"Is it the same when you feel like you know someone? Your brain misidentifies them?"

"I don't know." He took a step toward me. "I think that's something else. Something more . . . special. Don't you?"

We swam closer to each other until we were only inches apart, and suddenly the float seemed like a huge impediment. I ducked under it and pushed it away. When I surfaced, I realized that we were close enough to the shallow end that I could stand—the water hitting just below my shoulders. I walked on my toes closer to Russell, and let myself just drink him in for a moment. I liked seeing him like this—water dripping off his hair, lit by the moon and the glow of a neon cowboy hat, nothing between us. His kind eyes, his half smile that was growing as he noticed me looking at him.

"What?"

"Just you."

He touched my waist and looked at me. "Is this okay?"

I nodded, then I leaned forward and kissed him. He tasted like chlorine and pineapple soda, like sunshine and possibilities. While we were kissing, I touched his chest, and then his shoulders, and let my hands run down his arms, feeling the muscles underneath. He felt so strong—like he could hold me up if he needed to. (I couldn't imagine when that would be necessary, but it was somehow nice to know.) I broke away and looked into his eyes as my hands started to trace lower, over the ridges of his abs. "Is this okay?"

"Uh-huh," he said, kissing me again. "Very much so."

And we were kissing in the water, and there was suddenly so much *more* of him that I could touch—arms and legs and stomach and back, all exposed to me, and I couldn't get enough of it. He seemed to be feeling the same way, his touching my stomach, my back, my legs . . .

We were kissing faster now, and my legs were wrapped around his waist. Russell had one hand bracing against the side of the pool, one hand on my back, his fingers slipping under the band of my bralette. I was holding on to him, and somehow it didn't feel like the football field kissing anymore. It no longer felt like we had all night.

There was a hunger to our kissing now, a need I'd never felt before. It felt deeper, and more intense, like somehow, even though we were surrounded by water, a fire had started burning.

"Um," I said, when we'd both paused to take a breath. My legs were still wrapped around him, and I was above him, looking down. Russell leaned forward and kissed my collarbone. He slid my wet strap off my shoulder and kissed the skin there, his lips soft on me.

"Yes?" he asked, looking up at me. He smiled, then took a breath and pulled us both under. We surfaced together, and I was laughing and wiping water out of my eyes. "Sorry," he said, running his fingers up and down my arm. "Couldn't resist. What were you going to say?" he asked, even though he sounded a little bit dazed, which was exactly how I felt.

"Just—" I said, looking around. I unhooked my legs and stood on the pebbly bottom of the pool, flexing my feet. I wasn't sure what happened now. I suddenly wished that one of us had a car. "I wasn't sure if we should . . . go somewhere?" I realized this was the vaguest thing I could have said, but I wasn't sure how else to put it. I wasn't really sure what I even *meant*, just that I wanted this to continue, but maybe not in the pool.

"Well, we could . . ." He hesitated. When he spoke again, it was all in a rush. "I don't want this to sound presumptuous. And I'm not saying we even have to . . . not that I would expect—or that you would! Just . . . This is coming out all wrong." He looked at me and took a deep breath. "I was just thinking that—if you wanted—we could get a room."

"Here?" A second later, I realized what an inane question that was. *Of course* here. Here, at the hotel we were currently at that had vacancies.

But—*could* we even get a room? Were we allowed to? A second later, though, I realized that we probably could—we were both eighteen, and technically adults, so booking a hotel room was something I was actually, legally, allowed to do. I just had never done it before.

"Wait—you have enough money for a hotel room?"

I'd assumed that we were somewhat in the same boat at the moment, money-wise. As in, neither of us had very much. Otherwise, why would Russell have even been stuck in the bus station to begin with? Why wouldn't he have taken an Uber to Vegas with everyone else?

"I . . . have a credit card we can use. If you want! We don't have to at all, and nothing has to happen. I mean . . ." He let out a breath, then looked at me again. "We could just take hot showers and watch HBO."

"You know, I did see that they have it here. And for free!"

He laughed at that, but didn't look away from me, searching my face as though he was trying to figure out how I felt—which was exactly what I was doing.

Is this what you want? Didi whispered, her voice quiet.

And I was pretty sure it *was*. I knew Russell. I trusted him. And this seemed like the next step on a path that had just led me to more and more wonderful things. This was my epic night, after all. I was in my one-night, magical story—and this was just the next chapter. I felt an excited little thrill flutter somewhere inside my chest.

"I mean, I do love HBO. And hot showers." I met his eyes and nodded. "I think that sounds . . . like something we should do."

Russell smiled wide—it practically took over his whole face. "Yeah?"

I nodded, then took a breath. "I've never . . . um . . . stayed at a hotel with someone before." I felt heat creeping into my cheeks. It was embarrassing to have to admit this, but didn't we need to talk about it? Also—what if that changed something?

"Oh." Russell smoothed my wet hair back gently.

"Not that I haven't wanted to! I've just been . . . looking for the right one. Five stars, all the amenities." He smiled at that, and I made myself ask the question I was pretty sure I already knew the answer to. "Um . . . have you?"

Russell nodded, and I tried to figure out if I was disappointed or relieved. Somehow, it was a little bit of both. "I have," he said, then took a breath and looked right into my eyes. "But now I wish I hadn't. I wish I would have waited for this hotel. For right now." He ran his hand down my arm, picked up my hand, and kissed it. "I should have waited for Darcy Milligan."

I smiled at that—at the way he sounded saying my name. "I know this is kind of crazy," I said as I placed my hands on his face, looking into his eyes. "But it just feels right, doesn't it? Like . . . everything's been leading to this. Since that first moment." I smiled at him, feeling like my heart was cracked open, exposed—but I wasn't scared. Because I knew I could trust him. Like I could see him, and he could see me, and there was nothing to be afraid of. This was what Wylie Sanders and everyone else had been singing about all these years. And here, in a moonlit pool in Nevada, I finally got it.

"Maybe I've always been waiting for you," I said, cupping his cheek in my hand. "For Russell Henrion."

He took a step back, something I couldn't read passing over his face. "Look, Darcy," he said. Then he took a big breath. "There's actually something that I need to talk to you about. I'm—"

"Hey!"

All of a sudden, there was a flashlight beam pointing at us, and I drew in a sharp breath, squinting against the light that was blinding me. Russell stepped in front of me, which I was glad about, because there was an irritated-looking man in a security uniform glaring at us.

"Pool's closed."

"Ah," Russell said, nodding. "Right. Sorry. We'll get out."

"We've had some noise complaints," he said as he pointed his flashlight around.

I was suddenly very aware that I was in my underwear in front of a strange man, in a pool I wasn't supposed to be in.

"You're hotel guests?"

"Yeah," Russell said easily. "Guess we didn't see the time that the pool closed. We'll be on our way."

The guard's flashlight landed on the loungers and I watched as it moved around, every time landing on something that just seemed more suspicious. My bag, Russell's backpack, our clothes. I felt my heart sink. Actual hotel guests would have brought bathing suits, and changed into them in the rooms. Actual hotel guests would have towels, and wouldn't be swimming in their underwear. Suddenly, my big idea seemed incredibly stupid. All at once, I was getting to see the flip side of *why not*.

I looked at Russell—he looked as freaked out as I felt. "I . . . ," I started.

"Out of the pool," the security guy said, already reaching to talk into the walkie attached to his shoulder. *"Now."*

CHAPTER 7

Sunday
8:50 P.M.

Everything was awful.

We were standing in the office that was just behind the front desk, in the lobby, under bright fluorescent lights.

I had pulled my tank top and jean shorts on when we'd been ordered out of the pool. But we didn't have anything to dry off with—it turns out, security guards don't carry spare towels around with them. So my hair was dripping down my back, my tank top was sticking to me, and I had just learned the hard way that it is very uncomfortable to put on dry clothes over wet underwear. The AC in the hotel was also blasting, and I was shivering as I stood there, shifting my weight from foot to foot, watching goose bumps pop up on my arms.

Russell looked equally uncomfortable—and possibly more so, since he'd had to put on *jeans*. His black T-shirt was damp in patches, and in his haste, he'd put it on inside out—I could see the tag that read *Tom Ford*.

But worse than any of this—than standing under bright lights, clothes slowly getting wet, having just been caught in my underwear by a security guard—was the growing realization that we were *really* in trouble.

The red-haired woman I'd seen when I'd walked through the

lobby was behind the desk in the office, along with the security guard. There were two folding chairs leaning up against the wall under a calendar written on a whiteboard. But since they weren't unfolded, it would have seemed weird to set them up, so Russell and I were just standing in front of the desk, our bags at our feet.

This room really wasn't big enough for four people, especially if everyone was standing, and I could feel myself getting claustrophobic. Or maybe it was just the whole situation that was doing it.

I had never been this embarrassed in my life. I could feel the embarrassment in every cell of my body, like even my cuticles and pancreas were cringing. A guard with a flashlight had caught me and Russell kissing in a pool in our underwear, and then we'd had to climb out, dripping, as people in the upper floors of the hotel had watched from their windows. Before tonight, I had always thought that *died of embarrassment* was just an expression, but I knew better now, because it really felt possible.

"So let me get this straight," the woman said. Her name tag—it had a horseshoe on it—read *Lily*. "You're not hotel guests. I'm guessing you came from the festival?" She frowned down at my bracelets, then turned to the guard. *Josh*, his brass name tag read. "This is a problem every year. Festivalgoers crash here, eight to a room—which is a *fire hazard*. They create chaos; we get tons of noise complaints. People always hopping the fence to use the pool, keeping all the other guests up." She shook her head. Her voice had started rising with every word, like as she was describing all these things, she was getting more and more upset. "I've been dealing with this all weekend. And every year for the last three years. And I'm *done*."

I took a step back—even though there really wasn't anywhere

to go—and bumped into Russell, who was behind me. "Sorry," I whispered.

"It's fine," he whispered back. He put his hands on my shoulders, and I reached up and held one of his hands with mine, and he gave it a squeeze, letting me know that he was here, that I wasn't in this alone.

"So . . ." Josh said. He looked at us, then back at Lily, and spun the flashlight in his hand. "What do you want to do?"

Lily crossed her arms over her chest and looked at us for a long moment before reaching across the desk to grab the cordless phone. "There is clear signage. It says the pool is for hotel guests only, and that trespassers will be prosecuted."

"Prosecuted?" I whispered, and Russell's hand tightened on mine. Prosecuted as in . . . police and *jail*? That kind of prosecuted?

"Wait," Russell said. He dropped my hand and came to stand on the other side of me. He suddenly looked a lot paler than he had when we'd come in here. "We were actually just talking about this." He was speaking fast now. "About getting a room here for the night. We saw you had a vacancy?"

"Really," Lily said. She didn't ask it like a question.

"Yes," I said quickly. "We were. So maybe that would . . . fix this?"

Lily shook her head, looking even angrier now. "It's not retroactive! You two were trespassing. You don't get to buy your way out of it."

"You don't?" This was Josh the security guard. "Because my cousin got caught sneaking into a movie. But then he paid for the movie and so they just let him go watch it. So maybe—"

"Thanks, Josh," Lily said, cutting him off. She lifted the phone and it was like I was suddenly having trouble breathing. Because she was only going to make one call. She'd found trespassers; if she was calling anyone, it was the police.

A bleak thought flashed through my head—maybe if I was in jail, I wouldn't have to go to Stanwich College after all. But this thought was replaced a second later by a much worse one. I was going to have to tell my *dad*. He was going to be so disappointed in me.

I closed my eyes for a second. I knew, in my bones, that this was all my fault. I was the one who'd suggested the pool. I was the one who'd found the key card. Without me, none of this would be happening.

"It was my fault," I said, taking a step closer to the desk. "If anyone is going to get in trouble, it should be me. Not Russell."

"Darcy." Russell shook his head. "It's okay." He turned back to Lily. "I'm sure that we can work something out."

She let out a short laugh, the kind with no humor in it. "We're not *working anything out*. People need to know that there are consequences. This kind of behavior has gone on much too long."

It felt like we were being treated simultaneously as kids and adults—like we were kids who should have known better, but were also going to be subject to adult consequences. However, I knew better than to point this out at this particular moment.

"So I'm sorry," she said, even though she didn't sound particularly sorry. "This is happening." She was still holding the phone but hadn't turned it on or dialed it yet, which was all that was preventing me from spiraling into a full-blown panic attack.

"I promise," Russell said, "we can fix this." He turned to me, reached out and touched my hand for just a moment before letting it go. He gave me a sad smile, and then his face crumpled. "God-*damn* it," he whispered.

He bent down and started rifling through his bag, then pulled out his phone and stood up.

I took a breath, to remind him that his phone was dead—but then I saw Russell's home screen light up.

"Your . . . phone was charged?" I asked, even though the proof was in front of me. I just couldn't understand it. "This whole time?"

Russell winced, not looking at me. "Yeah," he said quietly.

"But . . . why would you . . ." I could see now very clearly—on a phone that was supposed to be dead—a picture of Russell, grinning, as he jumped off what looked like a very nice boat into an azure sea.

It felt like someone had shaken the earth beneath me, like the ground I'd assumed would hold me was riven with fault lines. What was *happening*?

"I'm going to call my dad," Russell said to Lily. "This will all get sorted. I promise." He said it with a kind of quiet authority, and even Lily must have heard it, because she set the phone down on the desk, though she kept her hand on it.

Russell pressed a number on his phone and raised it to his ear—and I clocked, for the very first time, that aside from his watch, his arms were bare. He didn't have a Silverspun bracelet on. The bracelet that everyone who'd attended the festival had to wear.

Things were starting to snap into place, forming a picture I really didn't want to see.

"Russell," I said slowly. "Who's your dad?"

He met my eyes—sadness and frustration mingled in his expression. He took a deep breath, and when he spoke, his voice was resigned. "Wylie Sanders."

II

A Little Less Conversation

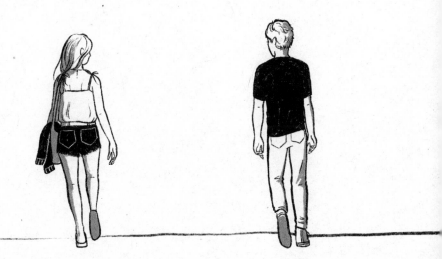

I pulled the car into the Chevron station and killed the engine. I was already sweating, which didn't seem fair. I glanced at the temperature on my dashboard and groaned. It was already seventy-nine degrees, and I had a feeling it was going to be worse as I drove through the desert.

I glanced into the back seat, where my duffel was, but resisted the urge to check it one last time. It was enough that I'd been getting messages all week—Don't forget to bring a sweater! It'll get cold at night!—R. It was time to just go.

I got out of the car and stepped into the bright sun, squinting and then flipping down my sunglasses. I definitely wasn't used to this. I headed into the mini-mart, welcoming the blast of air-conditioning that greeted me. Mariah Carey was playing over the store's speakers. I grabbed a sparkling water from the refrigerator case, then swung by the snack aisle for a bag of cheddar Ruffles—the best kind—as well as a granola bar and an Abba-Zaba.

My phone beeped again with a text as I picked up the candy bar, and I glanced at it. Did you get my email? We need to discuss what we're bringing! "Romy, give it a rest," I muttered as I shook my head and slid my phone into the back pocket of my jeans. If I didn't get moving, I was going to be seriously late.

I took everything up to the register, where the woman working behind it was humming along to Mariah. "Hot one," she said conversationally as she rang me up. I nodded. I was already dreading the moment I'd have to leave the store with its artic blast, and get back in my ancient Prius, whose air-conditioning was barely functional.

"I know," I said with a groan as I waved off her offer of a bag and handed her a ten. "And it's worse where I'm going."

She raised an eyebrow as she handed me back my change and receipt. "And where's that?"

I pocketed the change, crumpled the receipt, and gathered my snacks up. "Nevada."

CHAPTER 8

Sunday
9:30 P.M.

Two years ago, at the Raven Rock community pool, I'd fallen asleep in the shade on one of the loungers. Apparently, this made me an irresistible target. Didi had bought a jumbo cup of ice water from the concession counter, and she and Katy decided to wake me up by dribbling little drops on me.

And that's what they were doing until a kid ran past and bumped into Didi. She stumbled forward, and the entire cup of ice water was thrown on me. I'd woken at once, gasping and confused.

I had the same feeling now—startled and shaky, shocked out of a dream and back to reality with a jolt. Except now, I was not on a lounge chair at our community pool.

I was in Wylie Sanders's helicopter, flying toward Vegas.

I stared at my reflection in the helicopter window, meeting my own eyes in the darkness.

What had I been *doing*? Who had I thought I was? It was like I didn't even recognize the me from the last few hours. I wasn't a character in a book or a movie, but I'd pretended like I was. I'd just decided that I was having a perfect night and that this was the moment—and the guy—I'd been waiting for.

But none of it had been true—and things like that didn't happen in real life.

Because Russell had been lying to me, practically from the moment we'd met.

I glanced across the helicopter—he was in the seat opposite me. But then I immediately looked away again, my throat feeling tight. This was beyond humiliation. This was something I was pretty sure I'd never felt before—and never wanted to again.

I was cycling through shame, anger, embarrassment—then returning back to shame in a loop that was really a lot of fun for me. I had been about to *sleep* with this person—this stranger who had lied to me, over and over again.

Wylie Sanders.

Wylie Sanders was Russell's *dad*.

It explained so much—inconsistencies and red flags that I just hadn't wanted to see. It explained why he didn't have a bag or a tent with him. It explained the lack of a bracelet and the Tom Ford T-shirt and going to bars in Paris. It even explained *Jeopardy!*.

It was why his pool game sounded so familiar—it was a line in "Saturday Night Falls." *Kids playing Brontosaurus in the pool / hear the laughter slowly grow*. It wasn't just déjà vu—I knew about it because his *dad* had sung a *song* about it.

I closed my eyes as all the things I'd said to Russell flashed through my head, like a montage whose theme was humiliation. I thought about the way I'd gushed to him about Wylie Sanders— how great he was, how much his music meant to me. How important it was to me and my dad. The personal memories I'd shared, not realizing he'd probably been secretly laughing at me the whole time. I cringed as I thought about the way I'd proudly put on my dad's sweatshirt, understanding now why Russell had wanted me to take it off.

And all at once, I remembered what I'd said about his dad's personal life. How it was a train wreck—how Wylie Sanders had so many different kids with so many different women. I hadn't said anything that was untrue—but I'd said these things to his *son*. I could feel the creeping humiliation of being caught out, like in eighth grade when I'd been complaining in the bathroom to Didi about my lab partner—only to have her emerge from the stall, having heard everything.

I saw that Russell was mouthing something to me. We'd both been given headsets when we got on the helicopter and had been instructed to press the button on the side if we wanted to say anything, and be heard—it was too loud to understand anyone otherwise.

I shook my head at him, glad that I had this barrier, at least until we landed. If I didn't press the button, he wouldn't be able to talk to me. Wouldn't be able to try and lie to me again, and I wouldn't be tempted to believe it. I stared out the window, rubbing my arms—it was really cold in the helicopter. My sweatshirt was in my bag, but there was no *way* I was putting that on now. I hadn't even wanted to be on this helicopter, and I'd told Russell that. But when it came down to it, I didn't have much of a choice.

As he'd promised, once Russell talked to his dad—to *Wylie Sanders*—things started to move quickly. Suddenly, some lawyer was calling the hotel, followed shortly by some PR woman calling on the other line to see what could be done about this. Would the Silver Standard like a signed photo? A case of Sanders Vineyards champagne, or maybe some samples from the new tequila line? A shout-out on Instagram?

It started to become clear that we weren't going to be hauled off to the police station—at least, not at the moment. And only a few minutes earlier, that would have made me incredibly happy. And while I was still relieved not to be going to jail, it felt like everything was tainted now.

When I'd gotten the all-clear to leave—Lily had insisted that Russell and I write down our contact information and had photocopied our licenses, something I didn't love but didn't see a way around—I'd grabbed my bag, headed straight for the automatic hotel doors, and walked out into the night.

It was getting colder, my hair was still very wet, and I felt myself shiver as I looked around, trying to trace my steps back, find the most direct path to the bus station. I was teetering on the verge of some combination of hyperventilating or crying—potentially both simultaneously.

I just wanted to go home.

I wanted to curl up in my bed and pull the covers over me and let this all become a bad dream. I wanted to be back in a place where things made sense, where my life was quiet and boring again. Where I wasn't in the middle of nowhere in Nevada, trying to grapple with feelings that kept hitting me in waves, like I was caught in the ocean, unable to swim past the breakers.

"Wait," Russell had called, running out of the hotel after me, his voice raw. "Darcy!"

"What." I wheeled around on him, my voice catching in my throat. "What can you possibly—"

"My dad's lawyers." He held out his phone to me. "They need to talk to you."

"Oh." I took the phone from him—noting that it was almost

completely charged—and had a brief conversation with a paralegal named Sarah, who seemed remarkably awake and focused, given that it was getting late on a Sunday night. She told me that someone named C.J. would need just a smidge of my time when we got to the compound. Then she'd hung up and I'd handed Russell his phone back.

"C.J.," I said, folding my arms over my chest, "apparently needs to *circle up* with us when we get to the *compound*."

"Uh—yeah," Russell said. He ran his hands through his hair. It was drying funny, sticking up in places, and only twenty minutes ago I would have found it beyond endearing. "They want to talk to us, make sure everyone is clear on details in case the Silver Standard decides to press charges."

I nodded, even though just hearing *press charges* was enough to make me feel wobbly. Instead, I focused on the other part of my conversation with Sarah. "What's the compound?"

Russell sighed and looked at the ground. We were standing outside the front doors of the Silver Standard, the same place where, not that long ago, he'd kissed me as easily as anything. And now, everything was broken into pieces all around us.

"It's my dad's place in Vegas. He got it when he started his residency there. It's outside of town—half an hour from the Strip."

"And they expect me to go there?"

"My dad—" Russell started, then shook his head. "He's sending a helicopter for us." His voice was small.

The automatic doors opened, and stayed that way for a hopeful beat, before sliding closed again. When this happened a second time, I realized we must be in front of the sensor and walked to the side.

"I'm not going anywhere with you."

Russell took a step back, looking like I'd slapped him. "Darcy—"

"You *lied* to me!" I didn't know I was going to yell this until I was already doing it. "You told me your phone was dead—that your name was Russell Henrion—" I stopped suddenly, realizing what I'd just heard. "Did you say *helicopter*?"

So even though I hadn't wanted to be there, I also didn't want to have charges pressed against me for trespassing. I figured I would go talk to C.J., charge my phone, and then head to the bus station in Las Vegas. I still had my ticket and might even be able to get back to LA sooner now. And if not, I'd just wait there until I could get the first bus home. I had been planning on waiting all night at the bus station in Jesse, after all. So it's not like it made much difference. I knew it wasn't a great plan, but it was all I had, and I was clinging to it tight.

When the helicopter arrived, it touched down near the abandoned gas station—perhaps not surprisingly, the Jesse, Nevada, bus station was not outfitted with a helipad. I'd gone back in to get my things—they were still right where I'd left them under the bench. As I'd looked around, it felt like years, not just hours, had passed since I'd been there. Too much had changed for everything in it to look exactly the same, for the vending machine light to still be flickering on and off.

The couple who'd been watching the movie were asleep, curled up together under an unzipped sleeping bag. Sunburned Bald Man was still sleeping, and as I looked at him, I realized that he'd had the right idea all along. I should have followed his lead, just conked out on one of the benches and waited out my time until morning. I shouldn't have ventured beyond my comfort zone. I should have just stayed put.

But you had fun, Katy whispered.

I hadn't wanted to think about that, so I just grabbed the tent and my duffel and went outside to wait for the helicopter.

The pilot—Scott—had been cheerful and unfazed, like he was just always picking up teenagers in the middle of nowhere, late at night. And who knows, maybe he was. If anything had become clear to me in the last half hour, it was that I didn't know Russell at all. Scott had told us how to duck our heads to avoid the propellers, and once we were on board, had made sure we were buckled in. He explained about the headphones, and that we should be landing in twenty minutes.

Quite an upgrade for someone who couldn't afford an Uber, Didi had pointed out.

And in regular circumstances, I would have been really excited to ride in a helicopter for the first time. Especially *this* helicopter— the seats were soft dark-blue leather with a *WS* monogram stitched into all of them. But I just sat up straight with my legs twined around each other, trying to take up as little space as I could, staring out the window and willing us to land as soon as possible.

I felt someone tap my knee, and looked over to see Russell trying to get my attention, saying something I couldn't hear.

All at once, I flashed back to the pool, to his hands on my bare skin—my fingers, running over the ridges of his abs—the feel of him pressing against me as we kissed. I felt my face flood with heat, remembering what we'd done, what I'd said.

I'd told him that I was a virgin. I told him I'd been *waiting for him*. I told him about not getting into anywhere except two schools—I'd even told him about my brisket food poisoning. I'd opened myself up to him, had shown him my whole heart, assuming all the while he was doing the same. Never dreaming that he was hiding things from me, that he had his own agenda.

How could I have been so *stupid*?

Well..., Didi started.

You weren't stupid! Katy interrupted. *You were just taking a chance.*

Russell tapped his headphones again, and I finally turned them on.

"What."

"Darcy, listen," he said in a rush. It was disconcerting, to hear him like that, right in my ear. "I'm really sorry. I shouldn't have lied to you. I know that. I just . . ."

"Was it all just a game to you?" I wanted to sound tough and cool, but this failed spectacularly, and my voice started to shake three words in. "Were you trying to trick me?"

"No." Russell closed his eyes for just a moment. "I just wanted to be *me* for once. Not Wylie Sanders's kid. Not someone with all that baggage. I've never just gotten to be anonymous before tonight."

"But you weren't anonymous." I hugged my arms, because I was cold and because it felt like I was slowly coming apart. "You told me your name was Russell Henrion and that your dad was a structural engineer."

"It's a family name," he said quietly. "And I know I didn't tell you about my dad, but—"

"But what? That's not a little detail you forget to mention. It's not like my dad's in advertising, and instead, I told you he's in marketing. What your dad does is a *big fucking deal.*"

"Yes," Russell said, pointing at me. "Exactly. That's just what I'm talking about! The second anyone knows, it changes everything and I hate it. It's been my whole life, everyone having ideas about who I am before they've even met me. I never know how they actually feel about me." He took a shaky breath. "I mean you had my dad's face on your *sweatshirt*. You were telling me what a big fan you are. He's inescapable. It's like this shadow I've never been able to get out of. And tonight I thought . . . I guess I just wanted to see if you actually liked *me*."

"Well, at some point I think that was clear," I said. "I was going to *sleep with you!*"

"Guys, just jumping in here," Scott the pilot said, sounding uncomfortable. "Wanted to let you know I'm also on this channel and can hear this whole conversation. I'm switching to channel two; we should be landing in ten minutes."

"Thanks, Scott," Russell said faintly.

"Thank you," I echoed, wondering if maybe tonight was some kind of simulation just to see how much mortification one human being could take before they literally exploded or went mad.

"I was going to tell you," Russell said after a moment.

"When?"

"In the pool, right before the security guard showed up."

"Oh, that's *very* convenient."

"It's true!"

"But I can't believe anything you're telling me!" I yelled, and I felt tears prick my eyes.

Something in his face crumpled, and he looked out the window. I hated that he still looked so cute, that the sight of his inside-out T-shirt was making my heart hurt. I hated that I'd opened myself up to him, only to be slapped back down again.

"I don't understand about the phone," I said after a few moments of silence. "Why did you tell me that your phone was also dead when it was working?"

Russell looked over at me, then down at his sneakers, one of which, I saw now, was untied. "I just . . ." he said, mostly to his shoes. "I thought that maybe if we were in the same situation, we could just . . . hang out. I never expected anything like what we had, Darcy. And then you were so great, and we were having so much fun, and I . . . I shouldn't have done it," he said quietly. "And I'm sorry."

We banked slightly to the right, and suddenly there they were—the lights of Las Vegas. I'd been once before, when my dad had a conference when I was eight. Mostly what I remembered was riding the roller coaster at New York-New York, and the circus-themed hotel we'd stayed at.

But I'd never seen it like this—from the air, the sudden, dazzling brightness of it. We flew past the city, the lights dimming behind us.

"Um—Darcy?" I looked over at Russell, who was twisting his hands together. "Couldn't it be like the Ship of Theseus? Just like we talked about—the essence stays the same, right? You know something new about me, but the *me* you met is still the same. Could you maybe think of it like that?"

For half a second, I hesitated. Maybe—if I squinted—I could somehow return to the movie I'd been pretending we were in. But a moment later, I came back to reality. The bubble we were in had burst. I was awake now, and finally seeing things clearly.

"No," I said, and his face fell. "I was totally open with you—completely honest, and—"

"Really," he said. He didn't phrase it like a question. "You don't seem to want to talk about Stanwich, or why you're going there. You keep changing the subject. Why?"

I drew back against the seat. "That's my business," I said hotly. "Maybe I don't want to talk about everything—"

"And there it is," Russell said, pointing at me. "You can be mad at me if you want—I deserve it. But don't pretend that you were some open book tonight."

I knew that what he was saying was true, which just made me even more irritated. "Fine," I said, shaking my head. "Whatever. But we can just drop this, okay? There's no point."

"What—what do you mean?"

"I mean I'll talk to this lawyer because I don't want to get arrested. But then I'm leaving."

"Where are you going?"

"I'll go to the bus station in Vegas and get back home."

"You can't just leave. We have to—"

"What?" I snapped. I wished we weren't still talking about this. It was hard for me to hold on to just how hurt and betrayed I felt when he was looking across at me earnestly, his eyebrows drawn together. But he had lied to me and manipulated me. I'd been vulnerable with him, and had gotten practically naked with him, and had been a heartbeat away from sleeping with him. And the whole time, he had been keeping things from me. I couldn't let those facts slip away, no matter how regretful he suddenly seemed now. "Why are we even doing this? What's the point?"

"The *point*? The point is—we like each other. Right?"

I felt something in my resolve start to crack, and I tried to ignore it. The *who cares* Darcy of an hour ago was gone. If Russell still thought we were in a story where everything was fated, meant to be, and all worked out in the end, well, that was a *him* problem.

"This," I said, gesturing between us, "is done. We don't need to keep . . ." I shook my head. "I'll talk to this lawyer and then I'll be out of your hair, and we can just pretend this never happened."

"But I don't want to do that."

"Well, I do."

Russell took a breath, like he was going to say something, but then just sat back against his seat, his dad's initials emblazoned above his head. He was looking at me like he'd never seen me before, like he didn't know me—which wasn't inaccurate. I'd only known him for a handful of hours, after all.

So you were presenting a selective version of yourself, Katy pointed out. *Isn't that what you're getting mad at him for?*

"Wow."

"What?"

"It's just—really that black and white with you? All or nothing?"

I wrapped my arms around myself, not loving that he'd pinpointed what Didi and Katy—and my dad—were always saying. I took a breath to respond just as the helicopter seemed to stop. We hovered in the air for a moment, then started to descend.

We touched down, the noise in the cabin lessened, and when Russell took his headphones off, I took mine off too. I ran my hand through my still pool-damp hair, but I knew it was probably a lost cause.

I leaned out the window to try to see where we were just as Scott the pilot opened the door and motioned us out. Russell gestured for me to leave first. This would have charmed me an hour ago, but now it just made me roll my eyes. I ducked my head as I stepped off and walked out, even though it seemed like the propeller blades were slowing way down.

When I cleared the helicopter, I straightened up and looked around.

We had landed on the top of a building, even though it only

seemed like it was one or two stories. I could see that there was a *WS* painted in the center of a circle on the helipad, in the same font as had been stitched into the seats.

WS for *Wylie Sanders*. I had just arrived at a rock star's house. And my determination to be unfazed by any of this went out the window as I looked around and was immediately fazed.

As I tried to take it all in—not easy—I understood why Sarah the paralegal had called this a compound. Because *house* really wouldn't have been enough to fit all that was in front of me. There was a second building a ways away from the building I was currently standing on top of, and this seemed to be the main structure. It was an enormous, sprawling mansion, two stories, all glass and weathered wood. There was a huge pool, and the entire property was ringed with palm trees. It looked like most of the lights in the main building were on, the light spilling out onto the massive lawn that I just hoped was artificial grass—because Vegas. Behind the main house were a series of smaller structures that looked like they had been constructed to resemble mini versions of the bigger house. I had no idea what they were, but there were five of them. Guesthouses? I was just gobsmacked by the *scale* of it all—our whole house in Raven Rock probably could have fit into this helipad, with room to spare.

"Hello!" I turned around and saw two people standing just off the helipad—one guy, one girl, both in their twenties. They were both wearing khakis and half-zip black pullovers that had *WS* stitched on them in the same font from the helicopter and helipad. "Hey, Rusty," the guy said to Russell, as the girl gave me a nod and walked around to the back of the helicopter. "Welcome home."

"Hi, Kendrick," Russell said, giving him a smile. But I could see that *Rusty* had annoyed him. But then a second later, this annoyed *me*. I barely knew this guy—how was I intuiting what his unspoken feelings were? He gestured to me. "This is Darcy—"

"Darcy Milligan," the guy—Kendrick—said, giving me a crisp nod. "We got the full download from Bronwyn. Nice to meet you."

"Bronwyn?"

"My dad's publicist." It sounded like it pained Russell to say each of those words. "This is Kendrick, that's Bella—" He gestured to the girl who was now emerging from the other side of the helicopter, carrying my tent and duffel bag. She gave me a wave with her free hand.

"No," I said, taking a step closer to her. "I can get that—"

"No worries," she said cheerfully, not stopping. "I'll just bring them into the main residence for you while you guys meet with C.J. in SNF."

"Yes," Kendrick said, lifting up an iPad and scrolling through it. "C.J.'s en route now. Shall we?"

"I . . ." I looked for Bella, who had already disappeared. I didn't like that my stuff was suddenly gone, but what was I supposed to do about it?

"Great," Kendrick said, as though I'd just agreed with him. He typed something on his iPad, then nodded at us and walked toward a door at the far end of the helipad.

I followed him—it turned out the door wasn't a door, but an elevator, and we all stepped inside to go down one floor. I looked at Russell as we descended. He was staring resolutely at the floor, like he was trying to pretend none of this was happening.

My head was spinning as I tried to take it all in—the fact that Russell had grown up with this. Staff with iPads escorting you around, helicopters and main residences and publicists. I couldn't even fathom it.

The doors opened and we stepped out. It seemed like we had walked into an office building—there was a lobby-type area with couches and a coffee table, and then offices behind glass doors running down the hallway.

I blinked, feeling a little bit like Alice down the rabbit hole. I had thought we were going to Wylie Sanders's house—why did it suddenly look like we were in my dad's accountant's office? Even though his accountant didn't have a collection of bass guitars lined up in the waiting room.

"Sorry," I said to Kendrick. "But—where are we? I mean . . ." I gestured to the hallway, the couches, the offices, all of it.

"This is the Wylie Sanders management office," Kendrick said easily. "Where all Mr. Sanders's business operations are handled. Legal, publicity, accounting, touring, development . . ."

"Right," I faintly.

"This way," Kendrick said cheerfully as he headed down the hallway, swiping on his iPad as he went.

I followed Russell and Kendrick, trying to take in as much as I could, but it was all a little overwhelming. Most of the offices were dark, but even so, through the glass doors, I could see Wylie Sanders and Nighthawks merchandise and posters and pictures in all of them. Framed gold and platinum records lined the walls, along with blown-up album covers showing the sales figures in different countries, and pictures of Wylie and the band—in all its incarnations—everywhere I turned. What I'd thought were just black stripes on the beige carpet were, I could see now, music notes. I couldn't read music enough to tell, but they seemed specific enough that I was sure I was probably walking on one of the Nighthawks songs. I slowed my feet as I passed a glass-front cabinet that was filled with awards. I felt my mouth drop open as I looked at them—Grammys and Golden Globes and VMA Moon Men.

I knew even as I stared that there was a lot I was missing. And in that moment, as I made myself walk away from the trophy case, I felt sharply just how much my dad would have loved to see it. What he wouldn't have given to have been there—he would have been in heaven. If my phone had been charged, I wouldn't have cared if it seemed gauche or if Kendrick got mad at me. I would have taken every picture that I could to show him.

But of course, if my phone had been charged, I wouldn't have been here. None of this would have happened.

"Here we are," Kendrick said, stopping in front of a darkened conference room. SATURDAY NIGHT FALLS was written on the sign just outside it—the name of one of the Nighthawks' biggest hits. He opened the door, switched on the light, and I blinked.

It looked like a normal conference room—ergonomic chairs, large screen at one corner of the room. But unlike a regular conference room, there wasn't a table in the center of all the chairs. Instead, there was a large slab of rusty metal on legs that seemed to be standing in for a table. *Starline* was written on it in looping script. I just stared at it, but neither Russell or Kendrick seemed startled by this—but then, of course, they probably wouldn't be. Maybe they were used to pieces of rusted steel serving as their conference room tables, but I certainly was not.

Kendrick pushed open a stainless-steel cabinet in the corner of the room—which was apparently a fridge—and pulled out three cans of sparkling water. He set them down in the center of the table, then straightened up. "C.J. will be here shortly," he said, swiping on his tablet. "Security said they just had a car pull up to the gatehouse, so probably no more than five."

"Okay," Russell said with a nod. "Thanks, Kendrick. Um . . ." He hesitated, then took a deep breath before speaking. "Is my dad . . ."

Kendrick nodded. "He knows you've landed. And as soon as you're done with C.J., he wants a word at the house."

I looked over at Russell, trying to figure out if this was all just a normal occurrence for him. After all, he was a rock star's son. Maybe he spent every weekend nearly getting arrested and having to be bailed out. Maybe his dad was even proud of it. I had no idea—because I had no clue who this person actually *was*.

"Thanks," Russell said, his voice a little hollow.

Kendrick nodded and lowered his iPad. "I'll see you back at the house. Either of you need anything?"

I needed a lot of things at the moment—a hair dryer, a sweatshirt that didn't have Russell's dad's face on it, possibly a time machine. But even though Kendrick seemed very competent, I knew there was a limit to what he could pull off. So I just shook my head, and Russell shook his as well.

"Great," Kendrick said, then headed out, leaving the conference room door propped open.

Of course, the second after he'd left, I thought of something I could have asked him for—a phone charger.

"What?" Russell asked, looking over at me. And I realized that just like I'd been able to read him, he could now read me.

"Oh," I said, a little unnerved by this. "I was going to ask him for a phone charger." I narrowed my eyes, suddenly thinking of something. "Unless you had one with you this whole time?"

"No," he said, and I nodded, secretly relieved. "But hold on, I'll grab you one."

He hurried out of the conference room, and I took a cautious step over toward the "table." I knew my tetanus shot was up to date—I'd had to get everything verified to send my medical forms to school—but even so, I had no real desire to get much closer to it.

"Here," Russell said, returning a moment later with a phone charger and a plug. He slid them across the table to me, and I picked them up. There had been a line in one of the books my dad had read me when I was little that had always stayed with me, though I wasn't sure I'd understood the significance until now. *For want of a hammer, the kingdom was lost.* As I picked up the charger and turned it over in my hands, that was all I could think of. For want of a phone charger . . . well, all this had happened.

I located the closest wall socket I could find and plugged my phone in.

"You can sit if you want," Russell said. He was on one side of the table, and he'd already cracked open his can of sparkling water.

I took a step closer to the table. "What *is* this?"

Russell gave me a ghost of a smile—a pale imitation of the ones I'd seen earlier tonight. "It's the siding off the Nighthawks' first tour bus. Dad tracked it down in a scrapyard in Wichita."

"Ah," I said, feeling that my instinct to keep away from it had been correct.

"It's been sanded and sealed," Russell said, once again somehow intuiting what I'd been thinking. He ran his hand along the side of it. "See?"

"Okay." I took a seat opposite Russell, and picked up the can of sparkling water. I looked across the table at him—this suddenly seemed so *formal* after our night of parking lots and football fields. It was almost like we'd been dropped into a different movie, like we were getting divorced in a divorce drama.

No more movies, Didi said sharply. *That's what got you into trouble in the first place.*

She's not in trouble, Katy protested. *She's just having an adventure. And sometimes those get messy.*

I tentatively touched the table—sure enough, it was smooth, like it had been coated in plastic.

"Darcy," Russell said, sounding more serious now. He took a breath, his eyes not leaving mine. "I really am truly sorry."

I shrugged. "Okay."

"Okay . . . what?"

"Okay, I believe that you're sorry," I said slowly. "But . . . it doesn't change the fact that you lied to me."

"Not about anything that really mattered," he said. "Not about what I want to do, or my friends, or . . . how I feel about you. I was probably more honest with you than I've ever been with anyone."

I looked across the table at him and felt a crack start to spread in my resolve to be mad at him forever. "Well—except for the lying."

Russell nodded. "Except for that."

The side of my mouth was threatening to rise in a smile, and the more I tried to fight it, the harder it seemed.

Russell was smiling too. "So maybe we could—"

Just then, a woman strode through the door. She was tall, in a black suit and what had to be four-inch heels. "Hi," she said, looking at both of us and raising an eyebrow. "I'm C.J."

CHAPTER 9

Sunday
10:05 P.M.

I hadn't known what to expect from a rock star's lawyer, but I had not expected C.J. First of all, I'd expected her to be a *he*, which I was retroactively ashamed of.

Internalized misogyny is a real thing, Didi sighed. *It's something we could all work on.*

C.J. was all business, and seemed to speak faster than most people, her words coming out at a rapid clip. She'd walked right over to the table and started pulling documents and a laptop out of her bag, talking over Russell, who was trying to make introductions.

"Not necessary. I assumed you were Darcy," she said, giving me a curt nod. "How are you?" But she didn't wait for my answer, just took a seat at the head of the table and took out a phone, already starting to dial it.

"Well—I'm sorry to ruin your night, C.J.," Russell said, the tips of his ears turning red. "I hope you didn't have plans."

She waved this off. "The thing about anniversaries is that you have them every year," she said, and I saw Russell's eyes widen in dismay. She placed her phone in the center of the bus-table, right on the *A* in *Starline*. "We're just waiting for my assistant to get on; she'll be taking notes."

Russell frowned. "Why?"

"Just so that we can all be on the same page," C.J. said smoothly. "So that there's no confusion later . . . Sarah, are you on?"

"Here," the same voice I'd heard on the phone outside the Silver Standard piped up. "How is everyone?"

"I feel terrible about all this," Russell said, glancing down at his watch. "It's after ten—I'm so sorry to ruin your night."

"It's not ten," C.J. said, sliding on an oversize pair of glasses. "It's after one Sarah's time. She's in my New York office."

"Oh no," Russell said, looking horrified.

"It's fine!" Sarah said through the phone, her voice bright. "I made some coffee. It's all good."

"Babe?" a guy's voice—sleepy and confused—sounded through the phone. "Who are you talking to?"

"Sorry," Sarah said quickly. "That was just my partner. He'll . . . go away now."

C.J. rolled her eyes at the phone. "Well, take the call in the other room, Sarah."

"Right!" Sarah said, her voice getting a little higher. "The other room! We totally have one of those. I'll do that now."

"Okay," C.J. said, lifting a legal pad out of her pile of papers and looking from me to Russell. Even though she had a laptop out, I kind of liked to see legal pads being used by an actual lawyer. This was my first encounter with one who wasn't on TV. "Let's begin."

Ten minutes later, we'd gone through all the hotel stuff, and I was hoping that this was getting close to wrapped up. I wasn't tired yet—somehow—but my stomach was growling, and it seemed like a while ago that we'd eaten the tacos.

"So to recap," C.J. said, tapping her pen on the legal pad, "You first entered the Silver Standard to use the restroom. Which isn't trespassing, by the way—the lobby is open to the public, with no signage that the restrooms are for guests only. What you did next is dicier, but given that you didn't refuse to leave and complied with all that was asked of you, in addition to offering to purchase a room—they're not going to have much of a case."

"Really?" Russell asked, relief sweeping over his face. "They're not going to press charges?"

"Well," C.J. said, giving a one-shouldered shrug. "I don't have a crystal ball. But I'd be *very* surprised. The Silver Standard is part of the Pinnacle hotel chain, and your dad has agreed to play three songs at their corporate retreat next month, as well as do an hour of meet-and-greets. So! Everyone is happy." She paused for a second. "Well—maybe not your dad. But given what you've both told me, I think we're in the clear, and you aren't going to have to show up for a Nevada court date anytime soon."

"That's great!" Sarah said from the phone, speaking around a yawn.

"Sarah," C.J. admonished.

"Right," Sarah said. "I'll get some more coffee."

"Now," C.J. said. She set aside her legal pad and opened up her laptop. "Let's get down to business, shall we?"

"Oh," I said, glancing over at Russell. Wasn't that what we'd just been doing? "Um . . ."

"What do you mean?" Russell asked. "Aren't we done?"

"Almost," C.J. said breezily. "Just a few more things to clarify and then we can all go our separate ways, as charming as this has been." She looked from me to Russell, giving us a smile that didn't meet her eyes. "So you two had quite a whirlwind tonight! Quite the sudden romance."

I felt my face get hot. As embarrassing as it had been to go over everything that had happened with Russell in my head, I hadn't realized how much worse it would be to have to talk about it with a stranger in a business suit. And her paralegal, on the phone. (And possibly the paralegal's boyfriend.)

"Well," Russell said, and his face was bright red now. He looked exactly how I felt, like he was willing the floor to open up and swallow him whole. "I'm not sure how that's, um . . . relevant?"

"Well, your dad pays me to look at all the angles, kid," she said, giving him a smile that seemed genuinely sympathetic for just a moment. But then she turned to me, and all kindness was gone. Even though it was quite cold in the Saturday Night Falls conference room, I could feel my palms start to sweat. All at once, I knew that this woman didn't like me—and that she was not on my side. "Now, *Darcy*," she said, emphasizing my name in a way I didn't love. "You said you met Russell tonight at the bus station."

"Uh, yeah," I said, glancing across the table at him. "I . . . That's what happened."

"You'd never met before?"

"No," Russell said, sounding as baffled by this as I felt. "We hadn't."

"You're both based in LA," she said as she pulled something up on her laptop and scrolled down.

"No, we're not. Russell's in Ojai . . ." My voice trailed off as I looked over at him. He was staring down at his hands and I realized that he'd been lying about this, too. "You don't live in Ojai," I said, not phrasing it as a question.

"Let me see," C.J. continued, scrolling on her laptop. "You live with your father, your mother is in England . . ."

My head snapped up at this, and I looked at Russell, suddenly realizing that he must have told Sarah the paralegal this when he was on the phone with her. For a second I thought about correcting this, but then I let it go. Why should I be setting the record straight when Russell was lying to me left and right? "You and Russell are both the same age, the same grade, and you *do* have a mutual friend in common, according to your social media accounts, Darcy—Willa Curtis." I leaned forward to try and look at C.J.'s laptop screen. But the sides of buses are really long, which meant this table was too.

"How do you know Willa?" Russell asked me.

"We volunteered together." An image of Willa—blue hair, quick laugh, septum piercing—flashed across my mind. It had been a beach-cleanup project, and we'd been paired together. She was from Harvard-Westlake, one of the private schools in LA. Which, I realized a second later, probably meant Russell went there too. Knowing that he was actually a lot closer to where I lived, to people I knew, was making me feel his deception all the more strongly.

"Oh," Russell said. "Willa's in my class. Or was, I guess."

"So *not* total strangers," C.J. said with a nod.

"But wait—why are you looking at my social media?"

"Your accounts are public, aren't they?"

"Well . . . yes." I swallowed hard. It had never occurred to me that what I put online would be of any interest to someone who didn't already know me. It was all so personal and specific—pictures of Didi and Katy. A series in which I reviewed my daily lunch sandwich in a fake French accent, giving them a number grade with wildly shifting parameters. Way too many shots (according to Didi) of the jacaranda tree at the end of our street. Who else would care about these things?

But I truly got now what it meant for my accounts to be public. It meant all the stuff I'd put out there, intending it only for my friends, could be accessed by anyone with an internet connection and an interest in finding out about me. And this lawyer apparently had both.

"Why are you looking into Darcy?" Russell asked. "I thought you were just here about the hotel."

"My job is to protect the interests—and mitigate the legal exposure of—Wylie Sanders," C.J. said. "And, by extension, Russell here. And now," she said, looking at me over her glasses, "we need to figure out where you fit into the picture."

I blinked at her. "What . . . what is that supposed to mean?"

"You said you'd never met Russell before tonight. That you didn't know who he was."

"I didn't! He didn't tell me who he really was. In fact, he told me his dad was a structural engineer, he lived in Ojai, and his name was Russell Henrion." As I spoke, I was getting mad all over again.

"And you believed this?" C.J. asked. She gave me a smile that clearly said, *Nice try, kid.* "Because I understand you're a Nighthawks fan, right? According to a number of public comments you've made. As has your father, I believe. It seems like he's also a fan—Edward Milligan."

"Ted," I corrected automatically, then felt my stomach plunge. It was like my dad had suddenly walked in here, which was honestly the last thing I wanted. It was one thing for C.J. to know basic facts about *me*—it was another for her to be digging up things about my father. Because I hadn't ever told Russell my dad's name. I was pretty sure about that.

"I don't understand why you're doing this," Russell said, staring at C.J. "What's going on?"

C.J. took off her glasses and folded them, then turned to Russell. When she spoke, her voice was softer, like she was breaking bad news. "While we've done a good job of keeping you kids out of the public eye, you still can find information and pictures if you're so motivated. And Darcy here is an admitted Nighthawks fan." She turned and looked at me, her expression stony. "Which leads me to believe that she was not as in the dark as she claims."

"What?" I still felt like I was a beat behind. "You think I knew who Russell was—and pretended not to?"

C.J. nodded, looking relieved I'd finally caught up.

"Why would I—"

C.J. let out a short laugh and gestured around her. Like she was pointing out everything surrounding her—the conference room, the gold records on the walls—and the penny dropped.

"You think," I managed to get out, my voice a hoarse whisper, "that I was trying to—to trick him?" I could feel my face burn, and I didn't know how this had happened. I was the one who had been wronged here. He was the one who had tricked *me*!

"Darcy didn't know who I was," Russell said, his voice low and serious. "And for you to imply—"

"Then let's not imply it," C.J. said. "We can just say it straight-out. I'm finding it awfully coincidental that a huge Nighthawks fan runs into the son of her favorite rock star and then just *happens* to lure him into a compromising situation in which she has leverage for a potential financial windfall."

I closed my eyes for just a moment, like I could make this go away. My mind snagged on the word *lure*. It wouldn't stop reverberating in my head. Like nothing else that had happened with Russell and me tonight actually mattered. This lawyer—and her paralegal, on the phone—thought I was someone who had *lured* him to a hotel pool, not because I'd liked him, but for some kind of payday.

I felt suddenly like I needed to take a shower. The most personal thing that had ever happened to me was being dragged out into the light to be discussed by strangers. It made everything feel tainted. Like if my memories of tonight were on a piece of paper, it had just been crumpled up, and I'd never be able to get the creases out again.

"I didn't do that." My voice was shaking wildly, with some combination of anger and shame that was making it very hard to keep things together. And I knew I was about three seconds away from bursting into tears, which was the last thing I wanted.

"Nobody cares about me," Russell said, and I saw his face was bright red. "They care about my *dad*, but nobody has any interest in what his kids do."

On the phone, Sarah let out a quick laugh. "Sorry," she said immediately. "That was unprofessional. Carry on."

"Kid," C.J. said with a sigh, "we're living in a clickbait world, you know that. The pictures from Mallorca with Montana? You saw what happened there."

"My older sister," Russell muttered to me.

I realized two things in quick succession. The first was that—*of course*—Russell wasn't the only child he'd pretended to be when he wanted to have something in common with me. And the second was remembering the scandal, and how when it had broken and made headlines, I'd read the story like it was entertainment.

"She was photographed jumping off a yacht that didn't belong to her," C.J. explained.

"Naked," Sarah supplied from the phone. "Sorry—I just thought it might be relevant."

"One of Montana's so-called friends took pictures and sold them to DitesMoi," C.J. said, shaking her head. "And it didn't *matter* if anyone hadn't heard about Montana Sanders before then. All you needed to hear was that Wylie Sanders's daughter was behaving badly off the coast of Spain to get people to click on the article. Not to mention what happened with *your* friend, young man, earlier this year."

I looked over at Russell, who was staring down at the table, his shoulders tight.

"So I hear about this," she continued, gesturing to me, "and naturally—"

"No," I interrupted. I could feel the first hot tear threatening to tip over, like it was balanced on a precipice, and I tried to will it back. "I didn't do anything like that. I *wouldn't*." I crossed my arms in front of me, trying to hold myself together.

"I just—"

"*Stop*," Russell said. He sounded angrier, and more serious, than I had yet heard him. "Enough of this. I lied to Darcy about who I was. I was the one who deceived her, not the other way around."

I saw C.J. take a breath, like she was going to refute this, but Russell kept going.

"We met at a bus station," he said. "She didn't know who I was—I didn't *tell* her who I was. We were both stranded there and we started talking. We ended up walking around, and getting to know each other . . ." He took a shaky breath. "We had a really wonderful night. It was . . . great."

"That's so romantic," Sarah sighed from the phone.

"It really is," her boyfriend agreed.

"Sarah!" C.J. said sharply.

"Right. Sorry."

"So we're done talking about this," Russell said, a note of finality in his voice. "Nothing that you're implying happened. Okay?"

C.J. looked at him for a long moment, then nodded. "All right," she finally said. She glanced over at me, and I tried to glare back, but I felt my lip wobble and looked down at the metal, covered by a layer of lacquer, reflecting off the lights in the conference room.

"So can I go?" A second after I said it, I wondered if I even needed to ask permission. Maybe I could just get up, walk out, and start putting some distance between myself and this whole horrible situation. Could she actually stop me?

"One last thing." She flipped through her papers, then slid something across the table to me, followed a second later by a pen. "I'm just going to need you to sign that."

"What is it?" Russell asked as I picked up the paper. NON-DISCLOSURE AGREEMENT was printed at the top. My name and address had already been filled in, and there was a little yellow sticky flag on the bottom of the page pointing to where I should sign.

"Standard NDA," C.J. said, her eyes on me. "If Darcy really has no ulterior motive here, she won't mind signing it."

"She doesn't need to do that," Russell protested.

"I mean, you're right," C.J. said with a small shrug. "It's totally her choice. Absolutely. But. If she decides not to sign, all the strings we pulled to get you two out of trouble at the Silver Standard would no longer apply to her."

I looked up at C.J. sharply. "What?"

"We're happy to help as long as we're all on the same team. But if we're not . . ." She spread her hands, like there was nothing she could do.

"Fine," I muttered as I picked up the pen and uncapped it with shaky hands. Not telling anyone about this seemed like a great idea, frankly.

"You don't have to do that, Darcy," Russell said, looking from C.J. to the phone, like somehow Sarah could help him from her apartment in New York. "If Darcy says she's not going to talk about it . . ."

"That's sweet," C.J. said. "But we don't take people's word for it in my line of work. And I mean, let's be logical. You two have known each other for—what, four hours? Five?"

I looked across the table at Russell, then away again. Even though it was basically what I'd thought to myself on the helicopter, it somehow sounded worse coming from C.J. Like I'd been stupid to think anything different.

"Four hours isn't enough to know a basset hound," she said, "let alone a person. So I think it's better for everyone to just get it into a legally binding document."

I shook my head and scrawled my signature on the bottom of the paper. I pushed the paper and the pen back across the table to her and stood up. "I can go," I said, not exactly phrasing it as a question.

C.J. nodded. "We'll be in touch if anything comes up." I was about to ask how, when I realized that she probably had all the information on me that she needed. After all, she'd known my address and my dad's name and who I'd done ninth-grade community service with. My cell phone number was probably already in one of her files somewhere.

I unplugged my phone, then shoved the charger across the table at Russell. "Darcy—" he started, but I just shook my head.

I grabbed my bag and walked down the conference room hallway, the way we'd come in. I no longer wanted to stop and look at every single thing in the trophy cases and on the walls. I felt like I'd just seen behind the curtain—the machinations of how someone got to stay this successful, this long. They hired lawyers who were available late on Sunday nights to make problems go away. And who cares how it made people feel? *This*—this empire, everything hanging on the walls—was what needed to be protected. Not something as insignificant as someone's feelings.

I reached the lobby area, and saw the elevator where we'd come in. I looked around, then spotted a door a little farther down. I hurried toward it, pushed through into the cool night air, and took a deep, shaky breath.

My feeling of relief to be out of there only lasted a second, though, as I looked around and realized I didn't know what to do next. I was on a flagstone path, with gravel in between the paving stones. There were small, subtle lights lining the walkway. Toward the right, I could see the main house, the one I'd spotted from the top of the helipad.

I glanced to the left and took a few steps in that direction. There was what looked like a small parking lot and a long driveway that presumably led out to a road that would finally get me out of here. Could I just go? I didn't have my stuff, but my phone was at least a little charged now. Maybe I could just leave my duffel behind. I wasn't sure if there was anything in it that I desperately needed, or that couldn't be replaced. If it meant I didn't have to stay here any longer, I was willing to give it all up.

But I'd only gone a few steps before I remembered the tent—the one I'd borrowed from Didi and Katy. It was somewhere in the house, and I couldn't go back to Raven Rock without it.

I turned and began to walk in the direction of the main house. I wasn't thrilled about knocking on Wylie Sanders's door and demanding my stuff back, but I was also just *done*. I'd been insulted and humiliated and pressured into signing a legally binding document. If there was one more embarrassing thing to get through tonight, so be it. Anything to get me out of here, so I never had to see—or think about—any of these people ever again.

"Darcy."

I turned around and saw Russell standing behind me. "I'm so sorry about that." He shook his head. "I didn't know . . . I thought it was just going to be about the hotel. I never thought that she . . . she would . . ."

"Well, she did." I hated that my voice was shaking again, that I felt like I was going to cry.

"But I don't think that," Russell said quickly. "And I'm sure my dad doesn't, either. He just pays her to do stuff like that."

"Oh, well in *that* case, it's fine. That makes it *all* better." I walked a few steps away, fighting back the tears that were threatening to spill over, then turned back to him. "So you live in Ojai, huh? Only child? *Structural engineering?*"

He stared down at his feet. "We used to live in Ojai. And my dad always wanted to be a structural engineer. He still talks about it sometimes. Says he's still building bridges—just the musical kind."

I shook my head, not about to be charmed by any of this. "You could have told me the truth, you know. Even if you didn't want to tell me about your dad, you didn't have to make up the rest of it. What was even the point of that? Just to mess with me?"

"I'm so sorry, Darcy—"

"Yeah," I interrupted, cutting him off. "So you've said. But since I can't believe anything else you've told me, forgive me if I can't believe that, either."

Russell stepped back, a hurt look on his face. "Look, I've apologized over and over again. I defended you in there. I don't know what else you want."

"I don't want anything from you!" I snapped. "I just want to *go*. I'm pretty sure you've done enough."

"Okay," Russell said, his voice rising. "Sure. I mean, all I did was get us out of a situation where we could be in *jail* right now. I just got us out of Jesse and back to Vegas. So you're welcome for all that."

"*You* didn't do anything!" I yelled. "You just called your dad, and he did all of this. Don't pretend—"

"Would you prefer I hadn't?" Our voices were coming out raw and angry, overlapping, like we were throwing daggers at each other, pretending we didn't hurt where they connected. "Did you *want* to be in jail somewhere in Nevada right now? Just so you can prove some kind of point?"

I glared at him; the logic was making me even angrier. "No."

"And I wasn't going to bring it up, but—" He stopped himself a second later, and looked down at the paving stones.

"But what?"

"The pool was your idea!" he said, all in a rush. "You were the one who suggested breaking into it. You were the one who wanted to swim—"

"So this is *my* fault?"

"Oh, did I not make that clear? Of course it is! Who else's fault would it *be*, Darcy?"

I swallowed hard, feeling my cheeks flame. "Okay, fine, but you could have said no. You do have some choice in this matter. You didn't have to go along with it, you know."

"Well, I did! Because I liked you!"

It was like we both heard the past tense at the same time. And I knew that it shouldn't have bothered me—I was leaving! I never wanted to see this guy again!—but that didn't change the fact that it did.

"Well, then I'm *sooooo* sorry. Clearly, this is all my fault. What was I thinking? And I'm *so* grateful for your celebrity dad, and his millions of dollars, and his lawyers, coming in to rescue us. Thank you *so much*." I spat out the last word.

Russell nodded, folded his arms, and looked away.

I folded my arms too. I was breathing hard, already regretting some of the things I'd said.

"Right," he finally said, his tone cool. "Sure."

"I just want to go home."

"So what's stopping you?" It was like Russell was trying to sound tough . . . but not quite pulling it off.

"Well. My stuff has disappeared. And I don't know where I am, or how to get out of here."

"Your things are in the house," he said, nodding down the path. "And if you want to leave, we can get you a car into Vegas. But you could also stay in one of the guesthouses."

One of the guesthouses. The phrase seemed to hang in the air between us for a moment, and he must have heard it too, because the tips of his ears turned red and he looked down at the ground.

"That's not necessary." I decided I was going to be formal and businesslike and just get through this. It was the same way I'd handled any conversation I'd had to have with Gillian in the run-up to school starting.

"Fine," Russell said, matching my tone.

"Fine."

"This way." He pointed toward the house and started walking down the path. He was striding fast, not slowing down or waiting for me like I knew he would have done earlier tonight. But who cared? I didn't need for him to wait for me. In fact, the faster we got to the house, the faster I could get out of there.

But as we got closer, I slowed, then stopped short—shock piercing the red fog of my anger.

It wasn't like I'd never seen nice houses before. We lived in Los Angeles, the land of impressive homes. But I'd never quite seen anything like this.

The garage looked more like an airplane hangar. The house itself seemed to sprawl on as far as I could see. It was a mix of dark wood, steel, and glass, like a cabin crossed with a supermodern house—but somehow it worked. It was, above all, *impressive*. The kind of house that was designed, even though there was nothing gaudy about it, to let you know just how wealthy and important the owner was.

Russell walked toward the front door, still not waiting for me or looking to see if I was behind him. I hurried to keep pace—but then stopped short and just blinked at what was before me. There was a Jeff Koons balloon dog on the lawn. Fifteen feet high, purple, and reflecting the moonlight and the lights that lined the driveway.

The Broad museum in downtown LA had put on a Koons exhibit last year, and my dad and I had gone. We'd both loved the balloon dogs the best, but I had never seen his work outside of a museum. Until this moment, it hadn't occurred to me that you could *own* something like this. Art that was also in museums, the stuff that everyone else only got to look at for a few moments. But some people got to have it and see it whenever they wanted.

For just a second, I thought about our house in Raven Rock. The way that I could see the neighbors from my bedroom window, the way that my dad and I would sit on the front steps in the morning and wave to all the dog walkers and runners passing by. The creaky stairs and uneven floors. The slightly peeling paint my dad kept promising to get touched up but never actually did. Nobody was ever going to put it on the cover of a magazine. And the closest we'd ever come to having lawn art was when we put out Boney, our Halloween skeleton.

And as I tore my gaze away from the priceless art and climbed the front steps to stand next to Russell—but not too close—I was getting angry and embarrassed all over again. I'd talked to him about loans and trouble paying for college, assuming we were somewhat on the same page. Standing on the threshold of a mansion, I felt just how stupid I'd been.

Russell reached out and knocked on the door. "I went to Silverspun with my dad," he explained after a moment. "So I don't have my keys."

"That was the *friend* you went with?" Russell gave a short nod, and I realized the fight he'd mentioned must have been with his dad. But I wasn't about to give him the satisfaction of asking any follow-ups.

Russell sighed and knocked again, harder this time. "Come on," he muttered.

"Isn't that a doorbell?" I asked, nodding toward it, trying to move things along. After all, this house was huge, and the door was probably made of three-feet-thick reclaimed oak or whatever.

"Yeah. It's—embarrassing." He winced, then pressed the doorbell—and the first verse of "Darcy" started playing—*Darcy, tell me why / a love song ain't nothing but a lie.* It was much louder than normal doorbells.

"Wow."

"Yep."

Only a little while ago, I would have made a joke about how it was playing my song. But that moment was over. So I just looked straight ahead and made my plan. Surely Kendrick or Bella or someone would answer the door, and I'd grab my stuff and leave. If I was lucky, I could be heading for the Vegas bus station in under ten minutes. And then this night—and everything I'd gone through—would finally be over. It could move to the past tense, as opposed to something I was still in the middle of, struggling to get my bearings.

I took a breath, about to suggest Russell ring the bell again, when the door was flung open.

"So."

I blinked at the man who'd opened the door. He was barefoot and dressed all in black—black jeans, black leather belt, black cashmere Henley. He had on a huge, chunky silver watch, and rings on four of his fingers. He had long silver hair and was taller than I'd expected.

Wylie Sanders was standing in front of me.

CHAPTER 10

Sunday
10:30 P.M.

I stared at him.

It was like it took my brain a minute to click into gear. I'd seen images of this man my whole life—on album covers and magazines, in retrospective documentaries and music videos. I'd seen him on TV, at awards shows, and at the halftime show at the Super Bowl. I'd seen him hours ago—how was *that* possible?—onstage at Silverspun.

But until this moment, I'd never been just feet away from him—with him looking back at *me*.

Katy had gone down a bit of a rabbit hole last fall when she was working on a project for AP Psych about how our brains aren't wired for celebrities. She'd explained that, for most of human history, if you saw someone a lot, it meant they were in your village or tribe or whatever, and you *knew* them. And that in our brains, frequency builds affection. So that when we've seen pictures of celebrities for years and years, our brains code them as someone we know. As a *friend*. When, in actuality, they're total strangers.

I was feeling that now in real time, standing on the doorstep, as my mind tried to grapple with seeing Wylie Sanders close-up. In person, he looked older than I was expecting. Which made sense, since I was pretty sure he was in his sixties. Part of me—the part that Katy had talked about—was like, *Oh! You know him!* And the other, more rational part, was like, *Holy fuck, that's* Wylie Sanders.

We all just stood there for a moment, and then—Wylie? Mr. Sanders?—reached out and pulled Russell into a tight hug.

"I was so mad!" Wylie Sanders said while hugging his son. I could see that Russell was hugging him back. He tugged on the back of Russell's hair and then they stepped apart. "Don't do that again! You can't just leave like that! We were losing our minds—but I'm so glad you're okay." He smiled at his son, but this only lasted a second before it morphed into a frown. "But then you're getting arrested? And now I'm mad all over again!" He cupped Russell's face in his hands, kissed his cheek, then shook his head and sighed.

I looked between them, trying to process this—the warmth and worry and love that were as plain as anything on Wylie's impossibly famous face. This was not the Wylie Sanders I'd been expecting to see.

Wylie slung an arm around Russell's shoulders. "We're going to have a talk, kiddo."

Russell looked at his sneakers. A storm of emotions was crossing over his face—relief, anger, embarrassment. I didn't know what had happened with his dad—what their fight was about, or how Russell had even ended up in a bus station in the first place. But whatever was going on, I knew my being there to see it was making things worse.

Then Wylie Sanders turned to me and smiled, and it was like I could practically feel a charm offensive coming at me. Like stage lights were clicking on one by one, bathing me in warmth. "And you must be . . . Darcy." He seemed to twinkle when he said my name, and touched a hand to his heart in faux humility. "After my song, I presume." He said this like he was setting up a punch line, like he expected me to say, *No, it was from my grandmother,* or *I was named because of* Pride and Prejudice, or *My parents just liked it.*

I swallowed quickly before speaking—my words were caught against my throat. "Um—yes, actually."

Some of the practiced charm slipped a little bit, and a more surprised, genuine smile emerged. "Really?"

I nodded. "My dad—he's a really big fan. So he named me after the song." I took a breath and made myself say it, since I was very sure I wouldn't ever get this chance again. "I am too. A big fan, I mean."

He grinned, a totally genuine smile this time—big and a little dorky, and one I had never seen in any of his pictures or videos. "Really? That's great!" He jostled Russell—his arm was still around his son's shoulders. "See? Some kids your age like your dad's music."

"Um, okay," Russell said. The tips of his ears, I could see, were starting to turn red again.

"All right," Wylie Sanders said. He lifted his arm off Russell's shoulders and clapped his hands together—they made a metallic clicking sound, probably because of all the rings. I noticed that he was also wearing an impressive number of necklaces—a silver chain and what looked like an enormous shark tooth on a leather cord, and a tiny, dagger-looking thing encrusted with diamonds. "Let's go in and get all this sorted. Everything go okay with C.J.?"

Russell shook his head. "Not really. She was pretty aggressive. And I think she crossed some lines." He glanced at me for a moment, then looked away again. "She was really unfair to Darcy."

Wylie's face fell, and he winced. "I'm so sorry, Darcy. C.J.

sometimes forgets we're not opposing counsel. I'll have a talk with her. Okay?"

I nodded, even though I wasn't sure if he actually meant any of this. It was his job to be charming, after all—and his lawyer's job to make sure the machine kept running.

He stepped inside the house, gesturing for us to follow, pushing the door open wider, giving me a smile. "Darcy, please come in! I'm sure you're tired. And then I need to hear what happened at this hotel. And maybe one of you can explain to me why I'm apparently playing some kind of corporate retreat next month? And we should get some food in both of you. Priya's making some penne. And you're both just in time for Fishbowl!"

I wasn't sure what most of that meant, but before I could ask—or pluck up my courage to tell him that actually, I wouldn't be doing any of that, since I was about to leave—a brown-and-white bullet shot past me, brushing against my leg. It was a small dog, moving faster than I'd seen a dog move before—its legs were practically a blur. It took the three steps in a leap, seeming to hang in the air for just a moment before hitting the lawn and tearing across it.

"Oh, for fuck's sake—*Andy*!" Wylie Sanders yelled. Russell dropped his backpack and ran after the dog, and after only a second's hesitation, I did the same, dropping my canvas bag and running after him.

I hadn't gotten far before Russell reached the dog—Andy. He scooped him up and started walking him back to the house.

I'd expected the dog to struggle, try and get away—he had been *very* intent on leaving—but his stub of a tail just wagged furiously, and he tried to stretch up to lick Russell's face.

He was a small dog, probably ten or twelve pounds, with curly brown and white fur and a black nose. He ears flopped over, but it also seemed like he could lift them up, like he was doing now as he looked up at Russell beseechingly, as though asking why a belly rub wasn't happening. He was, in short, *very* cute.

I turned and headed back to the house too—which was when I saw Wylie had gone inside, and my bag and Russell's backpack had both disappeared. I didn't understand why, at this place, my possessions were constantly disappearing.

Russell stepped inside and gestured me in. "Shut the door." He nodded down at the dog in his arms. "Otherwise he'll try to get out again."

"Right."

Russell's voice was clipped and terse. I tried to remind myself that was how I'd resolved to talk to him as well, and I shouldn't be upset that he was doing this too.

Only after the door was shut did Russell put Andy down. The dog shook himself once, a full-body shake, then trotted off.

Russell glanced at me and frowned. "You okay?"

"Um," I said. My eyes were wide as I tried to take in everything around me. I was attempting to play it cool, but apparently I wasn't pulling it off.

We were in the entranceway of Wylie Sanders's house. But whereas my house's foyer—if you could even call it that—was the place where we kicked off shoes and dropped bags and keys and coats, this was different. The ceilings were incredibly high, and I needed to tilt my head back almost all the way to see up to the top. But that wasn't what I was staring at.

It was the art.

There was a Picasso across from me. A *Picasso.* It was hung on the wall, with no glass or anything, just the canvas in a wood frame. I automatically looked to the side of it, for the little white plaque that would give me the name and date of the painting, but of course it wasn't there. Because this was someone's *house*. There was a mobile hanging from the impossibly high ceiling, turning slowly this way and that. It was the kind I'd seen in museums before, even though I didn't know the name of the artist. But the most difficult thing to look away from wasn't the Picasso, or the mobile. It was the portrait right in front of me.

I didn't think this was an artist I was supposed to know, despite the fact that it was hung next to what I was pretty sure was a Kehinde Wiley. It was an oil painting, and huge—well over six feet. It looked like the kind of painting I'd seen on the covers of old paperback sci-fi novels. Wylie Sanders was depicted standing, shirtless, on some kind of desert planet—there were three moons and a sun behind him, at any rate. He was raising a sword above his head in triumph, his long hair blowing in the wind. There was a blond girl in some kind of desert-bikini thing pressed up against his well-oiled torso as a spaceship rose into the air behind them.

"Yeah," Russell said, seeing where I was looking. "Right. My stepmother had that commissioned. Ex-stepmother, now." He shrugged. "We've all just gotten used to it."

"Oh." I forced myself to look away, even though it was challenging. I glanced around the foyer—but didn't see my canvas bag anywhere, to say nothing of my tent or duffel. The last thing I wanted was to need anything from Russell—even information— but it didn't seem like I had a choice. I folded my arms and took a breath. "Do you know where my stuff is?"

"No idea. Probably inside." His voice was still cold, chilled all

the way through. He shook his head. "I'll see if I can track it down."
And with that, he walked inside the house and left me alone.

I hesitated for a moment—was I supposed to wait for Russell
to come back with it? Or follow him? Was I really supposed to
wander around a rock star's house? But I needed my stuff back, and
I didn't see any other way to make that happen.

It's okay. Didi's voice was surprisingly gentle. *It's almost over. Just
get your stuff and you can leave.*

I pushed my shoulders back and walked into the next room.
But I wasn't sure if *room* was the right word, since it seemed to
be basically the whole bottom floor of the house, just without any
dividing rooms or doors. The kitchen—enormous, with two islands
and no visible refrigerator—flowed into a dining area, which
became a huge TV room. The TV room had a fireplace, lots of
chairs, a coffee table, and was ringed with an enormous, squashy
sectional couch.

There was more impressive art on the walls, but there were also
family pictures, portraits and candids and Polaroids, hung up right
next to the Rothkos.

I could see Russell standing off to the side of the room, talking
to a dark-haired woman in her twenties who was holding an iPad.
In addition to them—there were a *lot* of people in this house—there
was a big group sitting around a massive dining table, which was
right in front of floor-to-ceiling glass windows. And through the
sliding glass doors I could see the backyard and a huge pool glowing
with soft, subtle lights.

There were at least eight people sitting around the table—
including Wylie Sanders—and most everyone seemed to be talking
at once, laughing and yelling, their voices overlapping. It had to be

getting close to eleven at night—why were all these people here? And who were they? What was going on?

The woman with the iPad walked across the room toward me, and I stepped quickly into her path. "Hi—do you know where my stuff is?"

She raised an eyebrow at me, and I realized a second later I'd asked this in the stupidest way possible. "Um—I'm Darcy," I said, and her eyes widened in recognition. "Kendrick and Bella brought my things somewhere?"

She nodded. "Russell just asked me the same thing." I looked over and saw that he'd now joined the group at the table. The woman gave me a nod and started to walk again. "I'll track it down. Are you staying for dinner?"

"No—" I began, but she was walking past me and into the kitchen. I started to follow, when a pony stepped into my path.

A second later, I processed that it wasn't a pony. But I wasn't that far off—it was a harlequin Great Dane, with ears that stood straight up. It was light gray and dappled, with black spots all over. This dog was *huge*—its head was higher than my waist, and as it plodded over to me, head cocked to the side, I just blinked at it, trying to make sense of this massive creature that had suddenly appeared.

"Oh—right," the woman with the iPad called, looking over at me from the kitchen. "That's Tidbit."

"Tidbit?"

"Darcy?" I looked over and saw Wylie Sanders walking from the table to the kitchen. He was motioning me over with a smile. "Come meet everyone!"

"Oh," I called to him, still trying to get my head around the fact that *Wylie Sanders* knew my name. "I just need my stuff?"

"Hm?" he asked, cupping a hand around his left ear. "Come on!" Maybe thinking he was being called, Tidbit padded gravely over to him. Wylie scratched his neck, without even having to lean down to do it. Clearly getting jealous, Andy stood up from under the table, shook himself, and ran over to Wylie, walking under Tidbit to accomplish this.

Feeling like I really didn't have a choice, I walked over to the kitchen, where I could see that in addition to the woman with the iPad, there was a South Asian woman in her thirties who was stirring something on the stove.

"Give us your opinion on this pasta sauce," Wylie Sanders said to me with a kind smile.

"Yes!" the girl at the stove said as she turned around, looking irritated. "Everyone keeps adding stuff to it and they're messing with its integrity."

"We just want to eat, Priya," the woman with the iPad said, a faint Southern accent lurking in her words. "We're trying to move the process along."

"And we will," Priya said, "when the sauce is right!" She looked at me expectantly.

"Oh," I said, shaking my head, even though my stomach growled in spite of myself. "I'm actually not staying—"

"Hey!" Wylie Sanders yelled to the room at large. When nobody at the table paid him any attention, he put two fingers in his mouth and let out an ear-piercing whistle. Every human in the room stopped talking, even as the dogs started barking frantically. "Hush," he said in the dogs' direction. "Everyone," he continued, raising his voice. He pointed at me. "This is Darcy. She's Russell's friend." Eleven people—and two dogs—turned to stare at me and

I felt my face get hot. Russell, I noticed, was deliberately not looking in my direction. Wylie smiled at me and took a comically large breath. "Ready?"

"Um," I said, not exactly sure what he was talking about.

"That's my daughter Montana," he said, starting at one end of the table. I tried not to do a double take when I realized I recognized her from her yacht escapades. She looked like she was in her late thirties, with long dark hair, and she waved at me cheerfully.

"My son Connor, her brother," Wylie continued. Connor looked like he was older than Montana—in his forties maybe, with a sandy beard—but I could see the resemblance between them. "His wife, Sydney," Wylie continued, pointing to an Asian woman next to Connor. She gave me a friendly, if slightly confused, wave. She was wearing a very cool jumpsuit and had perfect, straight-across blunt bangs. "My son Wallace," he continued, nodding at a guy in his late twenties who, bewilderingly, had a pile of small, folded pieces of paper in front of him. He was Black, with trendy oversized glasses.

"Russell you've met," he continued, and we made eye contact for half a second before looking away again. "I'm Wylie," he said, and then chuckled, like it was the best joke he'd heard in a while.

"Dad," Wallace, Montana, and Connor groaned in unison.

"Now," he said, gesturing to the other side of the table, where three women were sitting. They all looked back at me and I felt my eyes widen—because I *recognized* all of them. I was looking at three of Wylie Sanders's ex-wives, but what were they doing here? And sitting next to one another?

"This is Kenya," he said, nodding toward a regal-looking Black woman wearing a flowing caftan. I gave her a smile, hoping it wasn't clear that I recognized her from paparazzi photos and red-carpet pictures. "Wallace's mother and my ex-partner."

"Nice to meet you," Kenya said, sounding polite but confused.

"Connor and Montana's mother, Paula," he said, gesturing to the white woman sitting next to Kenya. She gave me a nod and a smile—the smile I recognized from when she'd been featured on the cover of the Nighthawks' second album, wearing a statement necklace and not much else. Now, though, she was wearing a button-up shirt over a bathing suit, her silver-streaked hair damp.

"And this is Chloe, my ex-wife." I nodded, still trying to get my head around all of this. Chloe was probably the ex of Wylie's I was most familiar with, just because she was the most recent. She was as stunning in person as she had been on the cover of *People* after she and Wylie had gotten married despite only knowing each other for a weekend—*Fifth Time's the Charm!* the headline had touted. She had long blond wavy hair and dark blue eyes. She had a dusting of freckles, and I could see a constellation of tiny earrings in her ear, multiple piercings. She was wearing slouchy sweatpants that said *Free City* on one leg and a white T-shirt. But somehow, these didn't look like the sweats and tees I normally wore—you could somehow just *tell* they were expensive.

And while I *knew* she was Wylie's ex-wife—I'd read all about their contentious divorce, the fight over their twins—sitting here, with no makeup that I could see, she looked incredibly young. Younger than most of the people at the table, and that included Wylie's *kids*. A second later, I also realized that she was the girl in the sci-fi oil painting in the foyer, the one who'd commissioned it.

"Hey," Chloe said, drawing one leg up. *"Darcy."* She raised her eyebrows at my name. "Pull up a chair. Allegedly, we're eating dinner."

"I'm working on it!" Priya called, sounding stressed.

I lifted my hand in a wave that I immediately regretted. "Uh, hi." I tried not to sound as baffled as I currently felt. But I was truly stunned by what was in front of me—the web of exes and kids and partners that had just been laid out. What was going on? Why were all Wylie's kids from different relationships hanging out together? Why were three of his ex-wives all sitting next to each other, none of them in a screaming match? Weren't Wylie and Chloe going rounds with lawyers over the custody of their twins? That was what I had heard was going on, at any rate. What was *happening* here?

I glanced over at Russell, and he met my eye for just a second before looking away. I felt my anger rise again as I thought about what he'd told me—that he was an only child. How he'd pretended to agree with me, to know what it was like. And here he was, surrounded by a family that was living proof of the lies he'd told me.

"This is Priya, Montana's partner," Wylie said, and the woman at the stove gave me a nod. "Bronwyn, who keeps the wolves at bay," he said, indicating the dark-haired woman in the kitchen who was still bent over an iPad. "Astrid and Artie and Dashiell are here too, but they're sleeping," he said, checking these off on his beringed fingers, then turned to me. "So! Any questions?"

I actually had a lot—including, but not limited to, where my possessions were—but before I could answer, Wylie was continuing.

"Everyone, please give Darcy a nice Sanders family welcome, okay? So she doesn't think we're complete savages and reprobates."

"She's going to be disappointed when she finds out, then," Montana said with a grin. She shot Russell a significant look, like she was indicating she thought I was a lot more than a friend. Russell, however, just stared pointedly out the window.

"Name a celebrity," Wallace said to me, adjusting his glasses, pen poised over a scrap of paper.

"Wallace," Kenya chided, taking a sip of her wine. "Is that how we welcome guests?"

He rolled his eyes. "Hi, welcome. Name a celebrity."

"I . . . what?" I looked around, but everyone was just looking at me expectantly, nobody explaining what was happening. Was this some sort of weird Sanders hazing ritual? Was I supposed to say *Wylie Sanders*? Or was I *not* supposed to say him?

"Just anyone," Connor said. "We need it for Fishbowl."

"First person that comes into your head," Sydney added, giving me a smile.

Wallace pointed at me. "Go."

"Um. Um. Steve Guttenberg?" The second I'd said it, I regretted it, and felt heat flood my face. *Steve Guttenberg?*

Deafening silence greeted this answer, and I saw Wallace widen his eyes at Connor before looking back at me. "Sure," he said, nodding. "Uh—thanks."

"Good pick," Wylie Sanders said cheerfully to me, which somehow made everything worse. I was getting pitied by a multiple Grammy winner because the only celebrity I could think of was *Steve Guttenberg*. It was like a nightmare, but one I hadn't had before because I hadn't been creative enough to think up these specifics. Wylie steered me away from the table and toward the kitchen. "Now, sauce help."

"I was actually—"

"Here." Priya was suddenly shoving a spoon at me. "Opinion, please."

I took the spoon from her, figuring it was the path of least resistance. It was a vodka sauce, and good—until the end, when it suddenly got very spicy. "Ah," I said, trying not to look like my mouth was on fire. "Um. Good. A little spicy?"

She whirled around to face the dark-haired woman who was still bent over her tablet. "I told you, Bronwyn! We didn't need that extra pinch of chili flakes."

She glanced up from her iPad. "I'm from Texas," she said. "Don't ask me about spice level if you don't want a real answer." I noticed she was dressed a little more professionally than everyone else, who were mostly in sweatpants or bathing suits with cover-ups. She set down her iPad with a relieved sigh. "Okay, there's no chatter about the hotel. We're monitoring the social media accounts of the Silver Standard employees and front-desk workers, but nothing so far. And C.J.'s going to be getting NDAs to them first thing tomorrow."

"Wait, what's happening?" Priya asked, frowning.

"Nothing," Bronwyn said cheerfully. "Because I'm *very* good at my job." She turned to me. "Bronwyn Taylor. I handle Mr. Sanders's PR. Just wanted you to know it looks like everything is locked down in Jesse."

"Where?" Priya asked, turning around from the stove. "Stop distracting me if you want to eat!"

"Are we eating?" A man in his fifties wandered in. He was Black, and wearing a sweatshirt that read *Sedona!* "It's getting late." He stopped when he saw Russell. "Russ is back!" he said, smiling at him. "Where did you come from?"

"That's Darcy," Kenya said, indicating me. "Darcy, this is my husband, Doug."

"Hi," Doug said, nodding at me. "Nice to meet you. Are you staying for dinner? Is dinner happening . . . anytime soon?"

"I'm working on it!" Priya cried from the stove. "I have to cook for all these people, you know, and then two more show up . . ."

"It's really okay." I took a breath, about to explain that I wouldn't be staying, or eating any more of her very spicy vodka sauce, so she didn't have to include me in her count.

"Don't pressure my girlfriend," Montana called from the table.

"I'm just *hungry*," Doug grumbled as he walked over to Kenya and kissed the top of her head. "I don't think it's unreasonable to expect dinner before eleven at night."

"Pretend we're in Spain," Chloe said with a smile.

"So we'll continue to monitor this," Bronwyn said to Wylie, her voice a little softer now. "But I don't think you need to be concerned. We've got the situation well in hand."

I suddenly realized that I had just been guilty of an egregious lapse in manners. But in my defense, nobody had ever used their celebrity status to get me out of a jam before. I knew I needed to thank Wylie Sanders—it should have been the first thing I'd done—but should I also offer to reimburse him for the helicopter ride? For the legal counsel?

"Um, Mr. Sanders," I said. "I just wanted to thank you. For . . . uh . . . helping out." Russell glanced over at me, and his mouth twisted in a frown. "I'm so sorry that we put you in that position. I never usually . . . I mean . . ." I didn't know why it was important to me that this rock star I'd never see again knew that I wasn't the kind of person who went around breaking into hotel pools, but for whatever reason, it seemed to be. "I'm really sorry. And really grateful."

He gave me a smile. "You're welcome, Darcy. I was happy to help."

Chloe snorted, got up from the table, and walked into the

kitchen with her wineglass. "Babes," she said to Wylie, rolling her eyes. "You were *livid*. You were not 'happy to help.'"

"I wouldn't say *livid*, Chloe," Wylie Sanders demurred.

She snorted again. "Sure. Is there more of the sauv blanc?"

"Mumma?" I looked over to see a small blond child in Spider-Man pajamas standing in the kitchen.

"Artie," she said with a sigh. "What are you doing out of bed?"

Russell had mentioned an Artie—but he'd told me that was his cool older cousin. Not a three-year-old—which meant this was one more lie Russell had told me. I glanced over at him, but he was laughing with Wallace about something. Probably about me picking Steve Guttenberg.

Chloe scooped Artie up and rested him on her hip, and I was jarred by it all over again—how *young* she looked. Too young to have been married, divorced, and the mother of a kid old enough to have superhero preferences.

"Artie, help us out," Wallace called across the room to him. "Name a celebrity."

"The Rock," Artie said immediately.

"Thanks, bud," Wallace said. He shot me a brief look, one that clearly said *Was that so hard?*

"Did you wake your sister up?" Chloe asked him.

"I didn't," he protested, trying to wriggle down. "I'm just hungry."

"Ooh, try my sauce!" Priya said. She turned around with a spoon, just as Artie spotted Russell across the room.

"Russell!" he yelled, and launched himself in his direction.

Russell grinned when he saw him coming, a real smile, one that opened up his whole face. He got out of his chair, picked up his little brother, and swung him around.

"Where were you?" Artie asked, even as he laughed, clearly delighted to be flying around in circles. "You didn't come back on the plane with everyone. And you promised me that you were going to play Brontosaurus."

"Sorry, bud," Russell said. He stopped spinning him and set him down. Artie took a few wobbly steps. "We can play tomorrow, okay?"

"Or now!"

"No," Wylie and Chloe said in unison.

Artie grabbed Russell's hand and started pulling him toward the kitchen. Russell met my eyes, and I could tell that this was the last place he wanted to be—anywhere in proximity to me. "Can we go swimming?" he practically yelled.

"Take it down a notch, bud," Wylie said.

"Yeah," Chloe agreed, glancing upstairs. "Your nephew is sleeping."

I bumped on *nephew* before I remembered how this worked. Presumably, one of Wylie's older children—like Connor—must have kids of their own. Which would mean that this three-year-old was someone's *uncle*.

"Want some pasta, kid?" Priya asked, taking her pot off the stove. Artie's eyes lit up.

"Yes, please," he said. "I like the bow kind. With a little butter and the cheese from the green can."

"I have this great sauce!"

"No thank you."

"At least *try* it?"

"Hey, buddy," Montana said, walking over to the kitchen. She tickle-lunged at Artie, who shrieked in delight and ran a few feet away. "Dinner almost ready, P?"

"*Fishbowl* is ready," Wallace called, sounding irritated. "Are we not playing?"

"After dinner," Sydney said, clapping her hands together. "I need to eat something or I'll get grumpy."

"*Get* grumpy?" Connor asked. She whacked him on the arm.

"Before we eat . . . ," Wylie Sanders said. He clapped his hand on Russell's shoulder. "We need to have a chat."

Russell sighed. "Yeah."

"What's happening?" Montana asked.

"Russ is in trouble," Chloe said in a low voice.

"Not trouble, exactly," Wylie said, then paused. "Well—actually, yeah. Trouble."

"Yikes," Priya said as she started pulling down bowls from a cabinet.

"And no offense," Doug said, hustling into the kitchen, "but we might not wait."

"Good luck," Montana said. She cleared her throat and rested her hand on her heart. "'It is a far, far better thing that I do than I have ever done. It is a far, far better rest that I go to—'"

"Okay," Russell said, shaking his head. "We don't need to make this worse." He headed out of the room, following his dad, but then stopped and turned back to me. "So you're going to go?" His voice was icy, but not believably so—like a lake that looked frozen but would crack with the first step.

"Yep." I made sure to keep my tone clipped. If I'd needed another reason to keep being mad at him, all I had to do was look around me. This whole life Russell had that he'd kept from me, spinning an entirely new picture just for kicks.

"So I guess this is it?"

"Guess it is."

"Don't go on my account."

"I wasn't ever going to stay. I'm leaving as soon as I get my stuff back. I'm not sure where it went."

"I'll find Kendrick," Bronwyn said, setting down her iPad and striding out of the kitchen. Her response made me all too aware that everyone around us could hear our conversation, and that nobody was making any effort to disguise the fact that they were listening.

"Well—bye."

I folded my arms. "Bye."

We looked at each other for a moment, but Russell didn't make any move to leave. And it hit me all at once that this was how it ended. That our night, fated and random, wonderful and terrible, was over.

"Okay," Wylie said after a moment in which the silence stretched on to the point of uncomfortable. He gave me a smile that seemed real. "Lovely to meet you, Darcy. Get home safe."

"Thank you for everything," I said, meaning it, trying to put all the warmth in my tone that I was keeping from Russell. Wylie gave me a nod and headed down the hallway.

Russell looked at me for a moment longer, his eyes searching mine. He took a breath—

"Russ!" Wylie called.

He hesitated for one second more, then turned and left the room, following his dad. I watched him go, trying to ignore the pull I felt in my stomach. This was what I wanted, after all. It *was*.

So why did this feel so awful?

"Where's home?" Chloe asked me. I jumped slightly—I hadn't realized she'd ended up right next to me.

"Oh—LA."

"How are you getting there?" She was watching me closely, her dark blue eyes slightly narrowed.

"I'll get a bus. I'm sure there will be one soon." And even if there wasn't, I would wait, but I didn't think I needed to share that part with Chloe.

"A *bus*?"

"Sorry," Kendrick said, hurrying into the kitchen. He was carrying my duffel, my canvas bag, and the tent. "These were put in the Bleecker Street guesthouse. I thought you were staying?"

I took them from him. "No, I'm heading out. But thanks so much."

"Want some pasta, Kendrick?" Priya called.

He shook his head. "I wish. I'm keto right now."

"Your loss."

"It literally is," he said, flexing a bicep. "Ten pounds and counting!"

"Wait," Chloe said, shaking her head. "I'm not sure we should let you just go to the bus station alone."

"It's really fine," I said as I pulled up my rideshare app. My phone was charged enough now for me to call an Uber, and though I didn't have a huge amount of money in my account, it looked like I had enough for the ride to the bus station. I'd just wait there for the next available bus, and be on my way back to LA.

"Let me drive you down to the gates," Kendrick said. "I can get the golf cart."

I shook my head, trying not to look exasperated. Maybe this was what having millions of dollars did to you. I was certainly capable of walking down a *driveway*. "That's okay. But thank you."

"It's a long driveway," Montana said, raising an eyebrow at me. "I'd take him up on it."

"I'm fine."

"Well," Kendrick said a little uncertainly, "just wave to the camera when you get to the bottom of the gates. Security will open the door for you. You have a ride coming?"

"Uh-huh," I lied. I saw that Chloe was looking at me closely, her expression skeptical. I was sure she was going to say something, but then Priya yelled that dinner was ready.

In the stampede for food that followed, I was able to shout a goodbye and thank-you in the general direction of the room, then grab my stuff and head back to the entrance hall.

In the foyer, I took one more look at the Chloe and Wiley sci-fi desert picture, then walked outside, closing the door quickly behind me so that Andy wouldn't get out.

I stood there on the step for just a moment—the quiet a contrast to the chaos in the house. I felt like I was turning off a movie halfway through, or leaving a play at intermission. Like the story was going to continue on without me—and I wouldn't know how it ended.

I shook my head and walked down the steps, pausing to look at the balloon dog for one last moment before crossing the lawn to the gravel driveway. The fact was, I needed to leave. And I was positive Russell wanted me to go just as badly as I wanted to.

But if that was the case, why had my stuff been brought to one of the guesthouses? I only let myself think about this for a second before I pushed it away—it was probably just crossed wires, nothing else. I looked up and suddenly understood why Kendrick had offered to drive me.

The driveway was gravel, impossibly long, with enormous palm trees planted on either side of it. It was the kind of driveway I'd only seen in movies—I half expected to see carriages arriving for a ball, or Ethan Hunt's sports car driving up it. At the end, a very long way off, I could see a set of metal gates—it looked like there was a *WS* worked into the iron.

"Okay," I said. Because what else was there to do except start the trek? But now that I was no longer inside a house with Wylie Sanders himself, I figured it would at least be okay to wear his merch. I set the duffel and tent down and dug my sweatshirt out of my canvas bag, looking at it for just a second, thinking how strange it was that I'd now met him. That Wylie was no longer just an image on a sweatshirt or a voice in a song—he was an actual person who'd really tried to make me feel welcome.

I pulled it on—it was a chilly, clear night, the sky an inky dark blue, with a few stars visible. Then I picked up the duffel and tent and walked down the driveway.

I couldn't help thinking back on how *nice* everyone had seemed. It was nothing like I'd thought it would be. They'd been bantering and joking together, exes and current partners and kids all sitting around a table as a family. All these siblings and half-siblings, getting along and hanging out. And it was clear they all really liked each other. . . .

Unbidden, I flashed back to the one and only meal I'd shared with my three half-siblings. How awkward it had been. How my defenses had been up going in, and how it only got worse every time I had to watch Gillian mothering *them*, laughing with them, helping to cut their food—not doing anything extraordinary, just being a regular mom. How I'd decided after that it was proof that it was better to keep things separated—me and my dad, Gillian and her real family. That trying to do stuff like have dinners was just too complicated.

Katy coughed discreetly. *More complicated than five ex-wives and millions of dollars and the world press reporting on it?*

Even as I tried to push it away, I thought about how Gillian's daughter Freya kept requesting to be my friend on Instagram. How I kept ignoring it. And all at once, it didn't feel like I was taking the high road or staying above it all. It just seemed small. And mean.

I shook my head and made myself keep walking, no sound except my sandals crunching over gravel. My thoughts kept returning to the happy, busy world I'd just left—everyone sitting down to a pasta dinner as a family, preparing to play Fishbowl (whatever that was). Now that I'd experienced it firsthand, it was like I could feel the *depth* of Russell's lies. All the people he'd just erased when he told me he was an only child.

I mean, it's not like you were being honest about Gillian, Katy pointed out. *Or Stanwich.*

But she wasn't actively lying, Didi countered. *She was just eliding the truth.*

I think it's the same thing, Katy said. *And that Darcy shouldn't be mad at him for something she was doing.*

Maybe that's why she is *mad,* Didi suggested.

I increased my pace, trying to ignore this. None of it mattered, after all. I wasn't going to see these people ever again. I was leaving tomorrow. I was off to the barren wasteland that was Connecticut. Even if I *could* understand a little more where Russell was coming from, what was the point of any of it?

We'd said goodbye. It was over.

What I needed now was to put all of this behind me and think about my next steps. I'd get to the gates, call my Uber. During the ride to the station, I could look up the next bus to LA. . . .

My phone rang in my bag, breaking the quiet of the night and startling me. It had been off for so much of tonight, it was almost like I'd forgotten that it was on and working now, and people could use it to reach me.

Gillian Beaulieu was the name on my screen. I stared at it for a moment, like this was a mirage that would disappear instantly. My mother's British husband, Anthony (Ant-ony)'s last name was pronounced Bewley, which was always hard to remember when I saw it written out. Most of the (very few) conversations I'd had with Anthony had revolved around him telling me not to pronounce certain letters in his name.

I stared down at my phone, trying to figure out what was happening. Why was Gillian calling me when it was getting close to two in the morning her time? Why was she calling me at all?

Unless—a cold fear gripped me—what if *she* wasn't calling me? What if something had happened?

I stopped walking and slid my finger across the screen, answering the call before it went to voicemail. "Hello?"

"Darcy." It was Gillian's voice, and I felt a clear flash of relief shoot through me.

"Hi," I said. "Um—it's late there."

"I know." Her voice was terse and angry, and my relief was immediately replaced with irritation, like someone had flipped a switch, changed electrical currents. "I've received a call from a lawyer in Las Vegas?"

"What?" I dropped my duffel and the tent onto the gravel—

they really were heavy. "C.J. called you?" Why was C.J. calling my mother when she'd made me sign a legally binding document that said I wasn't allowed to talk to anyone? Why would she be expanding the circle of people who knew about this, rather than trying to make it smaller?

"No. Some yawning person named Sarah." I could hear the anger in my mother's words, running just underneath them like water. "Waking me up. Waking Anthony up."

"I'm sorry that she woke up Anthony," I said, meaning it. After all, he didn't have anything to do with this. "But why would she call you?"

"I don't know!" Gillian snapped. "She seemed to think I would know something about what you've been up to. And when I asked why she was calling so late, it became clear she thought I was still in England."

"Oh." That one actually was on me, but I wasn't about to apologize for it. This situation was starting to make a little more sense— Sarah must have been trying to do damage control, make sure I hadn't talked to anyone before I signed the NDA.

"What is this, Darcy? What did you do?"

Just like that, I was irritated, my hackles up, the way I only ever felt when talking to Gillian. "I didn't do anything."

Well, Katy said.

Um, Didi added.

"I didn't do anything you need to concern yourself with," I amended.

"Well, clearly you did," Gillian snapped. And for just a second, I could hear something underneath her annoyance—*worry*. I remembered how my heart had seized when I'd thought, just for a moment, that something might have happened to her. Had she had the same thing when she'd gotten a middle-of-the-night call about me?

"I'm fine," I said, running my hand over my eyes.

All of a sudden, though, I felt just how long the night had been, everything hitting me at once. I was wrung out and exhausted, in a bone-deep way. I dropped the last thing I'd been holding, my canvas bag, and then I joined it, sinking down onto the gravel. I felt my lower lip tremble.

I wanted to be at home. In my own state, in my own bed. I wanted someone to bring me something to eat and brush my hair back from my forehead and tell me that everything would be okay.

I wanted my mother.

"Darcy?" Gillian's voice was a little more hesitant now, some of the anger gone.

And my mother was right there. She was with me now, just on the other end of the phone. But this was the whole problem, and always had been. Because while most of the time I told myself I was fine with the fact I didn't have a mother, that Gillian was never going to be what I wanted her to be—at certain moments, like now, it was as if the curtain was pulled back. And suddenly all I could see was the gulf between what I wanted and what I had.

And what I had was so little.

I shook my head, even though I knew Gillian couldn't see me, and sat up straighter. She didn't get to know anything about my night. It was information she wasn't entitled to, a level of clearance she hadn't earned.

"I'm *fine*," I repeated, even as I could feel that tears were incipient, threatening to spill.

"You don't sound fine."

"Oh, how would *you* know?" I snapped. "From all your experience with me? From the twelve hours total you've spent with me over the last ten years?"

I heard her draw in a sharp breath over the other end of the phone. The kind you take when someone sucker-punches you. "That's not fair. I'm trying—"

"Oh, you're *trying*? Alrighty, then. Great! So now everything is fixed."

"Look," Gillian said, and I could hear the irritation in her voice again. "I was woken up in the middle of the night—"

"I'm sorry, okay?" My voice was rising. "I didn't know they were going to call you. I didn't tell them to."

"Are you in trouble? I don't understand why they called me at all."

"I'm not in trouble. And they called you because they were under the mistaken impression that I had a mother. I'll be sure to correct them on that account, okay?"

She didn't say anything, but somehow I could hear the hurt in her silence, radiating out over the phone line, crossing the country from her in Connecticut to me in Nevada.

"Well." Her voice was going into cold-and-frosty mode, which always made her sound extra British. "The next four years will certainly be fun."

"That's your doing," I reminded her. "I didn't ask you for any favors."

"No, but you accepted them."

I blinked at that, surprised into silence. This was technically *true*, but . . .

"We can talk about this another time." Gillian sounded like she was trying to pull us back to more solid ground, not this dangerous place where we might accidentally tell the truth. "But . . . are you okay? Do you need something?"

That was all it took for my chin to start wobbling. I'd needed *so much* from her over the years—I'd needed things I'd never even admitted to myself, because it would just be that much harder when I never got them.

"No." I was trying to control my voice, even as I heard it crack. "Sorry that you were woken up. It won't happen again." Then I ended the call. I held the phone in my hand for a moment, tears balanced on the edge of my lashes, waiting to see if she'd call me back. Waiting to see if she would have heard something in my voice— known something; known that I needed her right then.

But the phone remained silent, and I could practically see it in my mind—Gillian setting the phone on her nightstand, getting back into bed, murmuring an apology to Anthony, not giving this another thought. . . .

I ran my hands through my hair and took a shaky breath. I was fine. I was more than fine. I was figuring things out on my own. I didn't need her.

Really? Katy whispered, her voice gentle.

And that was all it took. The tears spilled over, and I put my hands over my eyes and cried.

I didn't care, in that moment, that I was sobbing in the drive- way of an international celebrity. I gave up on caring if anyone saw me—because there was no stopping this.

I was crying for my mom. And all that I'd wanted and hadn't gotten. And how exhausting it was to pretend that I didn't need her or want her, when it was a flimsy lie that wasn't even fooling me. I was crying for the way that even when she was saying all the right things, I couldn't trust that she meant it. I was crying for the way I'd spoken to her, and how I already regretted it.

I cried for me, and for Russell, and the way it felt like we'd come close to something real, something special, for just a moment tonight before it all fell apart. I cried for the fear and exhaustion of the last three days, having to be so vigilant, while Romy got to run off and do whatever she wanted, because she knew that I would be there, holding down the fort and picking up the pieces. I cried for the way college already felt ruined and tainted, and for how I wasn't excited and optimistic about it like my friends—like this was just one more thing I didn't get. I cried because of the mess I'd made of everything, and the way I felt so trapped.

And finally, I cried because I was tired and cold and hungry and alone, and there were rocks digging into my legs.

I was just starting to pull it together a little when I felt something small and soft climb into my lap, and I froze.

Andy—who'd managed to escape again—was looking up at me.

CHAPTER 11

Sunday
11:00 P.M.

U m. Hi," I said. I ran my hand over the dog's head and just left it there for a moment. God, he was a comfort right now. I took a shaky breath and tried to pull myself together, running my hand over his ears. When I moved it, they popped straight up again. I pushed my hand down again, to flatten them—then lifted it up. After a moment, Andy's ears sprang back up and I laughed for what felt like the first time in hours.

I gave him one more pet, then pushed myself up to standing, lifting the dog with me. I moved the tent and the duffel onto the fake grass so they wouldn't be in the way in case anyone needed to drive out, then picked up my canvas bag and started the long walk up the driveway.

I wasn't sure how to get the dog back into the house—the last thing I wanted was to ring the "Darcy" doorbell, interrupt dinner, make a big fuss. But by the time I'd passed the balloon dog sculpture, I could see Chloe standing on the front steps.

I waved, incredibly relieved that I could just hand Andy off and go. "The dog got out again," I called as I held him up, like she needed proof.

"Huh. Weird." She seemed so unsurprised by this, I figured it must happen a lot. She opened the door and stepped through. "Let's get him in."

I'd been thinking I'd just hand him to her on the steps, but she was already in the foyer, so I didn't see any choice but to follow her back inside.

She shut the door once I was in, and I handed the dog back to her. "Good boy," she murmured to Andy before setting him down. He immediately tore off in the direction of the kitchen. I wasn't going to say anything to Chloe, but honestly, no wonder this dog was always escaping if he was getting these mixed messages. "Thanks for bringing him back," Chloe said, then her eyes widened as she looked at me. "Oh my god."

I looked down and remembered what I was wearing. "Oh, right. I can turn it inside out?"

"No, it's just that I can't believe he ever thought that hair was the way to go." Her smile faltered as she took a step closer to me. "Are you okay?"

"I'm fine," I said automatically. But I'd just cried harder than I had in years—of course it was going to show up on my face.

"I'm not sure you are."

"No, I'm good." My voice was getting high and tight, the way it always did when I was lying. But luckily, Chloe didn't know that.

"I kind of think you're lying."

"I've already taken up way too much of your time. I'll just—"

"Get an *Uber* to the *bus station*?" She made each of these things sound increasingly unappealing.

"Um, yes—"

"Last bus to LA leaves at midnight. It's half an hour from here to the Strip, more if there's traffic. *Maybe* you'll make it if you leave right now. But the closest Uber is twenty minutes away." She showed me her phone, and my heart sank as I looked at the distinct lack of cars around our little dot on the map.

"Oh well. That's okay. I can just wait."

"All night. At the *bus station*?"

"It's what I was going to do in Jesse," I pointed out. "Russell, too. We were going to wait there until the bus came at seven."

"Yeah, at a bus station in Bumblefuck, Nevada. You want to wait all night at a Vegas bus station?"

I shifted my feet, not quite sure how to get out of this. But I did know the longer we debated logistics, the small window for making the midnight bus to California was going to close. "I mean—maybe I can get there by midnight."

"You can't." Her voice was definitive. "And I *really* don't want to send you there and then you get murdered and the guilt of it haunts me my whole life."

"You could probably get a good true-crime podcast out of it, though?"

Chloe laughed at that, loudly, like I'd surprised her. "Just stay here. We've got more than enough room. One of the guesthouses is just sitting empty. You can have your own space; we won't bother you. Get a good night's sleep, and then we can drive you to the bus station in the morning."

"That's really generous of you. But I can't ask you to do that."

"You didn't ask me. I offered. So you'll stay."

"I mean . . ." I looked around, and discovered that it is very hard to come up with rational excuses when you're surrounded by Picassos and half-naked sci-fi portraits. I shook my head. "Russell—"

Chloe waved her hand in a gesture that somehow managed to

be dismissive but not unkind. "Leave him to me. I'd really feel a lot better if you stayed."

As I stood there in the foyer, the thought of a hot shower, a soft bed—things I hadn't had in days—was too tempting to pass up. I could take a moment to breathe, pull myself together. And if Russell thought it was weird that I was here—well, I would never have to see him again after tomorrow. "It's really kind of you."

Chloe shook her head. "It's nothing. And besides, I had to make it up to you. I heard you were dragged in front of C.J." She gave me a look that let me know she understood exactly what I'd gone through with the lawyer. "So you'll stay?"

I nodded. After all, wasn't this what I'd just wished for, sobbing out on the driveway? Someone to take me in hand, make things okay, take care of me? "I'll stay. Thank you so much. I left my stuff . . ."

"I'll get someone to grab it." She grinned at me and clapped her hands together. "This will be fun. Let's get you set up."

I'd been worried that it might be awkward to go back into the house after I'd left it. But it was like Chloe wasn't allowing for this possibility. Like she was bending the situation to her will.

We walked back into the main room, where everyone was sitting around the dining room table with half-eaten plates in front of them, laughing and talking, Artie on Sydney's lap, his face covered in sauce. Neither Russell or Wylie was there, and clocking their absence, I felt some of the tension leave my shoulders.

"Andy got out again," Chloe said as she breezed past the dining room table, me following in her wake. "Darcy got him, though. She's staying here tonight."

"What?" Wallace asked, looking up from his plate, but Montana gave me a smile.

"Good work, Darcy! Come back here and play Fishbowl when you're all settled."

Before I could answer that, Chloe was opening a glass door and stepping into the backyard, and I hurried to follow.

The backyard was just as stunning as the front—the pool was huge, and ringed with loungers and round covered chairs that seemed like mini cabanas. There was a connected hot tub, bubbling away. Bobbing in the pool was a huge float that seemed to be a punk-rock unicorn with wings, and a smaller circular float that looked like a bagel with a schmear. Striped towels were flung over the lounge chairs and the big circular chairs, but there were also baskets all around the perimeter with neatly rolled-up towels inside them. There was a huge, hulking piece of black metal to the side of the pool, which I was pretty sure was a Richard Serra.

"Darcy?"

"Yeah," I said, hurrying to catch up with Chloe.

I hadn't known what to expect when I'd heard *guesthouse*—but not this. It was one of the five guesthouses ringing the backyard. And the one I'd be staying in was a little smaller than our house in Raven Rock—but honestly, not by much. It looked like a one-story version of the main house, all wood and glass and sharp angles. There were three steps up and a small porch in front with two Adirondack chairs facing the pool.

Chloe headed inside, and I followed. It was a proper house— we were in the living room, with a couch and a TV, an open-plan kitchen behind it. There was a hallway where I assumed the bedrooms and bathroom were.

"Wiley misses being on tour, so he named all the guesthouses after his favorite places and decorated them accordingly. This one is Bleecker Street, in the Village."

I was about to ask what she meant by that—*what* village?—but then I took in the décor and realized, all at once, that she meant New York City.

Hanging above the couch was a large framed poster for *Metropolitan*. All over the walls were photographs and sketches of the city. There was even a huge, old-fashioned-looking metal sign hanging in the kitchen that read H&H BAGELS—NEW YORK'S FINEST.

Even the furniture seemed to somehow say *New York*, though I wouldn't have known that was a way to describe something until I saw it. The couch and chairs were a dark, soft-looking leather, and there were dark-red woven rugs on the wooden floors. Everything was angular and *cool*—it certainly no longer seemed like we were in the middle of the desert, outside Las Vegas.

"What?" Chloe asked. "Is it okay?"

"I—"

"Because normally, I could move you, but the other guest-houses are occupied at the moment, unfortch. Montana and Priya are staying in Hana Highway, and Kenya and Doug are in Beale Street."

"No, are you kidding? It's amazing. It's a whole house!"

"I know. Much nicer than any house I ever lived in before I met Wylie." She crossed into the kitchen, and I followed. There was a large basket of snacks and fruit on the counter, and just seeing it, I felt how hungry I was. But I didn't know how this worked—was I allowed to have these snacks? I was basically a pity guest—they were probably reserved for important visitors.

Chloe opened the fridge and pulled out a glass bottle. "Topo Chico?" I nodded. She took out two, opened them both, then slid one across the kitchen counter to me.

"So," I said, after I took a long drink, letting my canvas bag rest between my feet. My mind was turning over what she'd just told me about who was staying where, not to mention what I'd seen back in the house. Now that I was going to be here for a bit, my curiosity was starting to get the better of me. "How does it all work?"

Chloe reached into the snack basket and pulled out a bag of chips. I was relieved to see that it would apparently be okay for me to eat something from it too. "How does what work?" She opened the bag and held it out to me.

I ate three—salt and vinegar, *very* good—then wiped my hands on my jean shorts. "Well . . . that Kenya and Doug are here. And Paula, too . . ." And *you*, I thought but did not say. But she seemed to be . . . living here? Co-parenting with her ex-husband? And somehow on good terms with Wylie and his kids—many of whom were *older* than her—and his ex-wives.

She nodded as she crunched down on a chip and then shook the bag. "You think it's weird that we're all here together?"

"Well . . . yeah."

Chloe laughed, and I felt myself relax a little. Her phone beeped and she pulled it out of her sweatpants pocket. "Astrid's awake now too. I swear, the kids know the second I'm out of the house."

"Do you need to—check on her?" I didn't want to be the one who was taking up her time, even though she didn't seem like she was in any kind of a hurry to leave.

"I'm sure she's fine. And if she's not, there are a ton of people who can help. It's the benefit to all of us being together." She plucked another chip from the bag. "That's what you were asking, right? How we manage to do it?"

"I've just never . . . known about something like this, that's all. It's not what I would have expected."

"I mean, normally there aren't this many of us. We turned the festival into an occasion to all get together—but we do try to get together as much as we can. Wylie was very clear about it from the beginning. Said he had no interest in siloed families, everyone separate. He likes siblings to be in each other's lives, even if they don't all have the same parents. He likes the noise and the chaos, everyone running around together and getting into trouble."

"I can see that with the kids," I said slowly. "But . . ." Their mode of living just seemed so separate from anything I'd seen in my own family, or in my friends' families who were divorced, that I didn't quite understand how it was happening.

"Wylie just says that if you chose to partner with someone, it was for a reason. He was clear with me about the time he spends with his exes, all of the kids . . . and we all make it work." She arched an eyebrow and leaned forward, like she was about to give me the gossip. I leaned in to get it. "Sometimes, it works a little *too* well, in Paula's case."

"You mean . . ."

"Wylie and Paula got back together," she said with a laugh. "*After* we were divorced. We joke that he's had so many wives, he's back around to the first one. And it's better, honestly. He needs to be with someone his own age. He was getting tired of me not knowing who Burt Lancaster is. Was?"

"And everyone just . . . gets along?"

"I mean, for the most part. Like anything worth doing, you

have to work at it. It doesn't just *happen*. And his ex, Candace, *hates* him. As you've probably read. She's not on board with any of this. But for the most part . . . it just works."

I nodded slowly, trying to process this—that a millionaire rock star with a string of exes and a passel of kids could have these functional, happy relationships. But me and my dad were totally separate from Gillian and her new family—and I didn't know my half-siblings at all.

Well, Didi chimed in. *You've also never really . . . tried?*

"What?" Chloe asked, and I realized she was looking at me closely, like she was reading something on my face.

"Nothing—I was just thinking about how I wasn't sure that would be possible for me. With my mom's new husband and family, I mean."

Chloe nodded, crunched down on another chip, and held the bag back out to me. I'd just taken a bite when she asked, "Was that who you were yelling at in the driveway? It looked like mom yelling."

"You saw me?" I felt a dull flush creep into my cheeks. I just hoped that it was only Chloe, and not the entire household.

"Why do you think I sent Andy out to get you?"

"You—what?"

"I mean, he has an actual problem, don't get me wrong. He's always trying to make a break for it. But he's also a soft touch, and I knew you'd do the right thing and bring him back."

I finished my chip as I processed this. For a second I tried to figure out if I was angry about it, then decided I wasn't. Chloe had used the dog subterfuge for good, and now that I was here, and seeing where I was going to be staying tonight, I was grateful for it. "Well . . . thanks?"

"I know a mom fight when I see one," she said, setting down the chips and rooting around in the basket, finally coming up with an apple. "It's our most complex and primal relationship." I raised my eyebrows at that and she laughed. "Sorry, my psych major is showing."

"Psych major?"

Chloe nodded, looking proud and a little nervous. "Yeah, I just started at UNLV. Just part-time, though."

"You do have a very small child," I pointed out.

"Two of them, even. You'll meet Astrid in the morning." Chloe looked at the apple critically, set it down, and pulled out a chocolate bar. "Much better."

She held the bar out to me, and I broke myself off a square. She grinned at me, and I was struck again by just how *young* she looked. "Um . . . ," I started, cramming a piece of chocolate in my mouth to get my courage up.

"What?"

"Can I ask—how old you are? Sorry if that's rude."

Chloe laughed. "I'm twenty-four. I don't think it'll be rude for fifteen years or so."

I nodded, and broke myself off another piece of chocolate. Gillian had been twenty-four when she had me. And even though my dad had always talked about how young they had both been, I'd always shrugged this off. Twenty-four seemed *adult*. But looking at Chloe now, it was hitting me for the first time what that had meant for my dad. For Gillian.

Needing to think about something else for just a moment, I nodded back toward the main house. "Do you think Russell will be okay? Is he in big trouble?"

Chloe grimaced. "Russell normally *never* gets in trouble. He's the kid Wylie worries about the least. Not like Montana. She and Wylie could probably have a fight in shorthand by this point. But Russell and Wylie . . . it's new to them. I bet they're not having a fun conversation right now." She tucked her hair behind her ears. "Something happened at the festival. Right before Wylie's set—I saw the two of them arguing. And then after . . ." She sighed. "I don't know what happened. But they were both upset. And then we couldn't find Russell—he'd disappeared. He texted Connor that he wasn't coming back with us, and he was going to LA on his own. But we didn't know how, or where he was . . . Wylie was *not* happy. But he also refused to tell us what they were fighting about."

I nodded, thinking back to the times that Russell had alluded to the friend he'd come to Silverspun with, the one who he'd been fighting with—who was, it turned out, his dad.

"And then a few hours ago," Chloe went on, "Connor got another text from him. He said that he was okay and not to worry. That things were good with him, with like eight smiley faces. That did *not* go over well on our end, let me tell you. But then soon after that, Russell was calling Wylie and saying he was about to be arrested and needed help." She pushed herself off the counter and shrugged. "So all in all, I'd say they have some things to work out."

I turned this all over in my mind, realizing Russell must have texted Connor while I was in the bathroom at the Silver Standard. Russell had texted his brother, told him things were good, texted a row of smiley faces . . . because he was happy. Because of *me*. Because things had been going so well. . . .

It wasn't real, Didi reminded me.

It was *real,* Katy insisted. *Maybe the details were a little fudged.*

But everything that mattered was true. And you know it.

I suddenly wished that Russell would have told me the truth. So I could have known everything *real* about him, and he wouldn't have felt the need to keep any of it from me. I could have actually known about his parents, his stepparents, his half-siblings, this crazy circus life. What it had been like to grow up like this, and if he played any instruments, and if his dad liked his Fun Facts as much as I had. The real him.

Chloe finished her chocolate and clapped her hands together. "So! Let's get you settled in." She walked out of the kitchen, and I grabbed my sparkling water and hurried after her, pulling my canvas bag over my shoulder.

"Everything should be stocked," she said as she walked down the hallway, which was dotted with framed photographs on both sides. Central Park at night, the Brooklyn Bridge, Russell—

I stopped short and took a step closer to the photograph on the wall. Russell was standing on a New York sidewalk. He was wearing a suit—a dark jacket and pants, white shirt, no tie, his hair sharply parted. He looked so handsome it took my breath away. He was in profile, looking up at something. It seemed like maybe he was underneath a Broadway marquee? He looked so happy—just suffused with joy.

And I realized that I recognized it—it was how he'd looked for a lot of tonight. When we'd been happy. Together.

"Darcy?"

"Yeah," I called back. I pulled myself away from the picture, and continued down the hallway, past a framed poster of the famous Simon & Garfunkel concert in Central Park.

"Bathroom," Chloe said, opening a door and flipping on a light switch. "There should be everything you need in there. Towels, products, hair dryer . . ." She walked to the door just off the bathroom and opened it. "You can take whichever bedroom you want; they both should have sheets—"

She turned on the light and groaned. The room was bigger than my bedroom back home—upholstered headboard, fluffy-looking gray duvet cover, an explosion of pillows. And right in the middle of the bed, taking up most of it, was Tidbit.

He looked at us with his huge eyes, unimpressed, like he was wondering just why we were disturbing him.

"Tidbit!" Chloe sounded exasperated. "What are you doing here?"

"How did he even get in?"

"He can open doors," she said with a sigh. "He does it with his head. He was probably trying to escape Artie. He keeps trying to ride him." She looked back down the hallway, toward the house. "I should probably go investigate, actually. You okay?"

"I'm great—thank you so much."

"Come back to the house when you're settled," she said, then gave me a smile. "Or not! You might have had more than enough of us for one night. You're welcome either way." She turned to the dog. "Tidbit! Come."

Tidbit didn't even raise his head, just snuggled more deeply into the duvet.

"Maybe take the other bedroom? It's like trying to move a boulder."

"Um, okay. Do I need to . . . do anything?"

Chloe shook her head. "He'll let himself out when he wants to leave." She leaned over the bed and rubbed his ears. "You weirdo."

She straightened up and headed out of the room. "I'll leave you to it," she said, giving my arm a quick squeeze as she passed me.

"Thank you again," I called, even though I knew it was inadequate for everything that had just been handed to me.

"Sure," she called back to me. "See you in a bit."

"Uh-huh," I replied, figuring that this was easier than telling her that I was planning on locking the door and staying here for the rest of the night. Even though I *would* have liked to have tried Priya's pasta. And I was still curious about what Fishbowl actually was . . . but to go back up to the main house would be to risk running into Russell.

Chloe stepped out the front door, giving me a wave as she went. I kicked off my sandals and dropped my canvas bag next to them. And then, feeling like I had been in these clothes for *far* too long, I stepped out of my jean shorts and pulled off my Nighthawks sweatshirt and tank top. I tossed them onto the bed next to Tidbit, who seemed affronted by all of this. I smiled at him, then headed into the bathroom.

I felt like I could cry as I looked around—the bright white tiles, the sunken tub and glassed-in shower. The very idea that I was back to indoor plumbing felt like a miracle.

The bathroom was stocked with fancy products, the kind I'd seen on influencers' social media but had never tried out myself. I treated myself to them now, though, taking a long, hot shower. I washed my hair and then just stood under the warm water, eyes closed, until I felt something in my shoulders loosen, my neck unwind, like my body at last understood that I didn't have to stay on guard anymore. That I could finally set down some of what I'd been carrying.

There was a gray fluffy robe on the back of the door, and I wrapped myself in it. Chloe had been right—the bathroom was stocked with everything I could have needed. Brushes, combs, moisturizers . . .

I took the opportunity to dry my hair—I felt I needed to after letting it dry slowly with pool water in it for the last few hours. When my hair was dry and I felt like I was fit for civilization again, I headed back into the bedroom, feeling lighter and calmer than I had in days. I'd see if there was a phone charger in this house—there had to be one somewhere—and then I'd text Katy in her dorm at Scripps. I knew she'd still be up, and I wanted to go through all this with her. Didi would be upset, I knew, that she hadn't been looped in, but she went to Colgate, and it was very late on the East Coast. And maybe Bella would have brought my duffel, and I could change into my pajamas. They were creased and dusty, but it was still miles better than sleeping in my clothes at a bus station.

I stopped in the doorway of the bedroom and looked around. My sandals were still there, and my canvas bag. The dog was still there.

But my clothes had disappeared.

CHAPTER 12

Sunday
11:30 P.M.

I just stared for a second at the empty spot on the bed. I knew I'd taken a long shower, but it hadn't been *that* long. What could have happened to my clothes?

I gave Tidbit a look, but he just rolled over onto his side. He couldn't have *eaten* them, could he? But maybe he'd hidden them somewhere? This was a dog that was capable of opening doors, after all. And he was the size of a small subcompact. I felt like I shouldn't rule anything out.

"Tidbit?" I ventured. He raised his head slightly. "Did you . . ." The giant dog just looked at me, implacable, then set his head back down with a sigh. "Okay, never mind. As you were."

I checked the other bedroom, but the clothes weren't there, either. Walking down the hallway to the kitchen, I told myself there *had* to be some explanation. And as I looked around, I spotted a note, written in a curly, loopy hand, propped up against the snack basket. I hurried over to it and picked it up.

> Hi Darcy!!
> So Bella got your things from the driveway but
> everything was kind of all dusty so we're washing

your stuff! Left you something to wear on the couch.
Fishbowl at 11:30, don't be late!

xx

Chloe

I looked down at the note, wondering why I was even surprised. Every time I'd set something down at this house, it had been whisked away by someone.

I leaned over the couch and saw, neatly folded, a pair of sweatpants and a cashmere sweater. The sweatpants looked new—WYLIE FOR THE WYNN was written down the right leg—this was his Vegas residency, the one my dad had been so opposed to seeing. The cashmere sweater, though, I had a feeling was Chloe's. I picked it up carefully. It was a light camel color, and maybe the softest thing I'd ever felt.

Washing my clothes was a really nice gesture—as was leaving me these—but I couldn't help wishing they'd just dropped my stuff off and left me alone. Because now it felt like a ball had just been tossed into my court.

I traced my finger over the word *Fishbowl*. Somehow, knowing there was a time attached made this all so much harder to ignore. And made it impossible to just keep hiding out here, like I'd planned on.

Would Russell think it was weirder if I was staying in my guesthouse all night, refusing to come out? Or if I was playing some sort of game with his family members? And would it be too strange for him to see me back there again, with his family? After he'd already had what I was assuming was a hard talk with his dad?

You might not even see him, Didi pointed out, ever logical. *He might have gone to bed. It's late.*

It *was* late—and yet, I was wide-awake. And hungry. The chips had only seemed to make me hungrier—the tacos that Russell and I had eaten on the football field felt like a whole other lifetime ago. And I *had* blown my hair out . . .

Before I could talk myself out of it, I grabbed the clothes from the couch and then hurried into the bathroom to change.

I had assumed that Tidbit would stay where he was—he had barely moved at all since I'd been in the guesthouse—but as soon as I opened the door, I heard the sound of paws hitting the floor, and then the dog came walking down the hallway, his head level with the bottom of the picture frames. "Oh," I said, blinking at him. I honestly wasn't sure I would ever get used to being around a dog this big. "Are you coming too?"

He leaned his head against me, and as I gave him a tentative scratch on the forehead, he closed his eyes, like he liked it. When I stopped he just opened his eyes and looked at me, and I laughed and scratched behind his ears this time. "Okay," I said as I headed over to the door. "Shall we?" Now that he'd decided to come, I was actually pretty glad—because while Chloe had been clear that he could *open* doors, she hadn't said anything about his ability to close them.

We crossed the lawn to the house together, the giant dog padding next to me like an honor guard. I stepped in through the glass door, and Tidbit shook himself, a full-body shake, then headed in the direction of his water bowl in the kitchen. I pulled the door shut behind me, since the last thing I wanted was for Andy to get out and for it to be all my fault, then looked around.

There was no longer the full crowd that had been here when Chloe and I had breezed through. There was just Montana, sitting on top of one of the kitchen islands with a glass of wine, bent over her phone, and Connor, Sydney, and Wallace all sprawled on the couch. The TV was now showing some kind of medieval-set video game that Sydney and Wallace were playing while Connor read a book. I was relieved that there weren't quite so many people here now—and that the three-year-old had, hopefully, gone back to bed.

But most important—neither Russell or Wylie was anywhere to be seen.

"No! No! No! No! You absolute bellend!" Wallace yelled as he tossed his controller onto the giant ottoman coffee table.

"Don't swear at my wife," Connor said vaguely, turning a page in his book.

"I'm fine," Sydney said, grinning. "I'm better than fine, because I just destroyed Wallace's grain holdings and his dwarf fled his shire."

Connor looked up and frowned. "Explain this game to me again?"

"And it doesn't count if it's British swearing," Wallace explained, leaning back against the couch cushions. "Everyone knows that. I feel like your wife is taking advantage of my distracted state."

"Alyssa will call when she's free, Wallace," Sydney said.

He sighed, then nodded at the television. "Go again?"

"Darcy!" Montana looked up from her phone and smiled at me. "You're here. Oh, yay. Are you playing Fishbowl?"

"We're never going to play Fishbowl," Wallace grumbled from the couch. "I've given up even hoping. It's like *Waiting for Fishbowl* over here. We've had the game set up for literal hours, but *noooo*, we had to stop and eat pasta first. . . ."

"Do you want any?" Montana asked me as she pushed herself off the island. She headed toward what I thought was a cabinet until she pulled it open and I realized it was actually a refrigerator—just in disguise for some reason.

"Sure," I said, feeling my stomach rumble again. "That would be great."

"Priya will be so happy," Montana said as she pulled a glass container out of the fridge. "She hates when there's leftovers; she always sees it as an indictment of her cooking, even when she's made enough to feed an army." She pulled down a bowl, then looked back toward the couch. "Anyone else still hungry?"

"I'm good," Sydney said as she picked up her controller—apparently she and Wallace were going to play another round. "Hey, Darcy. Get settled okay?"

"Yeah," I said, glancing back toward the guesthouse. "Everything is really amazing. It's so nice of you guys to let me stay. And Chloe, um . . . gave me her clothes?"

Montana laughed. "She does that."

"I think it's just a loan, though, until mine get clean."

"Want to play?" Sydney asked, holding up her controller. "I could use some real competition."

"Hey," Wallace said, sounding wounded.

"I'm okay," I called to her. "But thanks." I looked over at Montana, who was bustling around the kitchen. "Can I do anything to help?"

"Just relax," she said, pulling out a container of parmesan and sprinkling some of it over the pasta. "Tell me about yourself!"

"Oh." My mind was suddenly a blank. Why was it whenever anyone asked you something like that, you couldn't think of *anything*? Like when someone wanted to know your top five movies, you suddenly couldn't remember any movie you'd ever seen. Or when you were asked to name a celebrity and all you could come up with was *Steve Guttenberg*. "Um . . ."

Montana put the bowl of pasta in what was apparently a microwave—it looked like another cabinet. Why was everything in this kitchen pretending it was just a cabinet? "Where are you from?"

"Los Angeles."

"So you know Russell from school?" She took a sip of her wine.

"No, we um . . . met in a bus station?"

Montana's eyes got wide. "Oh?"

A moment later, I heard how that sounded. "I was at Silverspun too," I added hurriedly so she wouldn't think some weird Nevada drifter had wandered into their home. "And then after the festival, we were both stranded. At least I was. I . . . um . . ."

"Oh, when he disappeared," Montana said, nodding. "He went to a *bus* station? So weird."

"Russell went to a bus station?" Connor asked, wandering up to us, carrying his book and a wineglass. "That's a choice." He reached for the bottle of white that was on the other island and poured himself a refill. I glanced at the book he'd set down—*The Last Holdfast* by C. B. McCallister. It was a thick hardcover that looked like a fantasy novel.

"No," I said quickly. "We were both on the bus from the festival to LA, but then it broke down, so we were stuck at the station. And we ended up walking around and talking. . . . We were only in the bus station by accident."

"Gotcha," Connor said as the microwaved beeped. He wandered away with his novel and his wine, and Montana set the bowl down on the island. She pulled up one of the stools, then gestured for me to do the same, placing a fork and a striped linen napkin in front of me.

"Thank you so much," I said, sitting on the stool and picking up my fork. I took a bite, then another. Whatever modifications the sauce had undergone were worth it—the spiciness had been tamped down, and it was *really* good.

"That's so cool," Montana said with a sigh as she picked up her glass. "The two of you, in the middle of nowhere by happenstance, meeting like that . . . it's like something out of a movie!"

I nodded as I concentrated on my pasta, keeping my face averted. Just because my romantic delusion bubble had been popped tonight didn't mean I had to wreck Montana's.

"I mean, it just seems . . . really romantic." Then she looked at me and raised an eyebrow. "Or not?"

I couldn't help but laugh at her expression, so nakedly interested. "I mean," I said, turning my fork between my fingers. I was very aware I was saying this to Russell's *sister*. "Russell is really great, but . . ."

"Not interested," Montana finished with a knowing nod. "I get it. Is it the hair? I keep telling him to cut it. I don't want him to make Wallace's mistakes."

"Wait, what?" Wallace called, not looking away from the game, where a very violent battle seemed to be taking place in front of a rain-swept castle. "I have a girlfriend, I'll have you know."

"She lives in Hawaii," Montana pointed out.

"She's still my girlfriend!"

"No," I said quickly, lowering my voice so that hopefully this would just be between me and Montana. I was suddenly seeing a downfall to open-plan houses. "I mean . . . we were, um . . . we did . . . I liked him."

"*Liked*, past tense?" Montana asked as she took a sip of her wine, her eyes above the glass not leaving mine.

"Well . . ." I looked down into my pasta bowl and took a breath. "He told me that he had a different last name. And he didn't tell me about his dad, or any of you. It wasn't until he had to call for help that I found out he'd been lying to me all night."

Montana set down her wineglass and raked a hand through her dark hair. "Yikes. Yeah, that's not good."

"What's not good?" Connor called.

"Lying about being Wylie Sanders's kid," Montana called to Connor.

Wallace paused the game and turned around to face the kitchen. "Oh, come on," he said, shaking his head at Montana. "Don't pretend you've never done it." Montana shrugged, but I could see that her cheeks had reddened. "But I do get it," Wallace continued, adjusting his glasses. "It can be a lot when you first meet someone. I mean, for you guys. Even with my last name, nobody assumes I'm Wylie's son, because racism." The game un-paused, and there was a squelching sound as Sydney's avatar swung her sword and Wallace's avatar fell to the ground, sans head. Wallace picked up his controller again with a sigh.

"I'm sure Russell didn't mean to trick you or anything," Montana said. "It can just be . . . a whole thing. Not that I'm condoning what he did!" she said quickly. "Just that I can understand the impulse, especially after what happened with Olivia."

What happened with Olivia? Didi asked sharply.

What happened with Olivia?! Katy echoed.

"Oh, um, right," I said, my mind spinning. Because Russell had never talked about an Olivia. Was this an ex? What had happened? Was this the thing C.J. had mentioned to Russell? I took a breath, trying to summon the courage to ask, just as Montana reached down and scooped up Andy, resting him on her lap. He immediately started licking her chin.

"So are you Russell's same age? Or in college already?"

I nodded, spearing another bite of pasta. "I'm about to start my freshman year. Stanwich College."

"Really?" Montana grinned at me and jostled the dog joyfully. "I love that school!"

All at once, I remembered Russell talking about his friend Montana, who knew about it. "How do you know it?"

"I was dating a professor there for a while when I was getting my master's in New Haven."

"You can say Yale," Connor said, looking over as he rolled his eyes.

"Oh, shut up," Montana laughed, and then turned to me. "That campus is just stunning, and it's right outside the city. And they have that great fall festival. . . ."

"They do?" In protest of going there, I had done almost no research into Stanwich, which was now seeming incredibly stupid.

"It's the best." She sighed happily as she scratched the dog under his chin. "God, I loved undergrad. I'd give anything to go back. Freshman year, everyone getting to know each other, hooking up in the dorms, people thinking they're actually going to continue with a philosophy major . . ."

"Which undergrad?" Wallace called, and Montana made a face at him.

"What do you mean?" I asked.

"My brother is referring to the fact that I bounced around a little. I transferred after my freshman year. And then I took a year off to do Habitat for Humanity. And then I studied abroad, and liked it so much I stayed another year—"

"Also known as, fell in love with a girl in her program," Connor said, turning a page in his book.

"And then I did my last year remotely because I got a great internship." She shrugged, and I nodded, feeling a little overwhelmed. Montana gave me a smile, then leaned forward, like she was about to tell me a secret. "Everyone expects you to do four years in the same place, but who wants to stick to a script? Things are *much* more interesting when you color outside the lines. And who's to say you need college at all? My dad never went, and he's doing okay."

I nodded, like I was taking this seriously. "So I'll put rock star down as my backup plan. Sounds good."

Montana laughed and I finished up my bowl of pasta. Somehow, as obvious as it was, this had never occurred to me. It was like I'd been on this path that had only pointed in one direction, trapped into going to Stanwich because I had no other options. But it suddenly felt like a window had just been opened, letting me see a view outside, one that had been there the whole time but I'd never bothered to look at. Because Stanwich didn't have to be the end of the story—if I hated it, and I kept my grades up, maybe I could transfer somewhere with a scholarship. Or study abroad. Maybe I wouldn't be stuck there for four years after all.

Or maybe you'll love it, Katy pointed out hopefully. *You don't know yet. Don't just* decide.

"All done?" Montana asked, looking down at my bowl.

I nodded. "It was so good. Thank you so much."

She smiled. "I'll have to tell Priya. She'll be so happy."

"While you're at it, tell her that we're finally playing Fishbowl," Wallace said, setting down his controller with a flourish.

"Is it because you lost again?" Connor asked.

"It's not *not* that," Wallace said. "But seriously. We worked so hard to set up this game and now we're not even going to play it? Unacceptable!"

Sydney shrugged. "Okay."

Wallace pointed to her. "Sydney's in!"

"I'll go get Priya," Montana said. She grabbed my bowl from the table and dropped it in the farmhouse sink on her way over to the doors that led to the pool. "Darcy, could you do me a favor?"

"Sure," I said immediately.

"Great. Could you just walk to the top of the stairs and yell 'Fishbowl'? Just to let people know the game is starting." She pointed toward the foyer, where I could now see there was a hallway and a staircase.

"Um." I glanced at the large wooden clock above the stove. It was *really* late. Did rock stars—and their families—just have a different internal clock? "Will I . . . wake people up?"

She waved this away, already opening the door. "All the adults are still up. And the kids will sleep through it. Thanks!"

She dashed across the lawn and I headed toward the stairs, wondering why I had to yell. Wasn't this why we all had phones?

I was halfway up the stairs, rounding the corner onto the second floor, when I nearly bumped into someone coming down—Russell.

"Oh," he said, stopping short and taking a step back.

"Sorry," I said automatically. I blinked at him. Just as I'd taken a shower and changed, it seemed like Russell had done the same. The jeans and T-shirt I'd seen on him all night were gone, replaced with a pair of khaki shorts and a light blue, soft-looking button-down. His hair looked wet and freshly combed, and we were standing close enough that I could tell he smelled like cedar and something else . . . like the woods after rain.

"I didn't—I thought that you left?"

"I did!" I said quickly. I didn't want him to think we'd had that awkward goodbye for nothing. "I absolutely left. But when I was half-way down the driveway, I saw Andy—he'd gotten out again. And then when I brought him back to the house, Chloe told me that there weren't any more buses to LA tonight and that I should stay here. So . . . I am." He was looking at the ground, and I wished I could see his face—to try to understand how he was feeling about this. "Is that . . . okay?"

"Of course! I said that you could stay, remember? I told you we had the guesthouses."

"I know," I said, then crossed my arms over my chest. "And—thank you. I just didn't want this to be . . . weird."

Russell looked down at what I was wearing, and then back up at me. "Nice pants."

"Oh," I said, glancing at the writing down my right leg. "Yeah. Chloe kind of . . . stole my clothes? She's washing them, I guess, so she gave me these."

"She does that. I came to visit one time, and she'd replaced all my clothes with a 'new direction' she wanted me to try. Consider yourself lucky you just ended up with sweatpants."

"What did she get you?"

"Leather pants," he said, his voice grim. "Like . . . so many. And I never wore them. Think of the cows!"

I could feel myself on the verge of laughter, a beat from tipping over into it. Just like that, I was remembering how easy it had been with him all night, up until the very end. How simple it had seemed for a while.

"So," Russell said. He looked up the staircase. "Were you . . ."

"Right," I said, remembering I'd been sent here on a mission. "Montana wanted me to go upstairs and yell that Fishbowl is starting."

"Finally!"

"Yeah. But I didn't want to wake people up. She said it would be okay, but . . ."

"Don't worry about it." Russell crossed in front of me and bounded up the stairs in what seemed like two steps. "Hey! Fishbowl is starting!" he yelled, then walked back down again.

I heard footsteps coming down the stairs, and a second later, there was Chloe, now in a pair of very fluffy-looking slippers. "Hey, Darcy!" she said as she breezed by, not stopping. "The sweater looks great on you."

She continued down, leaving Russell and me alone. We were standing closer than I'd realized—this landing was not particularly large to begin with, and probably not designed for people to just hang around on it, not going up or down, just stuck between two directions.

And in addition to that, I felt like I was stuck between the two versions of him—the Russell Henrion he'd pretended to be, and the Russell Sanders he actually was, who I didn't really know at all. I took a breath to say something—I wasn't sure what yet—when he took a step away from me and gestured to the stairs going down. "After you," he said, his tone polite.

"Thanks."

We walked down the stairs, me leading the way, not speaking— but with our feet falling at the same time.

. . .

"Fishbowl!" Wallace stood in front of the couches, looking happier than I'd yet seen him, in my brief experience. "Are you ready to play the best game of all time?"

"It's good you're not building it up," Priya said, giving him a thumbs-up. "Nice expectation-setting."

We were all on the couches to play this game that had still not adequately been explained to me, beyond putting celebrities' names in a bowl. Wylie, Kenya, and Paula had passed, so it was just (*just?*) me, Russell, Chloe, Doug, Montana, Priya, Wallace, Connor, and Sydney who were playing.

Wallace shook a giant ceramic bowl that had *Sanders Family Movie Night* stenciled on the side and looked at us expectantly. "Are we ready?"

"Guys?"

I looked over to see Wylie standing in the hallway.

He was wearing blue striped pajama pants and a sweatshirt that read *Harvard-Westlake*. But before I could even process that I was seeing Wylie Sanders in his pajamas, I noticed the expression on his face.

"What's up?" Wallace asked, lowering the bowl.

Wylie looked around the room, then back at us, his brows drawn together. "Has anyone seen Andy?"

CHAPTER 13

Monday
12:15 A.M.

O kay," Wiley said, looking around at all of us. "Everyone have flashlights?"

We were all standing by the gate at the end of the driveway. We'd been driven there in golf carts, since time was of the essence here and nobody had twenty minutes to hike down it. When Wylie hadn't been able to find Andy anywhere in the house, he'd come to ask us about it—which was when Montana realized that she'd accidentally left the door ajar when she went to get Priya for Fishbowl.

Everyone had fanned out across the yard, and when Connor saw a gap in the hedge on the border of the Sanders house, he realized that Andy was probably running around somewhere in the neighborhood. This was when all the searching had taken on a new, more serious level, as Kendrick handed out flashlights and Wylie assigned people roles. We would all take a different area of the neighborhood and search by foot in teams of two. Kendrick and Bella would search by golf cart—faster, but not so fast you couldn't spot a small dog. We needed to try and find Andy as soon as possible—before he wandered too far to be able to find his way home again, and before he could possibly run into a coyote.

So we'd gathered up the search party. Chloe and Paula stayed behind—so they could watch the sleeping kids, and also so there would be someone there in case Andy found his way back.

"We've got them," Connor said, holding up his flashlight. The happy, joking group from the couch was gone—everyone standing around the base of the driveway was serious, their faces grave and worried.

"Great," Wylie said, nodding. "Let's check in with each other in thirty minutes, if we haven't found him by then. Hopefully he hasn't gotten far."

Kendrick pointed a clicker at the huge black *WS* gates and they started to swing slowly outward. We all walked through, and as we did, it hit me that this was the first time I was going through them—I'd *flown* here, as crazy as that still seemed to me. So since I hadn't seen this road—or the rest of the neighborhood, except from the sky—I didn't know what I'd be walking out into.

But it was just a dark street—there wasn't a line painted down it, or many streetlights that I could see. There didn't even seem to be a house across from Wylie's, just a wall of hedges.

The second we'd made it out to the street, people started to organize themselves into pairs, mostly the couples—Montana and Priya, Kenya and Doug, Sydney and Connor. It wasn't until I saw Wylie clap Wallace on the shoulder that I realized it left me and Russell to pair up. I knew this wasn't a crazy assumption for everyone to have made—that Russell and I would *want* to be paired up. After all, I'd arrived with him, had been introduced as his friend—he was the only reason that I was even there. And frankly, everyone was probably too worried about the missing dog to give this much thought at all.

Russell seemed to realize this at the same moment that I did, turning his head as everyone else dispersed, flashlight beams bright against the blue-black night.

The golf carts pulled out of the driveway, each turning a different direction, and a second later, they were gone.

"You can go back to the house," Russell said, nodding at the gates. They were starting to close, with the *W* and the *S* coming closer together—but slowly, taking their time. "I didn't . . . I mean, I can go on my own."

"No, I want to help." And I did—even if that meant having to walk around with Russell.

"Okay," Russell said. The flashlight beams of his family were fading as they started to cover more ground, getting farther away from us. If you squinted, it was almost like we were back in Jesse—when it felt like we were the only two people on Earth. When it felt like we had all the time in the world.

"Which way?"

Russell pointed, and we started walking. "This is a gated neighborhood. So hopefully he's just on the street, or in someone's yard, and hasn't made it onto the main roads."

I nodded, pressing my lips together as I swung my flashlight beam over the hedges. I was determined not to speak first. Sometimes we'd hear faint calls of "Andy!" but aside from that, it was just Russell and me, walking along without speaking.

But after a few minutes of silent walking—and no dog in sight—my curiosity got the better of me. "So are these other houses . . . like your dad's?"

"I guess," Russell said, glancing over at me. "Why?"

"I was just wondering why we hadn't—you know—seen any."

There would occasionally be a house I could see, set way back from the road. But mostly it was just fences or high hedges or gates.

"Oh. Yeah, they're all pretty big. And people around here really like their privacy."

I turned my flashlight to the left side of the road, and Russell took the right. "Andy!"

"Andy!" Russell called. We both stopped, listening. I was straining my ears for the sound of a small terrier barreling toward us, but when nothing came, we started moving again.

"He does this a lot," Russell said, after we'd been walking in silence for a while.

"Runs away?"

"Yeah. My dad rescued him a few months ago, and Andy's been trying to escape ever since. He's brought trainers in, specialists, dog behavioralists—nobody can seem to get him to stop. Tidbit never goes anywhere, so my dad wasn't prepared for this."

I nodded—it was almost impossible to imagine Tidbit running away. Or running, period.

"And usually he doesn't do this more than once a day. But I guess he saw his chance."

"Has he ever come back on his own? When he's run away before?"

"No. We've always found him. And he always seems really happy to see us, and thrilled to be back home again. It's almost like he wants his freedom, but then gets turned around and can't find his way back."

"It seems like he's got a pretty good setup at your dad's. You wouldn't think he'd want to run away from all that."

"I guess if someone wants to leave, you can't convince them

otherwise. Even if they're running away from something pretty great. Anyway, after three escape attempts, my dad changed the dog's name."

"To Andy?" Russell nodded. "I don't get it."

"Well, his full name is Andy Dog-fresne."

It took me a moment, but then it clicked into place. "From *The Shawshank Redemption*?" I asked, and he nodded again. "My dad would *love* that. It's his favorite movie."

"My dad's, too."

"Really?"

"I think it's every dad's favorite movie."

"I know, I just . . ."

"He is just a dad," Russell said quietly after a few moments, like he'd understood what I'd been thinking. "I mean, despite . . ." He made a vague gesture, like it could encompass all of it—the modern art, the Grammys, the helicopter, the mansion. He sighed. "I know it can be a lot."

"Is that why?" I stopped walking and turned to him, lowering my flashlight so it made a small circle of light on the pavement. Russell stopped too.

"Why—what?"

"Why you lied to me." I could hear the hurt running through my voice like a crack. "Why you didn't tell me about him, or who you really were, or any of it."

Russell let out a shaky breath and looked down at the ground. "I think at first I just wanted . . . to not have to go into all of it. To not have to be *Wylie Sanders's son*, just for a little bit. When people find out, they look at you different, even if they don't mean to. And then when I thought you might—like me—" He glanced up for a second, meeting my eye before looking away again. "I was worried that if you found out, it might change things."

"It wouldn't have."

"But it did."

"Yeah, because you'd been *lying* to me about it! If you'd just told me from the beginning—"

"You think it would have been the same?" Russell raised his eyebrows at me. *"Really?"*

I opened my mouth to reply yes, absolutely, but then stopped. If I'd known the cute boy at the bus station was the son of a rock star, it *would* have changed things. I would have been dazzled by it. And it would have made everything a little more about his dad, and a little less about him. "Well—I certainly wouldn't have talked about your dad so much, if I'd known."

"I actually liked hearing you talk about the music. What you really thought. Most people don't tell me things like that. At least not to my face."

"Just behind your back?"

Russell laughed at that, and I felt myself fighting a laugh of my own as I tried to sort out what I was feeling. I had been *so* angry with him. And it wasn't like that had all gone away. It was more like a burn that had faded to a dull ache—you can still feel the pulse of it, you still know it's there, but it's no longer the only thing you can think about.

Russell looked at me, right in my eyes, and took a deep breath. "I really am sorry, Darcy. About the phone—about not telling you the truth. About lying. About all of it."

I nodded, finally letting myself take this in. I knew that he meant it. And most of all, I finally got that Russell not telling me the truth really wasn't about me at all. It was about him.

And also, it's what you were doing too, Didi pointed out.

I wasn't about to tell Russell it was okay—because I didn't think it was. But I wasn't going to keep being mad at him about it, holding on to this, doing what I always did—deciding something once and never changing my mind. "I know you're sorry," I finally said. "Thank you for saying it."

"Okay." Russell gave me a half smile and I gave him a nod back. It felt like a beginning—like the first piece of a rope bridge across the canyon that divided us.

"Okay." I started walking again and lifted my flashlight, sweeping it across the road.

"Do you think we could—start over?"

I shook my head. Even though I understood a little better now where Russell was coming from, I couldn't just forget everything that had come before. "I don't think so. I—" I stopped short. I'd just seen something run past my flashlight beam—a brown-and-white blur. "Did you see that?"

Russell nodded. "Andy!"

We started to run, sprinting across the road, both of us yelling for the dog who seemed to be gaining more ground than I would have thought possible in such a short time.

"ANDY!" Russell bellowed, the loudest I'd yet heard him. It seemed to work—Andy stopped in the middle of the road and looked back at us. He was still probably ten feet away, but he was *there*—the dog that everyone was looking for, just a few steps away, in the flesh. In the fur? Either way, he was there—not eaten by a coyote, not halfway to Reno—within our grasp.

Andy's tail was wagging, and he started to walk across the road toward us. "Good boy," Russell said, and I could hear the relief in his voice, exactly the same as I was currently feeling. "C'mere. I've got you." Andy was trotting toward Russell—just as headlights swept across the road, followed by a car barreling down it.

Russell darted toward the dog, but I stayed frozen in my spot on the other side. I closed my eyes tight, my heart hammering hard as I braced myself for the worst—a squeal of brakes, a frightened doggy yelp, blood on the asphalt.

"Darcy?" I opened my eyes—the car was gone, and so was Andy. "Is he . . . ?"

"It's okay," Russell said, starting to run, gesturing for me to follow. "He ran out of the way in time—I don't want to lose him again."

"Right." I was suddenly embarrassed by the way that I'd reacted when things had gotten scary. I hadn't helped or even been brave enough to watch—I'd just closed my eyes and tried to pretend it wasn't happening.

I dashed across the road, and then started sprinting full-out, trying to catch up with Russell, hoping I hadn't just cost us precious time.

"There," Russell said, sounding out of breath as we approached the gates of a mansion. They were open slightly—it didn't look like this was intentional, more like they hadn't latched properly—and I saw Andy run through and tear across the pristine lawn.

"Are we allowed to do this?" I asked as Russell squeezed through the gap in the gates and I took a step closer to follow. "Is it trespassing?"

"I think that it's okay in certain circumstances. In emergencies. Right?"

I wasn't sure about this—but I followed him through the gates. I was doing my best to look for the dog, but I was honestly distracted by the house in front of me. It made Wylie's house—which up until now was the biggest house I'd ever seen—look puny. There were a number of white marble statues placed across the lawn, but nothing as singular and striking as the balloon dog. "Who lives here?"

"Um. Well. You know Wyoming?"

"Yes?"

"This guy owns most of it."

"*What?*"

"There!" Russell pointed across the lawn, and I saw Andy sniffing around a particularly large white marble statue—it looked almost like it was a copy of a Rodin. And then I realized a moment later, my stomach plunging, that it probably *was* a Rodin. "I'm going to grab him," Russell said, pocketing his flashlight as he started to edge to the other side of the statue. "Keep him distracted."

"Okay," I said, even as I was internally screaming *How?!*

"Great."

"Andy," I called softly. The dog didn't look up, just continued sniffing, and I wondered if I'd been too quiet. I shot a glance at the house. I was all too aware that we were standing on someone else's private property. And I was sure, with a house this large, there were certainly cameras everywhere, possibly filming us right now. I saw Russell, crouching a little, come around the back of the statue.

Just as he did this, Andy's sniffing seemed to grow more focused, and I got a bad feeling. But I was too far away to stop him, and so was Russell, and as I watched in horror, the dog lifted his leg against the white marble. "No! Andy!" I hissed, but I was too far away—and too late—to stop what was already happening.

A second later, probably because there was a *dog peeing on a Rodin*—lights snapped on all over the property, making everything daylight-bright. Russell and I froze—even the dog seemed to freeze.

Russell reached out and grabbed him, and we both ran for the gate, which was slowly starting to close. If it shut before we could get through, we would be trapped in here and have to explain for the *second* time tonight why we were trespassing. Russell gestured for me to go through first, and he followed with the dog a second later, just as the gate closed behind us with a solid *thunk*.

Russell tucked Andy under his arm like a football, and without needing to discuss it first, we both started running. We didn't stop until we'd been running for a good five minutes. When we finally did slow down, my mouth was dry and I had a stitch in my side—but I was pretty sure that nobody was giving chase.

"Think we're okay?" I glanced behind us. I'd been following Russell's lead as he ducked down little winding side streets, so I was just hoping he knew how to get back home.

"Yeah, I think we're in the clear."

We slowed down, both of us out of breath. Andy didn't seem disappointed that his adventure was over—his tail wagged joyfully as he stretched up to lick Russell's face enthusiastically. "That was *not* a good boy," Russell said, lifting up the dog, but he was smiling at him. "You can't run off like that! I was so worried!" Andy's tail wagged even harder, and Russell laughed.

He held out Andy to me. "Do you mind? I want to text the family thread and let everyone know we've found him."

"Sure." I dropped the flashlight into the pocket of the sweatpants and took a step closer. I reached out for the dog, making sure to wrap my finger around his collar—blue stripes, a gold engraved disc hanging from it. I rubbed my hand over Andy's back, even as I made sure I had a firm grip on his collar. "I've got my eye on you," I assured the terrier. He just snuggled closer, his warm doggy breath on my neck.

"Great," Russell said as he looked down at his phone, which was buzzing and lighting up with texts. "Everyone knows and is heading back to the house."

"Are they all so happy?"

"Yeah." Then he frowned at his phone. "Well, except Wallace and Connor. It seems they had a bet on who would find Andy first and Connor is *not* happy he lost. Apparently, his money was on Montana." His phone buzzed again. "If we want to drop a pin, Kendrick or Bella will come pick us up. Or we could walk—it's probably about ten minutes."

"I don't mind walking. Unless you—"

"Walking is great," he said with a smile. He pocketed his phone and gestured toward the dog. "Want me to—?"

"I'm okay. I might give him to you in a little bit."

"Sounds good. We're heading this way."

I looked at Russell over the dog and gave him a tentative smile. "In that case—lead on."

CHAPTER 14

Monday
12:50 A.M.

We walked down the road to Wiley's house, falling into step together. And while Andy probably only weighed around ten pounds, I found it comforting to have his warm weight resting against me, his paws twitching as he dreamed, solid proof that he was safe and heading home.

Now that we were no longer searching, we'd both pocketed our flashlights and were walking by moonlight, the desert stars above us. Russell looked over at me and raised an eyebrow. "You were about to say something."

"When? I've been saying a lot of things."

"Before. Just as we spotted Andy. You were . . . telling me about how we couldn't start fresh. Right?"

"Oh." I rubbed one hand over Andy's head, trying to get back to the certainty I'd felt not even that long ago. I tried to find it—but it seemed out of reach. And maybe it was the relief, the lightness I felt now that we'd gotten the dog back. Or just that I had seen Russell dash in front of a car and across very expensive private property to try and save a tiny troublemaking dog. But for whatever reason, nothing was seeming as black and white right now. Or maybe it's just hard to hold a grudge when a tiny terrier is sleeping on your chest.

I knew it wouldn't be like it was back in Jesse—we were in reality now, the spell broken. And standing in the rubble of the fantasies of how it was *supposed* to be, I wanted to know the truth. Because I didn't know this Russell—the real one. But a moment later, I realized that I really wanted to.

I stopped walking, took a breath, and turned to him. "Hi."

"Hi?"

"I'm Darcy."

Understanding dawned on Russell's face, and he started to smile. "Darcy. Like the song?"

"Like the song."

"You know—my dad wrote that song."

"No way!"

"Way. I'm Russell Sanders." He held out his hand to me, and I shook it. When we touched, a thrill ran through me—but not the same one that had been there when we'd touched back in Jesse. There was memory in it now, and history.

"Nice to meet you, Russell."

"I live in LA. I have six siblings and two cats."

"Cats! You didn't mention the cats."

He gave me a guilty grimace. "I didn't mention a lot of things."

"Where do you live in LA?"

"Um—we're in Brentwood."

"Ah." I felt my cheeks get hot as I remembered how I'd described it, as a terrible place full of assholes. "Sorry about—what I said."

"I mean, you're not wrong."

"Is that why you told me you lived in Ojai?"

"We used to live there. When my mom and dad were together. It was one of my favorite times. We had this great house, and everyone pretty much accepted us as normal; we didn't get a ton of attention. And it was the three of us . . . until it wasn't. They split up when I was ten, and my mom and I moved to LA."

"And you met the Bens?"

"Exactly."

"So the Bens are real."

"Believe me, nobody could make them up."

I shook my head. "I can't believe we've both been in LA this whole time."

He laughed. "I know. It is wild to think about the fact that we've probably passed each other on the freeway."

"Or in line at Vidiots or the Bowl."

"No." Russell's voice was definitive. "I would have noticed you for sure. I would have remembered."

I raised an eyebrow at him. "Um, we *just met*."

"Right," Russell said, nodding. "Apologies."

The wind picked up, sending a chilly breeze across us and reminding me that even southern Nevada got cold at night.

"You okay? I should have brought a sweater or something. . . ."

"I'm all right," I said, "I have the dog keeping me warm. And I should get used to this, right? I'll be dealing with actual winter soon enough."

Russell grimaced. "Right."

"And you'll have it even worse in Michigan. . . ." I looked over at him sharply. "*Are* you going to Michigan?"

He let out a short laugh, the kind with no humor in it. "Yeah. I mean . . . maybe? It's . . ." His mouth twisted suddenly, like he'd just bitten into a lemon, and he took a breath. "I didn't get into the BFA program," he said quietly. "I lied about that, and

I'm sorry. I just . . . wanted it to be true, I guess. Even for a little while."

"Michigan's still a really good school, though. Even if you didn't get into the musical theater part of it."

"Yeah," Russell said, but not very convincingly. "I actually . . . That . . ." He trailed off, but I somehow knew that he was working through something—not to jump in just yet, but to let him get there. "It's what my dad and I fought about," he finally said. "At Silverspun. It's how I ended up in the bus station to begin with."

"You fought about . . . Michigan?"

"Yeah. When I first applied, I didn't get into the BFA program, but I got wait-listed for the regular admission. And then in May, I got a letter telling me I was off the wait list for the regular school. And it seemed like . . . what I should do. Like you said, it's a good school. Everyone was happy. My mom got to tell all her friends where I was going. It made sense, right?"

I nodded, recognizing something in his expression—the look of desperately trying to turn lemons into lemonade.

"So that was the plan. But then, right before my dad was taking the stage at Silverspun, I was backstage with him. He'd given me his phone to hold while he warmed up. And that's when I saw the email." He paused, then took a breath before he went on, the way you do before you jump into cold water—bracing yourself for what's coming. "It was from Michigan. They were giving him an update on their plans for the generous donation he'd pledged back in May."

"Oh."

"And it made me feel so stupid. I think that was the worst part, you know? I was so embarrassed that I'd let myself be *proud* I'd gotten in. Because of course I hadn't done it on my own. Of course my dad had pulled strings to make it happen. Of course they didn't want *me*—not without him."

"That's . . . a lot." All at once, I understood why the Russell I'd met shortly after this had all gone down wouldn't have wanted to tell me who he really was. Why being Wylie Sanders's son in that moment would be the last thing he'd want to claim.

"As soon as the show was over, I confronted him about it." Russell's voice was raw, like he was still processing this, present tense. "And the worst part was that he didn't seem to understand why I was upset—and then he was hurt because he'd done what he thought was a good thing and I was 'throwing it in his face.'" Russell stumbled over a loose piece of gravel. I reached out to him instinctively, but he righted himself and kicked the rock away angrily.

"Anyway, then I told him I didn't ask for this and I didn't want anything of his, and I didn't need him. That was me being very mature, by the way." I laughed at that, and Russell shook his head. "And then I ran out and found the buses that were going to LA, and I got on the first one."

"And *then* what happened?"

Russell stared at me for a second, then laughed. "Good one."

I walked next to him in silence for a moment as I thought through all this. I suddenly flashed to the way his face had crumpled, back in the Silver Standard office, when he'd finally pulled out his phone. I realized now what I hadn't known then—just how much it had cost him to make that call. "So did you guys—I don't know . . . clear the air?"

"I think we basically called a time-out. My dad and I don't fight much. It's like we don't have the skill set or something. So we weren't getting anywhere, just going around in circles . . ."

I nodded and we walked in silence for a moment—but the kind of silence that felt like an ellipsis, not a period.

"I just think the fundamental problem is that he doesn't understand *why* I'm upset. He just thinks I'm being ungrateful. And I *know* this is a ridiculous thing to be complaining about! I'm crazy lucky, and so privileged, and I know that. I *do*. But . . ." His voice trailed off.

"Yeah," I said slowly. I knew full well that I could just leave this here. I didn't have to talk about me, or my situation, even though they were actually kind of similar. But all at once—I *wanted* to. I took a big breath and made myself say it. "I . . . kind of know what that's like. To feel like it wasn't your choice. It *sucks*."

"It really does," Russell said, even though I could hear the question in his voice. "So is your dad *also* a huge rock star?"

"Oh, man—did I forget to mention that? So embarrassing. My name is actually Darcy Matthews Band."

Russell laughed. "You know *Band* isn't actually part of Dave's last name, right?"

"You call him *Dave*?" The second I asked it, I shook my head. "I mean, of course you do."

Russell cleared his throat. "Well—he is my godfather."

"Seriously?"

"Yep."

"Well, it was the first one I thought of. I couldn't remember Bono's real last name."

"Hewson."

"Okay. Is he also your godfather?"

"Nope. He's Connor's."

I smiled, shaking my head, and looked over at Russell. He was looking back at me steadily, like he knew I was stalling. I took a breath and twisted my fingers in the dog's fur. "It was just—I kind of understand—that is . . ." My voice was coming out halting and jerky, like a car I couldn't quite get to start. "What you were saying about Michigan," I finally said.

"Right."

"I'm kind of in a similar thing with Stanwich."

"Because you got that great financial-aid package?"

I nodded. And once again, it was like I could see my escape hatch—I could just leave this there. But I was done keeping it close to my chest. The thing that had been wrecking my sleep and churning my thoughts for months now—I wanted to share it with the one person who, I realized, might actually understand. "It's actually because of my mother."

"Your mother?"

"Yeah." I took a breath—and told him the truth. "She works in the HR department at Stanwich College."

Russell frowned. "But I thought . . . you said she was in England?"

"She *was*. But she moved back to the States last year." I started walking a little faster, and Russell sped up to keep pace with me.

"So—that was a fact about your life that *you* forgot to mention."

"Russell."

"Sorry." We walked in silence for a moment, and I could feel Russell looking over at me, waiting for me to continue, as I tried to figure out what, exactly, I wanted to say. "So your mom works at the college. And that's how you have such a great aid package. Right?"

He was laying out the facts, but I could also hear the question in his voice—he was struggling to understand why this was such a big deal. I suddenly flashed back to the Stanwich College brochure Gillian had sent to me, the Post-it with her handwriting on the front: *A perfect place for a fresh start!* As though it was that easy. As though it was a thing she got to decide.

"It's just—my mom left when I was two."

"Oh." I watched his face change, like he was shifting gears. "I—you said your parents got divorced—"

"They did. Eventually. After she walked out. She wanted to be an actress—and I guess we were holding her back?" I tried to toss this off, the way I always did when I talked about Gillian. But it wasn't working this time. The words were settling on me, heavy with their meaning. "I mean—who knows. She and my dad had me pretty young. I don't think I was part of either of their plans." I glanced over at Russell in the moonlight, his expression letting me know that it was okay, that I could go on.

"It's just . . ." This was something I tried not to think about too much but that would inevitably creep in, an insidious whisper whenever I was feeling particularly low. "It was probably me who wrecked their plans, actually. My dad trying to be a novelist, Gillian—my mother—trying to be an actress. But then I came along and my dad's temporary job became his real one. . . ." I shook my head. "Anyway. She left us and went to New York to make it—and then to London. Because there's *no* acting jobs in LA. And then once she was gone, Gillian didn't really make time for me when I was growing up. I didn't see her very much. Occasionally . . . but . . ."

"Darcy, I'm so sorry." I could practically feel Russell's eyes searching for mine, but to get through this, I needed to be looking at the asphalt or the tangly fur on Andy's back, not his blue-green eyes.

"I feel like . . . it almost would have been better if she had made it. If she had become a movie star like she always wanted. Like it at least would have *been* for something. But she just married a British guy and had three kids with him. Kids she actually takes care of."

I heard Russell draw in a sharp breath. Tears were starting to prickle my eyes and I held the dog a little closer. A part of me still couldn't believe that I was doing this—sharing things I never told people. Things I never even usually let myself *think*.

"But I was fine with how things were," I said, shifting Andy to one arm and brushing my hand across my eyes quickly. "I mean . . ." I adjusted the dog again—he was starting to get heavy.

Russell reached out and took him from me carefully, his eyes not leaving mine. He settled Andy in the crook of his arm—the dog blinked, unfazed, and yawned again—and gestured for me to keep going.

I looked up for just a moment at a cloud crossing the moon and took a breath. What was the point in lying? If I'd ever had a moment where I could be totally honest, it would seem to be now. "Okay, maybe I wasn't *fine*. I was pretty angry with her. I am," I corrected a second later. "But I'd really come to terms with it. I was okay with this status quo we'd found. You know?"

"But then something happened?"

"Yeah. When she and Ant-ony—that's her husband—"

"Why does everything sound better with a British accent?"

"It really does, doesn't it?"

"Sorry—go on."

"When they moved from the UK to Connecticut, Gillian got a job in Human Resources. At Stanwich College. And suddenly she's back in touch, insisting I apply to Stanwich. Making sure that I know that employees' kids get basically all their tuition paid."

"Right."

"And I didn't think I'd need it!" I heard the frustration explode in my voice as this came out, louder than I'd expected it to. "I applied to a whole bunch of other places—schools that I actually *wanted* to go to. And I kind of wish I would have looked at Stanwich before all this—so I would at least know how *I* felt about it."

"I get that."

"And then . . ."

"Brisket," Russell filled in, and I smiled.

"Brisket," I agreed. "So when I only got into two schools—it felt like it wasn't even really a choice. A free ride, or loans my whole life." I turned to face him more fully. "Oh, sorry. *Loans* are what you take out to pay for school when your father isn't a rock star."

"Hey now."

"And it just feels like I'm—trapped. But *then*, I feel so guilty, because I'm getting my college paid for, and who cares how it's happening, you know? I should be grateful."

"This is sounding familiar," Russell said, giving me a smile—the kind that actually makes you look sadder—over Andy's head.

"So tomorrow I start there. Just like she wanted. And me going there is like saying I forgive her, you know? That what she did is somehow okay. It's like she's bought me off, knowing I couldn't turn it down, and I just . . ." I let out a long, shaky breath. This was the problem with the whole situation—nothing was going to change. I could feel whatever I felt, but the reality was, I was getting on a plane tomorrow and this was happening. "She even offered to pick me up from the airport. Like she can just snap her fingers and pretend she's my mom."

Back when I'd first told her I'd gotten in, Gillian had sent me a series of excited emails, asking me for my flight information, saying she would come and get me, help show me around campus. I hadn't responded to any of them, and each subsequent email had fewer exclamation points, until they stopped coming altogether.

"That's a lot," Russell said quietly, echoing what I'd said to him.

"And the worst part is I'm dreading going to college. And that's not how it should be. I should be excited! I should be thrilled to be off on this whole new adventure, and instead I just want to pretend it's not happening and take a nap." I could see, down the street ahead of us, Wylie Sanders's gates. We'd almost made it back. "Like, I'm sure you would have gotten off the wait list even without your dad—"

"But I'll never know for sure."

"And I might have really liked Stanwich if I'd just come across it on my own. But now . . ."

"Yeah," Russell agreed. "I know what you mean. It's hard."

"Yeah."

We walked together, Wylie Sanders's house getting ever closer, and I realized I felt a bit . . . lighter. Not that anything had changed—I had just, in fact, been made aware of how intractable the problem actually was. But it did feel better to have shared it. That there wasn't some burden I was both hauling around with me *and* trying to keep hidden.

"Thanks for telling me," Russell said as we approached Wylie's gates.

I nodded. "And you too—for telling me, I mean."

Russell waved up at a camera, and a second later, there was a *whrrrr* of a motor and the gates started to swing slowly inward. We began our trek up the driveway, and a moment later, I realized I'd been entrusted with something. "Don't worry, I won't tell anyone about Michigan. I mean—" I flashed to the bus conference room table, C.J. pushing the document over to me. "I did sign that NDA, so I legally can't. But I wouldn't anyway."

"I never worried about that."

Russell looked over at me and gave me a smile. I returned it, holding his eye for just a moment before I looked away, back toward the house. The balloon dog was there, resplendent on the lawn. I was surprised by how happy I was to see the house—how familiar it seemed in not much time at all.

The door was unlocked, and as we made our way past the Picasso and the desert space portrait and into the main room, I was expecting that it would be full—that everyone would be hanging out in different groupings, and when they saw we'd returned bearing the dog, a cheer would go up hailing the Andy-rescuers.

But Wylie and Chloe were the only ones there—Chloe on the sofa and Wylie sitting on the ottoman coffee table across from her.

"Hey," Russell said as we stepped into the room. He held up Andy—who was wide-awake now and seemed desperate to get to Wylie, his tail wagging furiously. "Got him."

Wylie's face creased into a relieved smile, and Russell set the wriggling dog down. He crossed the room, running full-out, and leapt up onto the coffee table, climbing all over Wylie and trying to lick his face. "Okay, okay," Wylie said, even as he was laughing as he scooped up the dog. Wylie was in his pajama pants, with his reading glasses hooked over the collar of his sweatshirt. This was no longer the larger-than-life celebrity, impossibly cool, remote and removed. Wylie looked . . . like a *dad*. Like Russell had told me he actually was. Like all the rock star had been washed away and this was what was underneath.

"Good work," Chloe said, speaking quietly as she gave us a smile.

"I knew you'd be back," Wylie said. He raised the dog up above his head and Andy panted happily at him. "Tomorrow, we get you a new trainer."

"Where is everyone?" Russell asked, and I was glad, because it was exactly what I'd been wondering.

"They got rides back once we'd heard you'd got him, and then most everyone headed to bed." Wylie yawned and covered his mouth—and I noticed that even all his rings were gone. He was just wearing a normal silver band on his ring finger, nothing that would have been out of place in a suburban cul-de-sac. "Which is where I'm heading too."

"Thanks so much," Chloe said, giving me a smile, still speaking quietly. I took a step closer and saw that there was a tiny blond girl asleep on the couch in kitten pajamas next to her, thumb in her mouth and her head on Chloe's lap. "Astrid had a nightmare," she explained with a shrug.

"Funny how the only thing that seems to make the nightmare better is watching *Moana*," Wylie said, raising an eyebrow.

"She's just a girl who knows what she wants," Chloe said, smiling down at her daughter.

Russell yawned, and then a second later I did too, like I'd just been given permission. And just like that, I felt how tired I was. I'd been fine seconds earlier, but now it was like the events of the day— everything that had happened and just how long I'd been awake— were catching up with me all at once.

"Bedtime for you two as well, it looks like," Wylie said with another yawn. He glared at his son. "That one was your fault."

"Sorry," Russell said with a laugh.

"I'm heading up," Wylie said as he stood, taking Andy with him. He nodded down at Astrid. "Want me to grab her?"

"I'll trade you," Chloe said with a laugh as she scooped up Andy and kissed him on top of his head. Wylie picked up his sleeping daughter. She blinked twice but then closed her eyes again and settled herself onto Wylie's shoulder.

"Night," Wylie called as he headed toward the staircase.

"Good night," Chloe said as she followed behind him, giving my arm a squeeze as she passed me. "You have everything you need, Darcy?"

"And more," I assured her. "Thank you so much."

"Coming, Russ?" Wylie asked.

"I'm just going to walk Darcy to her guesthouse," Russell said, and Wylie headed up the staircase, waving with his free hand. "Um," he said, turning to me. "If that's . . . okay?"

Only a little while ago, I would have said that I'd be fine on my own. A little while ago, he wouldn't have offered. But now . . . I nodded.

Chloe shot me the tiniest of looks, one eyebrow raising up a half centimeter. "Night, guys," she said as she headed toward the stairs. "Thanks for bringing me home, mates!" she added in an Australian accent, making Andy wave as they disappeared from view.

I turned to Russell. "The dog is Australian?"

"Chloe seems to think so. When she does his voice, that's how he always sounds. I blame *Bluey*."

We walked to my guesthouse and climbed the steps to the front door together. Russell looked tired; his hair was sticking up in every direction. It suddenly seemed inconceivable to me that I hadn't known him when I woke up this morning. Because it felt like I could close my eyes and sketch his face from memory if I had a piece of paper. And any artistic talent.

I wasn't mad at him anymore—but I also couldn't imagine myself kissing him again. That felt like it belonged to a whole other version of me.

"So," I said as the silence between us started to stretch on. Like we were both trying to find our way in this new version of things, without a dog to chase or a destination to walk to or anything to distract us. "Thanks for walking me back."

"Well, it's a dangerous yard. Lots of hazards . . . rogue Great Danes . . ." Russell smiled and took a tiny step toward me. And for just a second, I hesitated. But then I stepped back.

"I think we should be friends," I said, and Russell's smile faltered a little.

"Friends?"

"Just friends," I said firmly.

"We could be . . . more than that?" he asked, his voice tentative. "I mean . . ." He glanced toward the pool, and I wondered if he, in that moment, was having the same flashback I was. A few hours ago, at the much less glamorous pool of the Silver Standard, my legs wrapped around his waist, the feeling that we couldn't get enough of each other.

"I'm leaving tomorrow. And you're starting school. And . . ." For just a second, I thought about trying to tell him. About the movies, and what I'd so foolishly believed about one magical night, and people being meant for each other, and love at first sight. Since I knew now that all of that was fake, getting a friend—an actual friend—out of all of this seemed like a great bargain. "It's just for the best."

Russell looked at me for a moment longer, then gave me a smile that didn't quite reach his eyes. "Okay," he said with a nod. "Sounds good."

"Okay," I said, nodding back.

He started to walk down the steps, then paused at the bottom one and looked up at me. "Sleep well, Darcy."

"You too, Russell. I'll see you tomorrow."

"I think it's already tomorrow," he said with a smile as he walked down the steps. "I'll see you later today."

I nodded and opened the door of the guesthouse and stepped inside. Before I closed the door I saw Russell walking across the lawn, breaking into a half jog as he got closer to the house.

Inside, I poured myself a glass of water, found a charger in the kitchen drawer, then plugged in my phone. I had texts from Katy and Didi that I knew I had to respond to, but at the moment, I didn't feel up to getting into everything—and I was sure both of them were long asleep. Instead, I just texted that Silverspun hadn't turned out how I had expected, but I was okay, and that we'd catch up tomorrow. Then I turned off the lights in the kitchen and living room and walked down the hallway, glancing at the Russell picture as I went—but not letting myself linger by it too long.

I saw that my duffel was there, and my clothes were washed and folded neatly on the bed—or at least, they probably had been at some point. Now, there was a Great Dane lying across them.

I eased them out from under Tidbit, grabbed my toiletry bag, and got ready for bed.

Since Tidbit was literally taking up the entire bed, I decided to let sleeping dogs lie, and gave his head a scratch before I headed into the other bedroom. This one was done in greens, with a huge photo of the Central Park Carousel, the lights slightly blurred, hung up above the bed.

I got under the covers and turned off the lights, my eyes closing as soon as my head hit the pillow. But a few moments later, the door swung open and Tidbit was standing in the doorway, looking at me with an expression I could only describe as *betrayed*.

"Um," I said to the dog. "Sorry. I—" But before I could finish, he'd clambered onto the bed and curled up—well, as much as he was able—along the foot of it, his giant head resting against my leg.

After a moment, I realized there was something so comforting about it—the warmth of him, the weight on my feet, his steady, snuffling breathing. I closed my eyes again, and felt myself falling asleep in the most literal sense—dropping into it as though from a great height.

And when I opened my eyes again, the sheets were twisted around my legs, the dog was snoring on the pillow next to me, and it was morning.

III
Waking Up in Vegas

I hadn't been driving on the freeway long when the line of cars ahead of me slowed, then slowed even more, and then finally came to a halt. It was early afternoon on a random Friday—the traffic shouldn't have been a problem, but welcome to Southern California. My dad, for a while, had done a bit about how he thought everyone's car out here should be outfitted with a little ticker where they could type in exactly where you were going, and why. So when you found yourself in a random, not-rush-hour traffic jam, you could at least understand the reason it was happening.

I checked the clock, and tried to assure myself that I was still okay on time—that I could still make it. But after everything—after all my big talk about schedules and commitments and timing, after all the texts to organize this weekend—I really didn't want to be the one who showed up late.

My phone buzzed in the console, and I saw Romy's number pop up on the screen. I hesitated for a moment, then pressed ignore. There would be a lot more Romy in my future, so I wasn't sure I wanted to engage with her sooner than I had to. And if it actually was an emergency, I reasoned, she'd leave a voicemail. It was enough that she'd been texting me constantly all week—I didn't need more of it.

I waited a second—no voicemail—then switched off the podcast I'd been listening to. I turned on the radio—Mariah Carey was playing, no surprise—and then switched to my most recent playlist.

I scrolled until I found my favorite song—the one that had been in heavy rotation for the last month. I pushed play, then rolled my window down.

I looked at the map and did a quick calculation in my head. I was okay on time. And by the end of today, I'd be in Nevada—and once I got there, everything would be smooth sailing. Hopefully.

The car in front of me started to move, and I turned up the volume. "Darcy!" Wylie Sanders wailed through the Prius's not-great speakers. I pressed on the gas and drove forward.

CHAPTER 15

Monday

6:30 A.M.

I stood by the door of the guesthouse, an impatient Great Dane next to me, feeling a distinct sense of déjà vu as I looked around, trying to remember if I'd forgotten anything.

After I'd woken up, I'd collected my—fully charged!—phone and saw an email from my dad. He had sent a picture of a giant fish he'd caught with my uncle, and told me he was planning on being home by three, but he'd call when he hit the road. He also mentioned that he hoped I'd gotten home okay last night, and that he couldn't wait to hear about the show.

My heart was hammering as I typed out a reply—well aware that as far as my dad was concerned, I'd arrived last night and had just been home this whole time. I kept things vague and upbeat, saying I was good and looking forward to seeing him later this afternoon. Then I'd found the bus terminal and looked up departure times from Vegas to Union Station. I was relieved to see they left almost every hour, but just to be safe, I knew I wanted to be on an early one—nine was probably the latest I could push it if I wanted to beat my dad home. I wasn't worried about missing my red-eye to New York—I didn't need to be at LAX until ten tonight, and that was probably even a little earlier than necessary.

Once I felt like I had a handle on what needed to happen—an Uber to the bus station, bus to LA, arrival home before my dad—I set my phone aside. Of course, there was a second part of my itinerary that came after I got home. I had to finish packing, and then my dad and I had a plan. Dinner at Town, our favorite pizza place, the one we'd been eating at on Friday nights since I could remember. Then back home to load up my bags. And we'd swing by the In-N-Out in Raven Rock for milkshakes for the drive to LAX. We'd park and my dad would go into the airport with me as far as he was allowed, to see me off. And then . . . I would get on the red-eye that would take me to the East Coast, and college.

I took a quick shower and got dressed (mentally thanking Chloe for the incredible luxury of clean clothes). Then I packed my things, grabbed a banana and a little bag of almonds from the basket in the kitchen, and dropped them, along with my charged phone, into my canvas bag. I picked up my duffel and tent, and gathered up the clothes Chloe had loaned me. Then I headed for the door, the dog trotting along with me.

I turned and gave the guesthouse one last look. I was still amazed that it somehow conjured up *New York* for me so easily, despite the fact that I'd only been there once in my life. And even though this shouldn't have been a surprise, it hit me that starting *tomorrow* I would be living somewhere that was only an hour from New York City. And as I looked at the city's iconography all around me, I felt a little excited thrill in my chest thinking it.

When Tidbit started to whine quietly—it seemed like the canine equivalent of clearing one's throat—I headed out and closed the door to the guesthouse behind me. Then I walked across the damp grass, Tidbit practically prancing as he led the way toward the main house. I'd leave a note on the counter, saying goodbye—and I'd just cross my fingers that the security people would be working this early and would see me when I waved, to open up the gates.

I pulled open the glass door to the kitchen, then closed it immediately once Tidbit and I were inside. He made a beeline for his food and water bowls, and I smiled as I realized this was probably why he'd been so eager to get indoors.

"Morning."

I jumped, turned, and saw that Wylie was sitting at the table with the newspaper and a cup of coffee. "Oh," I said, looking around. *Moana* was playing on the giant TV, but silently. I didn't understand why this was happening until I took a step closer and saw that Astrid and Artie were sitting side by side on the couch, sharing a bowl of dry Cheerios, watching the movie with headphones on and rapt expressions.

"It's our deal," Wylie said, and I turned back to him. "They can watch *Moana* as long as I don't have to hear it."

"I thought it was good," I offered, then a second later wondered if I should really be giving my opinion about a musical to a professional musician.

"I liked it too," he said with a grimace. "The first fifty times. It gets old after that."

I smiled. "I bet."

"You're up early," he said as he stood up from the table and padded into the kitchen. This morning, he looked halfway between the dad I'd seen last night and the rock star who'd first answered the door. He was wearing black jeans and a white tank top with a gray, soft-looking cardigan over it. He was barefoot, with a single necklace—the one that looked like a shark's tooth, edged in diamonds—and only three rings. "Sleep okay?"

I'd put on my now-clean jean shorts, a tank top I'd tie-dyed in Didi and Katy's backyard at the beginning of the summer, and over it, the long-sleeve Silverspun T-shirt I'd paid an exorbitant price for. But as I looked at Wylie, pouring himself more coffee, I was immensely relieved I wasn't wearing my Nighthawks sweatshirt, and we weren't having to have this conversation while I wore a garment with his face on it. He looked at me expectantly, and I realized a beat too late that he'd asked me a question.

"Yes," I said quickly. "I did." Tidbit shook himself and wandered away, and I was suddenly very aware that there was nobody else here—well, except for the two small children currently considering the coconut. That it was just me and Wylie Sanders, having a conversation.

"Early bird, huh?" Wylie asked as he opened the hidden fridge and pulled out a carton of milk. "I wish you'd give my kids some pointers. Well," he amended as he opened the milk and nodded toward the couch, "not these two. They're up at the crack of dawn every day. But these days you're lucky if you see Russell before noon. Coffee?"

"Please," I said, realizing as he said it just how good it sounded. I was also heartened to see the milk out—I liked my coffee about half milk and half coffee, and when I ordered at Starbucks, I was a sucker for the seasonal, pure sugar, no-coffee-required kinds of drinks. I set my things down by the door and crossed over to join him in the kitchen.

Wylie nodded and pulled a mug down from a cabinet. "I'm not really an early riser most of the time," I said, not wanting to take credit where it wasn't due. "I just needed to get moving—I have to get to the Vegas bus station so I can catch my bus back to LA."

Wylie's brows drew together as he poured me a cup of coffee, too fast for me to tell him to only fill it halfway. "Do you want to ride with us? We're flying back to LA tonight."

"Oh, really?" A moment later, I realized what he meant. He wasn't offering me a seat on a Southwest flight. He was offering me a seat on his *private jet.*

We call them PJs, Katy said, her tone blasé.

We really don't, Didi retorted, sounding appalled.

"That's—so nice of you. I wish I could," I said, really meaning it. I had a feeling it would probably be the last time a world-famous rock star was going to offer me a ride on a private plane. Or, if I was feeling optimistic about the kind of crowd I'd be running with in the future, the last time for a *while.* "But I actually have to get back sooner than that. I'm taking a red-eye tonight."

Wiley nodded. "Ah. I see. Milk?"

"Thank you," I said, crossing over to the counter to pick up my cup of coffee. He'd left the milk out, and I used the moment that he turned to open the fridge as my opportunity to pour some—okay, half—of the coffee out and fill the rest up with milk.

"What time is your bus?"

"I was thinking I'd get the eight o'clock? But I could probably also make the nine." I pulled out my phone. "Let me see how long the Uber's going to take."

"We can get someone to drive you."

"Oh—thank you so much," I said, surprised. Were all rock stars this generous with offering up forms of transportation? Between this, the plane offer, *and* the helicopter, it really was above and beyond. "But I can just get a car."

"It's not a problem," Wylie said, shaking his head. "Honestly, we try to limit the Ubers that come to the house—trying to keep the address under wraps."

"Oh," I said, nodding like this was just a normal thing. I thought about the gates, the *WS* three feet high. "I mean, I guess you could pretend it was someone else's house? Like . . ." I racked my brain for a celebrity. "Will Smith? Um . . . Wallace Shawn?"

Wylie grinned, and there was suddenly a flash of the rock star I'd seen onstage yesterday, like he'd just flipped a switch or put on a costume. "That's an excellent idea. I'll start spreading the rumor that *Wallace Shawn* has a spread outside Vegas." I laughed at that. "But in all seriousness, it's a bit of a trek, and I'd feel better about you not riding in a car with a stranger. If anything happened, your mom would never forgive me." He opened the secret fridge and emerged with a glass bottle of orange juice, the kind that looked fresh-squeezed. His smile faltered as he looked at me. "Did I say something wrong?"

"No," I said quickly, wishing my face hadn't betrayed me. Usually it was only people who knew me well who were able to read my expressions—it was why Didi always wanted to play poker with me. "I just—my mom isn't exactly . . ." I took a breath. "She lives in Connecticut." It was one thing to tell Russell all about my tangle of feelings about Gillian. I wasn't sure I really wanted to burden a literal member of the Rock & Roll Hall of Fame with them. "So I'm not really sure she'd be weighing in on Ubers. That's all."

"Got it," Wylie said, but he gave me a look that meant he'd clocked something and was putting a pin in it. "But we'll get you a ride to the bus station, deal? And this way you'll have time for breakfast. Are you hungry?" He set the orange juice on the table and then opened a different cabinet—one that, to my complete shock, contained a *second* fridge. How many fridges did this kitchen have? And why were they all disguised as something else?

"Um." I didn't know what the breakfast protocol was in a place where dinner was eaten at ten at night. I also didn't want *Wylie Sanders* to feel like he had to sit here and talk to me, just because I happened to wander into the kitchen before anyone else. He probably had much more important things to do. But the truth was, I *was* pretty hungry. "I am, actually."

"Great." A second later, he was setting the table—two plates, glasses, linen napkins, and forks. I sat down as Wylie headed back to the kitchen, pulling a carton of eggs out of one fridge, then crossed to the *other* fridge and took out the milk and butter. "Anything you don't eat?"

"I eat everything. Well, except oysters."

"Great," he said, huffy, as he picked up a dish towel and then threw it down again. "There go my plans for breakfast oysters. Thanks a lot."

I laughed. "Sorry to mess up your plans."

He pulled a spatula from a white ceramic crock of them sitting on the counter and pointed at me with it. "Don't let it happen again."

"I won't," I assured him. "Can I help?"

"Hm?" Wylie asked, turning around. "You say something?"

"Oh—nothing," I said, suddenly embarrassed. "Never mind."

"This ear's not so great," he said, pointing to his left one with a fork, and I remembered he'd done something like that when I'd first come into the house—back when I'd been trying to leave it immediately. "Blame three decades in front of terrible drummers. Just give me a second."

"Sure." As though they knew food was incoming, both dogs wandered into the kitchen, looking hopeful. I picked up Andy and gave him a scratch under the chin. Tidbit let out a huffy sigh, so I reached over with my free hand and gave his velvety ears a scritch too. Then I took out my phone and scrolled through my texts.

Didi

Happy Monday! It's justifiable homicide when your roommate is totally unreasonable, right? No jury would convict me. I'm feeling good about my chances.

Katy

NO. Also don't put this stuff in writing, because what if your roommate gets in an ACTUAL accident and then you have these incriminating texts? Haven't you ever heard a podcast?

Also Darce, we need to hear all about the festival!

Didi

We really do. Was Romy as bad as we'd predicted?

Katy

Was she even WORSE?

Didi

Oh god, was she?

I was about to reply, my hands hesitating over the keys. But then a second later, I locked my phone and set it down. There was no way I could go into everything—not here, not right now, while Wylie Sanders made me eggs a few feet away, humming what I was pretty sure was the bass line from "Saturday Night Falls" under his breath. This was a much longer conversation, and definitely not a text conversation—I'd have to get a FaceTime date on the books with them.

"Here we go," Wylie said, coming over to the table with a

skillet. I set Andy down, and he and Tidbit immediately crowded around Wylie, looking up at him expectantly.

He spooned what looked like a scramble onto my plate—eggs and tomatoes and onions and . . . mushrooms, maybe? It smelled delicious. He served himself some as well, then returned the skillet to the stove and came back a moment later bearing butter, jam, and a plate stacked with toast.

"This looks amazing," I said, placing my napkin on my lap. "Thank you so much."

"It's no trouble. Happy that you could stay over, Darcy." He paused, and it was like I could practically see my name lingering between us for a second. "It really is something that you're named after that song. It's one of my favorites, you know."

I nodded, even though I wasn't sure if he meant the name or the song. "I'm sure lots of people were named Darcy because of it, right? Like how after it came out, all these girls were named Jolene."

"You're too young for that reference."

"My dad told me about it. He's the one who picked Darcy."

"He's a fan?"

"The biggest," I said as I grabbed a piece of toast. For just a moment, I wished he could have been there. I knew it wasn't possible, but I would have loved it if he could have somehow just appeared at this kitchen table, getting to have eggs and toast with his idol too.

"What's his name?"

"Ted Milligan. Technically Edward, but he goes by Ted."

"And what does Ted do?"

"He's in advertising. Milligan Concepts."

Wylie nodded and raised his mug to me. "Well—tell Ted I appreciate the support."

"I love your music too," I said, all in a rush, like maybe I shouldn't be saying this. Was it breaking some kind of unspoken social contract? Did this only work if we pretended that he wasn't a gigantic megastar? "My dad played the Nighthawks all the time, so I just grew up on it. And I feel like I would have loved it even if I hadn't been named for the song, but since I was, it just made it so much more special. . . ." I felt my face get hot and I looked down and concentrated on buttering a piece of toast.

"Well, I appreciate that. Darcy." He smiled, then leaned forward. "If you want—I can tell you something. But only if you promise to only tell your dad, and nobody else."

"I mean, I did sign that NDA," I said, my voice faux serious. "Should we add an addendum?"

"I'll call C.J.," he said, matching my tone. "So." He speared a forkful of eggs but didn't eat them yet. "It's about the song, and where the name Darcy came from." He took a bite, then rested his fork across his plate. "If you're *sure* you want to know. This is real privileged information here."

"I do want to know."

"Okay. But this is just between you and me. And Ted. Right?"

"He won't say anything," I said, meaning it. Partially because I wasn't actually sure I was going to be able to tell my dad about any of this. I couldn't go into part of it without going into all of it. But was I really going to be able to keep this from him? That I'd not only *met* Wylie Sanders—which, twelve hours ago, would have been miracle enough—but that I'd talked to him, and stayed in his guesthouse, and eaten his very good breakfast scramble?

Wylie nodded, took a sip of his coffee, and then a deep breath, like he was preparing himself. "So it was about this girl—this was after Paula and I split, but before I got together with Kenya. I wrote the song all about what I was feeling for her, and I wrote it with her name. But at the last minute, in the booth, I changed my mind. It didn't seem fair to her—to say in a song what I hadn't yet told her in person. To put it all under a giant microscope."

"That makes sense."

"So I'm in the studio, I have the song, but I need a new name. And Laura, the sound engineer, was reading while she waited for me to get my act together—*Pride and Prejudice*. And I looked at the book, and just like that, there it was—Darcy. We did three takes, and had it in the can."

"So . . . it came from Mr. Darcy," I said, feeling like I needed to clarify this. "As in . . . *Fitzwilliam* Darcy?" I was a huge fan of the book and movie adaptations, but it had literally never occurred to me that this was where my name was from.

Wylie laughed. "Yep. You don't meet many Fitzwilliams these days."

"Sure don't." I kept my voice light even though my head was spinning as I tried to synthesize this information. It turned out, in the end, that all the people who asked if I'd been named after an Austen character had actually been right. "Wow. That's—not what I was expecting."

Wylie's brows drew together. "Should I not have told you?"

"No," I said after a moment. "I'm glad I know." As I said it, I realized it was true. How often do you get the origin of your name from the person responsible for it? And I did like the story behind it—that it had been created out of Wylie's integrity, wanting to shield this woman from too much scrutiny. And that the song had been more than just a love song, like I'd always assumed—it was a message in a bottle, intended for one recipient.

And I couldn't help liking that I was one of only a handful of people in the world who knew the truth about the song—and, in turn, my name. In the future, when people would inevitably ask me where my name came from, I would just tell them what I'd always told people—that it was from the song. But I would know the real story, from the only person who could have given it to me. "I feel like someone just told me who 'You're So Vain' is about."

Wylie laughed, shaking his head. "Your dad raised you right, that's for sure."

"He would very much appreciate you saying that."

"Feel free to pass it along."

I speared some eggs, then set my fork back down. "Wait, so what happened? With the girl who wasn't Darcy?"

Wylie leaned back in his chair, holding his mug. "Nothing really ever happened. We had one night—one of those epic dates." He smiled, and it was like I could sense that he was leaving this kitchen, this table, Nevada—and going to wherever this memory was located. "It was one of those dates that goes all day, and into the night, and you just have *so* much to say . . ."

"Um." I rolled up the corners of my napkin and then flattened them down on the table. "Right."

"But then . . ." The faraway smile that had been on Wylie's face dimmed out. "I don't know. It was almost like we couldn't move on from it. Like we'd had this perfect moment, and we didn't want to do anything to mess it up. Which is what I wrote the song about— the wonderful date, then followed by nothing."

"Oh." That was not how I'd expected the story to go, honestly. I sat with it for a moment. Wylie was staring down into his coffee cup, and in the light streaming in through the floor-to-ceiling windows, I could see the lines on his face. I somehow knew that he was no longer on that epic date with the girl, but back here, in the aftermath of what might have been.

"It's always better to know," he said after a moment. "You can't keep something on the shelf just to look at it. Even if it's not going to work—it's better to find out."

"Did she ever know? That 'Darcy' was about her?"

Wylie looked up from his mug and gave me a sad smile. "I thought it was going to be my big, grand gesture," he said. "But when I gave her a copy of the song—and told her—she'd moved on. And that was that." He shook his head and gave me a slightly forced smile. "Sorry—I thought I was just going to tell you the story of your name. I didn't mean to go into all that. . . ." He took a sip of his coffee, and it was like he was trying to shake himself out of this. "It all worked out for the best." He looked around, and it was like I could see him taking it in—mansion, dogs, two kids watching *Moana*. "Because if something had happened with us, I wouldn't have met Kenya, which means no Wallace, and probably not any of the rest of the monsters, either. But still . . ."

"What's that quote?" I asked. It was one of the ones that Katy really wanted to use for her senior yearbook quote, when she was in the throes of a breakup, and Didi and I had forcefully talked her out of it. "About how the saddest words are *It might have been*."

Wylie smiled. "Well, it's certainly true. I don't know the quote, though, but I bet Russell does."

"He does love his facts." I smiled as I thought about it—about how much I'd liked the way his face had lit up when he had one to share.

Wylie gestured to the table, and it was like we were turning a page, changing the subject. "Need anything else?"

"No," I said, snagging another piece of toast. "This is all great. Thanks so much."

Wylie leaned back in his chair and took a sip of coffee. "You said you're taking the red-eye? Tonight?" I nodded. "Where are you going?"

"New York," I said. "Well—Connecticut, but I'm flying into JFK. I start school—orientation is on Wednesday."

"Where are you going?"

"Stanwich College."

"Like Montana's ex!" He nodded, then shuddered. "She was kind of a nightmare, actually. You're not studying physics, are you?"

"Not planning on it," I assured him.

"Oh, good." He leaned back in his chair—or tried to, but Tidbit had placed both his paws on the arm of Wylie's chair and was staring at him with a forlorn expression. Andy was jumping up and down next him, clearly trying to achieve the height Tidbit had. These were two dogs who'd clearly waited what they thought was an unacceptably long time for food. "Okay, you beggars." He placed some eggs on the floor and the dogs snapped them up. "Too bad you're not driving."

"To *Connecticut*?"

My horror must have been apparent on my face, because Wylie laughed. "What? There's nothing better than a road trip."

"I guess?" I'd never really been on one, unless you counted driving up to San Francisco or visiting my uncle in Fresno. "That just seems like kind of a long one."

Wylie shook his head. "The longer the better, as far as I'm concerned. There wouldn't be the Nighthawks without a road trip."

"What do you mean?"

"That's where we first started talking about what a band could be—on a drive from Colorado to Chicago. And we were so excited, and so fired up, that once we got there we turned around again so we could keep the conversation going. It's the trip that changed all our lives."

"Well—maybe you and Russell can drive to Michigan?" The second I said it, Wylie's face changed, and I remembered, a moment too late, that this was not an uncontroversial topic.

"So you know . . . about Michigan." He studied me over the rim of his coffee cup. "I guess Russell told you?"

"He told me that he wrote a musical, but maybe that it needed more work? That he didn't get into any of his BFA programs." I looked at him and took a breath. "And . . . he mentioned the donation."

"Yeah," Wylie said with a deep sigh. "Probably I went about that the wrong way. He's really talented, you know. But he's the only one of my kids who's interested in music, which also makes it harder."

I nodded toward the couch and the three-year-olds. "Well—I mean, so far."

He gave me a ghost of a smile. "It's a good point. I don't know. I was trying to help, but clearly I made things worse."

"I think," I said, after I'd verified that Russell wasn't lurking in the doorway of the kitchen, listening in, "that the whole thing made Russell think that you didn't believe in him. Like you didn't trust that he would get in on his own."

"Of course I didn't think that." Wylie looked so alarmed by this, I knew he was telling the truth. "He's such a smart kid—"

"But now he'll never know," I pointed out. "If he could have done it on his own."

"I never thought of it like that—that he would think I didn't believe in him. I guess I just . . ." He hesitated, then ran a hand through his hair, his rings glinting under the kitchen lights. "It's stupid," he muttered, a flush starting to appear in his cheeks, which was truly shocking. Wylie Sanders, rock legend, was embarrassed to tell something to *me*?

"I'm sure it's not."

"It's just . . . Russell's so smart—all my kids are. They get it from their moms. But I was always terrible at school, I never went to college. . . . I thought that this was my way of contributing something. So that I would almost get to be there too, the only way I could . . ."

I shook my head. "It's not stupid. I just think that maybe . . . you should be telling this to Russell."

Wylie flashed me a smile. "I always knew you were smart." He shook his head. "I know I messed up. But I'm a parent. And you start out protecting your kids from everything—baby-proofing the house and making sure their laces are tied tight. And it's not like that goes away, even as they get older. And if you can step in—it's really hard not to."

I suddenly flashed back to the note Gillian had attached to the Stanwich College brochure—the way she'd reached out to me, extended a hand for a fresh start.

Maybe it hadn't been a bribe, or a trap. Maybe it had been a gift, imperfectly wrapped.

Wylie looked down into his cup. "Want another?"

"Um." I glanced at mine. "Yes? But just fill it halfway? I like a little coffee with my milk." He laughed at that and picked up my mug, navigating around the ever-hopeful dogs as he made his way back to the coffee maker.

I glanced outside, to the day that was dawning over Nevada, the light starting to stretch across the pool. Wylie returned to the table with a half-filled cup of coffee and a bottle of whole milk. I poured some into my cup as Wylie sat back down at the table.

"I do need to make sure I talk to him, so we can clear the air before he goes home," Wylie said, and I didn't have to ask which *he* Wylie was talking about. "You never leave a fight unresolved, you know?"

I nodded, even though I was thinking about Gillian and the things I'd said to her over the phone, the way I'd hung up on her.

"What?" Wylie asked, mug halfway to his lips as he looked at me.

"Oh—nothing," I said quickly, wishing once again that my expressions weren't quite so easily read on my face. "I just . . . kind of had a fight with my mother last night. And we didn't—you know, resolve things. That's all."

"Ah." Wylie sipped his coffee. "Is your mom in advertising too?"

"Oh—no. She's in HR. She wanted to be an actress, but it didn't work out. And she and my dad are divorced."

"That's hard," he said softly, turning his mug in his hands.

"I know. But I promise I'm fine."

"No," he said, looking up at me. "I mean—I'm sure you are." He gave me a quick smile. "I don't doubt that. You seem more than fine, and with a stellar musical education, to boot. I just meant . . ." He took a big breath, then let it out. "It's hard not to achieve your dream."

This was so unexpected that I just blinked at him for a moment.

"I'm the lucky one," he went on. "And I know it. I get to do what I love, and I'm thankful every day. But three steps in the wrong direction, a missed alarm clock, a bad show . . ." He snapped his fingers. "Poof. Just like that, all this never happens."

"But it did happen."

"But it doesn't for most people. Just think about all those songs we never got to hear. My first bassist—"

"Dustin Henry," I said automatically.

Wylie grinned at me. "I bet my own kids wouldn't have been able to make that pull. I knew I liked you, Darcy."

"Call me Fitzwilliam." He laughed at that. "Dustin Henry?" I prompted.

"Right! Dustin quit the band before we hit. He wanted to sing his own songs, thought we were holding him back." Wylie shrugged. "But then he was never able to make it happen, and I saw it eat him up. If you go off and chase your dream, the longer it doesn't happen, the harder it gets. And then to go home and admit you failed—that one is hardest of all, isn't it? To accept you can't do the thing you want to do the most."

I shook my head automatically, already starting to push back against this in my mind. But even as I was trying to deny it, I realized I'd never once thought about this from Gillian's point of view. "It's just . . . ," I started, as I heard loud, clompy footsteps from upstairs.

"Where is my *towel*?" someone yelled.

"The hordes descend," Wylie said, shaking his head.

"Thank you for breakfast."

Wylie smiled at me. It was the smile I'd seen last night, the one that seemed real, not a trace of rock star in it. He raised his mug to me. "Thanks for the conversation."

"Is there coffee?" Connor asked, coming into the kitchen. He was followed by Sydney, who was trailed by a yawning, dark-haired kid who still looked half-asleep. I was startled by the presence of yet another Sanders—like this house was a clown car that was just going to keep discharging people long after you'd thought it was impossible—until I remembered that I had heard about Sydney and Connor's son.

"Dashiell!" Astrid yelled. She paused *Moana* and yanked off her headphones.

"Morning, Aunt Astrid," Dashiell said with a yawn, and Astrid grinned.

"Want to go swimming? Want to watch a movie?"

"Listen to the dream I had last night!" Artie yelled as the kids—who were, somehow, aunt, uncle, and nephew—convened on the couch.

"Morning, all," Wallace said as he sailed into the kitchen, wearing a robe with a sleep mask pushed up on his forehead. "Who made coffee?"

"What's for breakfast?" Chloe asked as she followed behind Wallace, in workout clothes, her hair up in a ponytail. Andy hurled himself at her, tail wagging wildly, and she scooped him up. "Good morning, sunshine," she said to the dog. She glanced across at her children. "They're rotting their brains, I take it?"

"*Moana*," Wylie replied.

"Again?"

"There will never be anything else. I'm just resigned to it."

"Morning," Kenya said as she came into the kitchen through the sliding glass door. She was wearing a cover-up over a bathing suit. "Anyone want an early swim? The water's perfect."

"Please tell me there's coffee," Wallace said, pushing himself up to sit on the kitchen island. He yawned hugely. "I was up late trying to talk to Alyssa."

Kenya sighed. "You two need to get on a better schedule if you're going to make it work."

"Of course we're going to make it work," Wallace said, but I noticed that a worried expression had crossed his face, a flicker of doubt he was clearly working to keep at bay.

I put my plate and mug in the sink—considering the fridges had been a mystery, I wasn't even going to *attempt* to locate a dishwasher—and then pulled out my phone to check the time. Wylie, clocking this, gave me a nod.

"Let me see about finding you a ride," he said, getting up from the table. "You have all your luggage?" I nodded toward the stuff I'd left by the door. "Good."

"Um," I said, looking around, not exactly sure who to address this to, "if one of you could tell Russell goodbye for me?" I thought about saying I could text him, only to realize with a shock that I didn't have his phone number. Or email address, for that matter. "Or I could write a note . . ."

"Go tell him yourself," Chloe said, nodding upstairs.

"Really?" I looked down at my phone again. "It's kind of early."

"I know he wouldn't want to miss you," Wylie said, giving me a smile. "Third door on the left once you hit the top of the stairs."

I thought about protesting, saying that it was okay, that I didn't want to wake him up. After all, we'd had a nice goodbye last night in front of the guesthouse. But would this seem bizarre to everyone else here? Or even insulting to these people who'd offered me so much hospitality? And then a second later, I realized that I did want to see him one last time.

When I reached the top of the staircase I noticed this floor had a homier feeling—the downstairs might have been more impressive, but this was clearly where people actually *lived*. There were shoes and sweaters and dog-eared books on the couch in the little living room, and a scuff along one wall. The art here was less grand—more family portraits and drawings that looked like they'd been done by the younger kids. I paused in front of a large, framed black-and-white picture.

It was a family portrait. Everyone was wearing white, posed on a beach somewhere. Nobody seemed to be looking in the same direction, or at the camera, but somehow, despite that, you could feel the love and fun and chaos practically jumping out of the frame. I was a little taken aback by the sheer *number* of people in this picture—all these adults, all these kids—and how many of them I recognized. My dad and I had never had a formal family picture taken, I realized as I looked at it. Maybe because there's no point when your family portrait can fit in a selfie.

Or, you know, Katy said. *Not.*

You do *have more family than just Ted,* Didi pointed out.

I looked at the picture for a moment longer, finding Russell in the bottom right of the frame. He was standing next to a striking-looking woman—she had dark hair with a silver streak running through it. His mom, presumably—as the picture had been taken she was reaching up to flatten his hair.

I smiled, then headed down the hallway, stopping in front of the third door. I knocked, but nothing happened—no sound from inside. I pressed my ear to the wood, but all I could hear was the faint sound of ocean waves crashing. I knocked once more, this time pushing the door open as I did and just hoping this wasn't some giant violation of his privacy.

"Russell?" I called quietly as I stuck my head in. I blinked, trying to let my eyes adjust to the dimness of the room.

It was a large space, the blinds drawn against the morning sun. Not that I'd had a ton of experience seeing boys' rooms, but this one seemed neater and more picked up than I would have expected. There was an armchair in the corner, with the clothes Russell had been wearing last night—the shorts and button-down—draped over the arm of it. On the wall, there was a large framed piece of art—as my eyes adjusted I could see that it was a vintage-looking poster. *A Little Night Music*, it read. On the dresser, I could see a framed picture of Russell between two guys, one tall and one short—and I smiled as I realized that these must be the aforementioned Bens.

All the furniture in the room was dark wood, and there were rugs scattered artfully across the wood floors. The whole thing seemed really pulled together—sophisticated and adult, and I was suddenly embarrassed about my bedroom back at home, with my floral print comforter I'd picked out at Target when I was twelve and then never changed. I still had boy band and movie posters tacked up on my walls, and my mirror was crammed with Polaroids of me and my friends.

There was a king-size bed pushed against the far wall, with a blue-and-white-striped blanket on top—and Russell asleep underneath it. He was sleeping on his side, his back to me, facing the wall. The covers were pulled up around him, his breath rising and falling steadily.

As I looked at him, at his chest gently rising and falling, I knew I was seeing a part of him that was private and personal. This was Russell as his unguarded self, the person he was when he just *was*. I tried to tell myself that I needed to say something now, to break this spell, wake him up so this didn't seem creepy and *Twilight*-esque. But his name was caught in my throat.

I saw a white sound machine on Russell's nightstand, and I reached over and turned it off.

It was jarringly quiet in the room now that there was no artificial ocean being piped in. I hoped that maybe this would do it, that Russell would wake up and I could tell him goodbye and head back downstairs, job done. I was just about to say his name again when Russell sighed and rolled over, facing me. I took a step back, my heart beating hard.

He was shirtless, the blanket falling off one shoulder, his eyes closed, his lashes long on his cheeks, his expression peaceful. I could see now that he had white foam earplugs in—and I realized this, along with the fake ocean, explained why I'd had such a hard time waking him up.

For just a second, I had the strongest impulse. I wanted to reach over and brush his hair back from his forehead. I wanted to trace my fingers across his cheek. I wanted him to look at me the way he had yesterday, before everything had gotten wrecked.

But then I shook my head, trying to clear it. Russell and I were going to be *friends*. I'd decided it last night, and he'd agreed. These were just vestigial feelings from the day before, that was all.

I'd taken a breath to say his name again when Russell's eyes opened. He smiled lazily as they fluttered shut again, and he burrowed his head deeper into his pillow. I could see now that he had a crease across one cheek, making him look like a very cute pirate. "Darcy," he said with a yawn, smiling as he did so. "Hi there." His voice was slow and easy, like maybe he was on the verge of tipping back into sleep again. "What are you doing all the way over there?"

"I . . ." I blinked, trying to figure out what to do with this. What did *that* mean? I took a step closer and wiped my hands on my jean shorts. "Um . . ."

Russell's eyes snapped open again, and his happy, lazy expression was gone. "Hi," he said, sitting up. He took out his earplugs and raked a hand through his curls. Then he leaned over to the nightstand and picked up a pair of glasses—tortoiseshell, with rounded frames. He slipped them on, and I tried to hide my surprise. He looked different in them—younger, somehow, and more serious.

I tried not to stare at his chest or his stomach muscles, despite the fact that this was very challenging. "Darcy," he said again. His voice was still sleep-fogged, but it was sharper now, the languid earlier tone gone.

"Hi, sorry," I said quickly, feeling like I needed to explain my uninvited presence in his bedroom. "So—"

"That was so weird," Russell said, rubbing his eyes. "I thought I was still in my dream, and we were just continuing our conversation."

"So I was . . . in your dream?"

"Yeah . . . which is why this is so strange. Like I'm going from a dream and into reality, but without a break between?"

"Or maybe this is just another dream? And we're in some kind of *Inception* situation."

"That seems likely." He leaned over and looked at his bedside clock, and his eyes widened. "It's early."

"I know. And I'm sorry to wake you up. I just wanted to say goodbye."

Russell sat up even straighter. "Goodbye?"

"Yeah, I'm going to go to the bus station and then catch the bus back to LA. I was going to get an Uber, but your dad said he'd arrange a ride for me."

"You have to go this early? We're flying out later."

"I know, but I need to beat my dad home. He's getting in at

three, and as far as he's concerned, I rode a bus with absolutely no issues home from the festival last night."

"Right." Russell nodded a few times. "Got it."

I took a big breath, not really sure what I wanted to say. "I just—I hope you have a great time next year. And that Michigan isn't too cold. It's . . ."

"I can drive you," Russell said.

"Oh—that's not—"

"I'll just run you over to the bus station," he said, talking faster now. He swung his legs out of bed and stood up. And I could see that he was in long basketball-style shorts that sat low on his hips. After a moment, I made myself look away, concentrating on the poster on his wall. "It'll be no problem."

"You really don't have to."

"I want to," he said simply. "It's what friends do, right?" He held my gaze for a moment, and I nodded.

"Thank you. That's really nice." I was relieved I wouldn't have to ride with Kendrick or Bella—and that we wouldn't be saying goodbye like this, in his bedroom with its rumpled sheets where he'd just been sleeping—and dreaming, apparently, of me. Better to say goodbye outside, with other people around. And the fact that he'd have to drive me to the bus station meant this, right now, wouldn't be the last time that we saw each other.

"Of course."

I headed for the door, and I'd just reached it when I turned back. "What was your dream about? The one—I was in?"

Russell took a breath. "I—"

"Russell!" Artie was pushing past me in the doorway, Andy at his heels. Andy raced across the room and jumped onto the bed, climbing up on Russell and trying to lick his face. "You have to go downstairs! Doug said he'd make his special pancakes and Tidbit fell in the pool!"

Russell laughed. "It's been quite a morning, huh, kid?"

I pointed to the door and stepped out, and Russell nodded. "Want to play a game?" I heard Artie ask as I headed back down the hallway.

I reached the landing, hearing the sound of laughter and conversation floating up from the kitchen. As I started to head down the stairs, a wave of sadness that I hadn't been expecting washed over me. The thought that I'd never see Russell—or any of these other people—again suddenly seemed both impossible and unfair.

You hadn't even met *Russell this time yesterday,* Didi pointed out.

But yesterday was a long time ago, Katy chimed in. *A lot has happened since then.*

As I walked down the staircase, I decided that Didi was right. I'd known Russell less than twenty-four hours. So, really, it shouldn't be that big a deal that I wouldn't see him again after today. I shouldn't be acting ridiculous—I'd done enough of that yesterday. And it was time to go.

I pushed my hair behind my ears, let out a breath, then took the rest of the stairs down to the first floor two at a time.

CHAPTER 16

Monday

8:00 A.M.

O kay!" Chloe said, smiling at me. "You all set?"

We were standing in the huge garage that, as I'd guessed the night before, resembled more of an airplane hangar than a regular garage, and I could see now was filled with cars—low-slung sports cars; luxury SUVs; a huge, mud-spattered truck. I'd said goodbye to the dogs back in the house, giving Tidbit's silky ears a last rub and telling Andy to behave himself as he wagged his tail furiously and tried to lick my face.

And then after the dogs, I'd said my goodbyes to everyone else (Doug called a goodbye from the hot tub). Montana had told me to have a great time at school, and took my email so that she could send me a list of her favorite Stanwich recommendations. Wallace had been on the phone with his girlfriend, the long-distance Alyssa, but waved at me before going back to his conversation. I'd given the priceless art one last look, and then I'd left the house with Chloe to join Wiley and Russell, who'd gone out before us.

They were standing next to a vintage-looking blue Bronco with wood paneling along the sides. Russell was wearing shorts and a light-yellow button-down, the cuffs rolled up over his forearms, and when he'd come down that morning, he looked freshly showered, his glasses gone, his dark curls damp. It looked like Wylie was saying something to him about the car, but I couldn't make it out from across the garage.

"Darcy?" Chloe prompted.

I swiveled my attention back to her. "Right!" I said quickly. "And yes. I'm all set." I tipped my head toward Russell and his dad. "Is everything okay over there?"

She waved this off. "The Bronco is Wylie's baby. He never wants anyone to drive it, which never made sense to me. Why have a car if it's just going to sit in a garage?"

"I guess . . . if you don't want anything to happen to it?"

"Then don't buy it," she said, her voice definitive. "Otherwise it's just a waste. Do you have everything?"

"Yes," I said, suddenly remembering. "But I need to give you your clothes back."

She waved this off. "It's nothing. I want you to keep them. Consider it my way of atoning for the bus thing."

"What bus thing?"

She raised an eyebrow at me. "Buses leave practically every hour from Vegas going to LA. I know for a fact there's one that leaves at three a.m. so that people can be back in time for work in the morning."

"That's . . . really troubling."

"I know," Chloe said with a sigh. "The gambling industry is truly terrible."

"But—why did you tell me they stopped running?"

"Because I didn't want you to be alone in a bus station in Vegas," Chloe said. "Also, I thought maybe you and Russell had stuff to clear up." I gave her a look and she shrugged. "But obviously, that's your business, not mine."

"Yeah." I glanced over to Russell and Wylie. "I just . . ."

Russell was now wearing sunglasses—they were black Wayfarers. It hadn't been bright enough yesterday for either of us to need sunglasses, and wearing them now, backlit by the sun, he looked like a Paul Newman dream.

"You just what?" Chloe asked, her voice soft.

"Nothing. Russell and I are just friends, that's all." Chloe gave me a look that plainly said *come on*. "We're just friends *now*," I amended. "And okay, sure, yesterday I thought maybe it was something else, but I was very stupid yesterday."

I'm not arguing, Didi chimed in.

"I mean, it was ridiculous. I got caught up in an idea of something and convinced myself it was true. But there's no such thing as falling for someone at first sight."

"What? Of course there is."

"But—"

"It's just not the *only* thing," she said. "The rest of story is more important than the beginning."

"Have you ever—I mean . . . ?"

Chloe looked over at Wylie, her expression softening. "Oh yeah," she said. "I was a goner from minute one. He was too. It was like lightning."

"But it didn't work out," I said, even though I had a feeling she was more than aware of this. That lightning lights up the whole sky—but then disappears.

She turned back to me. "*Most* things don't work out," she said, like it should have been obvious. "But if you don't try, you don't know. Right?"

"Okay," Wylie called. Chloe headed over toward him, and I

followed, turning her words over in my head. Wylie handed Russell a set of keys with what looked like great reluctance. "Russell has assured me that he will treat my baby with respect and care."

Russell gave me a smile, then got into the driver's seat and started adjusting the mirrors. Wylie put my duffel and tent into the back seat, then came to join me and Chloe.

"Well, um . . . It was really great to meet you, and thank you so much—"

"It was great to meet *you*," Chole said as she pulled me in for a quick hug, then took a step back and looked at me critically. "Have you ever thought about bangs?"

"Um. Not really?"

"I think they'd look great," she said with a nod as she headed back toward the house. "Get home safe!"

I waved at her, then turned to Wylie. "Thank you. For everything."

He waved this off. "Just drive safe, okay? And good luck." He held out his hand to me, and I shook it. Wylie smiled at me, his real smile, his eyes crinkling at the corners. "Darcy."

I gave him one back, trying to freeze this moment in my mind. And even though I had a charged phone now, and I knew I could have taken it out and asked him for a picture, I also knew I wasn't going to do that. Not only because it seemed incredibly gauche, but also because I kind of liked that, for once, I didn't have any pictures marking this time. It was just something I'd have to remember, and hold on tight to.

I headed for the car and pulled open the passenger-side door. Russell was in the driver's seat, one elbow resting against the open window, his curls falling over his forehead and his black Wayfarers reflecting the sun.

As I settled into the car, dropping my canvas bag at my feet, I realized I'd never been in a car quite like this. It looked like it was probably from the seventies or eighties. Russell and I didn't even have our own seats—the front seat was just one long bench seat that stretched across, with nothing separating or dividing us. And the seat belts just went across our laps—which I knew was a thing from older cars but wasn't anything I'd experienced outside of a plane. The windows went down with a manual crank, which was also something I'd never seen before.

"Ready to do this?" Russell asked, starting the car.

I nodded. "Ready. Do you need the address? It's the South Strip Transfer Terminal." I looked around and realized—of course—this car wouldn't have any kind of screen you could see directions on. "I can navigate, if you want?"

"I'm good to get us in the general direction—I might need some help as we get closer."

"For sure." I pulled out my phone and typed the address in. "And thanks again for the ride."

"Of course." He shifted the car into gear and pulled forward, down the driveway and toward the gates. I glanced back and saw Wylie standing in place watching us. He raised a hand in a wave, and I raised one back. "You should definitely be there in time for the nine o'clock bus."

"Oh, good." As Russell approached the gates, they swung inward, and when they'd opened all the way, he drove through them. I turned around for a last look at the mansion, this impossible place where I'd literally landed last night, taking one last picture in my mind before we drove forward and it passed out of sight. I leaned back against the seat, which was covered in a kind of soft maroon fabric. "I would have a lot of explaining to do if my dad came home and found I hadn't been there."

"He really thinks you got in last night?"

"He's not home yet, so I think I'm in the clear."

"Yeah, I talked to my mom a little bit this morning—she's not thrilled with me either. When you disappear after a music festival and don't reach out for hours, it seems to make people upset. Who knew?" We approached a gatehouse, and Russell slowed the car. The woman inside nodded at him, and a second later, this gate rose up. "She says we're going to have a discussion about it when I get home tonight," he said with a wince.

We drove in silence for a little while. I unrolled my window and let the morning breeze lift my hair, then looked across the car at him—he was just an arm's length away.

"What?" he asked, glancing over at me.

"Nothing. I just realized that this is the first time we've been in a car together. We did a helicopter before a car. We're doing things all out of order."

"We were on that bus, though. Does that count?"

"Maybe. It's just funny that this is the first time I'm seeing you drive."

"And? Verdict?"

I turned a little bit to face him more, drawing one leg up. These lap belts really did make it easier to move around.

That's because they don't work as well, Didi pointed out. *You get that, right?*

"Very safe." He was driving carefully, if a bit slowly, his hands gripping the wheel at ten and two. "You're a driving instructor's dream."

"Yeah," Russell said with a short laugh. "I, um, was in a car accident right after I got my license. I was with the Bens, and Tall Ben was driving. This car ran the red, slammed into us—we spun around in the intersection, and hit another car. . . ."

"Oh my god. Was everyone okay?"

"Ben broke his collarbone when the airbag deployed. I got pretty scratched up. One cut was so deep they actually had to take a skin graft for it."

"Really? I didn't see anything."

"It was actually from, uh, my butt." I could see that Russell was blushing, his cheeks turning red.

"Right, then I guess I wouldn't have . . ." I trailed off as I suddenly remembered just how much of Russell's skin I had, in fact, seen, feeling like my face was probably matching his.

"So, ever since then, I drive pretty slowly. My friends always make fun of me. Actually Tall Ben calls me the Little Old Lady from Pasadena."

"But—the whole point of that song is that she drives fast." Every time summer rolled around, like clockwork, my dad went on a Beach Boys kick. "Summer in California music," he'd call it, grooving in the kitchen as he made dinner to "Fun, Fun, Fun" or "Wouldn't It Be Nice" or "God Only Knows." Just like I'd absorbed all the Nighthawks songs as though through osmosis, it was the same with the Beach Boys. There wasn't a moment I remembered learning them, but in my brain was every word on *Pet Sounds*, in there along with my ABCs. "She's *the terror of Colorado Boulevard*. Remember?"

Russell shook his head. "Don't tell my dad. He'll never forgive me."

"I mean—the Bens might have been calling you that for some other reason that had nothing to do with your driving."

Russell laughed again. "I'm okay now, but it used to stress me out to drive on surface streets. Too many intersections, too much stopping and starting—too many red lights. But on the highway, it's always just been easier. It's why I normally drive out here."

"You mean—to Vegas? From LA?"

Russell nodded. "It's the perfect road trip, as far as I'm concerned. Four and a half hours, the scenery is beautiful—and just about the time you're getting sick of driving, you're home."

"Don't tell Jesse, Nevada."

Russell laughed. "I won't."

"Well, I'll try to appreciate it from the bus."

"Speaking of buses—how do you think they're doing?" Russell asked as he changed lanes.

"Who?"

"Our friends from the bus station. The movie couple and Sunburned Dude."

"Probably halfway to LA by now, right?"

Russell nodded, but then smiled. "Unless."

"Unless?"

"*Unless* it turns out that Jesse is a magic town that only appears once every hundred years and we actually dodged a bullet, leaving when we did."

I frowned and leaned my head back against the window. "Why does that sound familiar?"

"Why does—it's *Brigadoon*!" he sputtered. He glanced over at me for a second, then back at the road. "The musical?"

"Oh, right. I knew I knew that from somewhere."

"You're definitely going to need to check it out. It's one of the best."

"Or I could hear *your* musical." This car didn't have anything like a normal console—or cupholders—but above the vents and an *ashtray* there was a little kind of tray that folded down, and that's where Russell's phone was currently riding. I had a feeling this car was way too old to have any kind of connection to our phones, but I figured Russell could just play it from his phone and turn up the volume.

"Um." Russell glanced down at his watch. "Maybe."

"Right," I said a second later, as I remembered what our situation actually was. I looked at my phone and saw that we would be at the bus station in five minutes. Not enough time to hear a whole musical. Barely enough time to hear a song. "So the next turn is George Crockett Road, and then a left on Gillespie Street."

"Great," Russell said, giving me a quick smile.

We must have been getting closer to the Las Vegas Strip—there were suddenly billboards popping up, advertising casinos and comedians and buffets. I tried to concentrate on them as I looked out the window, attempting to ignore the last-day-of-school feeling that had started churning inside me. I now only had three minutes left. Was this really going to be—it? Three minutes from now, I'd be on a bus and this whole thing with Russell would just be over?

Well—yeah, Katy said, sounding confused.

What did you think was going to happen? Didi asked.

"Is this it?" Russell slowed the car down and I looked around. Sure enough, there was a sign—black letters on beige tiles reading SOUTH STRIP TRANSFER TERMINAL.

"I think that's it." It looked like a big building—and from the sound of the plane roaring by above my head, I had a feeling we must be pretty near the airport. Russell swung the car into the lot and shifted into park.

"You're good on time?"

I nodded. I was—but even though I had a little bit of a cushion, I was well aware I still had to go talk to someone, figure out about making sure my ticket from last night transferred over. "I should be okay." I ran a hand through my hair—it was like I could practically hear the ticking of the clock. There was so much it felt like we hadn't said—and absolutely no time left to say it in.

Russell held out his phone to me. "Do—you want to put your number in? And then I could text you with mine?"

I took his phone, nodding. "Right. Sure, good idea." It seemed crazy that we didn't have each other's numbers—but then, until now, there wouldn't have been a moment that we needed them. I typed my number into his phone, then handed it back. "And Montana has my email. And probably C.J., too, now that I think about it."

Russell laughed. "I'm sure she does."

We looked across the car at each other—the whole space filled up with everything we weren't saying. I broke the look first, reaching down for my bag. "I should grab my stuff."

"Right," Russell said. He killed the engine and we both got out of the car. He helped me take out my tent and duffel bag. "I'll wait here for a bit? In case something goes wrong?"

"That's really nice of you. But I'm sure I'll be okay." I glanced across the asphalt toward the main building. It wasn't even that far a distance. But I knew that the second I crossed it, this would be over.

"Well—okay," Russell said. "I guess . . ."

"Yeah," I said. I reached over and gave him a quick hug, barely touching, over before it started. "I guess . . . I'll see you?" But even as I was saying the words, I knew I wouldn't, most likely.

Russell gave me a smile that let me know he was thinking the same thing. "Sure," he said with a nod. "Absolutely."

"Okay," I said, hating every minute of what was happening now—and hating that there wasn't time to make it better. I gave him a nod, then turned and walked toward the bus station on legs that suddenly felt heavy.

As I got closer to the sliding doors, I tried to tell myself that this was just what had to happen. And that everything was fine. Because it *was*. I'd be home in more than enough time to get my car and get back home before my dad. Things were working out. This was what I wanted.

And yet.

And yet what? This was Didi, her voice unexpectedly gentle.

The doors to the station slid open, and I was hit with a wave of air-conditioning. But I only got two steps in before I stopped short. And before I could think about what I was doing, I turned around and walked back out into the parking lot.

Russell was leaning against the side of the car, and when I reached him he straightened up, his brow furrowed. "You okay? Did you forget something?"

"Not exactly. Kind of? I just . . ." I twisted my hands together, balancing on the precipice of my idea. Was I really going to do this? It was also a *big* ask.

The worst he can say is no, Didi pointed out.

"What?" Russell came a step closer, and tucked his sunglasses into the V of his button-down.

"Just . . . what if I didn't get on the bus?"

"I thought you had to get home before your dad."

"I do! But since you said it was your favorite—I guess I was wondering if maybe . . ."

"Maybe . . . ?"

I took a breath and made myself ask. "Maybe instead, you wanted to take a road trip."

Russell's jaw dropped open. "Wait, *what*?"

IV
Going Away to College

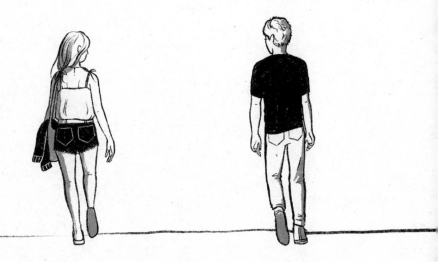

had planned on driving straight there—I was under a time crunch, after all. But that was before I saw it off the side of the highway, in bright red and yellow, a beacon of hope and secret sauce—the In-N-Out arrow.

I signaled to take the next exit, telling myself that I still had plenty of time, that I'd still make it with no problem, even though I knew I had been cutting it close to begin with, without burger stops. But I needed sustenance—it's not like Nevada was just around the corner. And, true, I'd bought snacks when I'd stopped for gas, but that was before I'd seen the In-N-Out sign and my priorities had shifted.

Normally at In-N-Out, I'd go in and order at the counter, since the drive-thru line was usually insanely long. My dad and I always felt very smug as we'd leave with our white delicious-smelling bags, and see the people in the drive-thru line who still hadn't moved. But right now, at this particular In-N-Out—it was one I'd never been to before—there was almost no line at the drive-thru, so I swung in. I pulled to a stop behind a minivan with a stick-figure family marching across the back windshield. Even with my windows closed, I could hear the Mariah Carey blasting from their car.

My phone buzzed in the cupholder, and I saw the text pop up on my *screen.* Everything okay?—R. *I shifted the car into park and texted back.* All good! *Then a second later, I added* I MIGHT have stopped at In-N-Out but still okay on time. *A second later, the response popped up.* Bring me some? *I laughed as I texted back.* I really don't think it'll keep. *I was searching for the green-faced barfing emoji when my phone rang. I smiled at the contact and pressed the button on the screen to answer it.*

"Hey, Didi."

"Darce! Finally. Katy's here too."

"She is?"

"Hi hi hi," *Katy said through the phone, her words tumbling out quickly.* "I'm here! We're both here. Where are you?"

"I'm driving," *I said, shifting into drive to pull up a few feet. The people in the Mariah Carey–loving minivan in front of me—it sounded like they were playing the song again, clearly trying to get as much use out of it while they still could—were giving their order to the In-N-Out employee with her tablet.* "I'm not stopped or anything."

"That's a weird thing to say," *Didi said, and even through the phone, I could practically hear her raising her eyebrow.*

"Hi, welcome to In-N-Out!" *The girl with her tablet hadn't waited for me to get to her—she'd come to me. And totally blown my cover.*

"Traitor!" *Didi hissed through the screen loud enough that the In-N-Out employee took a concerned step back.* "Bastard traitor!"

"One sec." *I muted the call, then gave her my order—Double-Double extra toast, extra sauce, fries well, Neapolitan shake.*

"Great," *she said, punching it in.* "Got it. Pull up to the first window to pay."

"Thanks so much," *I said. I started to drive forward and unmuted the call.* "I'm back. You scared the nice In-N-Out employee."

"Darcy never agreed to your meat ban, Deeds," Katy pointed out, as ever the reasonable one. "You're the one who chose to date a vegan."

"All I promised was not to eat meat in front of you," I reminded her. "Plus, how do you know I didn't order a grilled cheese?"

"Did you?"

"Of course not."

"Don't be ridiculous," Katy laughed. "Also—don't give Darcy grief about In-N-Out. You know it's not as available to her."

"Thank you."

"So," Didi said in what, since seventh grade, had been her getting-down-to-business voice. "How are you feeling?"

"Excited. Nervous?" I glanced in the rearview mirror and played with my bangs—they were maybe a smidge too long.

"Of course you're nervous," Katy said. "But you've got this. You'll call us the whole time, right?"

"She's not going to Nevada to talk to us," Didi admonished. "But that being said, we do want updates."

"Yes," Katy said, and I could tell that she was smiling. "Have fun! Be safe!"

I felt my cheeks get hot. "Katy. Stop."

"What?"

The car in front of me drove forward, and I saw I'd gotten three texts while we'd been talking. "I promise I'll drive carefully, and I'll call when I can."

"And let us know when you're back," Didi said. "We have a lot of catching up to do."

"Of course," I said, pulling up to the first window. "Gotta go—I'm paying."

"Later," Didi said.

"Byeeee!" Katy practically yelled into the phone.

"Hi, that'll be eight sixty-five," the girl behind the window said as I reached her. I rifled through my wallet, and handed her a twenty. She dropped it into the register, then gave me a smile as she handed me back my change. "That's eleven thirty-five," she said, dropping the coins in my palm. I could hear, faintly, the In-N-Out soundtrack—Mariah Carey fading out, Kelly Clarkson starting up.

"Thanks a lot," I said as I dropped the change into my cupholder.

"Please pull forward to the next window," she said. I gave her a nod, but before I drove away she smiled and added, "And happy holidays!"

CHAPTER 17

Monday
9:45 A.M.

I held my hair back from where the wind was blowing it around, and looked across the car at Russell.

"I know," he said into the phone. It was on the console between us, on speaker, since Bluetooth hadn't even been thought of when this car was built. "I know, Dad. But—"

"I did not give you permission to drive my car to *California*," Wylie huffed. "I barely like to take it to the casino! And I have my own parking spot there."

"I've seen it," Russell assured him. He had waited to call Wylie until we'd been driving on the highway for about ten minutes. When I'd first proposed a road trip—using someone else's vehicle—it had only taken Russell a beat to process the change of plans before he grinned and told me he was in. I had wanted him to call his dad then and there, in the parking lot of the bus station, to make sure it was okay.

But Russell had shot this down. "It's better to ask forgiveness than permission," he'd said. But now, listening to what had been a mostly one-sided conversation with a very displeased Wylie, I wasn't so sure.

Russell looked over at me and I mouthed, *Sorry*. He shook his head and mouthed, *It's fine*, then rolled his eyes.

"What even gave you this idea?" Wylie demanded.

"I'm really sorry, Mr. Sanders," I said, leaning across to speak into the phone. "It's my fault."

"I'm sure it isn't."

"No, it was. It was all my idea. I guess I just remembered what you said about that road trip you took? And . . ."

"Look, it's just four and a half hours to LA," Russell interjected. "Nothing's going to happen to the Bronco."

There was a silence, then Wylie sighed. "Fine," he finally said, sounding resigned. "This is what comes of talking up my youthful road trips. I want you to drive the car back by Thursday at the latest."

"Great," Russell said, giving me a smile. "That's—"

"And you and I are going to go to Michigan together."

The relief that had washed across Russell's face was replaced by something more complicated. "I don't know, Dad. I think—maybe Mom? I . . ."

"I'd like to be there with you. It's a real moment. Okay?"

Russell let out a breath, then nodded. "Okay. It's a deal."

"Good. Okay—Darcy, take notes." Wylie cleared his throat, then started giving us increasingly detailed instructions about the car. He reminded us that we were driving through the desert, in *August*, and that we should be careful not to let the Bronco overheat, not to let the gas get too low, things like that. Then he'd made Russell promise to call the second he was back inside the LA city limits.

Then he said goodbye, and Russell hung up and glanced at me. "Sorry about that."

"No, *I'm* sorry. Now I've gotten you roped into a trip with your dad."

"Well, it's appropriate, right? The only reason I even got into Michigan is because of my dad's donation. And so it's probably good that he goes with me and shows his face on campus. They can at least get their money's worth."

I glanced over at him, taking in the unhappy twist of his mouth, the way he was trying to sound like this was just no big deal, but not pulling it off. "It's just . . . I mean . . ."

"What?"

I thought about it before I spoke, replaying the conversation I'd had with Wylie. He'd never told me I wasn't supposed to relay it back to Russell. And it just felt like something that he should know. "I actually . . . had a talk with him this morning. Your dad, I mean. He made me breakfast."

Russell gave me a look—like he was smiling in spite of himself. "Did he make you a scramble?"

I nodded.

"He only makes those for the most important people. It's a compliment."

"We got to talking. About you and him. And I just . . ." I took a deep breath. "I think that in terms of Michigan . . . he was just trying to do something nice for you. To give you a gift. To . . . let you know how much he loves you."

Russell flushed, his hands tightening on the wheel for just a moment before he released them.

"I don't think he ever thought you couldn't do it on your own. He's really proud of you."

Russell nodded, still not looking at me. "Thanks, Darcy."

"Should I not have told you?"

"No," Russell said immediately, shaking his head. "I'm glad to know it." He changed lanes on the highway, going around a slow Tesla.

I looked out the window, taking it all in. We were still in the Vegas proximity bubble, because all the exit signs and billboards were telling us about things we could do and places we could stay back on the Strip. I kicked off my Birks and stretched my feet toward the dashboard, then hesitated. "Sorry—is this okay?"

"Fine with me."

I rested my feet against the glove compartment and looked out the window, taking in the huge swath of sky, the mountains in the distance, the vastness and *scope* of it all. I was going to trade all this for New England? Church spires and leaves turning and cold winters? "I, like, logically know it's happening. But I can't actually believe that soon, I won't live in California anymore."

"It is kind of wild that you're starting school tomorrow."

"I know. I'd wanted this weekend to be a distraction from it happening, but this might have been pushing things a little too far."

"Was . . . I part of that too?" Russell's voice was light, like he really didn't care about the answer, but I could see his hands were gripping the wheel hard. "Just—another distraction?"

It suddenly felt like we were approaching something real— something true. Like we were in a giant game of Operation and nearing the electronic sides, about to hear the beep warning you from getting too close. I thought about just saying no, changing the subject, moving on. But wasn't this the whole *point*, being on the road, getting more time together? To actually talk about this stuff?

"So I'm in this film club with Didi and Katy," I said slowly, realizing this was actually the best way to explain what my head-space had been. "Friday Night Movie Club. We've been doing it forever. We rotate our picks, to keep it fair. Katy always picks action movies. Didi picks horror or animated movies. And I always choose—"

"Sci-fi? Experimental Danish dramas?"

"No," I said with a laugh, lowering my legs and turning to face him a little more, leaning against the car door. I took a breath and made myself say it. "Romance."

"Oh." Russell sounded surprised.

"Yeah. And when this weekend started, all I wanted was to pretend my real life wasn't happening—that everything wasn't about to change. And then you showed up—the cutest guy in the bus station."

"I mean, thank you? But it's not like there was a lot of competition."

I was about to make a joke about Sunburned Bald Guy, but knew that I had to keep going if I was going to get this out. I took a shaky breath. "Do you remember the first thing you said? You said, 'I heard you were looking for me.'"

"Ah," Russell said, and I could see him flushing slightly. "I did, didn't I? Sorry."

"But the thing is—I *was*. You had no idea how much. You were what I thought I'd been waiting for. And then you were so great, and everything seemed so perfect . . ." I shook my head. "It was like I cast you in my head as the lead of a movie I thought I was in."

"*Romantic hero* isn't the worst box to be put in," Russell said with a ghost of a smile.

"Maybe not. But it's also not fair to you. And then when things didn't go the way I expected . . ."

"You had every right to be upset. I *lied* to you."

"And while I was upset about that too—as you might have noticed . . ."

Russell laughed.

"I think I was mostly angry that all these things I'd believed weren't real. And then I was mad at myself for putting so much stock in them."

"We should definitely blame the movies. And the stories."

"And the songs! We should blame your dad, actually."

"No arguments here."

I shook my head. "And it really is a ridiculous concept when you think of it—love at first sight."

Russell glanced over at me. He started to say something, then hesitated. "You think?"

"I mean, there's no such thing as *friendship* as first sight, right? It's understood that it takes a long time to get to know someone. Hanging out and eating meals and having adventures and talking . . ."

"And taking road trips?"

I glanced over at Russell and smiled. "Well, exactly."

We drove in silence for a bit, like we were both thinking over everything we'd just talked about. "So," I said as we passed a sign that informed us there would be a rest stop in three miles, and then no more services for thirty. "I think I'm done with romantic movies. At least for a while."

Russell shook his head. "I bet musicals are actually worse, because in a musical, when two people fall in love, they *break into song*. I mean, talk about setting a high bar."

"And I guess there aren't many musicals about relationships that don't work out."

"Seriously?" He looked over at me with an expression of surprise. "Sorry—I forget you've seen, like, one musical."

"Three! At least. Probably. So you're saying that's wrong? There's lots of breakup musicals out there, winning the . . . musical award?"

"The Tony," Russell said, his voice patient. "And there definitely are some. *The Last Five Years* is all about a relationship falling apart. *Six*, certainly. And *Merrily We Roll Along*. *Passion*. Most of Sondheim, now that I think about it. And even going back further, *Show Boat*, *Carousel* . . ."

"Okay, you have to make me a playlist. And then I'll understand all these references."

"But you're definitely right about most musicals centering around love, with usually a happy ending. For the most part, things work out. I'm sure it also gave me a skewed perception of things. . . ."

His voice trailed off, and I realized I could tell that there was something he was thinking about, but not quite able to say yet. And I knew that if I just gave him a little bit of space, he'd tell me when he was ready.

So I looked out the window, taking in the scenery. There were starting to be fewer signs and billboards, and it was becoming clear we were *really* in the desert. This shouldn't have been a shock—I was well aware where Las Vegas was located. But it was one thing to know it—it was another thing to be taking in the vastness of what that actually meant. And it meant *desert*, on both sides of the car and all we could see in front of us.

"That's actually kind of the problem with my musical," Russell finally said. "It started out as a love story. Kind of, um, autobiographical. But then the love story I'd thought I was a part of collapsed. And so the story changed—it turned into a whole mess.

I should have started over, most likely. Instead, I tried to kind of Frankenstein it."

"You mean Frankenstein's monster it?"

"No, because in this case *I'm* the mad scientist putting things together that don't belong and trying to breathe life into a corpse. So for once, Frankenstein is accurate."

"A *Frankenstein* musical would be a good idea, though."

"There is one. It was only ever on the West End in London, though. I liked some of the songs."

"Please tell me one of them is called 'Nuts and Bolts.'"

"I *wish*. Where were you when it was being written?"

"Well, I'll add *Frankenstein*—the musical!—to my list."

Russell smiled, but it didn't last long. I watched as it faded slowly from his face. "I probably shouldn't have submitted it for my applications. I knew there were issues with it. I had other samples I could have sent in, things that were more polished. And I was too close to have any perspective . . ."

"This relationship the musical was based on," I said, pulling my legs underneath me so that I was sitting cross-legged—I was really becoming a fan of this bench-seat thing. "Was it with—Olivia?"

Russell glanced at me, looking surprised. "What?"

"Montana, um, mentioned something."

"My siblings like to gossip."

"She didn't tell me any specifics," I said quickly. "Just that there was some . . . drama."

"Yeah." He sighed, his hands tightening on the wheel again.

"Sorry—you don't have to—"

"No. It's . . . it's okay." He took a breath and let it out. "Just—give me a second."

I nodded, looked out the window again, and four billboards later, I heard Russell draw in a sharp breath—the kind you take just before plunging underwater or getting a shot. "So her name was Olivia—which you know. We were together seven months."

"Oh." I hesitated—there was a question I really wanted to ask, but I was suddenly dreading the answer. Because what if they'd broken up last week? What if this whole thing had just been a giant rebound? My stomach plunged at the thought of it—but I took a breath and made myself ask it. "How long . . . I mean, when did you guys break up?"

"Back in October," Russell said, and relief flooded through me. "It, um . . . ended kind of badly."

I nodded. Montana had said something to this effect, and now, looking at the tense set of Russell's shoulders, the way his brow was furrowed, I wished I would have asked for more specifics.

"I had thought that things were good with us. But . . . then I found out she'd been giving out information about my dad to DitesMoi."

"She . . . what?"

He let out a short laugh. "Yeah."

I suddenly remembered the way he'd reacted when I'd brought up DitesMoi. Not to mention all the times I'd looked at it when I was bored or wanted a distraction—using other people's real lives for entertainment, never worrying about who it was hurting or if it was even true.

"It was when he and Chloe were deciding to separate. And of course I was talking to Olivia about it, because she was my *girlfriend* and I thought I could do that."

I drew in a breath. "Oh no. Russell. I'm so sorry."

"And it sucked because I know my dad and Chloe wanted to do it on their own time, you know? But suddenly the news was breaking, and C.J. was getting called in, and Bronwyn . . . and it was all because of me."

"Not *you*," I pointed out. "You didn't leak information to some trashy gossip site."

He sighed. "Even so. Obviously, we broke up after that."

"It's so awful that she would do that," I said, feeling my stomach clench with anger.

"Yeah. Not great." He switched lanes, even though I couldn't see that there was any need to—maybe it was just to have something to do. "So then the musical, which had been all about love, suddenly took a really big turn in act 2. I probably should have just scrapped it, but . . ."

"What was it called?"

"*Crystalline Lies.*" I couldn't stop myself from making a face, and Russell laughed. "Yeah. I know. My dad tried to get me to change it too. That should have been my first clue it wasn't working."

I looked across the car at Russell, wondering if he felt the same I had last night, when I'd finally told him about Gillian—like I'd just put down something heavy. "Thank you for telling me."

"Has . . . anything like that ever happened to you?"

"I mean, just last week I caught Didi trying to auction off my personal information. . . ." I was trying to make a joke, but Russell only gave me a ghost of a smile, and I knew it had fallen flat. "Sorry."

"I didn't mean about that."

"No, I know."

"I meant . . ." He glanced over at me. "Have you ever had your heart broken?"

I shook my head, suddenly feeling woefully inexperienced. Russell had written a whole angsty (and possibly not all that good?) musical about his ex. And all my actual feelings about my short-lived relationships probably wouldn't even have been enough for a jingle.

"No. But I've never really been in a serious relationship like that. I think," I said slowly, "I've been spending way too much time waiting for my meet-cute, or whatever. And missing out in the meantime."

You mean like we've been telling you for ages? Didi huffed.

I mean, at least she's getting there now, Katy said.

"Or maybe you had your heart broken a lot earlier." I looked over at him, confused, and he shrugged. "Heartbreak isn't always because of romance."

Just like that, the specter of Gillian appeared in the car between us. "You mean my mom?" Russell shot me a sympathetic smile and a shrug. And for once, I didn't try to push my feelings about her away—I just sat with the idea for a moment. I'd spent so long telling everyone I was *fine*, that she didn't matter to me. Lying to myself and everyone else. Ignoring the giant gash in my heart I wasn't allowing to heal. "Maybe you're right."

"It happens occasionally. Not often, but . . ."

I smiled. "It's funny."

"What is?"

"Just—when we were back in Jesse, I thought it was good we weren't talking about anything really real. Like how you never know what people are saying in those rom-com montages—I thought if you had to talk about serious things it meant there wasn't some kind of immediate connection." I shook my head. "But I don't think you *should* zoom past it, really. Like, this is the important stuff."

"Maybe we're just getting everything in the wrong order. It's helicopters before cars all over again."

I laughed. "I mean, I don't even know your middle name."

"I have two."

"Two middle names?"

"I got off lucky. Wallace has, like, four. Apparently Kenya's labor was so bad, she said she was never doing it again, so they gave him every name they'd considered."

"So what are they?"

"Wallace's?" Russell took a breath.

"I meant yours."

"Oh—Russell Jennings Henrion Sanders." He glanced over at me. "And you are?"

"Darcy Cecilia Milligan."

"You were named after *two* songs?"

"I mean, my dad says the Cecilia was after my great-aunt. But I have my suspicions."

"If there was a Layla in there, you'd know for sure."

I laughed. "Well—thanks for telling me. I really should have asked you yesterday, though."

Russell frowned and looked over at me. "Why yesterday?"

"You know, because—" I suddenly realized the cliff I was heading for and stopped abruptly, staring out the window as though I was fascinated by the FOOD GAS LODGING sign up ahead.

"Because?"

"Just . . ." I could feel my cheeks heating up. "Didi has a rule that you should never sleep with someone unless you know their middle name."

"Ah." I glanced over and saw that Russell's ears were starting to turn red.

"Not that we did—"

"We didn't—"

"But we were, you know. Almost . . ." I cleared my throat and looked out the window again.

"Right. I remember." I glanced over and saw that Russell was smiling.

"Anyway!" I said, trying to hold back a smile of my own.

It's a good policy, Didi said magnanimously. *You're welcome.*

We drove in silence for a few miles. The highway was busy, but not so many cars that we were crawling through traffic. We were coasting at around seventy—when a car in the left lane suddenly swerved in front of us, making a break for the exit. Russell slammed on his brakes, sending his phone flying down to my footwell.

"Shit—sorry," he said, sounding shaken. "You okay?"

"I'm fine," I said, wincing slightly. I'd just found out when your seat belt doesn't have a shoulder strap, your waist basically gets bisected by the lap belt. So maybe there were some downsides to it.

I set the phone back on the little shelf, even though that clearly wasn't the safest place for it. The longer I was in this car, the more it was bothering me that there weren't any cupholders. What had people in the seventies or whatever done when they got thirsty?

I looked out the window, feeling the sun on my face. I was definitely going to have to dig my sunglasses out of my bag whenever we stopped next. Which I hoped was going to be soon; it was seeming like a long time ago that I had my scramble, and I was getting hungry.

And like I'd willed it into being, I suddenly saw it off the highway—a red-and-yellow arrow, as familiar to me as anything. I knew it was early, but I just hoped Russell would be on board. "What do you think?" I asked as I nodded toward it. "Hungry?"

Russell glanced at it, then grinned at me. "Starving," he said. He hit the turn signal and pulled off the highway, heading for the In-N-Out Burger.

CHAPTER 18

Monday
11:00 A.M.

So." I looked over at Russell and raised my eyebrows. "What do you think?"

Russell picked up a fry and bit into it with great ceremony. Then he popped the rest of it into his mouth and turned to me with a nod. "Yeah. You were right."

We were sitting in the back of the Bronco, the hatch open and our legs dangling over the bumper. When I'd proposed my favorite In-N-Out option—the *box for your car*—Russell had agreed. And while we'd been waiting in line to order—even though it was still before noon, on a *Monday*, the restaurant was packed—we'd covered the basics.

"So." Russell's voice had the gravity to it that befitted such an important topic. "What's your order?"

"Right now it's a double-double, extra sauce, fries well, extra ketchup, strawberry shake. But since I'm getting one with my dad later, maybe I should skip it now."

"Or you could have a two-milkshake day."

"You make a good point."

"I've never heard of anyone ordering fries *well* before."

"It's just getting your fries well done. You didn't know they could do that?"

"No!" Russell looked shocked by this. "You mean all this time I've just been hoping to get the crispier fries and I could have just been ordering them like this?"

"At least you know now," I said, trying not to laugh at the disgruntled expression on his face, like he was mentally reliving every trip to In-N-Out he'd taken, and finding them wanting. "You can also get them *light*, or underdone, but that seems less like a way to order fries and more like a crime against humanity."

"I'll say."

"So what about you?" I gave him a nudge with my shoulder, then froze, wondering if this was okay. It had just been an instinct—but was this going outside of my *just friends* decision? But a second later, I figured it was fine—surely, friends shoved each other sometimes.

You've certainly shoved me, Didi cut in, sounding irritated.

The line moved up, and I used the excuse to walk forward and try to pretend it hadn't happened. "Your order, I mean."

Russell just gave me a smile, like he'd seen through my whole silent mini-spiral. "Double double, extra pickle, no onion, fries animal style. And I always ask for extra toast."

"Extra *toast*?"

"It just means your hamburger buns are extra toasted. Oh—and a Neapolitan shake."

"What's that?"

"It's a shake with all three milkshake flavors—chocolate, vanilla, and strawberry."

"I didn't know that was a thing! I thought I knew everything on the secret menu."

"Next!" The In-N-Out employee called, and we stepped forward to order.

Now, back in the car, I tried not to be too satisfied with the expression on Russell's face as he ate his crispy fries. I pulled out my phone and checked the map and our ETA.

"We're still okay on time?"

"Right now we're getting there with over an hour to spare," I said. "I think we're good."

"Awesome."

I picked up my burger and took a bite—I'd tried his extra-toasted tip—and nodded. "Yep."

"Good, right?" Russell asked, looking pleased with himself.

"Basically, what we've discovered is that everything here just needs to be cooked more."

Russell laughed. "Exactly."

"I also feel like it holds the ketchup better," I said, taking another big bite of my extra-toasted bun. "This is an excellent hack."

"Fun fact—unless they've overstayed their welcome?"

"Never," I assured him, dipping a perfectly crispy fry in the secret sauce.

"Okay, so the fifty-seven in Heinz 57 isn't actually about the number of varieties they have. That was just a marketing campaign that came later. It was because five was Heinz's lucky number, and seven was his wife's."

"So did they then have to make fifty-seven varieties? So they weren't lying on the label?"

Russell shrugged. "Clearly, I need to do more research." He took a bite of his burger, then wiped his mouth carefully. "This was a good call. The last time I had this was with the Bens, and that was two weeks ago now—before they both left."

"They're at school already? The Bens?"

"Yeah. Tall Ben is at Tulane, and Actually Tall Ben is at Emory. Apparently, he spent the first week going around pretending he thought he got into *Emerson*, and asking everyone where Walden Pond was."

"They sound great."

Russell smiled. "They really are. You'll have to meet them someday."

The words hung in the air between us, and I saw immediately that Russell had just registered what he'd said. "Right," I said quickly, picking up my drink. "Sure."

I took a sip of my Arnold Palmer—I'd decided a two-milkshake day might put me in a sugar coma—but it didn't taste quite as sweet as before. We finished up quietly, both of us suddenly occupied with our fries or burger remnants. "Ready?"

Russell nodded, then held up his milkshake cup. "I'm going to keep working on this, though."

"There aren't any cupholders," I pointed out. "Just something to keep in mind."

"How did I not notice that?" he asked, turning around to look at the front of the car. "Also, did nobody get thirsty in the olden days?"

"That's what I was thinking!" I gathered up our lunch detritus. "I'll just toss this out."

"I can get it."

"I don't mind." I started to slide off the back of the car, my hands full, when Russell frowned.

"Darcy—you've got . . ." He nodded toward my face.

"Oh." Did I have a glob of ketchup or something on my face? Had it been there for a *while* now? This was the problem with eating with boys. Didi and Katy would have pointed it out as soon as it happened. I went to put down the boxes in my arms just as my cup threatened to fall, and I grabbed for it. "Just . . . a second."

"It's . . . I can," Russell said, moving in a little closer to me. He raised his eyebrows, asking if it was okay. I nodded, my heart suddenly beating harder as he leaned forward and closed the space between us.

He reached over, his fingers brushing against my cheek gently. "Got it," he said. He lowered his hand but didn't move away.

"What was it?"

"Tiny piece of lettuce," he said with a smile. "Nothing to worry about."

"Well—thank you." I was having trouble concentrating—he was suddenly so much closer. I'd gotten used to it in the car, but this was different. This was leaning-forward-four-inches-and-kissing-him nearness. This was seeing-the-freckles-on-his-forearms nearness. The last time we'd been this near, we'd been half-naked and kissing furiously.

A moment passed between us—one that felt different. It wasn't like earlier, when it seemed like just a look, a touch, was enough to generate a spark between us—exciting and ever-changing and volatile. This felt more like an ember—warm and steady and keeping watch, ready to catch if conditions were right, but not until then.

"Darcy," Russell said softly. He took a breath—just as his phone started to ring. "Sorry," he said, stepping back and pulling his phone out of his pocket. "That's my dad."

"He's probably checking on the car."

"Undoubtedly. I'll just be a second." Russell took a few steps toward the restaurant, and I found the nearest trash can to dump our stuff in. Then I made my way back to the Bronco, leaning against the back, trying not to think about the fact that when Russell and I had been so close, everything in me had been yelling to kiss him.

So kiss him! Katy screamed at me.

She decided *they're just going to be friends,* Didi reminded her, and I could practically hear her rolling her eyes.

Yeah, like, five seconds ago. It's not a binding treaty. She can un-decide it. Kiss this cute boy who obviously wants to kiss you!

I looked out at the highway, at the cars rushing past, while just for a moment, I got to stand still. I pulled out my phone to check our ETA. There was a tiny bit of red coming up on the map, but we would still make it in time. But even so, I could practically hear a ticking clock, one that was starting to get louder. Last night, in Jesse, it had felt like we were the only two people on the planet— and like nothing needed to be rushed, like time was stretching out endlessly before us. But now, it felt like it was counting down, sand through the hourglass disappearing until soon there would be nothing left.

"Hey." I turned and saw Russell walking toward me. His sunglasses were on, but even without being able to see his eyes, I could tell that something was bothering him.

"Hey. Everything okay?"

"Kind of? I'm not sure. It's . . . a thing. I'll tell you on the road." Russell headed for the driver's side.

"I can take a turn driving."

"I don't mind."

"I can't let you do this the whole time. We should share it, right?" A second later, I suddenly worried that, given the way Wylie had talked about the Bronco, this might not be allowed. "Unless your dad doesn't want me to—that's fine too."

"No, it's not that," he said, taking the keys out of his pocket. "I was just trying to be gallant."

"It was very gallant," I assured him. "In a, um, friendly way." Russell handed me the keys, I fished my sunglasses out of my bag, got into the driver's seat—and then we had to figure out how to move the bench seat up so that I could actually reach the pedals. Russell wasn't that much taller than me, but I was realizing that he liked to sit farther back from the wheel than I did.

"Nice," he said nodding at me, and it took me a moment to realize that he was talking about my scratched aviators.

"Thanks," I said, giving him a smile before starting the car. "Whoa." I had an old Prius and my dad had an electric car, so it felt like it had been a while since I'd driven a car like this—the steering wheel seemed to be shaking from the vibrations of the engine.

"I know," Russell said. "You get used to it, I promise."

I backed up carefully, then pulled out of the parking lot, Russell giving me directions to get back on the freeway. The steering wheel was wider than I was used to, and thinner, but I liked it—it made me feel like I was driving a truck.

And despite the growling engine, it was a pretty easy car to handle, which I was glad about. I could feel myself relaxing back against the seats, not gripping the steering wheel quite so hard. After five minutes in which I drove in silence so I could concentrate, very aware of *don't crash the rock star's car*, I felt like I had a handle on things. "Should we listen to music?"

"Sure—want me to play something of yours?"

"You be the DJ. Clearly, I need to increase my musical theater knowledge."

"How about we trade off? I'll DJ for a while and then when I start driving again, you can do it?"

I nodded, and gave him a quick smile before switching to the middle lane so I could speed up a bit. "Sounds good." I nodded down at his phone. "Hit me with your best shot."

But ten minutes later, there still had been no music. "Sorry," Russell said, sounding flustered. "I've almost narrowed it down."

"Anything is fine," I assured him, trying not to laugh at the expression on his face. He'd spent the last few minutes hunched over his phone, scrolling through it furiously and muttering to himself.

"No, it's *not*. Darcy."

"Russell?"

"This is one of the finest American art forms, and it is one that you have shockingly little knowledge of."

"I wouldn't say *shocking*—"

"So I need to make sure I'm playing the right songs, or I might miss my window to make you fall in love." I looked over at him, and he blinked for just a moment before adding quickly, "With musical theater. If I play you the wrong songs, you might think you don't like it, and you'll continue to only know the three musicals that you do."

"And god knows, we can't have that."

"We really can't. Okay," he said, holding up his phone. "I think I've got it."

"Great."

"Wait." He paused, his thumb hesitating over his phone screen. "How do you feel about cannibalism?"

"Cannibalism? In . . . a musical?"

"Okay, maybe we table *Sweeney Todd* for the moment. Maybe *In the Heights*?"

"What is that?"

A shocked expression passed across Russell's face for just a moment before he took a deep breath and composed himself. "It's the first Lin-Manuel Miranda musical—it all takes place over twenty-four hours in Washington Heights, and I frankly think it got unfairly eclipsed—"

"It takes place in a day?"

"Yeah," he said, nodding. "Why?"

"I just didn't know that could happen. I thought they were all—I don't know, more epic or something."

"Twenty-four hours can be plenty epic."

I smiled at that. "That's true."

"But there's a few of them. *How to Succeed in Business*, I'm pretty sure. And I think *Forum* all takes place in one day. . . ."

"Huh."

"What?"

"Nothing," I said, giving him a smile, even as my mind was filing this away as useful information. "What's next?"

We drove across the desert, and Russell played me highlights from the last one hundred years of musical theater—songs about love, and loss, and carnivorous plants, and *Lion King* ushers. About turning thirty-five, and mythical towns that exist just for one day, and meat pies made of people (I'd relented about the cannibal thing, mostly because I was curious). About the wives of Henry VIII, and MI5 during World War II, and Mormon missionaries. With every song, I knew Russell was watching me, looking for my reaction, trying to see how I felt about it. I could practically see him cataloging the songs I liked and tailoring the next song accordingly.

I listened as I drove, sometimes requesting repeats or complaining about the logic jumps I was expected to make (like, why were the people in River City so excited about a boys' band? And why couldn't girls be in the band too?). And while the songs played, or while Russell cued up the next one, we talked—sharing the details we hadn't gotten to before, filling in some of the gaps and missing pieces in both our lives.

"What are your cats named?" I asked, looking over at him as he scrolled through the songs on his phone. "You said you had two?"

"We do. Bisou and Dameron."

"I'm guessing you named Dameron?"

"He was always taking flying leaps as a kitten!" Russell said, sounding a little defensive. "So he had to be named after a space pilot."

"Well, *obviously*."

"Do you guys have any pets? You and your dad?"

"No. I always wanted a dog, but we never had one."

"Maybe he'll get one now," Russell suggested. "Keep him company when you're gone?"

"If he gets a dog when I've left, after denying me one for my entire childhood, I'm going to be *so* mad."

"It's a catch-22." Russell glanced over at me and raised an eyebrow. "A fetch-22?"

"Nicely done."

"Fun fact—it's been proven that dogs are stress reducers. That when you pet them, your cortisone levels drop."

"I'm not sure I would put Andy in the stress-reducing category."

"Well, he might be the exception." Russell stopped scrolling on his phone and looked at me. "How familiar are you with Jonathan Larson?"

"Who?"

"Oh my god. Hold on."

"Let me get this straight," I said as I cranked down my window—it was starting to get really hot in the car. Russell had just played me songs from *Pal Joey, Carousel, Once Upon a Mattress*, and *The Light in the Piazza*. "All these people are related?"

"Yeah. It was Rodgers and Hart, then Rodgers and Hammerstein. Then Richard Rodgers's daughter, Mary Rodgers. Then her son, Adam Guettel."

"Talented family."

"I'll say."

I looked away from the road for a second and across the car at him as he scrolled though his phone, totally absorbed. "Is that hard for you?"

He looked up, frowning. "Is what hard?"

"I mean . . . with your dad. And you wanting to do music too." I shook my head, knowing *do music* was not the best way to put this.

Russell lowered his phone and looked out the window for a moment. "It's both really great and really hard," he said slowly. "Like, he's the first person I play stuff for because he just gets it on a different level than my mom or any of my friends. But at the same time—I know whatever I do will be compared to him, and probably not favorably. It's just . . . a lot to live up to. I think it's the reason I was drawn to musicals in the first place."

"What do you mean?"

"Just as a way to separate myself, since it's not what he does. But also—I always loved the storytelling aspect of it. How you can really tell the story of a triumph, or failure, or great love . . ."

"Or how hard it is to be Spider-Man."

Russell laughed. "Well, exactly." There was a pause in which we just listened to Jeremy Jordan sing about unionizing. I was about to ask him to turn it up when Russell spoke again, his voice hesitant. "I actually . . . talked to my dad about it when he called. About what he did to get me in. The whole Michigan thing."

"You did?"

"Yeah. I mentioned what you told me he said—and that I could see he was trying to do a good thing. And that I shouldn't have thrown it back at him."

"Oh, wow."

"But then he said he hadn't seen it from my point of view. And that I don't have to go if I don't want to. If what he did really changes how I feel about it, it's my choice if I want to go or not. He said he'd still donate the money."

"Oh, well, *that's* good. That school is famously underfunded." Russell smiled and looked out the window, turning his phone over and over in his hands. "So what are you thinking?"

"I'm not sure. I just . . . I wish there was some way I could know. If I could do it on my own."

"Well . . . you could do that, right?"

"What do you mean?"

"You didn't get into the Michigan theater program, right? Just—the regular school?"

Russell sighed. "Yeah."

"But you said you really wanted to do a BFA track somewhere."

"I did," he said, and I could hear some frustration coming out in his voice. "But I didn't get in."

"No, I know. But since you're not even going to the part of

Michigan that you wanted to go to, couldn't you just, I don't know . . . defer for a year? Write a different musical and then apply to where you really wanted to go? USC and . . . what were the other schools?"

"Temple. And NYU," he said slowly. "I guess I could. . . ."

"I thought about it when I only got in two places," I said, remembering the very long, sleepless night I'd spent on my laptop, trying to figure out if I had any options and if I could do anything in a year to help myself. "But the most I can really do at this point is get good grades and then transfer. I wouldn't be able to change my application all that much. It's not like I have a musical to write."

"*Yet.*"

"Yet," I acknowledged with a laugh.

We drove in silence for a beat, Russell's fingers tapping restlessly on the steering wheel. "I don't know," he finally said, his voice hesitant. "It's strange to even consider not starting next week—like stepping off the path. You know. All my friends are going to school—most have already started—"

"Mine too."

"But if I had a year—to work on a new show . . ." It was like I could practically see his wheels turning. "Is it crazy that never occurred to me until you said it? Am I just very stupid?"

I laughed. "No, I think it's just the funnel we're all put through. It's probably the same with you, but my whole life, it's been do *this* to get *that* so you can get into college. It's like you're on a treadmill and you're not encouraged to ever get off or look around or go wander."

"Exactly!"

"Didi was thinking about maybe taking a gap year. And her parents lost their *minds*. Like even the thought that she might not go right to college really freaked them out."

"So what did she do?"

"She's currently at Colgate, stealing her roommate's Twizzlers."

Russell nodded. We slowed down—I could see there was road-work ahead, everyone being pushed over into the left lane. "What about you?" He looked across the car at me. "How are you feeling about starting tomorrow?"

"It feels—too soon. Like, we're here now, in the middle of the desert, and tomorrow I'm going to be in Connecticut? I want more of a transition or something."

"Fun fact!"

"Bring it on."

"I'll play that one next." When I just stared at him, he shook his head. "Musical joke. Never mind. But! One of the reasons it's called 'jet lag' is that it didn't exist before planes. When you would, like, cross the ocean to get to Europe, you'd have enough time to be fully adjusted by the time you arrived."

"Unless you hit an iceberg."

"Well, exactly. But . . . is it going to be hard, tomorrow—seeing your mom?"

"I won't be seeing her tomorrow. She did offer to get me from the airport, but I said no."

I waited for the surge of anger I always felt when Gillian came up, the one that I invariably pushed away a second later and pretended I wasn't bothered by. But for the first time in a long time, it didn't come. I could feel the vestige of it, an outline. Like a crime-scene chalk drawing, representing something that once had been there but wasn't any longer.

I looked over at the window—this normally would have been the moment I would have played with the button, pressing it up and down. But there really didn't seem to be much point to that with nonautomatic windows. What was I supposed to do, crank it up and back down again? Russell glanced over at me, like he was waiting for me to say more. I just gave him a shrug, and he gave me a nod—like he was somehow letting me know that when I was ready to talk more about it, he'd be here.

We headed down the highway, the desert unspooling before us. There were rest stops and service stations, but they were getting fewer and farther between, and most of the signs now were telling us when the next service station was—so that we could prepare accordingly.

And as we drove, an idea was flitting around in my head—and not going away, to the point where I absorbed very little of Russell's favorite song from *A Little Night Music*, and when he asked me what I thought, I struggled to find an answer.

"It's okay," Russell said, shaking his head. "We don't have to keep listening to these. I might have hit you with *too* much Sondheim. It actually helps if you can read the lyrics while listening—"

"I don't want to stop," I said, and saw a flicker of relief pass over his face. "I was just thinking . . . has anyone ever made a musical of *Theseus's Sailboat*?"

"No. I kind of think we might be the only two people who've ever read it."

"Don't you think it would make a good one, though? You did say that musicals can take place over one night. There could be a great love ballad when they first meet. And the campers could have their own songs. And the cat, too."

"The *cat*?"

"Snoopy sings." I honestly hadn't known there was a Peanuts musical until Russell had played me songs from *You're a Good Man, Charlie Brown*.

"That's true. I can't argue with that."

"So what do you think?"

"I mean—I'm sure it would," he said slowly, like he was trying to figure out what I was talking about.

"So you could write it. If you wanted to do a new musical—you could base it on the book." I glanced over at him to see what he thought about this, but he was already shaking his head.

"I don't have the rights."

"I'm not saying that you need to get it produced. But just to have something to reapply with—if you wanted to do that—you could, right? Isn't there some kind of exception for students, if you're not going to try to sell it?"

I looked across the car at Russell and smiled when I saw that his eyes had lit up.

"Okay. I had a thought," Russell said. He'd taken out his copy of *Theseus's Sailboat* and was using it for reference, talking through plot points as we tossed around ideas. I'd secretly been hoping that when he pulled out the book, he'd put his glasses back on, but it seemed like maybe he had his contacts in now, and I might not get to see him in glasses again, which honestly was incredibly disappointing.

We were on a stretch of highway that was a straight shot toward the horizon, mountains in the distance that we kept driving toward but somehow never seemed to get any closer to. Three lanes and a shoulder, with short, scrubby green bushes on the side of the road. The sky was huge and blue and endless above us, wispy white clouds drifting across it. The road wasn't very busy—I was staying in the middle lane, mostly to avoid the trucks barreling past in the right lane and the cars on the left whipping past us at speeds that seemed, even on a fairly deserted highway, really ill-advised. But the openness of the road—and the real lack of traffic—made me feel like I could relax into the drive, leaning back against the cloth-covered seat and resting my elbow on the window, occasionally letting the wind drift through my open fingers.

"Darcy?"

"Sorry," I said, glancing away from the road for a moment to look at Russell. He was bent over his book, the way he had been the very first time I'd seen him. "What did you say?"

"Just that I had an idea. What do you think about this—the camp song can be a motif we keep revisiting; it can be threaded through the whole show. And then in act 2, when the campers sing, Will can actually be having a duet with his younger self."

"We've gone through this." I laughed. "They're not the same person."

"Okay, except they totally are."

"Give me some proof."

"What about the scar they both have on their left hand?"

I frowned. "Remind me?"

"Here, I'll read it." He leaned back against the door, one leg bent. He cleared his throat, then started to read out loud. And as he did, I had to catch my breath.

I was in a vintage car, windows down, driving across the desert. A very cute guy was reading to me from my favorite book. I'd wanted to go to Silverspun so I could have some memories to hang on to before I left—of mountains and sunshine and music.

But that all seemed so shortsighted now. As I let the familiar words wash over me, I knew that Silverspun was only going to be a blip in my memory—more a means to an end than anything else. *This* was what I would remember, and take with me, and think about in November. The wind in my hair, the sun on my legs, Russell in his sunglasses reading to me, the endless horizon in front of us.

"Emma traced her hand over the small, crescent-shaped scar on William's thumb, letting her fingers rest there for just a moment before—"
BANG.

A sound like a gunshot ripped through the car. I jumped, and Russell yelped, the book tumbling to the floor. "Fuck! Darcy, what was—"

But before I could even think about answering, the Bronco swerved to the right, out of my control. "Ohmygodohmygod," I said, all one word. I gripped the wheel hard and tried to swerve back, but overcompensated and veered into the left lane. There had hardly been any cars on the road but there were some now—in my peripheral vision, I saw a blue sports car barely get out of our way in time.

Everything seemed to be happening very fast and very slow, all at once. My heart was racing—I could feel the adrenaline coursing through me, everything in my body screaming *danger danger danger*. The car was shaking, the steering wheel getting hard to hold on to, the wheel pulling right even though I wasn't turning it that way.

"Gonna pull over," I managed, and Russell turned to glance behind him.

"You're clear."

I put on my turn signal, then slowed down, feeling the jerky movement of the car that I knew couldn't be good, and then pulled off the road, the steering wheel fighting me the whole time. When we were on the shoulder, I shifted into park, shut off the engine, then lifted my trembling hands from the steering wheel.

The whole thing had probably only taken thirty seconds, but I felt like I'd just run a marathon.

"What happened?" Russell asked, sounding as shaken as I felt. "What—was that?"

"I think—it was the tire," I said slowly. That sound, the gunshot sound—I knew it. I'd heard it once before. And just like that, a memory was nudging at the corners of my mind, one I hadn't let myself replay in a long time.

I had been seven. Gillian had been in Ashland, Oregon, for the summer, understudying in the Shakespeare festival. My dad had taken me up for the weekend, after I'd begged. That was when I still wanted to see her whenever I could; when I was still so sure that if I did everything right, and said everything right, she'd change her mind and come back to California, and me. I no longer believed in Santa Claus or the Easter Bunny or the tooth fairy—I was going into second grade, after all—but at that moment in time, I still believed in my mother.

I was in the front seat, even though I knew I wasn't supposed to be, but she didn't have a booster seat, or seem to know about them, so I was feeling grown-up and maybe only a little bit scared as we drove to get lunch together.

She'd been reciting Masha's monologue from *Three Sisters*— she told me how you always have to be ready to go on; you never know what's going to happen—when a sound like a shot had echoed through the car. I'd screamed, but Gillian hadn't been scared, I remembered that—at the most, she was a little annoyed as she pulled off to the shoulder. She got out to investigate, and I scrambled out after her.

"It's a flat," she'd announced, twisting her hair up into a knot on top of her head and pulling the end through so it stayed.

"So we—call a tow truck?" My only experience with flat tires at that point had been seeing them happen in movies or TV shows.

She raised an eyebrow at me. "Of course we don't. We change it ourselves."

"You know how to do that?"

"Your grandfather ran a garage. He taught me everything." She frowned, her face falling slightly. "You knew that, right?"

Before I could answer, she was walking around to the trunk.

"I'll show you. Everyone should know how to change a tire."

And she'd done it. In what seemed like only a few minutes, she'd removed the hubcap, loosened the lug nuts, jacked up the car, and put the spare on.

And when it was finished and we were back in the car, she looked across at me and held her hand up for a high five.

Over the whole drive back to the theater—we didn't have time for a sit-down lunch, so we just got McDonald's drive-thru—I played it out in my mind. How everything would be different now. Oregon was pretty close to California, after all, and I was sure I'd see her more. I didn't know that a month later she'd move to London and I wouldn't see her for two years. In that moment—in the car, with my mother, a bag of warm fries between us and a mission completed together—everything had been perfect.

"The tire?" Russell echoed. I focused back on him, reminding myself where we were. I wasn't in Oregon with my mother. I was in California with Russell, and we needed to figure this out.

"I think so."

Russell located the hazards, turned them on, and we both got out. The second we did, I was hit with a wave of heat and the rush of the wind from the cars speeding by on the freeway, dust flying up in their wake. I crossed around the hood of the car to see that I'd been right—the tire was blown out, the car already listing to one side. "I'm so sorry," I said, my throat tight. Wylie had made it clear just how precious this car was to him—and I'd still managed to run over a rock, or whatever it had been, and damage it.

"It's not your fault," Russell said immediately.

"I can't believe this." I'd just wrecked Wylie Sanders's beloved car, the one he hadn't wanted us to take in the first place. Even though I was surrounded by more horizon than I had ever seen, it was like I could feel walls starting to press in on me.

We had a flat tire on the side of the highway in the middle of the desert. Not only did this strongly resemble the premise of one of Didi's horror movies—it also meant the very thin buffer of time we had to get home before my dad was going to disappear.

Just like that, it was playing out in my mind—my dad would come back to an empty house. It wouldn't take him long to realize I still hadn't returned from Silverspun—which meant he would realize I'd been lying to him for multiple days now. He was going to be furious. And worse than that, he was going to be disappointed in me. And then I was going to leave. Were we going to have to say goodbye like that—in the midst of a fight? The thought made my stomach hurt.

"It's fixable, though, right?" Russell asked. He knelt down to look at it. "People get these things fixed."

"I'm so screwed," I said, my voice hollow. "My dad—when he gets back ahead of me . . ."

"It's okay," Russell said, already pulling out his phone. "I'll call AAA. My dad made me get it after I was in that accident."

"Do you even have service?" I could hear my voice going high and panicky. Reception had been patchy the whole drive—when Russell had been driving, I'd sometimes look down at my phone and see no bars at all.

"I do," he said, and I felt myself breathe a little bit easier. "Let me just try to find my card."

I nodded, and Russell went back to the Bronco. Not even sure why I was doing it, I crossed around to the back of the car. I lifted out the tent and my duffel and raised up the fabric panel. And there it was—a spare tire. And inside it, a jack and lug wrench.

"Darcy?" I looked around and saw Russell holding his phone. "I got my card. And it looks like there's a 76 station a few miles from here, and they have a garage. So I'll call AAA, and they can tow us there. We're kind of in the middle of nowhere, so it might take them a while to get to us, but I think it's the best we're going to do."

I looked back down into the trunk for a moment. "Or," I said, before I even knew I was going to, "we could change it."

"We—could?" Russell stared at me. "I mean—I can't. Have you changed a tire before?"

"I've seen someone do it." I knew this wasn't the same thing at all—and the last thing I wanted to do was mess up Wylie's prized Bronco. But if we could do this, it would save us a *lot* of time. We wouldn't have to wait for a tow truck to come and find us on the side of the highway. Maybe I'd even make it home before my dad—maybe this could all still be okay.

"I mean—if you think you can, that's amazing," he said. "My mom would be so impressed with you."

"Well—I haven't actually done it. But I know it *can* be done. So maybe we could find a YouTube video, just to be on the safe side?"

Russell nodded. "That I can do."

I gave him a smile, then twisted my hair up into a knot on the top of my head and pulled the end through so it stayed.

Russell googled *change tire how to video easy*, and we watched it three times in a row before we even attempted it. The host was a cheerful Texan guy who made the whole thing seem simple—and even like a fun adventure.

But what had seemed so easy, watching it as a kid, was a *lot* harder in real life. It took both me and Russell several tries with the wrench to even get the lug nuts to loosen a little. The longer everything took, the more I was starting to feel myself getting nervous. I was hot, and dusty, and wondering if this was just a huge mistake. "Let me try again," I said, reaching for the wrench. The sweat was beading on my forehead and dripping down my back, and I couldn't stop myself from pulling out my phone to check the time on the map, once again. As I looked, my stomach clenched. I could see just how much time had been added to our arrival—and we weren't even on the road yet.

Russell wasn't saying anything, but what if I'd messed this up? What if we had to call AAA *now*, and had to wait all this time for them to come? If I hadn't suggested this—would we have already been to a garage by now with the tire halfway to getting fixed by a professional?

"I think I've almost . . . got it . . . ." Russell said, putting all his weight on the wrench—and finally, I saw the last lug nut grudgingly turn. "Okay," he said, smiling up at me. "According to the video, now we jack up the car."

"I'll get it," I said as I hurried to the trunk. I was doing the math in my head—if we could get the tire on and get on the road, *maybe* we could get there in time. I had just reached for the jack when my phone started to ring. It was "Fun, Fun, Fun"—my dad's ringtone. "Fuck," I muttered as I pulled my phone out of my back pocket. My heart was pounding as I slid my finger across the screen. "Hi, Dad! I'm just driving," I said quickly, knowing he'd be able to hear the sound of the cars. "Near home. Good old 134." My voice was too high and shrill, and I had a feeling he'd be able to tell something was wrong.

Russell glanced over at me, his eyes going wide, and I knew he'd just had the same thought I had—that I was in *trouble*.

"Darcy," my dad said. "So—"

"Are you home?" I asked, my words tumbling out. "I mean, where are you?" There might still be a chance we could make it back—unless he was already there, in which case, there was no chance and I was screwed.

"No, that's the thing." I straightened up, clocking his tone. I wasn't in trouble, I could tell that much. But something else was happening.

"What's wrong?"

"So I got on the road this morning, and hadn't gone far before the check-engine light went on."

"So you left late?" I held my phone away from my ear for a moment to see the time, trying to do the calculations.

"I'm still at Uncle Jeff's." My dad's voice was resigned. "I can't get the car into a shop until tomorrow morning."

I felt an immediate, giddy surge of happiness. I'd get away with this! My dad wouldn't have to know about the fact that I was currently on the side of the highway with a flat, that I'd still not made it back, that I'd almost gotten arrested. At least, he wouldn't have to know about any of it *right now*. I was pretty sure I was going to have to tell him at some point, but that day would not have to be today. Relief washed over me like a cool wave. I could stop panicking. I could stop doing the time math. I was home free.

But then a second later, with a crash of disappointment, I realized what this actually meant.

"So you're not—coming home tonight."

"I'm so sorry, honey," my dad said, and I could hear in his voice that he really was. "I asked your uncle if I could use his car, but he needs it for work. And—"

"It's fine," I said quickly, trying to ignore the pit that felt like it had just formed in my stomach. "Really. I can get myself to the airport. I'll get an Uber. It's not a big deal."

Russell straightened up, his eyes on me, giving me a sympathetic wince.

"It *is*, though," my dad said, and I could hear how frustrated he was. "We had our whole plan—pizza and milkshakes and then short-term parking and the discreet corner where I'd sob while you went off to start your life without me."

"I know we did." In all my worry about my dad getting home before me, I'd never once entertained the thought that he wouldn't *be* there. I had wanted to get away with this—I'd wanted there to be some way I'd get home before my dad, undetected. And now I was getting my wish, but in a terrible monkey's-paw way. I took a few steps away and rubbed my sandal over the crumbling asphalt.

"I'm so sorry, kiddo."

"It's not your fault." Mechanical problems happened, after all.

Mechanical problems were the whole reason I was standing here right now, and the whole reason Russell and I had even met in the first place.

"I'm still sorry. Why don't you call me at the airport and I'll give you the speech I prepared?"

I laughed in spite of myself. "You did *not* write a speech."

"I did so! So just FaceTime me and I'll tell it to you."

"It's a plan."

"So how was the festival? I want to hear all about it."

"Well." I started to try to organize my thoughts, then gave up when I realized there was no simple way to even start doing this. "It was really—different than I expected. But good."

"Okay, I'll have to get the whole story later."

"For sure."

I heard my dad take a breath and let it out. "I love you, kid."

I smiled. "I love you, too."

"We'll talk tonight, okay? When you're at the gate."

"Sounds good."

I hung up and just stood there for a moment, breathing in the dust and gasoline fumes, trying to push down the disappointment and sadness that was threating to bubble up.

Or, you know, Didi suggested. *You could just let yourself feel it.*

That works too! Katy chimed in.

"That really sucks." Russell's voice was soft. I turned around and saw he was standing in front of me, his sunglasses pushed on top of his head.

"It's really okay. I'll get an Uber to the airport."

"I'm sorry, Darcy."

"It's fine." I said this automatically, but then a second later, wondered if it really was. "It's just a stupid rite of passage, you know? Saying goodbye at the airport. And it's probably not that important. I think I've just seen too many movies about it, so I was attaching all this meaning to it."

"But maybe we have these rites of passage for a reason. It was important to you."

I shrugged even as I nodded. "I'll FaceTime with my dad at the gate, and we'll just do it remotely. If it's really important that the person who drives me to the airport is sad to see me go, I can really try to dazzle my Uber driver or something." Russell laughed at that, but when I followed the thought to its logical end—that I would be hauling my suitcase out of a stranger's car myself, heading off to college without anyone to hug me and tell me they'd miss me—I felt a lump in my throat.

And for once, I didn't try to just push the feeling away.

Finally, Katy cheered.

About time, Didi added.

"But it does suck," I agreed with a sigh. "Like—I know things sometimes don't turn out the way you expected, but I thought I would get this, at least. Before everything else started, you know?" I felt my chin tremble, and I pressed my lips together.

Russell took a step closer to me. He closed the distance between us and pulled me into his arms. I leaned against him, my cheek resting on the soft fabric of his yellow shirt, warmed by the sun. I closed my eyes and let out a shaky breath, and he ran his hand over my hair, stroking it gently.

After a few moments, I straightened up again. Even though it felt like I could have stayed there for a lot longer, I knew we needed to finish this. "We better get moving. We don't have a minute to *spare.*"

Russell took a step back himself and smiled at me. "The puns have returned, I see."

"I mean, doing this ourselves is better than getting a professional. They'd just *jack up* the prices."

"Very nice."

"You're not *tire-d* of them?"

"Okay," he said, shaking his head. "That might have been a bridge too far."

"I knew it would fall *flat*." He groaned, and I smiled at him, even though my heart wasn't quite in it. With the help of Russell's video, we got the car jacked up and the spare on. When we'd tightened the lug nuts and put the hubcap back on, we looked at each other in silent amazement.

"Did we just—do that?" Russell asked.

"I think we did." I was still sweaty, and my back was sore, but we'd changed a tire.

And in that moment, the only person I wanted to tell was Gillian.

"Go team," Russell said, holding up his hand.

"Go team," I said, laughing as I slapped his palm.

Russell drove us—very slowly, hazards on—to the 76 with the garage that he'd found. We didn't play any music, or even talk—both of us were sitting very still, listening for any signs of trouble, or indications that the tire had been put back on wrong and was currently detaching itself and rolling down the highway.

I didn't start to breathe easier until we pulled into the garage part of the gas station and Russell cut the engine. Even if we'd done things wrong, we'd made it this far.

Russell went to the garage, to see if he could find a mechanic to look at the tire and check if we'd done it okay, and I headed into the mini-mart, enjoying the blast of air-conditioning that hit me as I stepped inside. I used the bathroom and washed my hands for much longer than usual, trying to get the grease off them.

When I came back out, I could see Russell still in the garage area, talking to a 76 employee in coveralls. Feeling like I needed to stretch my legs, I walked in the opposite direction, toward the parking lot, and just beyond it, the highway. I pulled out my phone to check the time on the map, automatically—before I remembered there was no need for this. We didn't have to hurry anymore. I was definitely going to get home before my dad now. Because I wasn't going to see him before I went to college. I had to draw in a breath as a wave of sadness walloped me.

To have to do this on my own, on both ends, suddenly felt really unfair, and the tears that had been lurking behind my eyes edged closer to falling.

Gillian did offer to pick you up, Katy reminded me, her voice gentle. *You shut it down.*

I *had* shut it down. Because I hadn't wanted to—what? Give her the . . . satisfaction of helping me? It seemed so stupid now, and so childish.

All at once, my thoughts were racing, going as fast as the cars tearing down the highway. Images and flashes of memories were flooding my mind. Gillian smiling across the car at me, McDonald's bag between us. Chloe, looking impossibly young, picking up her daughter. Wylie in the morning sunlight, talking about dashed dreams. And Andy, running away and not being able to find his way home again.

Something that Didi and Katy had said was echoing in my mind—

Darcy.

You know we're not actually here, right?

That we've never been here?

That there's actually nobody here but you?

I took a breath, then let it out.

Of course I knew this—I'd always known it. I wasn't disassociating or anything. Didi was at Colgate, in upstate New York. Katy was at Scripps in Claremont. I hadn't talked to either of them— neither one had any idea about anything that had happened over the course of the last day. They'd never even heard of Russell. It had just seemed easier—less lonely—to imagine what they would say in this situation.

But it had been me, this whole time.

Which meant I actually knew what I wanted to do, even if I needed to pretend to be my best friends in order to hear it.

I unlocked my phone, my hand hesitating over the screen for only a moment.

Then I pressed the button to call my mother.

CHAPTER 19

Monday
1:45 P.M.

held the phone against my ear, listening to it ring. What if I
finally got up the courage to call her—and it went right to voicemail? I had just resigned myself to this when Gillian picked up,
sounding out of breath.

"Hello? Darcy?"

"Hi." I hated that tears had sprung to my eyes at the very sound
of her voice, and I blinked them back impatiently.

"Is everything okay? Did something happen?" I could hear she
sounded worried, which was understandable—I never called her up
just to chat.

"No, everything's fine." I swallowed hard. "I just, um . . ." I
looked out at the cars flying past, everyone heading somewhere. For
a second I got overwhelmed by it all—all the stories contained in all
of them, all the loves and losses and heartbreaks.

Focus, I reminded myself, since I didn't want to rely on Didi and
Katy to do this anymore.

"I changed a tire."

"You—what?" Gillian sounded utterly thrown by this, and I
didn't blame her.

"I'm on a drive with a—a friend, and the tire went flat and we changed it. You showed me how. Remember? In Oregon?"

"I do," Gillian said slowly, like she was also pulling this memory, over a decade old, from the recesses of her mind.

"But that's not really why I called. I . . ." I pressed my lips together and made myself say it. "I wanted to apologize for last night. I shouldn't . . . have said those things to you. And I'm sorry."

"Wow. Okay," Gillian said. It was like I could practically feel her regrouping over the phone. "That's not what I was expecting. Um . . . thank you."

"I guess," I said, making myself go on, knowing that if I stopped to think about what I was doing, I wouldn't get through it. This was walking on a balance beam, or doing a backflip off a diving board. If you thought too hard about how impossible the thing you were doing was, you'd never accomplish it. "I've been . . . really mad at you. For a while now. And I probably should have just talked to you about it, but—" I shook my head. I was now regretting not figuring out what I was going to say before I started this, but that ship had sailed, and here we were. There was no way out but through.

"I was mad that you left, that I didn't get to see you, like, ever, and then you started a whole new family with someone else and forgot all about me. And then it seemed—it seemed—" My voice was hitching in my throat, and hot tears had started to snake down my cheeks. I took a shaky breath. "It seemed like you wanted me to just forget about it all when I said I'd go to Stanwich, like that made up for everything. Like you were trying to buy me off or something? Like—a bribe? And I just—" I swallowed hard and lifted my sunglasses up to wipe my face.

"Darcy. I never forgot about you. Never *ever*." Her voice was fierce, and it sounded like maybe there were tears on her end as well.

"You're my daughter, and not a day goes by that I don't wish . . . that I would have done some things differently." I heard her take a hitching breath on the other end of the phone, three thousand miles away from me. "I was so happy when I heard you got into Stanwich. And so *proud*. And I thought that maybe it could be a fresh start for you and me."

"I was talking to . . ." The words *Wylie Sanders* floated through my mind, but I didn't want to derail this conversation by bringing a rock star into it. ". . . to someone this morning, and they said that as a parent, you just want to do what you can to help your kids. And I hadn't thought of it like that until now."

"Oh, Darcy." Gillian sighed. "I never meant for you to see it as a bribe. It was just . . ."

There was a pause, and for a second I wished I knew what she looked like right now, where she was. At work? In her kitchen, in her house in Connecticut? I couldn't even picture it—but maybe soon, I would be able to. I'd been so dismissive of her, so angry that she didn't know anything about my life—not factoring in, until now, that this went both ways. That I also didn't know nearly enough about hers.

After a moment, she went on, a slight tremble in her voice. "There's so much I wasn't there for. So much I didn't give you. And I just thought that this was finally *something* I could do for you."

I looked out at the traffic as the warm breeze lifted my hair—the hair I'd inherited from her—and blew it all around me. "I didn't understand just how young you and Dad were—when you had me. And I know I probably got in the way of things you wanted to do—"

"No." Gillian's voice was firm. "You were the best thing I ever did, Darcy. And I might regret what I did—and how I handled things—but I never regretted you. Not once."

My eyes filled with fresh tears, like the ones I was already crying weren't quite enough.

I heard her take a halting breath, and then continue. "And I know I probably don't deserve one—but if you could see your way to giving me a second chance, that would make me . . . really happy."

I wiped the tears from my eyes. It felt like all the things I'd so firmly believed were breaking up and floating away. Suddenly, it was like I could see everything from a new angle. What if being around Gillian this year *wasn't* going to be the worst thing in the world, some kind of punishment? What if it could actually be an opportunity to finally get to know my mother? Because this was all I'd wanted when I was younger—more time with my mom. To actually be in the same place that she was. It suddenly seemed beyond petty that I was turning my back on this because it wasn't happening in the timeline I'd wanted.

"I think I'd like that too." I pushed my sunglasses on top of my head, wiped under my eyes, and took a deep breath. "I'm not sure what that looks like, though."

"Me either," Gillian said immediately, and I laughed—and heard, through the phone, that she was laughing too. "But maybe we can figure it out? We don't have to do everything all at once."

I nodded, feeling this hit me somewhere deep in my chest. "That sounds good."

"Well. Okay."

"Okay," I echoed. There was a beat of comfortable silence, and I just took a moment to note how nice even that was—a conversation with Gillian that wasn't fraught and testy, me snapping and angry and resenting her for everything I wanted from her but wasn't getting.

"So now that that's out of the way," she said, clearing her throat, "maybe you want to tell me why Wylie Sanders's lawyer was calling me last night?"

"Oh." I glanced back at Russell, who was standing by the car. He gave me a look that even from a distance I could tell meant *Everything okay?* I nodded and pointed to my phone, and he nodded as well. "Well . . ."

"Did you *meet* him?" Gillian's voice was high and fangirly.

"Wait—you're a Nighthawks fan?"

"What!" She sounded affronted by this. "Of course I'm a—who do you think got your father into them in the first place?"

"Wait, *what*?"

"I gave him a mix tape in college! He'd never even heard them before; he was refusing to let ska go, and listening to all these bands with *saxophones*, and it was like, no."

"Dad is a Nighthawks fan because of *you*?"

"Why do you think you're named Darcy?"

"I thought—it was on the playlist when I was born. . . ."

"Yes! *My* playlist."

"Oh." I shook my head, just trying to get my mind around this truly world-shaking news. Whenever I'd listened to their songs or played albums on a loop, there had been a connection between me and my mother—I just hadn't known about it until this minute. "Well—in that case, do I have a story to tell you." Maybe it wasn't only my dad who was going to get to hear about my adventure. Because it seemed like Gillian—my mom—would appreciate it too.

She laughed. "It sounds like it. I have to get to a meeting, but you'll be on campus tomorrow, right?"

"Yeah. My plane lands in the morning."

"Unless . . ." She hesitated, and when she spoke again, it was all in a rush. "I mean, the offer still stands if you want a ride from the airport. It's no trouble."

"Oh. Um . . ."

"But if you'd rather come on your own, I understand."

"No, that would be . . . really nice, actually."

"Wow. Okay." I could hear in her voice how surprised—but pleased—she was. "Great. So—just text me your flight information."

"Okay. Will do. Um . . . thank you."

"Of course. I'll see you tomorrow, Darcy."

"See you . . ." For just a second, I thought about trying *Mom* but rejected it immediately. "Gillian."

She hung up and I just stood with the phone in my hand for a moment. I thought of what Russell had said to me when we were fighting—what Katy and Didi were always saying—and what my dad was always trying to get me to change. That I saw things in black and white. That everything was always all or nothing.

And maybe—just maybe—it didn't have to be that way.

Maybe I could dislike the way I'd ended up at my college but still be able to see some good things about it. Maybe Wylie could be a rock star but also have a sprawling, loving, close-knit family.

Maybe I *didn't* have to solve my relationship with my mother immediately, or even know what it would look like. Maybe we could figure it out—together.

Maybe Russell could be a good guy who'd made a mistake. Maybe it didn't have to be either love at first sight or just friends— maybe there was something in between the two.

I stood there for a moment longer, watching the cars on the highway pass me by. I knew that nothing had changed with the view—it was the same one I'd seen minutes ago. But I couldn't help thinking it looked different now. Like everything did. Like I was now in a world where impossible things could happen.

Russell drove the rest of the way back to LA. The mechanic had tightened some of the lug nuts but declared it a good job otherwise, which I'd felt a rush of pride upon hearing. He told us not to drive too fast on the spare, and to get a real tire on the Bronco as soon as possible. Russell filled up the car with gas, and after hitting the mini-mart for some snacks and sodas—it turned out Russell liked pretzels and Coke Zero—we were back on the road.

I took over the DJ duties—occasionally going back to throw in one of the musical songs I particularly liked (Russell always smiled when this happened, even though he was clearly trying to be nonchalant about it). But the closer we got to home, the more it seemed like every song I picked was about saying goodbye, people missing each other, letting each other go. It was like I was only just now fully realizing how many songs are about painful separations, even the upbeat ones.

"You okay?" Russell asked, glancing over at me when we had half an hour left before we hit Union Station. I'd just zipped through six songs, not letting any of them play for more than a few seconds, once I really realized what they were about.

"Yep," I said, desperately searching my Spotify for something that wasn't about saying goodbye forever to someone. "Um—want to hear a podcast about the history of fonts?"

"*Go to Helvetica*? Already heard it."

"Of course you have."

"I have to get my fun facts from somewhere, after all. But—happy to listen to it if you want."

"No, it's okay." I pulled up the newest AJR album, figuring that this was one of the safer bands I could go with, and pressed play.

"Nice," Russell said with a smile as I rested my phone on the seat between us.

I glanced out the window—traffic was starting to creep back up, and it seemed to be getting worse the closer we got to Los Angeles. As soon as I'd gotten back to the car at the gas station, I'd told Russell what had happened with Gillian—and I realized, as I was taking him through the conversation, that he was the person I *wanted* to tell.

He'd been surprised to hear about the revelation that she was actually the original Nighthawks fan in the family. And as I was telling Russell about this, I thought about the sweatshirt—the one my dad had had forever. Had it first been my mom's? It was somehow easier to picture her buying a sweatshirt with a shirtless Wylie Sanders on it than my dad, now that I really thought about it. But it didn't have to be a complete mystery—I could ask my mother tomorrow. When I saw her.

Now, I looked across the car at Russell, at his excellent posture and careful driving and the way he kept checking in with me. Was I really going to say goodbye to him in less than an hour? Possibly forever?

He was so close to me, really. I could have taken off my lap belt and slid across the seat and rested my head on his shoulder. I could have threaded my fingers through his. I could have rested my hand on his leg and kept time to the music, played drums on his knee.

I was no longer even trying to pretend to myself that I only wanted to be his friend—and from the way he kept glancing over at me, I was pretty sure he felt the same way.

But was there any point? We'd be at Union Station before this album was over. And then . . . that would probably be it.

So even though I really, really wanted to reach out and touch him—even though I wanted to kiss him again—I clasped my hands in my lap and looked out the window. I hadn't even known this person twenty-four hours ago. So would it really be that hard to say goodbye to him, let this day fade into memory, the details and specifics getting fuzzy?

Even without my inner Didi and Katy to point it out, I knew I was kidding myself.

The second we got into LA proper, traffic slowed to practically a crawl, but in contrast to this, time seemed to be moving faster. And before I'd really prepared for it, we were taking the exit for Union Station.

Russell pulled around the front circle to drop me off. "I'll just get my car and meet you here," I said, shouldering my canvas bag. "And then I can get my stuff from you and load it into my car." That was also when we'd have to say goodbye—which suddenly seemed like it had arrived a lot faster than I'd been prepared for it to.

Russell nodded, shifted the car into park, and turned his hazards on. "Sounds good."

I walked fast through the parking garage, trying to remember where I'd left my car. I was having trouble getting my head around the fact that on Friday, three nights ago, I'd parked here, not knowing anything that was about to happen. Then, I'd been excited to go to Silverspun, while dreading the future that was barreling toward me. And while it was still coming—it felt now like I was getting to choose it. Like I was barreling along with it.

I found my car, got in, and just sat there for a moment. It seemed somehow like it should be different. So much had happened—it didn't make any sense that my car was exactly the same, maybe a little dustier. I glanced at myself quickly in the rearview mirror—I'd never had bangs, but if Chloe thought they were a good idea, I was certainly going to take that into consideration—and started the car. I'd just shifted into drive when my phone rang.

Russell was flashing on the screen and I felt a little thrill as I answered it—somehow, this would be the first time we'd talked on the phone. "Hi," I said.

"Hey, Darcy," Russell said, speaking fast. "So they're telling me I have to move my car. I can't stay here."

"Keep it moving!" I heard the unmistakable voice of a parking attendant, blowing a whistle that made me wince.

"Oh," I said, trying to think fast. "Okay—I'm coming." I pulled forward, driving toward the exit—and then slammed on my brakes. There was a line to pay at least five cars deep. "It might take me a minute to get out of here."

"They're definitely not going to let me stay," Russell said, and I could hear the stress in his voice. "Maybe I could meet you somewhere?"

"Do you want to just meet at my house?" I asked, after trying and failing to think of a place near the station. "It's just ten minutes away."

"Great," Russell said, and I could hear the relief in his voice, now that we had a plan. "Just text me the address."

I did, and I had plenty of time to do it as I crawled forward, trying to get to the payment kiosk. When I finally made it, I paid using the cash I'd been keeping folded in my pocket, feeling my shoulders relax when the attendant nodded at me and the gate rose up. I no longer had to be quite so worried about money—at home, I would be reunited with my debit card and my in-case-of-emergency credit card and the three hundred-dollar bills in my sock drawer. I no longer had to be living in a state of counting my cash and trying to do parking-lot math. It was a burden I could finally put down. I pulled out of the Union Station garage and headed for home, feeling a lot lighter.

I turned onto Raven Rock's main drag, and then I took the familiar streets to my house, the neighborhood I knew like the back of my hand. *My last day here* flashed into my head as I waved at our two-doors-down neighbor, who was out walking her beagle. But I didn't want to go there quite yet. I'd spent so long thinking about tomorrow, and the next few months, what they would or would not look like. For a little while longer, while I still could, I just wanted it to be *now*.

I pulled up into our driveway and saw Russell standing by the Bronco, which he'd parked on the side of the street. As I got out of the car, I looked at our craftsman, with its slightly overgrown lawn and the sign that had been there since May—RAVEN ROCK HIGH SCHOOL GRADUATE __DARCY__ IS ON TO GREAT THINGS! For just a second, I wondered if I should be embarrassed for Russell to see my house, now that I'd seen his dad's mansion, with its helipad and its pool and its guesthouses. But that only lasted a second as affection for it rose up in me, trumping all of that. It was home. Familiar and comfortable and mine.

I looked over to see Russell leaning against the vintage Bronco, sunglasses on, and so handsome it took my breath away. There was a piece of me that was still getting my head around the fact that this guy was waiting for me. That when he smiled it was because I'd come into view, and even though I hadn't been gone long, he was happy to see me again. Was I honestly looking for more than that? Wasn't this what it was about, at the most elemental level?

Russell came to meet me on the driveway, holding the Merediths' tent and my duffel bag. "This is home?"

I smiled at him as I took my stuff from him. "This is home."

We stood there for a moment, a few feet apart. I was acutely aware that I didn't have a script for anything that happened next. As I looked at him, standing in the sun, it was as though he was coming into focus, like when you look through the lenses in the optometrist's office, when you don't realize how blurry things have been until the right ones fit into place. And suddenly everything is clear, and you can read the line of letters with confidence.

And I knew I didn't want to say goodbye—not yet.

I took a step closer to him, closer than we'd been since Jesse, just hoping he wasn't ready for this to be the end either. I took one more step and then I was right there, in front of him, with my heart on my sleeve and nothing left to lose. "Hi."

"Hi," he said, looking down at me, happiness and surprise mingling on his face. We weren't touching—not yet—but it felt like we were just a beat away from it.

"I didn't know if you wanted to—come inside? It's a long drive back to Brentwood."

"It is a long drive," Russell said, taking a step closer to me, his eyes on mine.

"I thought we could hang out in my house for a bit."

A smile was pulling at the corners of his mouth, like a boat straining against its ropes. "You mean the house where your dad isn't home?"

"The very same."

"I thought you said—you just wanted to be friends."

"I did say that." I nodded, then looked up at him and smiled, my heart beating hard. He reached out and touched my cheek, so softly. "And yet . . ."

And then I moved toward him and he moved toward me and caught me up in his arms, and we were kissing.

V
The Ballad of Darcy & Russell

I was almost there.

Jesse was just twenty minutes away, and time seemed to be compressing and expanding simultaneously. I'd turned my music off an hour ago. It was like I couldn't even hear my favorite songs right now. Music was too distracting, spinning my thoughts in too many directions. I needed to focus on where I was going and what I was heading to.

My heat was cranked up—the temperature had been steadily dropping as I'd gone north, but even so, I could still feel my palms sweat when I thought about what I was moving toward.

Because Russell would either be there, in the place we'd decided on back in August, waiting for me—or he wouldn't.

And if he wasn't, then I'd just be a girl alone in a bus station who'd driven seven hours with nothing to show for it except a slight sunburn across her cheeks.

But I had to take the risk. I had to show up and just hope that he would be there too, that he'd missed me as much as I'd missed him. That his heart was also pounding an excited, nervous metronome in his ears right now.

I saw the exit for Jesse and signaled to take it, flexing my hands against the wheel.

I was almost there.

CHAPTER 20

Monday
4:19 P.M.

We were kissing as though we'd never stopped, picking up without missing a beat. His hands slipped under my T-shirt to rest on my waist, warm against my bare skin. My arms were around his neck, pulling him as close to me as I could.

It was wonderful to be kissing him again—because now the nervous energy from back in Jesse was gone. This was a kiss that remembered everything that came before and promised what would come next. And even though it had only been twenty-four hours, I knew him now. I knew who he really was, in all senses of the phrase.

I'd met his family and his dogs. I'd seen him when he woke up in the morning. We'd had a terrible fight and had come out the other end. I'd told him my biggest fears and worries, shown him the worst side of myself, and he was still here.

All of that was there as we kissed—my canvas bag falling down at my feet, forgotten; his strong arms around me, lifting me up for just a second before returning me to the ground on legs that felt unsteady.

A sharp bark shook me out of this reverie, and I broke away from Russell and looked over to see my neighbor—and her beagle—

walking back up the street. She gave me a nod, even though it looked like she was trying very hard not to smile.

"Um," I said as I clasped my hands behind his neck and looked up at him. "Maybe we should . . ."

He smiled at me, his thumbs tracing circles on my waist. "I think that sounds like an excellent idea."

Russell grabbed my tent and duffel, and we hurried up to the front door. I flashed for just a second to Wylie's endless driveway and priceless art. But just for a second. It looked like my dad had forgotten to cancel the papers, and I scooped up copies of the *Times*—both New York and Los Angeles—and pulled my keys out of my bag.

I stepped inside and held the door open for Russell, who set down my things and pulled it closed behind him, and then we were kissing again, and I was lost in his lips and his hands and his arms around me. I started to walk backward toward the stairs, while also continuing to kiss him, but Russell pulled back. "Shoes-off house?"

"Oh," I said, trying to focus. "Um—sure." I kicked off my Birkenstocks, and Russell took off his sneakers by stepping on the backs of them. He then quickly stripped off his socks, rolled them together, and rested them in his empty left Nike.

He stood up and looked at me a little questioningly, and I just smiled at him and ran up the stairs, hearing him following right behind me.

The door to my room was ajar and as I walked inside, I was relieved that it wasn't a gigantic disaster, and that I'd even made my bed.

"This is your room?" Russell asked, stepping in behind me.

"Uh-huh." And even though I knew we were alone in the house, that my dad was stuck up in Fresno with car troubles, even though nobody else would be coming in, I closed the door.

Russell held on to my hand, his fingers drawing circles along the inside of my wrist, but all the while looking around, like he was drinking everything in, which seemed only fair. I'd had access to so much of his life, after all—now he was the one getting to see my front lawn, my house, my bedroom.

"Let me guess," Russell said as he looked at the Polaroids stuck around my dresser mirror. He pointed at the one from the prom— me, Katy, and Didi, all of us looking in a slightly different direction, all of us laughing. He pointed at Katy. "Katy?"

I nodded.

"So that's Didi."

I smiled. "*Very* impressive. They'll be incredibly pleased to hear you got it in one." I reached over and picked the photo up. My hair had been blown out and put in a half updo, and Katy had spent almost on hour on my makeup. "This is what I look like when I actually have my hair done and makeup on."

Russell shook his head as he looked at me. "You look beautiful." He said it in such a steady, simple way, like there was no other answer.

My heart started to beat a little harder, a little more joyfully. He took my head in his hands and smoothed my hair back from my forehead. He traced his fingers under my jaw, like he was taking in every detail of me. "So beautiful."

My instinct was to make a joke, or brush this off—but then I looked into his eyes and saw how much he meant it, and so I just let myself take it in. I stretched up to kiss him, and took my hand in his, pulling him with me until we tumbled back together onto my bed.

CHAPTER 21

Monday

6:00 P.M.

Kissing Russell on a football field, and in the hotel pool, had been great.

But it was nothing compared to this.

Getting to kiss him on my bed, in my room, with the door closed. With nowhere to be but right here and hours ahead of us.

No AstroTurf, no smell of chlorine, no worry that we were going to be discovered. Just the two of us under my covers, finally getting to breathe a little and take our time.

And after so much talk—so many conversations and tangents and jokes and puns and fun facts—it all dropped away.

We were still talking. But we were no longer doing it with words.

There were still *some* words, of course. We checked in with each other at every stage, making sure we were both okay, that this was what we both wanted and were comfortable with. Russell went on a mini rant about my bra clasp and I had a moment of nervously babbling while my fingers fumbled with the buttons on his shirt.

But for the most part, it was just us and a different kind of conversation—his lips and his hands and my arms and our feet tangling together and getting to see every inch of him, and letting him see me.

It all just felt so natural, and so right. And I somehow knew that despite—or because of—four days of missed connections and mistakes; buses, helicopters, and cars; lucky accidents and twists of fate, I'd somehow found myself just where I was supposed to be.

And so when Russell asked me if I was okay—if I was sure—I nodded without hesitation.

I stretched up to kiss him, and gave him a smile. "I'm ready."

CHAPTER 22

Monday
9:00 P.M.

Darcy." I woke up and felt Russell's arms around me. He kissed my bare shoulder and I smiled without opening my eyes.

"Hi," I said, cuddling back into him. We were under my sheets—we'd tossed the blanket off at some point; I'm sure it was on the floor somewhere—fitted together like two spoons. I sighed and snuggled down deeper into my pillow. Sleep was just around the corner, and I was sure I could fall back into it in just a few seconds. And when I woke up, Russell would be there. How wonderful was that?

"I think we need to wake up," he said, even though I could tell from his voice he'd only just woken up too. "We should probably get going?"

My eyes flew open—just like that, reality crashed down on me. It was dark in my room, and I sat up with the discombobulating feeling that comes with oversleeping—when you're not quite sure where or when you are. I looked at the clock on the bedside table—it was nine at night. Which meant I only had half an hour, at most, before I needed to leave for the airport.

"Oh, god." Russell was absolutely right that I needed to get up and start getting myself organized. But instead, I just lay back down and rolled onto my other side, so I was facing him. I twined my feet with his and just took him in for a second—he was right there, sharing my pillow, his hair sticking up in all directions from where I'd been running my fingers through it. "You're right," I said with a sigh. "We should go."

"Yeah." He ran his hand up and down my back, letting it rest on my hip. I somehow knew that the second we got up and had to start dealing with the world again—bags, car, airport—all of this would be gone. We were in a tiny bubble, a kingdom we'd made in my room. And when we got out of the bed, there would be conversations to have and things to decide and this magical moment would be over.

I reached across and stroked his cheek, and Russell smiled. "Remember this morning?" he asked.

"Vaguely." I ran my thumb over his cheek, tracing the constellation of his freckles.

"I said I had a dream about you. And you asked me what it was."

"Oh, right." That was when it had seemed so incredibly intimate to see Russell in his bedroom, in his element. And now here he was in *mine*, with his arm around me and nothing between us. "So what was it?"

He opened his eyes and looked right into mine. "This," he said with a smile, half disbelieving. "That we were just sleeping next to each other, and I woke up and reached out for you and you were there."

I wound a strand of his hair around my finger. "That was the dream?"

"You sound surprised."

"I guess I just thought it would be something more . . . exciting."

He turned his head so that he could kiss my hand. "There's nothing more exciting than this."

We just looked at each other for another moment, our heads sharing a pillow, and suddenly I wondered—should we have done this just as I was leaving? It had seemed absolutely right and romantic a few hours ago—but was this the absolute worst timing? A beginning and an ending, all mixed up together?

"We should get going," he said, even as he made absolutely no move to get up.

"Yeah," I agreed, equally not moving, and he smiled. But then reality hit me like a wave as I looked around my room. My suitcase was half packed on the floor by my desk, and the sheer amount of *stuff* I had to do in the next half hour was suddenly overwhelming. "I still need to finish packing."

"For college? You haven't packed?" A second later, Russell shook his head. "Sorry—didn't mean for that to sound judgmental. You haven't packed!" he repeated, now making this sound like a fun idea.

"I guess I thought . . . if I didn't pack, maybe I wouldn't have to go?" I sighed, and grabbed my robe from where it had been flung over my desk chair. "It won't take me that long." I pulled open my closet, flipping through my dresses, looking for the warmest ones.

Russell pulled his T-shirt on and stood up, now—disappointingly—dressed. "Bathroom?"

"Just down the hall." I pulled three dresses off their hangers, almost at random, and dropped them in my suitcase. I grabbed a pile of T-shirts and placed them in my bag, then pulled out pajamas, underwear, socks . . . with every item I tossed in my bag, it was like the reality of what I was heading to was getting sharper, and the dreaminess of what we'd just had was starting to fade away. The whole last day had been a respite from all of the reality that was now rushing toward me like a wave, all the more jarring because I'd been pretending it wouldn't happen. But maybe, I reasoned as I threw in a Milligan Concepts sweatshirt and my favorite sweatpants, it wouldn't be so bad. Maybe I could even start to see it as an adventure.

"Can I help?" I turned to see Russell leaning against the doorframe, and smiled automatically when I saw him, like a reflex.

"I think I'm okay." I took my makeup bag off the counter and added it to the suitcase, then grabbed two of my favorite Kelly Tipton novels from my desk and placed them inside too. "Nearly there." He walked a little farther into the room and I raised an eyebrow at him. "I assume you're already packed up?"

He shook his head. "You can't in our house. The cats don't like it when you take out suitcases, so we all avoid taking them out until the last minute."

"What . . . do they do?"

"Unspeakable things. You don't want to know."

I laughed at that and started pulling out my jeans. Were five pairs enough? There would also be, I reasoned, stores in Connecticut. Probably.

"You did Mock Trial?" I looked up from my suitcase to see Russell looking at the plaque I'd gotten at graduation.

"Oh—yeah," I said. "All four years."

"Huh." Russell leaned forward to look at it more closely, and I realized that we hadn't talked much about this—who we were only a few months ago.

"What—I mean, what did you do? At school?"

"I played lacrosse."

"Lacrosse?" Somehow this didn't make any sense with the Russell I thought I knew. "Really?"

"Absolutely. And I was in the band as well—I played piano for all the musicals. Guitar, too. . . ."

I nodded. "Right." That made more sense to me—but it was like I'd just realized that there was a lot more of Russell than I'd seen so far—like I'd just been downstairs in a house that had whole other wings and rooms. I gave the suitcase one last look, then zipped it up. I was *really* not sure if I'd packed properly, but I told myself that I could have my dad send me anything I'd forgotten that was essential.

"All set?" Russell crossed over to me and helped me lift my suitcase.

"I think so? Hopefully?" I glanced at the clock on my dresser—if I was going to make it to the airport, I really needed to leave. "I should see how long an Uber's going to take."

Russell shook his head. "What do you mean? Of course I'm going to drive you."

"Oh—that's so nice, but—"

"Darcy." Russell shook his head, like this should have been obvious. "Don't be ridiculous."

"Oh." I smiled at him, and it felt a little bit like someone had just hit snooze on our goodbye—that we'd been able to push it off, at least for a little bit. "Well—thank you. That's really nice of you."

He leaned over and gave me a kiss, and we lingered there for just a moment. "Five stars," he said when we finally broke away, winding a strand of my hair around his finger. "That's all I ask."

Twenty minutes later, I'd gotten dressed and we'd loaded my suit-case into the car. I'd emptied out my canvas bag of the stuff I'd needed for Silverspun and instead put in my wallet, phone, phone *charger*, laptop, and sweater for the plane. I'd also added my Nighthawks sweatshirt to my suitcase. I wasn't going to wear it in front of Russell, but I also wasn't going to leave it behind.

"Is that everything?" Russell asked me as he shut the back of the Bronco.

"I think so." I dropped my bag onto the seat and glanced back at the house. I knew that time was ticking, but I needed just one more moment. "I'm just going to lock up. Be right back."

I ran across the lawn and up to the front door—but then opened it and stepped inside. I couldn't help but wonder what would have happened by the next time I was in this spot, a semester of college under my belt. Who would I be then? I didn't even know that Darcy, but in three months' time, she'd be here. The house would be the same, but I wouldn't.

I took the stairs up to my room two at a time, and quickly smoothed the covers over my bed, picking up the blanket from the floor. Then I reached under the bed and pulled out the shoebox with the picture of my mother in it. It was the two of us—I was standing on the sidewalk, reaching up for something, as my mother smiled at whoever was taking the picture—my dad, probably. Her hands were holding tight to mine, like she was never going to let me go.

I looked at it for just a moment longer, then glanced around my room. I saw my copy of *Theseus's Sailboat* on my bookcase and grabbed it. I tucked the picture inside and headed downstairs.

In the kitchen, I paused. It seemed impossible that a few days from now my dad would be doing his crossword puzzle like usual, only I wouldn't be there to help.

A line from my namesake song—that I now knew both the

true origin of, *and* that it was my mother who'd helped give it to me—floated through my head. *Has there ever been a day when Darcy wasn't here?* Like it or not, starting tomorrow, it would be what was happening.

I grabbed the Milligan Concepts notepad from where it always lived on the kitchen counter, and wrote a quick note.

> Thank you for everything.
> I love you.
> Darcy

I propped it up against the TV—the place where we'd always left messages for each other—and headed for the door. I locked it behind me and rattled the doorknob once to make sure.

Then I tucked the book under my arm and hurried across the lawn to where Russell was waiting by the car.

"Ready?" he asked when we were both inside, ignition on.

I looked back at the house, taking it all in. Trying to freeze it in my mind. The whole time I'd been going through the admissions process, all my recommendations and applications and paperwork, the reality of *and then you leave the only home you've ever known* had somehow not really registered with me. But of course this was happening. There was no other way for it to go—but I let myself feel it for just a moment, this goodbye that was always going to happen, one way or another.

And when I'd gotten my fill, I turned to Russell and gave him a slightly quavery smile, and nodded. "Let's do it."

CHAPTER 23

Monday
10:15 P.M.

Luckily, there was very little traffic on the way to LAX. And as we flew down the half-empty freeway, I was torn over whether that was a good thing.

I knew it was good in the sense that I really didn't have a lot of time to spare before getting on this plane, especially since I had to check a bag. But it was bad because time seemed to be speeding up, counting down the minutes I had left to spend here—both in LA and with Russell.

It was like we had so much to say that we weren't saying any of it, just focusing on the logistics—which lane was moving faster, and if he could get over to it. But once we hit the 105—the freeway that would take us to the airport—the moment had finally arrived.

"Is your mom going to be mad?" I glanced down at my phone to look at the time—the Bronco had an analog clock, and this was just easier. "I bet she expected you home hours ago. When was your dad's plane supposed to land?"

"I called her while you were locking up the house and got Gordon instead. He promised he'd tell her I was on my way, so hopefully he'll soften the blow."

I blinked, feeling like I'd missed something. "Wait—who's Gordon?"

"He's my mom's partner. I mentioned him, didn't I?"

"No," I said, shaking my head. "He—lives with you?"

"Most of the time. He's an artist, and has a place in Taos. . . ."

"Oh. Well—that's cool." I looked out the window, trying to get my head around it. So Russell basically had a stepfather he hadn't mentioned. It was fine—we just hadn't had that much time, that's all.

Russell tapped his fingers on the steering wheel, looking at the freeway—wide-open and empty—ahead of us. "But my mom is *really* not going to be happy if I tell her I'm not going to Michigan in a week."

"Really?" I turned on the seat so that I could face him a little more fully. "You're—considering it?"

Russell glanced away from the road and gave me a half smile. "Turning it over in my mind. I am going to have to make a decision soon, though, huh?"

"I mean, you can probably take a day," I said, and Russell laughed. "Maybe two?"

"But," he said, glancing over at me. "If I decide not to go, my dad's in New York all the time. It's where Sydney and Connor and Dashiell live. So I could see you really easily. And even if I'm in Michigan, we can figure it out. Right?"

"Right," I said automatically. "Totally." I knew that Russell was saying everything right. He was following what, a day ago, I would have believed was the best and most romantic way for this story to go. Two people meeting by chance and then building something lasting off that one magical night. It was in all the stories I always swooned over—everything I wanted to believe was true. But now . . .

"You could come to campus and stay in my . . . dorm," I said, hesitating over the last word when I realized I didn't even know what to imagine when I said it. I had no idea what the campus would be like, or where I would be unpacking my things tomorrow morning. I couldn't even picture myself there—how could I picture Russell?

"Totally," Russell echoed, his voice slightly strained as he gave me a quick smile, then turned back to the road.

I looked out the window, waiting for a surge of excitement to follow this, butterflies swooping around in my stomach. But it didn't come.

And even though it went against every movie I'd watched and what my instincts only yesterday would have been, I realized that this probably shouldn't happen. That I shouldn't be trying to figure out a brand-new potential relationship while also starting one of the biggest transitions of my life at the same time.

"That all sounds . . . really wonderful," I said after a moment, finding my words as I was speaking them. "It sounds like just what I would have wanted, not that long ago."

Russell glanced over at me, his smile falling away from his face, like a wave retreating from shore. "But?"

"I don't know." I looked down at my hands, twisting together in my lap, and tried to gather my thoughts. "I really like you. So much. It's just . . ." I took a breath, trying to get this in some kind of order. "How long have Wallace and his girlfriend been together? The one who's in Hawaii?"

"Uh," Russell said, looking a little thrown by this change of subject as he put on his turn signal for the exit that would take us to the airport. "Two years, I think? Why?"

"It just kind of seems like they were having some trouble keep-ing things going."

"What are you saying?" There was a red light at the intersection of Aviation and Century, and Russell looked over at me.

"Just that . . . a potential long-distance thing is hard enough when you have some kind of foundation. And we would have a day."

"Not a normal day, though," he pointed out, shaking his head. "Come on."

"No, I know," I said, nodding.

There was a honk behind us, and we both looked to see that the light had turned green. Russell drove forward, and I moved a little closer to him on the bench seat. "It's just . . . I'm going to have to get settled at school, and see what things look like with Gillian. And you're either going to be starting school or writing the next Great American Musical." A smile flitted across Russell's face, and then it was gone. "And that's a lot of pressure to put on something really new."

"So, what," Russell asked, moving into the right lane for the airport entrance. "This is just . . . over? Right now?"

"I don't know," I said unhappily, my heart clenching at the thought of it. "I'm just not sure what the right thing to do here is." I didn't know if I could take the idea that I would never see him or talk to him again. However, I also had a feeling that if we tried to stretch our time together—our one day—over weeks and months, it would all start to fall apart and taint the memory of what we'd had. I wanted there to be some other solution—I just wasn't sure that I could see one.

When we'd first started driving, Russell had asked me what airline I was flying—JetBlue. And as we made our way through the warren of terminals at LAX, I'd expected he would just drop me off. But he signaled to turn into short-term parking, right across from the terminal. "You don't have to park. I can just get off at the curb."

"Didn't you say you wanted someone at the airport to watch you go, and be sad you were leaving?"

I smiled at that, and Russell found parking on the second level of the structure. He lifted my roller-bag suitcase out of the car easily, which was impressive because it was not light. I reached out to take it, but he just smiled as he raised up the handle. "Let me be gallant for just a little while longer."

I nodded and gave him a smile that couldn't help but turn sad at the edges. "Thank you."

We took the elevator down, along with a bickering couple and their small dog, and when we stepped out to walk across the street to the terminal, he reached over and took my hand in his.

I realized, as we stood there holding hands, waiting for the light to change, that this was the first time we'd done this. Just held hands, walking next to each other. It felt so simple, and so right, our palms lining up perfectly and fitting together so easily. I gave his hand a squeeze just as the light changed and we walked across the crosswalk together.

For a second, I wondered how we would look to someone else. Probably just like a normal couple, saying goodbye at the airport. Probably nobody would have guessed we'd only met a day and change ago. That we'd been through so much together and had somehow ended up here, in a crowd of travelers, everyone else flying off as well—to their own adventures or weddings or business trips or funerals. Just one story among so many.

We walked together through the automatic doors and were hit

with a blast of air-conditioning. The lines to check in and drop off bags thankfully weren't terrible—which was good, since I had a feeling I was nearing the cutoff time.

I had expected that this was where Russell and I would say goodbye, but he just stepped into the line with me. When we reached the front of the line, he hung back as I approached the counter and handed them my ID and heaved my bag onto the scale.

"Red-eye to JFK?" the woman behind the counter asked, her fingers flying over her keyboard. "You just made it for checked bags."

"That's great," I said, breathing out a sigh of relief.

"Here you go," she said, handing me a boarding pass and my license back. "Boarding in half an hour."

"Thank you," I said as I walked away from the counter.

"No problems?" Russell asked.

"We made it under the wire."

"Oh good."

We stood there for a second—very much in the way and not where we were supposed to be standing. When a guy in a sweat suit, pulling a rolling suitcase, sighed very loudly as he went around us, I knew we had to find someplace else to be.

I nodded toward the area that led to the security line—there were a few little benches, tucked away in a darkened corner, and that seemed like as good a place as any to have an un-fun conversation.

"Fun fact," Russell said. He gave me a smile, but I could tell his heart wasn't really in it. "Back in the olden days, you used to be able to go with people right up to their gates and say goodbye. Doesn't that sound nice?"

I nodded. It really did. I could barely picture it, but it truly would have been better to have this conversation sitting in chairs by a gate, maybe with a Jamba Juice, knowing that we could talk up until the minute my flight was called, not having to try to calculate how long the security line would be and how far away my gate was. Or maybe not. Maybe this was going to be hard no matter where we were and if we had smoothies or not.

"Do you—regret what happened?" he asked, his brow furrowed as he looked down at me.

"No," I said immediately, knowing it was the truth. "Not at *all*. It was a day I'll never, ever forget."

"Me neither," Russell said, giving me a sad smile.

"I really do care about you so much. And it's not like I want this to be the end," I said, needing to make sure that he understood me. "I just don't think it makes sense to try to stretch this out. Do you?"

"I do need to decide what I'm going to do next year," he said slowly. "And even though everything in me is saying we should just go for this, it . . ." He shook his head and drew in a shaky breath.

"What is it?"

"I think I need to get out of my own way a bit," he said, his voice hesitant, like this was a brand-new thought he was exploring. "I turned in the last musical, even though I knew it wasn't ready. Because if it wasn't my best, I wouldn't actually have to see how I compared with my dad. And while it's so tempting to just jump into this with you . . . maybe I should actually focus on writing a new sample. So that I can change things in my life and stop hiding from it."

"Yeah." I looked over at his hands, hanging by his side, and thought about how easily he'd taken mine in his just moments ago. Was that done now? Would I ever hold his hand again? "We could . . . go back to being friends?"

"I don't think we were very good at being just friends."

"We really weren't," I said with a laugh. And then it faded out, and it was just the two of us, standing across an ever-widening chasm from each other.

"Well," Russell said after a moment. He nodded up toward the security line, which was starting to get worryingly long. "I guess you should go."

"Yeah," I said, even as my throat closed around the word. I knew all too well that I'd brought this on myself. I'd invited him in the house, I'd kissed him, I'd brought him up to my room and made this all that much harder for both of us.

I stepped toward Russell and he stepped toward me, and pulled me into a tight hug. I hugged him back, and let my head rest on his shoulder for just a moment, breathing him in. His arms tightened around me and he lifted me off my feet. But then he set me back down and took a step away.

"You're going to crush it. Connecticut isn't going to know what hit it."

"You too," I said. "Whatever you decide to do. It's going to be so great. I know it."

He gave me a sad smile. "Fly safe."

I nodded and gave him a smile back, one I didn't at all feel. "Thanks. I will. I mean—I'll try? It's really not up to me, but I'll mention your request to the pilot."

He laughed, then gestured to the uncomfortable-looking metal benches. "I'll just wait here, in case you need anything. Just for a few minutes."

I nodded, even as I could feel tears pricking my eyes. People passed by on either side of us, nobody paying the slightest bit of attention. An emotional goodbye in an airport was probably as ordinary as seven-dollar bottles of water. And for a second, I flashed to all the running-through-the-airport scenes that were a staple of my romantic movies. It always ended with an airport chase, right? It was only when someone was about to fly away that you found the courage to tell them how you felt. "That's really nice of you."

He gave me a smile and a half nod. "Take care, okay?"

"You too." I reached out and gave his hand a squeeze, and he lifted mine to his lips and kissed it, not breaking eye contact with me. I stayed there for just a moment longer—my hand in Russell's, our eyes saying all the things we weren't—but then took a step back. I really did need to go. "Bye," I made myself say.

And then I turned and headed for the stairs that would take me up to the security line, feeling like my heart was much heavier than it had been just minutes before. I told myself I wasn't going to look back. It was cliché and trite, and also I had a feeling that if I did, and saw Russell looking after me, watching me go, waiting to see that I was all right, it would be that much harder to actually leave. But there was no alternative—the plane was going to take off, and I was going to be on it.

I glanced down at the check-in line, where the guy in the sweat suit was having an argument with the same woman who'd checked me in. Probably he'd brought his bag in too late, and missed his window.

As I climbed the stairs, I tried to think about what would have happened if I'd also been too late. What could even be done at that point? But a second later, the answer came to me, as clear as anything. Russell would have volunteered to help me. He would have driven my bag back, even though it was the opposite direction for him, and left it at my house so my dad could get it to me.

Of course he would have volunteered to do it—he wouldn't even have hesitated. I somehow knew that this was the way it would have gone, as surely as if it had actually happened. And that revelation was enough to literally stop me in my tracks.

What a good person he was. How if he could have done something to help me, he would. And how if our situations had been reversed, I would have done the same for him.

And realizing this, it felt like something I shouldn't push away or let go by.

Was this me, once again, seeing everything in black and white? Thinking that something either had to be a long-distance relationship or nothing?

And just like that, I could see beyond the black and white to a potential shade of gray.

Looking around, I saw Russell get up and start to walk away.

For once, I didn't overthink it or hesitate.

I just turned so I was heading down the stairs, toward him.

And then I ran.

CHAPTER 24

Monday
10:40 P.M.

R ussell!" I yelled as I ran through the airport.

And I didn't even mind that it was a trope from my favorite movies. They weren't a good blueprint for basing your life off of—I knew that now. But it was clear to me that they'd gotten one thing right: when someone's about to slip away, possibly forever, you do what you can to get them back.

Even if it's running through the airport.

Especially if it's running through the airport.

I saw Russell just outside the sliding glass doors, walking away, and I picked up my pace, stepping back out into the cool California night. "Russell!"

"Darcy?" He turned, his brow furrowed, and walked toward me. "Is everything okay?"

"Yes. And also no. I just . . ." I closed the space between us and looked at him, seeing all the variations at once.

All the Russells I'd known over the last day. Russell sharing my pillow, reaching over to stroke my cheek. Lifting my suitcase out of the car, refusing to let me help. Reading to me as we drove across the Nevada desert. Helping me change a tire, patient and joking the whole time. Walking in the moonlight, holding a small, tired dog.

Fighting with me outside his dad's offices, both of us yelling, neither one of us backing down. Crossing the football field in step with me, a bag of tacos under his arm. And finally, the stranger in the bus station, the cute boy who heard I'd been looking for him. I took a deep breath and reached up to touch his face, my hands on either side of it. "I don't want this to be goodbye."

A smile flashed across Russell's face like lightning—just as bright, gone just as quickly. "Me either," he said. "But you actually did make some good points—"

"Why did you say *actually*?" I asked in a tone of faux outrage, and he laughed.

"—about what this year is going to look like for us."

"I know," I said. I dropped my hands and twisted them together and got my courage up. All I could do was ask. If he said no, he said no, but at least I would have tried. "But what if we didn't have to decide right now what it's going to be?" Russell looked at me, his eyebrows raised. I took a breath and went on.

"How about this? We're not in touch for the next few months. We live our own lives, we do our own thing, we're not tied to anything. But if we're still feeling this way, we'll meet back at the bus station in Jesse in December, over Christmas break. And if we both show up there, we'll know we should give it a try. But we won't be holding ourselves back or trying to stretch something out. And if only one of us—or neither of us—shows up, we'll know it wasn't meant to be, and no hard feelings."

Russell had started to smile. He tilted his head to the side. "Isn't this from a movie?"

"Um," I said, looking down and tucking my hair behind my ear. "Possibly."

"Isn't it *Before Sunrise*?"

"Maybe," I said, wanting to move past this. "But it's *An Affair to Remember* and *Sleepless in Seattle*, too. There's a long tradition."

"But didn't all of those take place before people could, you know—text each other?"

"I kind of like the idea," I pointed out as I searched Russell's face, trying to discern what he was feeling.

"No communication," he said slowly—thinking it over. "Jesse bus station in December."

"The twenty-first?" I asked, just picking a date at random. "Six o'clock?"

Russell shook his head. "I have something at six. Can we shift it?"

I started to reply, then realized a second later he was kidding. "What do you think?"

He took a step closer to me, cupping my chin in his hand. "I'm in if you are."

I stretched up to kiss him just as he bent down to kiss me, and I didn't care that we were in public or possibly blocking the doors to the airport. I needed this kiss to be the bridge between now and three months from now, giving me something to hold on to.

We broke apart after a while—I'd truly lost all sense of time—and I pulled my phone out of my pocket and groaned. "I really have to go."

"You have a flight to catch," he said, smiling down at me. "And a world to conquer."

I smiled at him. "Well—maybe I'll see you in a few months? Or not."

"Jesse bus station. December twenty-first. Six o'clock."

"I'll see you then." I kissed him one more time, then stepped away. We were still holding hands, and I gave his a squeeze, holding it for one more beat before I let it go.

"It's not a goodbye," Russell said, shaking his head. "It's a *see you later*."

I smiled at that. I wondered if he felt like I did—suddenly a little bit lighter. I knew that this plan wasn't perfect, and a million things could—and probably would—happen before December. But for now, it felt like the right thing to do. It would mean I could move forward, not feeling like I'd made a huge mistake or committed myself too quickly. But like we'd actually have time to figure out what we wanted. "See you later," I echoed.

He gave me a smile and a nod, and I gave him one back.

And then there was nothing left to do . . . but go.

I turned and walked back up the stairs toward the security line, tempted to take them two at a time, feeling a buoyancy in my step, still tasting Russell's kiss on my lips.

When I reached the top, I turned around. I could still see him, but barely, through the glass doors. They were sliding open and shut. I saw him, through the crowds and the doors and the distance, meet my eye.

He raised a hand in a wave and I raised one back.

I stood there for just a second longer, memorizing this moment.

And then I turned and walked forward, toward whatever the future would bring.

CHAPTER 25

Friday, December 21st
5:45 P.M.

I pulled into a space in the Jesse Bus Terminal lot and shifted the Prius into park.

As I'd gotten closer to Jesse, and the temperature had dropped, I'd seen that the mountains that surrounded the town were now snow-capped and stunningly beautiful—making it both familiar and completely different.

The lot wasn't hugely full—a smattering of cars and trucks, the occasional van, and a motorcycle parked right by the entrance. I looked around for the Bronco, before I realized a second later that of course Russell wouldn't have been driving it. But I actually had no idea what he would be driving.

I tilted the rearview mirror down and ran a brush through my bangs. Chloe had been right—they worked on my face, and I really liked them a lot—but it was the highest-maintenance haircut I'd ever had, something I was still getting used to. But Didi and Katy both loved it—I'd FaceTimed them right after I'd left Visible Changes, the salon in Stanwich that Gillian had recommended.

In the first few days after I'd gotten to the Stanwich campus and met Mirabella, my very flaky roommate (she would go on to drop out after twenty days, leaving me with the enviable position of being a freshman with a single, even though I was assured by the housing office that this would *not* be the case second semester), I found myself checking my phone a little too often, always hoping to see a message from Russell, that he'd decided to forgo our agreement and reach out. And at first, the silence did bother me, in a low-hum kind of way, in the background but still present. But this really didn't last long—because there was a *lot* going on.

I had to get my class schedule and navigate the campus and try to make friends and sort out the dining hall etiquette and get a handle on my hair, which was encountering sustained humidity for the first time ever.

And more than anything else—I was figuring out what a relationship with my mother looked like. For the first time since I was quite tiny, we were in the same place at the same time. And it wasn't like things had been easy—the ride when she'd picked me up from JFK had not been a great start. I'd been exhausted from barely sleeping on the plane, in addition to my emotional hangover from the previous twenty-four hours with Russell. We were stilted and awkward with each other until, unprompted, Gillian pulled off the highway and into a McDonald's drive-thru. I got a sausage, egg, and cheese McMuffin, she got a McGriddle, and we both got hash browns and coffee. We drove the rest of the way with the bag on the seat between us, eating in silence. But not super-strained silence. More like we were just getting our bearings.

We started with a once-a-week coffee date on campus that then grew to include a standing Sunday dinner at her house. "That's so *Gilmore Girls*," Didi had groaned. "You're even in Connecticut! On the nose much?"

These dinners meant I was also getting to know my half-siblings, and even Anthony a little (though he still seemed to travel a lot for work, going back to the UK pretty frequently, so he was only there around half the time). It was a strange concept, essentially meeting three people that I was related to. We were easing into what our relationship could look like—so far, it involved watching a lot of animated movies and playing a needlessly complicated board game about building railroads. We didn't yet have the kind of relationship that Russell had had with his half-siblings. But it was a start—and for now, that was enough.

I knew what Gillian and I had didn't look like a traditional mother-daughter relationship, and maybe it never would. But we were finding out what it looked like for *us*, and maybe that was all that was needed. We were just taking it one coffee date, one dinner, one conversation and text exchange at a time. Rebuilding our bridge slowly, so that it would be strong enough to withstand a storm if the weather got rough again.

And it wasn't like my dad had been absent from all of this. My first day on campus, we'd had a very long conversation in which I told him everything—the bus station and Russell and the helicopter and Wylie Sanders and staying in the guesthouse and the road trip home.

He had not been happy about this, to say the least. But he did seem somewhat mollified when a huge box of Nighthawks merchandise had shown up at the house—including a note from Wylie that was addressed *To Ted*. My dad wrote him back a thank-you—which led, in a twist I truly hadn't seen coming, to my dad and Wylie becoming friends. They'd started hanging out whenever Wylie was in California, going on hikes and to baseball games, and there was talk of my dad going out to see him at the Wynn.

I heard from Montana occasionally—she was always sending me Connecticut recommendations and funny memes. She was supportive of our dads becoming buddies, telling me that her dad needed a friend his own age. And when I pointed out that my dad was twenty years younger than Wylie, she'd waved this off, calling it "rock-star math."

And not only did my dad have a new, burgeoning friendship with Wylie—he was also no longer alone in our house.

He'd sent me a picture in late September, him holding up a yellow-white puppy with a squashed face and huge paws. It turned out the dog had been a rescue hired for one of my dad's ad campaigns, and he'd fallen in love with him on set, especially when the dog refused to take any sort of direction and ended up toppling the craft services table, then joyfully eating the spoils that hit the ground.

He'd taken the dog home that night, just calling him the name of the product as a stopgap, even though I'd told my dad in no uncertain terms not to do this, in case the dog got attached to it. Which of course he did, so now we were stuck with it. And while my first instinct was to be mad about the fact that I hadn't had a dog my whole childhood, and that my dad got one basically the second I was out of the house, I was just so won over by his cute face and high-pitched bark and whappy tail, it was impossible to be mad. The dog was *so* cute that with all the updates and pictures I was getting, it had taken all my self-control not to clean out my savings and book a flight home immediately to cuddle him. But my dad assured me that he would be there waiting for me when I came home for Christmas. And when I'd finally met him three days earlier, Zyrtec the dog had more than lived up to expectations.

I gave my bangs one last brush, then dropped the brush into my purse. My heart was starting to beat a low, steady pulse in my throat. I wasn't nervous—I was excited.

Because unless something had gone very wrong in the last few hours, I knew Russell would be there.

I had thought, as we'd moved into October and I got my first glimpse of the wonder that is fall in New England, that this would just be it. That we would keep to the terms of our agreement and have no communication until December. And Russell had faded out, slightly, from the forefront of my mind. I made friends, I took weekend trips into New York City, I found that I loved my sociology professor and hated everything about Statistics, I fell hard for East Coast bagels, and I inadvertently got into a feud with my RA when I left a note on their whiteboard that accidentally led their girlfriend to figure out they were cheating. So there was a lot going on. And when, on a random Tuesday, I opened my inbox, I wasn't at all expecting to see an email from Russell—with the subject line THE BALLAD OF DARCY & RUSSELL.

It was lyrics to a song. A song about two people finding each other against the odds, connecting over one night, going their separate ways, but always thinking of each other—usually at the same time, though they didn't realize it, thousands of miles apart.

It was beautiful. Even without being able to hear the music, just reading the lyrics, I felt tears spring to my eyes.

I called Russell immediately, and he answered on the second ring. And I hadn't realized until that moment just how much I'd missed hearing his voice.

And we started a marathon phone call that lasted all that afternoon (I decided I didn't really need to go to Statistics) and into the evening, talking on the phone, headphones in, curled up on my bed as it got later and later—and I was beyond grateful, once again, that Mirabella was gone and I didn't have to do this while pacing around the quad or in one of the soundproof cubbies in the library. It turned out that Russell had deferred Michigan after all—he was bouncing between LA with his mom and Nevada with his dad as he worked on his musical adaptation of *Theseus's Sailboat*. But the Darcy and Russell song was a one-off—he told me he hadn't been able to stop thinking about it until he got it down on paper.

I told him about my friends, and my classes, and the escalating feud with my RA. And it was like we were picking up where we'd left off—we could have been walking around Jesse, or driving in his dad's Bronco, or sitting with bags of well-done fries in front of us.

Finally, I had to hang up to go to sleep, but as we said goodbye, I knew this wouldn't be the end of things. And I was right—as October moved into November, we fell into a routine. We would have long conversations on the phone, usually at night. We had an open text thread that we just kept going—the perfect place to drop in an observation, or a meme, or a picture of Tidbit and Andy.

And as we shared stories and observations and our daily minutia, I *actually* got to know him—got to know him in a way that you can't in twenty-four hours, no matter how jam-packed they are. I knew which emojis he liked, which Spider-Man meme he would inevitably send, how his voice sounded at night when he was sleepy and talking to me with his eyes closed. I got to learn about his day-to-day, and he did the same with me. And as we moved into the middle of November, it was crazy to realize that I thought I'd known him back in August. Because while I'd gotten a sense of him, it was still just the outline. But we were filling in the rest now, one late-night conversation, one text exchange, one FaceTime chat at a time.

So it probably shouldn't have been a surprise when Russell mentioned that his dad was going to be back in New York in November. And maybe . . . ?

But what did surprise me was how quickly I said no. Even though we'd broken every other part of our arrangement, I wanted to keep our December meeting as it was.

"You want us both to drive, separately, to Nevada? All the way from California? And meet at a bus station?" Russell had asked me, incredulous, when I'd put the kibosh on a November meeting.

"You're going to be coming from your dad's," I pointed out. "You only have to drive three hours. I'm the one who has to drive seven hours."

"But neither of us has to drive any hours! We can just meet in LA."

And while I knew that made a lot of sense, I held the line. I liked the romance of it—even though I knew that he would be there waiting for me, I wanted the road trip to meet the boy I'd been separated from. The drive across the desert as night started to fall. The reconnecting in the place we'd first met.

Russell finally agreed, and November continued apace. My dad flew out for Thanksgiving—he stayed in a hotel, but we had Thanksgiving dinner at Gillian and Anthony's. It was something that I wouldn't have believed could even be possible a few months ago—but there we all were, sitting around a table, passing the gravy and arguing over whether marshmallows belonged in sweet potatoes (I was a resounding yes).

And before the month was over, I got another equally ground-shaking surprise. Russell sent me a link to a song—the Darcy and Russell song. With Wylie singing it. It was a little pre-holiday present, just for me. There weren't any plans to release it, and it was just for the three of us—which made it all the more special. And ever since he'd sent it, I'd been listening to it pretty much nonstop.

So it felt like things were working out as I'd flown home to California three days earlier. Well—despite the small wrinkle that Romy Andreoni was going to be my roommate come January. She emailed to tell me that she was "like, *so* over California" and had applied to transfer to Stanwich from UC Santa Cruz. And when she'd mentioned she knew me—and the housing office saw the vacancy that they weren't thrilled about to begin with—it must have been a done deal. So I was preparing myself to lose my single room and have to share it with one of the most chaotic people I knew. And while Katy and Didi were horrified, I also figured that if Romy and I could survive sharing a tent together at a music festival, we would probably be okay in a dorm room.

I checked the time, then my teeth in the rearview mirror. In a few minutes—just a handful of seconds—I would be seeing Russell again. We hadn't made any plans beyond this—I honestly didn't know what was going to happen. I'd promised my dad I'd be back home on the twenty-third, but that was the closest I'd come to planning. Maybe we'd stay at the Silver Standard, or drive to Wylie's house, or get a room somewhere in Vegas.

But it was okay that we didn't have a plan. I was going to see him again soon, for the first time in months, and that was all that mattered. And I knew we'd figure everything else out from there.

I'd changed into a nicer outfit at a rest stop on 93 North—I was no longer in the cutoffs and T-shirt from my drive. Not only because they'd gotten slightly sweaty and ketchup-stained, but they were really not going to work with the weather—it was in the high forties, with the temperature dropping. So I was now wearing my favorite short blue knit dress with a gray cardigan over it. I gave myself one last look in the mirror, then got out of the car.

The bus station, I was surprised to see, was different than I remembered.

It seemed smaller, somehow. The flickering light in the vending machine had been fixed. But most of all, there were now other people in it. There were people working behind the ticket windows, and sitting on the benches killing time, and waiting in line for the bathroom. The Sunday-night quiet that we'd found when we'd washed up here was gone, replaced by the bustle of pre-Christmas travel.

Russell wasn't anywhere in the bus station, but that was okay. I knew he'd be here soon. I walked over to the spot where I'd camped out—the one under the WHEN YOU'RE HERE—YOU'RE HOME mirror. For just a second, I flashed back to the girl I'd been back in August. Trying to pretend I didn't care about Gillian, dreading the future, scared to go up and ask strangers for a phone charger. And I realized, with a kind of wonder, just how much can change in a few months. Even though I was in the same place, it seemed like a million years ago.

I felt a tap on my shoulder, turned around—and there he was.

Russell.

My Russell.

He was wearing a light-blue button-down, dark jeans, sneakers, and his hair was a little longer. He was so handsome, he made it hard to breathe for a second. "Hi," he said, his eyes steady on mine. "I heard you were looking for me?"

I smiled, simultaneously wanting to laugh and to cry. But instead, I just nodded. "I sure am." I practically threw myself at him as he swept me into his arms and gave me a kiss that let me know he'd been missing me these last few months just as much as I'd been missing him.

We broke apart and I hugged him tightly, realizing that the mirror, of all things, was right. I *was* home. I was with him.

"Hey," I whispered into his ear. "Fun fact." Russell drew back slightly to look at me, one eyebrow raised, expectant. I took a deep breath and made myself say it. "I think I'm in love with you."

Russell was smiling at me with his eyes, his lips—with his entire face. "That *is* a fun fact," he said, "because I *know* I'm in love with you."

And we kissed again, a little less frenzied, because I knew we had time. We had all night, and the next few days, and then whatever came after that. Maybe Russell would get into NYU, and we'd be just a train ride apart. Maybe he'd go to USC, or Temple, or Michigan, and we'd continue to figure it out. Maybe this was all going to fall apart next week. Maybe it never would. The only way to find out, I'd finally realized, was to jump in.

"So," Russell said, when we stepped away. He took my hand in his and raised it to his lips. "What comes next?"

I smiled at him. "Whatever we want. We get to write our own story."

He grinned. "Can I pick the genre?"

I laughed at that as he swung our hands between us and we started walking across the bus station, toward the doors.

I knew that our love story—the story of Darcy and Russell—wasn't anything like the love stories I'd seen in the movies.

It was better.

It was *ours*.

Russell squeezed my hand in his, and then held open the door for me.

And we walked out, into the December twilight, together.

ACKNOWLEDGMENTS

The very first book I published with Simon & Schuster was *Amy & Roger's Epic Detour*. It was a story with an ampersand title about California kids falling for each other and a road trip. And while that book and this one are very different, I was thrilled when I realized my seventh teen book is an ampersand title about California kids falling for each other and a road trip. It's always lovely when you can see a full-circle moment and appreciate just how far you've come.

And I couldn't have gotten anywhere without the amazing team at S&S. I have been so lucky to work with all of you, especially Justin Chanda—aka the world's best editor. Thank you for always letting me follow the story where it led me and for the confidence that it would take us to just the right place.

Thank you to Lucy Ruth Cummins for facilitating the covers of my dreams—this one vaults over your impossibly high bar. Thank you to Jessica Cruickshank for the stunning illustrations. All the people at S&S are just a murderers' row of kindness and talent. Thank you to Amy Beaudoin, Nicole Benevento, Amy Lavigne, Michelle Leo, Brendon MacDonald, Morgan Maple, Ashley Mitchell, Lisa Moraleda, Chrissy Noh, Emily Ritter, Roberta Stout, Erin Toller, Daniela Villegas Valle, Amanda Brenner, Chava Wolin, and Anne Zafian.

Emily Van Beek, thank you so much for all you do. Thank you to Sydney Meve, Melissa Sarver White, Katherine Odom-Tomchin, and the whole team at Folio. Thank you to Corrine Aquino at Artists First, and Austin Denesuk and Ellen Jones at CAA for all your amazing work.

Thank you to Adele, Anna, Jen, Julie, Maux, Rebecca, Robin,

Sarah, and Siobhan—Wednesday Crew. Thanks to Diya and Sneha, Walt's Crew. Thanks to Derick and Sarah, TCMC Crew. Thanks to Jenny, Travel Crew. And thanks to Kate, Americana Crew.

Thank you to Jason Matson, Katie Genereux, and Jane Finn—my family.

And finally, thanks to Jesse and Annie for the inspiration.